THE MACHINE

BOOK TWO OF THE GRID TRILOGY

CLIVE HARDWICK

Also available from Amazon by Clive Hardwick

CHANTER'S HIDE

THE RIFT (Book One of The Grid Trilogy)

THE FLIP SIDE

(A Nick Blades Story)

All characters in this book are fictitious and any resemblance to actual persons, living or dead, is purely coincidental

Imagine there's no Heaven
John Lennon - 1971

Final chapter of The Grid – Book One

Their guide reached forward and pushed the oak door and it swung inward. She nodded to Seth and left them to their own devices. The inside of the cottage appeared dark and gloomy through the partially opened portal.

Seth pushed it open wide and, the light it let in, showed a hallway with four doors, two on either side and the bottom of a staircase at the end of the passage. Seth knocked on the first door on the right, waited about thirty seconds and opened it. The curtains covering the window opposite were worn and thin and allowed in a little light. The room reminded Dave of his Nan's sitting room.

"This is just an old woman's home," said Ringo. "It's just like my Nan's."

'Copycat,' Dave thought.

The other three doors continued the theme, a small dining room, a spacious kitchen and a tiny toilet. Going from defending a tribe of diminutive, blue people from something from 'Clash of the Titans' to this throwback to fifties Britain was peculiar, to say the least. They followed Seth to the staircase and Dave, seriously, thought they might find an old woman lying in bed, in the dark, suffering from a migraine.

"Maybe she's got a migraine," he said. Seth gave him one of his 'why don't you shut the fuck up' looks. Dave didn't think he liked him very much.

"Or a hangover," said Phil with a grin, receiving a similar glare from the big man. That made Dave feel better; it wasn't just him; it was all flippant, young punks. He could live with that.

"You need to chill a bit," Dave said to Seth, giving him a wink. He always liked to push his luck; it had been a thing of his for as long as he could remember. It had earned him a few good hidings from the old man, in his younger days. Some people never learn.

"And you need to take life a little more seriously, young man," Seth said sharply. "Not everything is a laughing matter. Have you any idea how vital our mission is?"

Dave shook his head. "As you haven't told me – no I don't. And, one other thing, I hate patronizing bastards." Seth was starting to get on his tits with his high and mighty attitude. The way he had dealt with that big, ugly fucker impressed the shit out of Dave, but that didn't give him the right to talk to him like a was a snotty nosed, little kid.

Seth looked him up and down as if he were a pair of jeans, he was thinking of shelling out for. "I wasn't being patronizing."

The geezer with the dog, Sebastian, Dave thought Danny said he was called, opened his mouth, and Dave thought, here we go. He surprised him.

"You may not have intended it, Seth, but I'm afraid it sounded pretty patronizing to me."

Seth was taken aback. "Well, if that was indeed the case, I apologise."

"Dave," Dave said. "The name's Dave."

Seth sighed. "Okay, I apologise Dave. Now can we get on, please."

Dave gestured forward. "Go for it."

Danny and Ringo listened to the exchange between Seth and Dave. Ringo frowned. "Man, he's so uptight," he whispered. "I mean, what is his problem?"

"I think Dave might be a little too jocular for him," Danny replied. "He's not one for youthful humour."

"That's obvious."

"He's a good bloke though," Danny said. "Bloody useful in a scrap, as well. As you've already seen. He saved your arse."

Ringo held up his hands. "Okay, okay, I agree. He's a legend, a fucking hero and I wouldn't fancy going up against him. All I'm saying is – it wouldn't hurt him to lighten up a bit, that's all."

"He has his moments," Danny said. "Few and far between, I admit."

"This could get ugly," Sebastian said suddenly. "I think a little mediation wouldn't go amiss." He stepped forward.

After he'd poured oil on troubled waters, Sebastian re-joined them, and they followed Seth, Dave and Phil into the house, Harry, Jack, and Pete bringing up the rear.

"This is just totally out of character," Pete said. "Does anyone else feel uneasy about this whole situation?"

They all shrugged. "You should be used to it, by now mate," said Harry. "Nothing is logical anymore. Just when you think you might be getting a bit of a handle on things; you get another curveball lobbed at you. Like Ringo says, you've just got to accept it."

Pete shook his head. "No, I know all that. I've just got a feeling, that's all"

"Oh no, not another of your famous feelings," Jack said with a sigh.

Ringo wasn't quite so dismissive. "What d'you mean Pete? What sort of feeling – good, bad, indifferent?"

"It's not a good feeling, put it that way."

Seth, Phil and Dave didn't hear this exchange, Seth already making his way to the staircase. The little group at the rear shared a look, Jack rolling his eyes, Ringo's brow furrowed, Pete concerned, Danny and Harry non-committal.

Danny nudged Ringo. "You don't think he has a sixth sense, do you?"

He shrugged. "I don't know." He paused. "All I do know is that I'm starting to get a similar feeling."

"What happened to taking everything as it comes?" Danny asked him.

He shrugged again. "What can I tell you? Despite the lunacy that now passes for our lives, I'm getting this feeling of.......foreboding, I suppose is the best word to describe it."

"You're both mental," Jack said, and, as they neared the bottom of the staircase, he moved forward to join Seth's group.

"Hey, Jack." Ringo reached out to him, but Pete grabbed the Liverpudlian's arm.

4

"Let him go," he said softly, nodding; his smile, one of resignation.

Ringo looked at him. "Why?" His expression became one of concern. "I think you're starting to freak me out a bit, Pete. You're not starting to see.... like.... visions, are you?"

Pete shook his head. "No. Like I said, it's just a feeling. I can't really explain it."

Watching the exchange between these two, and the way Jack had rushed to be with Seth & co. had got Danny thinking, so he waded in. "The dynamics are switching, aren't they? We came together as two separate units. Those are splitting and new ones forming. That's why you want Jack to go with Seth. Is that it?"

Pete shrugged. "I don't know. Honestly, I don't. I just get the feeling he needs to be away from Ringo and me. I don't know anything about new groups."

Danny thought Ringo would take the opportunity to start on again about how any of the new bands paled into insignificance compared to his beloved Beatles, but he didn't. He was looking from Danny to Pete, confusion dragging down the corners of his mouth and furrowing his brow.

"This whole, fucking thing is spooky enough without this shit," he said.

"I think," said Sebastian. "That you might be right, Danny. We have already split into two different parties; only separated by a foot or so, granted. But, nevertheless, we have, inadvertently, formed new alliances. Over a longer period, that would not

5

be unusual, but within the space of an hour or so, it becomes yet another extraordinary development."

"Does he always talk like that?" Ringo asked Danny.

"If you mean, properly," Sebastian answered. "Yes, I do. If, in future, you have a question relating to me, I would appreciate it if you would refrain from directing it elsewhere."

Ringo nodded. "Um....yeah......sorry. I guess."

"Apology accepted," said Sebastian.

As they climbed the stairs, Jack had pushed himself up to the front.

"Hello mate," Dave said. "Getting fed up with Beatle-head?"

"Nah, it's Pete and his psychic shit. Mind you Ringo ain't helping."

"What? Is the old parsnip getting his funny feelings again?"

Jack sniggered. "You got it. He's starting to do my head in."

"Ah, come on, he's harmless," Dave said. "And to be fair, he was right about us meeting these nice people." He smiled at Phil; she grinned and gave him the finger again.

"Let's forget about it," Jack said and shivered.

"Man, you're severely uptight about it," Dave said, shocked. "I didn't realize it was creeping you out so much."

He shook his head. "I had an Auntie, who was a medium. She used to scare me to death. She used to wear this bright, red lipstick and thick, black eye liner and call me 'little Jacky'. She'd stick her face right in mine, her breath stunk of rotten onions." He shivered again. "It makes my skin crawl, just thinking about it."

Dave laughed. "Poor little Jacky."

"Don't," he pleaded. "It's not funny. One afternoon, I crept into the room just before she did this séance thing. Halfway through, she threw her head back and this......stuff, came out of her mouth. It was fucking horrible, man."

"Ectoplasm," Phil said.

"Whatever," said Jack. "It's not the sort of thing a nine-year-old should see, believe me."

Dave nodded. "I'm sure. I don't think Pete's going to go down that route though, mate. Do you?"

He shrugged. "You never know, Dave. You just never know. Especially now. Let's face it, anything's possible."

Dave had to agree. Recently, everything they had taken for granted had been blown to fuck. Up was down, left was right, fantasy was reality – or was it? At that precise moment in time, he could, quite honestly, say, he had no idea what was real and what wasn't. For all he knew, it could all be a weird dream, but he didn't think so. He looked at Phil's posterior in those tight pants and hoped it wasn't. Once a shallow bastard, always a shallow bastard but then, nobody's perfect.

By this time Seth had reached the top of the stairs. Maybe the blue queen could shed some light on their current situation."

7

Danny tried to peer around Seth and the others as he pushed open the door on the left and then quickly reached for the handle of the door directly in front of him. From their position he couldn't really see what was going on. He did, however, hear him say, 'follow the path of the spider' and turn to his right.

"What's he doing?" Ringo whispered.

Danny shrugged. "I don't know. I think he was going to open the door at the top of the stairs, but something, someone said to us earlier, changed his mind, for some reason."

Dave must have heard him. "A bloody big spider came out of the bathroom and scuttled under that door," he said, pointing to the right.

"And he's following it?" Ringo asked.

"I think he's got a bee in his bonnet about following them," Dave said. "That's spiders not bees."

Seth reached forward, grabbed the door handle, took a deep breath, and twisted the knob. The door swung inward silently. The room beyond was black and Dave couldn't see a bloody thing. It was like a solid wall of thick, impenetrable darkness. He felt like they were in one of those horror films where some young tart's about to enter a room where everyone knows she's going to meet her end. The music's building and then it suddenly stops and the only thing that can be heard is her breathing. Most people are on the edge of their seats, mentally screaming – *Don't go in there, you silly bitch.*

Like the silly bitch, Seth entered and, ridiculously, they followed. It was the blind leading the blind. Dave had his hands out in front of him, unable to see his shuffling feet. As soon as he entered the room, it was as if the dark closed in around, mummifying him.

"This is taking the piss," whispered Phil, unable to hide the fear in her voice.

"I don't like this, one bit," added Jack, reaching out and grabbing Dave's arm. His grip was like iron.

"Steady on, feller," Dave said. "You're strangling my arm."

Just as he started to ease off on the pressure the door slammed shut behind them and it re-intensified.

"Shit," a number of voices blurted in unison.

"Try and keep calm," Seth said softly. "Are we all here?"

After a verbal roll call, it appeared their group of ten had been reduced to four, Seth, Dave, Phil and Jack.

"Try the door," Dave urged anyone.

"It's fucking locked," yelled Jack, rattling the handle. "It's fucking, bastard locked. Oh God, what's happening?"

The poor sod was practically in tears. Dave wasn't best pleased himself, He had to say. "Calm down, mate. We'll be fine. Seth?" He was after a bit of assurance from the big man. Jack was on route to becoming a gibbering wreck.

Normally when in a darkened room, a person's eyes become accustomed to the gloom. They begin to make out shapes and stuff; this just wasn't happening. They were in a big bottle of black ink. "Seth?" He tried again.

"I'm as much in the dark as you," he said.

"Did you just make a joke?" Dave asked him, then to Phil. "Did he just make a joke?"

Phil was about to answer, Jack was back, wringing the life out of his bicep when a deep, ethereal gasp washed through the room like surround-sound.

"Oh m...m...y G...God," stammered Jack.

'You are the four rangers. The spider will guide you. Never stray from his path." The words seemed to be in Dave's head, formless but intense.

"Where are our friends?" Seth asked the darkness.

'The spider will guide you'. The communication faded to a breathless notion.

To their left a crack of light appeared as a, previously, unseen door swung outwards a tad. Their old friend, the spider disappeared through the chink. Jack was after him, in a shot, pushing the door wide and falling through. The room, this block of black ended at the new doorway but the light from beyond didn't penetrate it. Seth, Phil and Dave followed Jack into the light.

Danny and Ringo were standing on the top couple of stairs when Seth opened the bedroom door. Over Jack's shoulder, Danny saw only darkness, no glimmer of light. He began to share Ringo's feeling of foreboding.

"It's pitch black in there," he shared. Blue began to whine.

"Sshh, girl," whispered Sebastian, rubbing her ears. She leant into his leg.

Danny looked back and watched Seth enter the room, Dave, Phil and Jack on his heels.

"This is turning into a horror film," Ringo said.

"I think we're about to start a new chapter," said Sebastian.

"And, what the fuck's that supposed to mean, Einstein?" Ringo hissed.

"Do you have a problem with me?" Sebastian asked him.

"As it happens, yeah. You, either talk in riddles or you act like a fucking teacher, and it's getting on my tits. Any more questions?"

Their new 'group' seemed to be having some teething problems. "Come on, Ringo. We're all getting stressed, and we're all dealing with it differently," Danny said quietly. Blue's hackles were up and, if a dog can glare, that's what she was doing – Ringo, the focus of her attention. To add a little menace, she emitted a low growl and twitched her muzzle, flashing her teeth.

"Easy girl," Sebastian said softly.

"Stop being a twat," Pete said. "There are some people who know more than you, and don't need to eff and blind all the time. Try acting more like John Lennon and less like John Dillinger."

Ringo looked as though he was about to launch into another verbal assault, then reason kicked in. He let out a heavy sigh and held up his hands.

"Sorry man," he said to Sebastian. "I thought I was dealing with this shit pretty well. Obviously, I was wrong."

Sebastian held out his hand. "I have met many 'twats' in the past." It was clear that he was uncomfortable using vulgar slang. "Plus, I pride myself in being a good judge of character. I've forgotten it already." As if to reinforce his words, Blue became quiet and started to wag her tail, slowly. Apparently, she wasn't totally convinced. Ringo shook his hand and muttered another apology.

This exchange had taken their attention and, by the time harmony was restored, Jack was crossing the threshold of the bedroom. The gloom swallowed him. Danny went to follow him when the door was slammed in his face.

"Christ, Jack," he said, grabbing the doorknob. The door was locked or jammed. Either way, it wouldn't budge.

"Open the door, Danny," yelled Ringo.

He rattled the knob and it rattled back but the door stayed firmly shut.

"You try," he suggested, stepping away from the door.

Ringo rushed forward, grabbed, pushed and grunted but to no avail. The door remained shut.

"What the fuck," was all he could manage.

"Wait," said Pete. "It'll open in a minute."

Ringo shook his head. "Oh Pete, man. You're starting to......"

There was a sharp click and a gap appeared between the door and the frame.

"I think," said Sebastian. "It's our turn."

While the rest of them stared tentatively at the door, Pete stepped forward, pushed it open and entered the bedroom. He disappeared beyond what appeared to be a dense, black curtain.

"Well, here goes," said Sebastian. "Come on girl." He followed Pete, Blue by his side.

"There could be anything in there," said Harry.

"We haven't heard any screams," Ringo said. "I guess that's a good thing, yeah?"

"We can't stay here," Danny said.

"We could go back," Harry said.

"Nah, you should never go back," Ringo said, wiping his palms on his trousers. "Who dares wins." He vanished into the blackness.

"Come on Harry, best foot forward." Danny grabbed his arm and they almost stumbled through the door.

THE GRID - BOOK TWO

THE MACHINE

PART ONE - SEPARATION

ONE

The sun was startling, and they all squinted as their eyes adjusted to the complete change. A few feet in front of them a ten-foot wall of lush green hedgerow blocked their path, stretching, seemingly, for miles to both left and right. Dave turned to look back at the house they had just left and gasped.

"Jesus Christ," was all he could manage.

Redstone cliffs reached into the blue sky, their surface sheer and forbidding. Of the house, there was no sign.

"Ah, for fuck's sake," said Phil, shaking her head. "This really is taking the piss now."

Jack had just about stopped gibbering and now looked as if he'd seen a ghost.

"What are we supposed to do now?" He asked, looking around at Dave, the cliff-face, the wall of brush and the sky for an answer.

"I guess we follow him," said Seth.

They followed his gaze and saw their little buddy, the spider, disappearing into the greenery.

"We'll get ripped to bits," Dave said.

Seth took a couple of steps to the left. "I think it's a maze," he said, following the spider's route. He disappeared into the hedge and they hurried after him.

Sure enough, three beautifully manicured pathways presented themselves to them, all directly ahead, separated by slim, leafy partitions.

"Which way did the little feller go," Dave asked Seth.

He shrugged. "I don't know," he replied. "Maybe his job was to show us the entrance. I imagine the rest is up to us. It would take all of the fun out of it if we had something to guide us all the way through, wouldn't it?"

Jack had finally regained his composure. "Somehow, I would be surprised if we encountered anything remotely resembling fun," he said.

Dave nodded. None of them knew what they would meet inside this verdant puzzle, but all agreed; it was unlikely to be pleasurable.

"Well, which way?" Phil asked Seth. "Doesn't your sonic thingy tell you?"

Seth raised his detector and switched the switch. He waved it around and shrugged. "Sorry, but wherever we are now, this isn't going to help. We're on our own."

"I vote we do the old paper, scissors, stone thing," Dave said.

"It seems as good as anything," Seth said.

Dave felt a tiny glow of pride that the big man had sanctioned one of his ideas. "Okay, left is paper, middle – scissors, right – stone. Ready?"

He received another three nods and counted them in. Seth weighed in with stone, Jack – scissors, Phil – stone, and Dave – scissors."

"Well, that didn't work, did it, smart-arse?" Phil jeered.

"It will," Dave insisted. "Just keep doing it until we get a majority."

Seth shrugged. "Suits me."

Dave counted them in again. On the third attempt they nearly got a full house with three papers and one stone.

"Left it is then," said Seth. The others trailed after him, trepidation, their companion.

"This is getting to be like a really bad 'B' movie," Dave said to Phil.

"I doubt it could be classed that high," said Jack.

Phil shook her head. "I just don't know what to think anymore," she said, shaking her head.

"So, what's new?" Dave said with a wink.

His right bicep was becoming very sore and, probably, bruised by the constant pummelling it was receiving. He winced at the latest attack.

"You'd better learn to watch your mouth, young Davey," she said. "Before you get yourself into serious trouble."

He smiled. "You love me really."

She shook her head again but, this time there was a glint in her eye. He gave her another wink and his best cheeky, Potter grin.

"You are a tosser," she said, unable to hide the smile.

"There's a path to the right about twenty yards up," Seth called back.

He was about the same distance in front of them. Dave hadn't been taking much notice of where they were going. He had been too busy treating Phil to a good, old dose of the tried and tested Potter charm. She was proving a little harder to crack than normal, but she was definitely thawing. Give it a month or two and he'd have her eating out of his hand.

Seth turned. "Shall we carry straight on or take the turn?"

"Shall we do the old paper...?" He didn't get chance to finish before Phil said.

"We ain't doing that bollocks again. Seth – you decide. None of us know the right way, anyway. We'll trust you."

She is thawing, no two ways about it, Dave thought.

Seth shrugged. "Let's give it a shot." Once more he disappeared into the bushes. They caught up and followed. The scenery was becoming extremely boring; there's only so much privet you can take. They walked for about three hundred yards before hitting a dead end.

"I told you we should have done the......." This time Dave got a slap around the head before he could finish his sentence. The old charm was starting to work; she couldn't keep her hands off him.

They turned around and Jack led them back to the main path. Dave held off on the chat, he thought he had better let her calm down. He didn't want to get her too excited.

"We could be in this fucking thing forever," Jack said. "I don't know about anybody else but I'm starving."

With the banter, Dave hadn't thought about food. Now Jack had brought up the subject, his stomach grumbled, and he started to see plates of steak and chips and bowls of apple crumble. He wondered if they would have to start eating their way out. At the moment the thought of munching on privet wasn't too appealing. In a week or so though, it could be a different story.

"Somehow, I don't think we'll be allowed to starve to death," Seth said.

"You don't know," said Jack. "You've already told us that."

Seth shrugged. "We've been cut off from the others and planted here. It must be for a reason. We are, after all, the four rangers." A smile drifted across his features, as if he were taking the piss. Maybe he was.

He strode off in their original direction, a purpose to his step. They followed, as purposefully as they could manage, under the circumstances. Jack's mention of hunger had really pissed Dave off. He couldn't stop thinking of Sunday roasts and Friday night curries, which, in turn, got him onto pints of his beloved Strongbow. He was amazed at how a body could go from not even considering its stomach to becoming totally obsessed with it.

"You're a bastard," Dave said to Jack.

"Yeah," said Phil. "A total bastard."

"What have I done now?" he wailed.

19

"You could have kept the fact that you're starving to yourself," Dave said, a little more harshly than he deserved.

"I was only saying," Jack said.

Phil pointed her finger at him. "Next time, think before you speak."

Poor old Jack looked crestfallen and Dave suddenly felt sorry for him.

"Eh, we're only pulling your pisser, mate. Don't take it to heart. Aren't we, Phil?"

He gave her his serious stare.

"Er, yeah, just jesting, man," she said, her brow creased in bewilderment.

"Come on troops, best foot forward," Dave said, quickening his pace, trying to rid his mind of a vivid image of a plate of bangers and mash with lashings of onion gravy. It wasn't easy.

The privet didn't become any more interesting; the path meandered on, sometimes taking a left turn, then a right, then straight on again. No more junctions appeared for, at least, an hour. By now his belly was complaining audibly and Dave could not keep pictures of various victuals from racing around his brain. He was starting to feel actual, physical pain. It was like the time he gave up fags; the only thing he could think about was having a fucker. The craving he'd felt for nicotine then was like that for food, now.

He looked up when Seth muttered, "Ah."

He stood at a 'T' junction. "Someone else's choice this time," he said, turning and facing them. Who's going for it?"

"We could always do the pap........." Dave began again.

"Take the right," said Phil, cutting him off again.

"I wish you'd stop doing that," he said.

"Stop being a dick and I will," she said sharply. She stared at him, hands on hips, breasts thrust forward, long legs parted, those dark, brown eyes blazing. Lust overpowered the hunger.

"You're gorgeous when you're angry," he said, unable to prevent a leer. It earned him another slap around the head. "I'm getting to quite like that," he said, with a wink. She gave him a left hook – a real punch.

"How about that?" She asked, with a very exaggerated wink.

He rubbed his chin. "That's going to bruise,"

"Can we focus?" Seth said forcefully. He swung round and dove down the path, his coattails trailing.

"I think he's getting a bit pissed off with you," Jack said.

"Ah, he's got no sense of humour," Dave said.

"He probably thinks the same as me," said Phil.

"You're a tit."

"You just need to give in to your true feelings, darling." He was about to give her another wink but thought better of it. He couldn't be sure which other part of his body she may decide to be playful with. She didn't know her own strength, that was the problem.

"Call me darling again and I'll kick you where you don't want to be kicked. Understood?"

He winced and crossed his legs. "Understood."

He couldn't understand why the Potter charm was taking so long to work. All right, it was a bit on the rusty side, but it had never earned him a smack in the mouth before. It was as if he were irritating her but, surely, that couldn't be the case. They'd hit it off fairly well, initially. He needed a second opinion. Phil marched off after Seth. Dave grabbed Jack's arm and pulled him back.

"Do you think she fancies me?" he asked him.

Jack chuckled. "If she does, she's got a weird way of showing it."

"She's just a bit playful, that's all." Dave said.

"I certainly wouldn't want to go out with a girl whose idea of playful was a smack in the gob," Jack said.

"What? Do you think I ought to tone it down a bit?"

Jack grinned. "Unless you want to have your cobblers kicked into the middle of next week, I think it might be a good idea. Yes."

Dave carried on rubbing his sore chin, wondering where it had all gone wrong. Maybe he would have to try a different approach, more conventional, maybe. He was sure she liked him. He fancied *her* like mad. "Perhaps a bit of old-fashioned wooing?" He said.

"It might be safer," Jack agreed. "Or maybe play hard to get?"

Dave nodded. "Yeah – hard to get, I like that. To be honest, I wouldn't know where to start with the old wooing business, anyway."

Jack glanced at him, shook his head and smiled.

"What?" Dave said.

"Nothing. No-one has ever asked me for relationship advice before. You must be really desperate."

"Desperate, me? Nah, just shooting the breeze, that's all," Dave said, a little too forcefully. "We'd better catch up with the others."

"I was fine before you dragged me back," Jack said with a wider grin.

"Well, I didn't actually drag you, but...eh, it don't matter. Come on, let's get a wiggle on, otherwise Seth'll be giving us a bollocking again."

"Us?" Jack said, and then sighed. "Whatever."

They increased their pace and were soon back with the leaders of the pack.

They carried on, Dave feeling a little put out that he appeared to be viewed by the other three as a total twat. He had always classed himself as a bit of a loveable rogue, a geezer with a wicked sense of humour. When he was with the others, they had a good laugh – now it was like being with his dad and some ice queen. Even Jack had changed and become sensible. And he was fucking sick of privet walls. Man, all this shit was becoming depressing. They had been slung back eight centuries, chucked into some sort of parallel dimension and now, it was all........garbage.

"You've gone quiet," Jack said.

"No point in being anything else," he said morosely.

Jack gave a shrug and they fell silent again. Dave wondered how long they were going to have to traipse through this bloody maze before they came to the pissing exit. It was doing his head in – that, Seth and frosty knickers. He'd never been one for self-pity before, but he was certainly making up for it now. He slouched along, feeling hard done by and unwanted. He didn't even notice the snow-queen herself, slow her pace, until she slapped him on the back.

"Why the long face, donkey?" She asked with a grin.

"Very funny," he said, not looking up.

"I'm not like one of the bimbos you normally give your silly spiel to, you know."

Then he did look up. "I never said you were," he protested. "Not that I'm in the habit of associating with bimbos, anyway."

She laughed. "'Course not. Silly me."

He gave her his best hurt expression.

"You're doing it again," she said sharply. "Look Dave, I like you, but if you carry on acting like a knob, you're just going to piss me off."

He looked into her beautiful, brown eyes. "Sorry," he said, and he meant it. "New start? " He held up his right palm.

She slapped him a high five. "New start," she said. Suddenly, the depression lifted, even the privet appeared to be gaining a floral tinge.

"Has Seth said anything?" He asked her.

She shook her head. "No. I think he's pissed off that he has no clue what's going on, though. I get the impression he's used to being in control of his own destiny. All this is doing his crust in, though he won't admit it."

"He thinks I'm a dick, doesn't he?" he said.

"Pretty much, yeah," she said.

"I'm going to talk to him." The decision made; he quickened his pace.

"Hey Seth," he called. Seth turned his head, and then disappeared.

"What...the..." Dave said. He turned to Phil, but she darted past him. He followed, Jack at his heels. They all disappeared – then re-appeared – somewhere else.

TWO

It was a picture from one of those old westerns, when the gunslinger rides into town, a neckerchief tied around his mouth to stop the dust going down his throat. And the tumble weed is blowing eerily down the main street. It seemed; they were the gunslingers.

"You got to be kidding me," Dave said, shaking his head. "The Wild, fucking West."

They looked around. Sure enough, there was a saloon, a sheriff's office, a barber's shop, a wash house, an undertaker's, and a load of other wooden structures whose function was a mystery to Dave. Seth's expression was priceless. It was a mixture of disbelief, confusion and total helplessness.

"What's going on now, big man?" Phil asked him. He just shrugged and moved his lips. No sound came out.

Out of the corner of his eye, Dave saw one of the Saloon's swing doors open a touch. "I think we're being watched," he said. "The saloon."

"Let's go and see who's watching us then, shall we?" Seth was a man on a mission.

"He's really pissed off," Dave said to Phil.

"I think it's starting to get to him big time," she replied. "Come on, we can't let him go in there on his own."

Although none of them knew what they were getting into this time, they were all in it together.

They ran across the dirt road and caught Seth up as he pushed open the saloon door.

The place was packed, like Wetherspoons on a Saturday night. Only the people here were not throwing pints down their necks and swearing like troupers. The room was full of men, women and children. There was a plethora of ten-gallon hats and women's bonnets. Every set of eyes was on them. The fear was almost tangible. A woman's voice suddenly whispered, "Is it them?"

A man in a stovepipe hat walked slowly towards them. "Are you the ones?"

He asked.

Seth immediately stood tall. "We are the rangers," he said. All confusion seemed to have left his features.

'It is them; it is them', rumbled around the room as if it were on a loop. The man took off his stovepipe and bowed. "We have waited so long," he said, tears in his eyes. "A great many of us had given up all hope."

"We're here now," Seth assured him.

"Is he on drugs or something?" Dave whispered to Phil.

"Search me," she said. "This lot seem pretty pleased to see us though."

"That's because we're the rangers," said Jack. "Apparently."

"You'll get them all back, won't you?" pleaded another woman. "Promise, you'll bring them home."

"Where is your sheriff," Seth asked.

A timid looking chap shuffled forward. His ten-gallon hat seemed to drown him. A geezer, less like a sheriff, you would struggle to find.

"We are in need of sustenance," Seth told him. "Once we have eaten, we will discuss the situation and devise a solution to your problem."

Within minutes, a table was placed in the centre of the room and food and drink appeared, as if by magic.

"Nice one Seth," Dave congratulated him. Seth looked at him and shook his head. Dave was still something he had trodden in.

They sat and tucked into a mini feast of cold meats, salads and home baked bread. As for the butter, Dave had never tasted anything like it. To call it creamy would be like calling Hattie Jacques a pound or two overweight: no offense Hat. Jugs of foaming ale were plonked in front of them. Dave poured himself a mug and drained it in one go, belched and gave their hosts a double thumbs up. It seemed the universal language of this simple sign straddled all dimensions as he received smiles and reciprocal thumbs.

"Do you have anything other than beer?" Jack asked a young woman, who bore more than a passing resemblance to a young Ursula Andress.

"We have juice, lemonade, or my mother's blueberry punch," she replied with a smile that would melt the heart of any red-blooded male. Dave was waiting for the old western favourite – sarsaparilla but was disappointed.

"Is the blueberry punch, non-alcoholic?" Jack persisted.

"What's with the non-alcoholic business," Dave asked him.

"You know what happened at the spit and sawdust place," Jack said. "I'd just rather play it safe, for a while, that's all."

Dave gave him a 'please yourself' shrug and let him get on with it. Ursula answered his question.

"It is, and it's delicious. I can vouch for that." The smile broadened, revealing the most perfect set of gnashers Dave had ever seen. He was falling in love again. That was, until he sustained a Doc Marten to the ankle.

"Close your mouth David, you look simple." Phil said with what Dave hoped was a hint of jealousy. He winced and was about to protest but seeing Phil's expression changed his mind. She was mad, that was for sure, only underneath that anger there did appear to be a green seam of jealousy glowing, plain as the nose on her face. And she had called him 'David'.

"I was just looking at her teeth," he said quietly, unable to keep the satisfied grin off his mush.

When Ursula came back with Jack's punch, Dave didn't look up from his plate. Everyone else had moved away to the bar or sat at the tables around the edge of the room, giving them some space. They ate the rest of their meal in silence, and Dave enjoyed every mouthful. Seth was the first to push his plate away, followed by Jack. Dave shovelled the last piece of ham in and joined them. Phil wasn't far behind. When it was obvious to their hosts that they had finished, the table was cleared and they were given a few minutes to themselves before the sheriff and a tall bloke in a black suit came up, carrying a chair each.

"My name is Emitt Tulder," said the sheriff, holding out his hand to Seth. "This is Jonas Garrow, our padre." Both shook hands with Seth and nodded to the rest of them. Dave was a little miffed about that, he had to admit. They were, after all, in this thing together. They pulled their chairs up to the table, sat down and Dave thought, 'it's official, there's no such thing as a free lunch'.

"Padre told us you'd come," Emitt said, shifting in his chair. "Some of us weren't......erm.... convinced, shall we say."

Seth looked at Garrow. "And how did you know?" He asked him. "Did God tell you?"

The priest laughed. "God? We all gave up on him a long time ago."

"But you're a.......man of the cloth," Dave said, choosing his words carefully.

Garrow shrugged. "I have no other clothes, and these are quite serviceable." He turned his gaze on Dave. His eyes were a strange shade of blue, almost grey. "You must be the one described as the jester."

Phil burst into laughter. "You're not wrong there, Padre."

He shifted his gaze to her, a wry smile touching his lips. "No," he said, and after a pause, he shook his head. "I won't embarrass you."

30

"What?" She said, the hilarity suddenly fading.

"Never mind," Seth cut in impatiently. "I reiterate. How did you know we were coming?"

Jonas Garrow looked at Seth and took a deep breath. "I dreamt of a spider," he said softly.

"Here we go again," Dave muttered, shaking his head. "I think we're down to 'D' movie now."

Seth shot him a look. "Be quiet, jester," he said sharply, with, what could only be described as, a satisfied smile. The smile took the sting out of the sharpness but, together, they were taking the piss, and enjoying it.

"Continue," Seth said to the Padre.

"I was compelled to follow the spider. It took me to the valley where they take the children. You were there fighting to save them. Words came, like pictures, in my mind, and I knew. I knew you would come. Unfortunately, I didn't know when."

"The valley where they take the children? Who takes the children?" Seth asked him.

A woman rushed forward and fell to her knees before Seth. Torture lined her face. It was obvious she was the mother of one or more of these children.

"The dead ones," she cried. "The dead ones take them. You will get them back. Promise, you'll get them back."

"We call them the dead ones, because they cannot be killed," explained Tulder. "Bullets bounce off them and their eyes are black as midnight. Each one has the strength of ten men. We have tried to fight, but it's useless. They cannot be hurt."

"Better and better," Dave said.

"Why do they take the children?" Seth asked.

"We don't know," admitted Garrow. "Many men have gone to the valley, fathers of the sons and daughters taken. None have returned."

"But I bet we're going to the valley. Am I right?" Dave asked Seth.

Seth gave him a wink and a nod. "We are the rangers," he said.

Dave had to admit, being a ranger wasn't all it was cracked up to be. It might have been slightly better if there were about fifty of them, strength in numbers and all that. But, come on, who in their right mind would even consider fighting bastards that can't be hurt. You're on a loser from the start, right?

"You got a plan then?" He asked the big man.

"Not yet," Seth said. "We'll formulate one of those once we're in situ."

"In what?" Jack asked.

"When we're overlooking the valley," Seth explained. "On site, in situ, actually there."

"Okay, I only asked." Jack muttered.

Dave looked around the room and saw a few kids, clinging to their mothers and fathers. "How many children have they taken?" He asked Garrow.

"They come every few weeks and take three each time," he said. "We've tried to hide them but it's as if they already know where they are. They never have to search; they go directly to our hiding places."

"So far they've taken nine, five boys and four girls," said Tulder.

The woman, who had beseeched Seth, grabbed his hands. "Can you bring them home?" Her expression was a mixture of hope and doubt.

"What is your name?" Seth asked her softly.

"Mary Conway, sir."

"My name's Seth, Mary. I give you my word that we will return all of the children unharmed."

She smothered his hands in kisses, her tears falling on the table." Thank you, sir, thank you. May God go with you."

"It's unlikely," Phil said softly.

Dave was still trying to get over Seth's ridiculous promise. Number one – they were about to walk into sudden death, number two – dead people don't perform rescues and number three – even if they could, how did Seth know those kids were not dead already.

"A little optimistic, I feel," he whispered. "You shouldn't go making promises, you can't keep. Didn't your mother ever tell you that?"

"If it wasn't within our power, we wouldn't be here," Seth said, matter of factly.

"I know." Dave sighed. "We are the rangers."

"And we have a job to do," Seth said. "So please, less negativity David, if you don't mind."

"Just Dave will do." Dave said. "My mother was the only one to call me David, and that was only when I'd done something she didn't like."

"Well then David. Let's have more positivity, eh?"

"When do we start?" Dave asked him. 'If you can't beat 'em, join 'em', he thought.

"There's no time like the present. Are we all in agreement?"

They all nodded, although Dave failed to see a glimmer of enthusiasm from either Phil or Jack. He was just resigned to an early death.

"How far away is the valley?" Seth asked Tulder.

"Half a day's ride," the sheriff replied.

"Do you have horses we could take?"

"None of the men returned," Garrow said. "But all of their horses trotted back into town, like homing pigeons."

"We'll need supplies," said Seth. "Food, water and guns."

"They'll do you no good," Tulder insisted. "Did you not listen?"

"Can their horses be killed?" Seth asked.

"Well......yes. Dan Thatcher killed one once. He was aiming for the rider, but his eyes aren't what they used to be."

"Do you have any explosives?" Seth enquired.

"We have a few sticks of dynamite left from blowing up the mine," Tulder said.

"Blowing up the mine?" Phil said.

Tulder waved a hand. "That's another story," he said. "Maybe when you bring the kids back, we'll chew the fat." It was obvious, by his tone, that he didn't believe they would be coming back.

"Well, if you could get together all the things we need, we'll be on our way," said Seth, ignoring

Tulder's pessimism. "In which direction do we ride?"

"Don't worry about that," Garrow said. "I'm coming with you."

Seth shook his head. "We'll have our hands full, as it is. We can't worry about anyone else."

"You needn't worry about me," Garrow said through clenched teeth. "I don't intend coming back. I just want to see those kids alive before I go. And maybe take a couple of them bastards with me if that's possible."

Seth looked at the preacher. "You're a good man, Garrow. If you come, you're on your own. We won't be able to watch your back, you know that."

Garrow nodded. "I wouldn't expect you to. The kids are the only ones that are important here. Maybe I could create some kind of diversion?"

Seth sighed. "All right, you're in; but you do as I tell you. Understood?"

Garrow nodded, a grim smile creasing his lined features. "You bet," he said.

Tulder nodded to a couple of the women and they scurried off. He turned back to Seth. "All the guns and ammo are in the jailhouse."

Dave kept expecting Clint Eastwood to barge through the saloon doors with a cheroot hanging from his gob and tell someone that his mule didn't like folks laughing at him. This was getting more surreal by the minute. He was now in some John Houston western. Only he didn't feel much like a movie star. One thing was bothering him more than everything else about this suicide mission, and he felt he had to get it off his chest.

"There's one thing that's worrying me," he said. Seth let out one of those real, heavy sighs. "What now?"

"I've never ridden a horse," Dave admitted. "If I'm honest, they frighten me a bit."

By the laughter that went round the room, he realised why Garrow had called him the jester.

The six of them meandered over to the sheriff's gaff – jailhouse – or whatever you want to call it. Dave was feeling a little hurt by the severe derision he had suffered after his recent admission. He had grown up on a council estate in Croydon – there weren't a lot of horses about.

"You are a bell end," Phil said.

"Oh thanks, that's very fucking nice. Especially after being made to feel like some twat who'd gone to a fancy-dress party in his Batman costume only to find it was some old dear's wake."

"That's what I mean," she whispered. "I've never ridden a bloody horse either, but I'm not about to admit it to the inhabitants of Yellow Gulch here."

"Is that what it's c....," He nearly said, before realising she was taking the piss.

She grinned and shook her head. "I despair."

It seemed Dave was on a roll. To make himself the biggest donkey in the wild west. At least Clint Eastwood wouldn't laugh at him.

They stepped up from the dirt track, that passed for the town's main drag, onto the wooden platform that would be called, in England, the pavement. It really was like all the westerns he had seen on the box. If their stay wasn't going to be so short, he'd probably have enjoyed it.

"Hope you like beans," he said to Jack, unable to stop the scene from 'Blazing Saddles' springing into his head.

"Love 'em," Jack said, letting out a little Tommy Squeaker. They both fell about.

Seth glanced over his shoulder and gave them the evil eye.

"Just a little joke, oh great one," Dave said between chuckles. "I am the jester, after all."

Tulder pushed open the door to his office, there was as much dust on the floor inside as there was outside. The cleaner must have been on holiday. They all piled in. It was extremely basic, as would be expected. Directly in front was a cell with a barred door, it was empty. A rickety looking desk and a similar looking chair were placed against the right-hand wall, giving a good view of the cell and the door. A few papers lay on the desk with a pot of ink and an old wooden pen, with a severe nib. There were some drawers to the left of the chair. On the opposite wall was a cabinet, with a lock dangling from it. Tulder walked over to it, took a key from his pocket and unlocked it.

He swung open the door, revealing a row of ten rifles.

"I'll bet they're Winchesters, " Dave said, it being the only name he could remember from the cowboy movies he'd seen.

37

"You might not be a horseman," said Tulder. "But you know your firearms." There was a definite hint of respect in his tone. He grabbed one, turned and threw it to Dave. Luckily, he'd always had rather good reflexes and was renowned for his catching skills when he and the boys used to have a game of estate cricket. He caught it by the barrel. Okay, maybe he was a bit rusty.

"Harvey Jackson, the smith, will be round with the horses shortly, as will Mary with the vittles." Garrow informed them.

'Vittles'! – this got better and better.

"Tell us a bit more about 'the dead ones'," Seth said as they waited.

Tulder stared into space for a few seconds. "Not much more to tell. They look like regular riders." He thought a little more. "They don't speak to each other much, I guess. Just come into town, get the kids and ride on out."

"Looking into their eyes is like looking at a dead horse," said Garrow. "No emotion. Not even anger, when we try and hide the children. There is just nothing. Like Tulder says – they come, get what they want and leave."

"Sound like robots," Dave said.

"What're robots?" Tulder asked.

Seth waved a hand. "Never mind." He was obviously on the same wavelength as Dave. Trying to explain artificial intelligence to cowboys would be difficult, to say the least. A film Dave saw years ago came into his mind; it starred that bald bloke – Yul Brynner. All about this theme park where

38

people went to relive the Wild West, full of robot gunslingers.

"Have we entered 'Westworld'?" Phil asked.

"That was the feller," he said. "Westworld – with Yul Brynner."

She gave him a sideways glance. "That's what I just said."

He wished it were only recently that he'd seen the film, it might give them some ideas. As it was, all he could remember was old baldy waltzing about shooting the fuck out of everybody. He couldn't remember how they got rid of him, but he was sure they must have.

The door opened and a bloke with a beard like Father Christmas and arms like Arnold Schwarzenegger entered the room. Dave guessed this was the blacksmith.

"Horses are out front," Santa said to Tulder.

"Thanks Harvey."

"Mary's on the way with the provisions," Harvey continued. He looked at Seth. "They took my boy, Frank. I'd like to tag along if you have no complaints."

Seth let out a sigh. "I'm sorry Harvey; I'm going to have to say no. This must be done as quietly as possible. If we go in mob handed, we'll be spotted before we get near enough to even assess the situation. We'll bring your son back; I give you my word." He held out his hand and the blacksmith shook it.

"Me and Janey are counting on you, Mister. Don't you go letting us down now." As he turned to leave, he had tears in his eyes. Dave just hoped that Seth's faith in their abilities wasn't misplaced. If it was, there were going to a lot of distraught people here.

Just after Harvey left, Mary came in with the 'vittles'. There were five large cloth covered packages. She laid them on Tulder's desk, walked over to Seth and hugged him. "Thank you, sir." She turned and looked at the rest of them. "Thank you, all. May God help you defeat these devils."

Dave nodded. They were going to need all the help they could get, and he was hoping the big man was going to prove Seth wrong. At this precise moment, he kind of liked the idea that the Almighty was in their corner.

Their supplies were packed into saddle bags – what else! They said goodbye to the townsfolk and then came the scary part. Being the gentleman that he was, Dave let Phil mount her horse first, a huge black monster with wild eyes. She placed her right foot in the stirrup and swung her left leg over the beast, like Annie Oakley. He was beginning to wonder if she'd been having him on, when she said she'd never ridden a horse before, but then the animal did a quick shuffle and, although she tried, she couldn't stifle a whimper escaping. Seth was up in a jiffy, followed by Garrow. Jack was a little hesitant but seemed pretty comfortable, once in the saddle.

"Come along David," said Seth with what Dave could only describe as, a cruel grin. "Show him who's boss."

"You're enjoying this, aren't you," Dave said. His
horse was a little smaller than Phil's and a glossy
brown with a white flash on his forehead.

"He's a good, old boy," Tulder put in. "His name's
'Billy'. We picked him especially for you."

Dave looked at Billy and Billy looked at him. Dave
said, "Hey, Billy, I'm Dave."

Billy snorted, nodded his head and dragged his left,
front hoof along the ground.

"I think he likes you," Seth said, still grinning.

"Just stroke his neck," said Garrow. "Put your
head close to his."

Dave did as he was told, and Billy nuzzled his
cheek. Despite his fear, he couldn't help chuckling.
"Love you too, Billy," he whispered in the horse's
ear. Billy nuzzled again.

"Come on, Horse Whisperer," said Phil. "The
introductions are over, get up."

Dave patted him again, raised his right foot and
placed it gingerly in the stirrup, grabbed hold of
the pommel, took a deep breath and swung his left
leg over. He held his breath waiting for Billy to rear
or buck, or whatever horses do, who don't want
stupid bastards on their backs. Billy snorted and
nodded again but otherwise remained still.

"Good boy, Billy," Dave said softly, rubbing his
mane. He could have sworn the horse made a
strange purring sound, like a cat.

"Right. Are we ready?" Seth asked. Everybody
nodded or muttered assent. He urged his horse
forward, a sleek, white stallion with an aristocratic
air.

"He thinks he's fucking Gandalf," Dave whispered to Phil.

"Maybe he is," she replied with a wink.

She spurred her horse forward with a gentle caress of her Doc Marten's. Her nag jumped a little before easing into a trot. Garrow was already up with Seth and Jack was just behind the two of them.

"Our turn Billy," Dave said to his new best friend, touching him slightly with his feet. "Me and you are going to get on just fine," he added. "Let's go get the bastards, boy."

THREE

After about an hour Billy and he were as one – a unit. Dave jabbered away continually to him, and he was sure Billy understood every word he said. His nan used to say that about her mangy mongrel, Sasha and Dave used to think it was probably the early stages of dementia. Now he and Billy were best buddies, he had to rethink the whole thing. Or, then again, maybe it was him; perhaps he was a natural horseman, and never knew it. He looked over to Phil – she was looking a little stiff, obviously not totally happy in the saddle.

"You all right, girl?"

She glared at him. "Firstly," she snarled. "Call me 'girl' again and I'll rip your lungs out. Secondly, I haven't been given some old Dobbin, like you have. This fucker's like a coiled spring."

Dave shrugged. "Honesty is always the best policy." He gave her a big smile. "By the way, animals sense when you're uptight. Try and chill out a bit." He nudged Billy and the horse trotted a couple of miles per hour faster. 'Good boy', Dave whispered.

He was that confident he mooched up, next to Seth. "So, what's the plan, big man?"

Seth glanced at him with that - not this twat again – sort of look. "There is no plan, until we know what we're dealing with," he said with a tired sigh. "When I've formulated a plan, I'll be sure to let you know." He looked at Dave squarely now, that cruel grin back. "I think Garrow's idea of a decoy may be a good one. Are you up for the role?"

Dave reined Billy in a little and dropped back by Jack. "What is it about me?" He asked him. "Why does he hate me so much?"

"He doesn't hate you," Jack said soothingly. "He just thinks you're a moron."

"That's all right then," Dave said. "I was getting worried. Bastard."

Jack laughed. "Don't take it to heart. When we hit the valley, you can show him what you're really made of."

"Can't wait."

They trotted along in silence for a time. They were in what Dave supposed they called 'the prairie'. In the distance the ground climbed up to a rocky ridge. Although it seemed closer, it was probably three or four miles away.

He heard Seth ask Garrow if the valley was beyond the ridge. Garrow told him it was 'aways' past that ridge to the next. Dave loved this western speak. He was starting to yearn for chaps, cowboy boots, holsters and a couple of Buntline specials. He'd even got a nice line in Eastwood stubble about the chops. He was riding taller in the saddle, and that was no lie. Tulder had given him one of the Winchesters and he was waiting for some lowlife laughing at Billy, so he could plug him full of lead. It was a shame he couldn't carry on living the fantasy instead of facing the real thing. From all accounts, the bastards they were about to encounter were not easily plugged.

"Any thoughts?" He asked Phil.

"At the moment, just one," she replied, through gritted teeth. "Keeping my arse in this saddle."

He was becoming so comfortable with Billy; he was starting to nod off when Seth waved them over to the bottom of the ridge.

"We'll wait here until the sun goes down," he said.

"Break out the vittles?" Dave said.

He didn't know what he was expecting – no that's a lie – pork and beans was what he was expecting. That's what they eat in all these movies where they're heading 'em on in and moving 'em on out. It's a cowboy staple, like pie and mash in London, pasties in Cornwall and Balti in Birmingham. What he wasn't expecting was something from the Great British Bake Off. Seth and Garrow cracked out the grub, like a Wild West version of Mary Berry and Paul Hard…something or other. In fact, thinking about it, Seth didn't look dissimilar to old Paul, with the silver hair and matching stubble, and was just as annoying and self-centred.

There were several pastry-type things, like sausage rolls, but nothing like sausage rolls, wraps but not wraps. Everything seemed off kilter. Apart from pork and beans, he'd never known much about the old cowboy nosh. Garrow unwrapped a large pie. It was golden brown and cause for salivation, even though none of the rednecks knew what was in it. He took out a penknife.

"Who's for a slice of Mary's delicious pie?" He asked.

"What's in it?" enquired Jack.

"The same as always," Garrow replied. "Pork and beans."

Dave couldn't stop a fist-pump, he just couldn't. It was like watching a James Bond film, when he introduced himself, you know – the name's Bond, James Bond. It was like everything was right in the world again.

"It'd be rude not to," he said.

Garrow looked at him and shook his head. "You don't want any?"

"No, I mean…yes…please."

Seth raised his eyebrows in a – see what I have to put up with – expression. Garrow nodded but cut Dave a generous slice anyway. He looked up at Phil and Jack; they both nodded and received a similar sized slice.

Dave took a bite. He'd been expecting pastry filled with tinned baked beans with frankfurters. He wasn't an authority on old west cooking, after all was said and done. It was beautiful. Both the pork and beans were soft and tender and spicy. The pastry melted in the mouth. Mary, of Bake-Off fame, would struggle to equal this masterpiece. It was one of the best pies he'd ever tasted.

"This is bloody good," Phil said through a mouthful.

"Mmm," was all Jack could add.

So, for the next half-hour, they sat in the fading light, munching on, what could possibly be, their last meal. The other little, curious pastries were just as good, some savoury and some sweet. Dave

would have liked a nice bottle of 'Pinot' to wash it
down – or a Strongbow, he wouldn't have been
fussed. Unfortunately, all they could do was crack
out the water. Beggars, as they say. Once they'd
had their fill, Seth lay down.
"The sun's almost down," he said. "We'll get a few
hours' sleep, before we go any further."
So, out came the rough blankets, no tog 5 duvets
here. They un-slung their saddlebags for pillows
and the job was a good 'un. Seth was down and out
within minutes, Garrow not far behind, their
breathing soft and steady. Dave lay down, put his
hands behind his head and watched the sun go
down. As it disappeared beyond the horizon, it
turned the rugged landscape into burnished gold.
He glanced over to where Phil lay on her side, her
back towards him. Jack was like the other
bookend, his back towards him as well. Suddenly,
he felt lonely. He watched the sun drag its golden
rug away as it sunk from view and felt totally alone.
He was starting to miss Ringo and the others.
They'd been a team, a band of brothers and he
yearned for the banter, the piss-taking. Old Jack
was all right, but he'd always been the quiet one.
Seth thought he was a bad joke, and he was sure he
was a pain in the arse, as far as Phil was concerned.
He felt like he was losing his identity, trying to be
different things for different people. As the
darkness deepened, he vowed to stop trying to
impress. If they didn't like him the way he was,
fuck 'em. That was the way he'd always been, so
why change now? He rolled over onto his side,

closed his eyes and pulled the blanket up to his chin. One thing was for sure – when the sun went down, in these parts, it got bloody cold.

He managed to get about an hour's kip before Seth was jabbing him with his boot. It was still dark. "Come on, time to open those baby blues," he said sarcastically.

He'd just about had enough. "Has anybody ever told you, you're a pompous twat?" He said sharply. Seth shook his head. "I don't believe they have." "Well they have now," Dave said. "From now on, talk to me civilly, or don't talk to me at all. Is that clear?"

Seth opened his mouth, closed it again and nodded. Dave threw back his blanket and shivered. Phil was by his side, rubbing her arms to keep warm. As Seth went to re-saddle his horse, she punched him in the arm. "Good on ya," she said. "He needed telling."

He turned and faced her. "And so do you, I'm tired of you treating me like shit and taking the piss." He paused. "So, what goes for him. That goes for you too. I'm done being treated like the poor relation. Got it?"

She looked shocked but he thought he saw the dawning of respect as well. "Got it," she said quietly.

He went over to Billy and readied him for the off. Billy nuzzled him and Dave nuzzled him back and chuckled. "You're a lovely boy," he whispered in his ear. "Why can't humans be as simple and honest as you, Billy?" He rubbed his ears and stroked his neck and Billy did that purring sort of sound again. "I'm sure you've got some cat in you," Dave said. He could have sworn the horse winked at him.

"Is everybody ready?" Seth asked quietly. They all nodded. "We'll ride to the bottom of the ridge and then make the ascent on foot. Okay?" They nodded again. Game on.

They rode slowly, the horses seeming to know their need for stealth, especially Billy. Dave patted his neck and leant forward, his face next to Billy's, and kissed his cheek. You knew where you stood with animals. There was never any one-upmanship bollocks or deviousness; they were as they were, they either liked you or they didn't – no pretence. He and Billy were best buds, no two ways about it. In fact, at that precise moment in time, he felt closer to him than any of his human companions – and he felt quite happy about the fact. After his straight talking with Seth and Phil, everybody was a little wary and not interacting too much with him, which was fine. He was in no mood to have folks trying to blow smoke up his arse, and he was done blowing it up theirs. No, he was fine trundling along with Billy, getting himself psyched up for the carnage to come, and he wasn't too bothered. When those who can be killed go up against those who can't, there can be only one outcome and he was resigned to that. He just wished he could be with Ringo, Harry and Pete as they went down, fighting to the end. Even at a time like this, there

49

would have been banter, bravado and downright camaraderie. They'd have been bulling each other up, telling each other how they were going to kick their robotic arses. As it was, they rode in silence, the chill of the early morning seeping into their bones, morose and resigned. Dave just wanted it over. To say Goodnight Vienna, close his eyes and drift into the big sleep. At this point, the existence or non-existence of the big man didn't concern him. He was tired and disinterested in life. He used to be Jack-the-lad, now the sun was going down on his life and he wasn't bothered if it came up again or not.

"Hey, I'm sorry if I've been a bitch," said Phil.
He shrugged. "Forget it," was all he could muster.
"No, Dave, I really mean it. Are we cool?"
"As ice," he replied, thinking he'd never felt so out of place before.
"Sure?" There was concern in her voice.
He felt disconnected, going through the motions. "We're good, Phil. Don't sweat it. I just don't like being woken up after an hour's kip, that's all."
She got the message and left him in peace. The bottom of the ridge was close, about another half mile and silence became more imperative, for which he was grateful. As they neared, Seth waved his hand in a 'dismount' gesture. They all dropped to the ground as quietly as possible and tied their horses up to the ragged trees and bushes running along the base of the incline.

From now on, everything was done by signals from Seth and soon they were all creeping up to the top of the ridge, the dampness of the hour limiting the fall of rubble. As they neared the top Dave heard a soft humming and felt a constant vibration through the earth. He looked up to see a sky, vibrant with stars, the moon, an all-seeing eye. He took a deep breath and prepared to meet his maker, whoever or whatever he or it might be.

Seth held out a hand as he reached the lip of the ridge. They all stopped in their tracks and waited. Seth turned his head and mouthed 'quietly', and they resumed what was left of their ascent. Dave climbed up beside Garrow and looked down into a valley, buzzing with activity. Nine John Wayne look-a-likes were beavering away like stink. It was like the cast of 'Auf Wiedersehen Pet' on speed. It was a very orderly building site. Slabs of stone were cut meticulously from the quarry below them with, what appeared to be, laser technology. They were hoisted into wagons on rails that took them to the other end of the quarry where a tower like structure was being built. Dave looked around for the missing kids. There was no sign. A group of ten more of the cowboy droids were inert at the east end of the valley, whilst, close to the tower, someone seemed to be conducting operations – literally. A tall geezer, with flowing, black locks and neatly trimmed facial hair was flinging his arms around as though he was conducting an orchestra. His feet were planted precariously upon the wall of the quarry. He wore a black suit, a frock coat, swaying as he swung from side to side, his features rapturous as he led the robotic 'Dukes' in their 'Fantasia' type efficiency. Dave heard Seth groan softly. He motioned for them to go back down the ridge. They crept back to halfway house and he fell back against the rock and let out a heavy sigh.

FOUR

"I thought he was a myth," he said.

"Who?" Dave asked him. "Who was a myth?"

Seth looked at him, as if seeing him for the first time. "In your old world, he would probably be the Devil." He thought for a moment and then said. "I suppose within The Grid, he could be called similar."

"Well, hell's a lot smaller than I thought it would be," Dave said. "Not many inmates, either."

Seth was deep in thought, shaking his head continually.

"I'm guessing this is not good news," Phil said.

He didn't even look at her, just carried on shaking his head.

"I hate to be the one to say this," Jack said. "But I didn't see any children."

Seth glanced at him. "You did," he said softly. "And, if you looked properly, you will have seen where another ten will go."

"Those things are controlled by kids?" Dave said.

"No, they're controlled by him. The children are their life-force – their batteries if you prefer."

"How do you know all of this?" Garrow asked him.

"I've seen many things throughout my long life and heard a great deal more." He looked up at the sky. "I never imagined, however, seeing what I just have."

"Which is?" Dave asked.

"The last of the exiles."

'The man in black isn't Johnny Cash then', Dave thought. "I think an explanation might be in order," he said.

Seth looked shell shocked. This geezer was obviously something else, to bug him so much. He gazed around the group for a time before taking a deep breath and launching into his story.

"Some time after our people came to earth and began their work, creating The Machine and The Grid, the negative force I mentioned to you before Phil, affected a small faction."

"Hold up, " Dave interrupted. "Phil might know what you're talking about but I'm afraid the rest of us are still playing catch up here." Garrow looked totally bemused. "Especially him," he said, jerking a thumb in the padre's direction.

"His folks came here from somewhere out there," Phil said impatiently, gesturing towards the sky. "Made The Machine, created The Grid and started what we know as mankind. That's it in a nutshell. We can put a bit of flesh on the bones later. Let him just tell us who this bastard is – yeah?"

Dave shrugged. "Do we have a choice?"

"I promise I'll explain everything in depth at a later date, when we have a little more time," said Seth. "If you'll just bear with me and accept what I'll be telling you as the truth, I'd appreciate it."

"Just get on with it Seth, will you," said Phil.

"To put it simply, ours was a peaceful race. Anger and aggression were emotions unknown to them. My forefathers set to work to make this planet our new paradise, developing a living mechanism and framework to ensure its safety and our endurance. Soon it became clear that a small number of the group were being affected by some force produced by the planet or elements in its atmosphere. At first, it was minor – a disagreement or two, which was not unusual, but it was the way some of the people reacted that caused concern. It escalated quite quickly and soon it was clear that something had to be done. The leaders assembled and, after much deliberation and with great regret, they decided that those concerned would be exiled." He paused and took another deep breath. "You must realise that this was a terrible course of action for them to take, against all of their beliefs and principles. Nothing like this had ever happened before. But it was apparent that to do nothing would be destructive to everything they were trying to achieve. Though it was deplorable to them, the remainder of the group forced the faction into a capsule. It was sealed and sent off into the cosmos. Our race was never really the same again."

"I don't get it, "Dave said. "If he was one of them, why is he here now?"

"As I said before, I thought it was a myth." Seth shook his head. "Many years after, a rumour began to circulate. One of the exiles had escaped the capsule before it was sealed. The rumour has it that, over the ages, he developed certain powers."

"Such as?" Phil asked.

"Apart from, apparently, eternal youth; I dread to think," said Seth.

"So, what's the plan?" Dave asked him.

"This puts a whole new complexion on things," Seth replied. "I have no idea what he is capable of."

"He's only some weirdo in a long coat," said Phil. "I've seen you in action; you could kick his ass, no sweat."

"Thanks for your vote of confidence, Phil. But I'm afraid we might be dealing with a being, who, somehow, has managed to tap into the old magic."

Dave sighed. "Okay, lay it on us. What the fuck is the 'old magic'?"

Seth looked at him and Dave could see the expletive had annoyed him. He was sort of glad about that. "It was alleged that our ancestors possessed ethereal powers. It was said they could bend time, control the elements. It was thought to be another myth, a tale told to children – like a fairy story."

Garrow was gazing, wide eyed, as the conversation progressed. It was bad enough for the rest of them; he must have thought they'd started speaking a foreign language. Dave patted him on the shoulder. "We've all seen some pretty strange things recently," he said to him. "I know this must be screwing with your head, big style, but you just have to go with it. Expect the unexpected, believe the unbelievable. I'm telling you, it's the only way to keep your sanity."

Garrow stared at him, open mouthed and then nodded slowly. "Right," he said.

"So, I guess we've got to find out what Mr. Exile can do," Dave said. "We can't just sit here on our thumbs. After all, we've got kids to rescue."

Seth's expression changed from annoyance to a semblance of respect. "Of course. It was a bit of a shock, that's all."

"Maybe a little more surveillance?" Dave proposed.

"Indeed," Seth agreed. "We'll go back up and appraise the situation."

For the second time they began their ascent. Dave turned to Jack. "You've been quiet."

Jack shrugged. "You seem to have things under control." He shook his head. "I can't get over the new Dave. What happened to the joker, I kind of liked him better."

Dave punched his shoulder. "Don't worry, he's still there. I just got pissed off with being treated like the village idiot by the big man. I needed him to see that I was capable of cognitive thought."

"Cog...what?"

"Never mind Jack, my old buddleia. Let's go and get ourselves killed."

"That's more like it," Jack said with a grin.

They reached the top of the ridge and looked down at the scene below. The last of the exiles was still conducting the escapees of Westworld in the construction of his tower.

"What's that thing for?" Dave asked Seth.

"I'm not sure," Seth replied. "But I don't like it. Can you see the rails behind it? This is not just something he's building for his personal use. It has a purpose, and, although I don't know what that is, it won't be good."

The general feeling wasn't brilliant, Dave had to admit. Not only did they have to face robotic monstrosities containing kids, but now, they had some latter day
'Dynamo' sort to worry about, as well.
"Could this be any worse?" He asked anyone who was listening.
"I suppose there could be twice as many of them and two of the mad magician dudes," said Jack, holding out his hands.
Dave nodded. "I guess we ought to count our blessings, then."
"What's happening?" Phil asked.
The exile toned down his conducting and his android minions began to march off to the other side of the tower.
"Must be tea break," Dave said.
"Your flippancy may not be too far off the mark this time, David," said Seth.
Dave was getting used to Seth's use of his full name and it didn't annoy him anymore, which, he was sure showed, and irritated the big man. Win, win.
They watched as LOTE (last of the exiles, get it?) followed his workers and disappeared behind the tower.
"I suggest one of us creep down there and suss out what goes on at break time. The information could be useful," Dave said.

"I agree," Seth said.

"I'd like to go," Dave added. "It would be stupid for you to go." He nodded at Seth. "If things go pear shaped, I'm a lot more dispensable than you are."

"I'll go with him," said Phil. "You can't let him go on his own." She held out her hands in a 'am I right or am I right' gesture.

Seth looked from one to the other, and Dave could practically see the cogs turning, as he weighed up the options. Finally, he nodded. "Just get close enough to see what's going on, do not make a sound, and get yourselves back here safely. Understand?"

"I was just going to barge in there, singing a Beatles medley. How about you Phil?" Dave said sarcastically.

"Sure, what else?"

Seth sighed. "I'm showing concern," he said softly. "Not trying to treat you like children. Will you give an old man a break?"

Dave suddenly felt a total dick. He'd been too involved in this ridiculous one-upmanship rubbish and lost all perspective. "Sorry," he said, holding out his hand. "Truce?"

Seth smiled and took his hand. "Truce, Dave. Now go on and be careful. Please."

Dave winked at him, looked at Phil. "You ready?"

"I was born ready," she replied, returning the wink. "You should know that by now, Davey boy."

They waited a couple of minutes, just to make sure the coast was clear.

"Here goes nothing," Dave said, climbing over the top of the ridge. Phil followed. There were plenty of rocky outcrops and fallen scree to hide behind as they made their way down into the valley, and they used them. There was no telling if LOTE would pop back out to assess the state of play, check if he needed to give his child fuelled androids a kick up the arse. They moved slowly and quietly, edging nearer to the tower. Now they were closer, the walls of the tower appeared slate-like or metallic and possessed a strange sheen. They had seen the large slabs being cut and transported but, looking at the construction now, in the words of Eric Morecombe – you couldn't see the join. The walls sloped upwards and inwards like continuous sheets of steel. They carried on until they reached the valley floor and were only feet away from the tower. Dave turned to Phil.

"You okay?" He whispered.

"Never better," she whispered back. "Now stop asking stupid questions and move your arse."

Dave grinned, nodded and set himself back to the task in hand, moving forward. He reached out and touched the tower. He nearly let out a cry of surprise but managed to stifle it as he pulled his hand back.

"What's the matter," Phil asked.

"It feels like skin," he said with a look of disgust. "It's fucking weird."

"So, what's new?" Phil whispered. She reached behind him and put her index finger to the tower.

She pulled it back quickly. "Urgh," she said. "That's horrible."

They moved to the back edge, careful not to come into contact with the fleshy structure. Dave thought, because he'd resigned himself to an early death, he'd said goodbye to fear but unfortunately, towers built from stone, that looked like steel and felt like human skin still put the willies up him. They reached the corner and he peered around to the back of the structure. The wall was sheer, once more, but there was a doorway in the centre, where a pair of rails emerged and disappeared over the horizon, to their left. There was no sign of LOTE or any of his minions. He beckoned Phil and they began to creep along the rear of the building. Before they set off, Garrow had given them both a pistol each and he never took his hand off his. It was rammed into his belt, even though he doubted it would do him any good. Bullets, they'd been told, were no use against the robots and he, somehow, suspected the same would apply to the last of the exiles. Hopefully, they could do what they'd come to do; size up the situation, without being sussed and get back up to where the others waited in one piece. Hope is a wonderful thing, if, many times, ridiculous. They were now only a couple of metres from the far edge of the tower and the side where LOTE and the robots waited. He stopped, looked at Phil and nodded. She nodded back,

He eased forward, not wanting to touch the walls of the tower, crouched and peered around the

61

corner. Five of the robots were sat, their chests and stomachs wide open, showing printed circuits and multi –coloured wiring with domes hanging loosely. Five kids sat, spooning thin soup into their mouths, looking weak and exhausted. It didn't take Einstein to work out the situation. The domes were caps that fitted over the children's heads, that much was obvious, and by the look of it, they took their toll on the poor little buggers. Dave was not ashamed to say that more than one tear rolled down his cheeks as he gazed at the pitiful picture before him. How could anyone treat kids like this? The last of the exiles was perched on a slab of the weird slate/stone/skin shit, glaring at them, as if daring one to try and run for freedom.

Dave had been aware of Phil leaning on his back, her head above his. She suddenly drew back and let out a muffled sob. He pulled back as well and looked at her. They both shook their heads and hugged, her tears dripping on his shoulder, his on hers. "Fucking, dirty bastard," she murmured through gritted teeth. He patted her back. "We'll get them back," he whispered. She drew back and looked into his eyes, searching for the lie. From that moment, Dave swore to himself that he would give his life gladly to save those kids. "We'd better," she said.

They went back to the corner and resumed their surveillance. The kids who had been fed were ushered back into position by the other robots, the headset dropping automatically as they took their seats amongst the circuitry. Once the dome was in place, their expressions changed immediately, the weakness and fatigue leaving their features, replaced by a savage resignation. Their eyes became bright, as the walls of the cavity closed over them. The last of the exiles ushered them back to work and beckoned the next four robots forward. They sat and, after a wave of his hand, their cavities opened, and the domes lifted. Six more bemused and terrified children fell out of the robotic cockpits. LOTE made them sit and fed them more of the thin soup. It was obviously just enough to keep them alive, as they looked so frail and thin.

Dave motioned Phil to move back behind the wall. "I think we've got enough," he whispered to her. Her expression told everything. There was intense hurt, extreme anger and maternal sadness, chasing each other across her features. It didn't take a psychologist to see it. For him, he was set on running around the corner, drawing his sword and ramming it through the bastard's chest, and, if it had been that easy, he would have done it. Even after what Seth had said about this loony, he was still tempted.

They crept back the way they had come, and it wasn't until they were halfway up the incline that Phil broke down. She wept uncontrollably for a couple of minutes before she could get herself back in check.

"No kid should have to go through that," she croaked.

"And they won't for much longer," Dave said. "I promise you that."

They retraced their steps, keeping an eye on what was going on below, making sure they weren't spotted. They reached the top of the valley and dropped over to the other side, where Seth and the other two waited anxiously. There was an audible, communal sigh of relief as they appeared over the ridge. They slid down to their position and Phil could hold it in no longer.

"That bastard has to die," she snarled. She stared at Seth. "You'd better not be scared of the fucker, Seth." The tears started to roll down again. "You'd j... just b... better not," she sobbed. Seth put his arms around her.

"I'm not scared of him, Phil," he said. "I've just got to find out how to deal with him, that's all." He turned his attention to Dave. "Tell me everything you saw." Dave filled him in, getting almost as emotional as Phil as he told him about the state of the kids and how the last of the exiles was treating them; the meagre rations they were given, the misery, bordering on emptiness, in their eyes. Seth showed no emotion, just sat in silence as Dave described the terrible scene on the other side of the ridge. When he'd finished, Seth stared into space for a time before standing. "I need to be alone," he said softly.

"And what good's that going to do?" Phil asked angrily. "Those kids need our help now. Don't you dare go pussy on me."

"I'm not 'going pussy' on you," Seth replied, his distaste at the phrase obvious.

"If we go in there as we are, we are going to be no help to those children."

"So – what do we do?" She asked, the anger undiminished.

"You do nothing," Seth said. "I have to attempt something that could, potentially, be my last act."

"You're not making any sense," Dave said.

"I have to try and tap into the old magic. Without it, we're doomed to failure."

"Can you do that?" Dave asked him.

Seth shrugged. "I have no idea. Until I saw him." He gestured towards the top of the ridge. "I didn't know it was possible. Whether I can do it or not – I haven't a clue. There are tales of members of our race reaching out for the power and it destroying them. If the old stories are to be believed, and I see no reason to doubt them now, some have the resilience to accept the force and some don't. I must hope that, in the parlance of one of your popular film franchises, the force will be with me. If not, we have no chance of rescuing those children."

"But you promised," said Phil.

"The sooner I start this, the sooner we will know, "said Seth. "One thing I will say to you – whatever you see – do not – I repeat – do not, try to intervene."

"What's likely to happen?" Dave asked.

"I really don't know Dave. Just let me be. I must try to switch off consciousness to find something that may or may not be there. If anyone tries to rouse me once I'm in a catatonic state – it will be the end – believe me. Have I made myself clear?" They all nodded. Seth walked away and sat down about fifty yards from them. He rested his arms on his knees and let his head fall to his chest.

FIVE

They watched and waited. No-one dared say a word in case they disturbed whatever was going on. Dave imagined the big man was trying to sink himself into some kind of meditative state. It occurred to Dave that maybe one of *them* could tap into this ancient force. Perhaps Seth wasn't the only one that could. He was about to whisper his thoughts to Phil but then thought better of it. It was probably only members of Seth's race that would be able to access it; it made sense. But then he thought – if the power comes from The Grid, and we're all part of The Grid – why not? He debated with himself for a while before deciding to give it a go. Hell, he didn't even know what to do. He glanced over to Seth, who appeared to be in a deep sleep, his fingers twitching, as if he were dreaming about playing guitar or something. Dave leant back against the incline and closed his eyes, regulating his breathing. It suddenly hit him, how shattered he was. He tried to clear his head, mentally setting the thoughts that flashed into his brain into boxes and closing the lids until they were all sealed away. He sank deeper, his mind free to roam.

He no longer felt anchored to his body. He was exhilarated, a feather floating on waves of calm. A strand of light, like cotton drifted towards him. He attached his mind to the thread and became one with it, feeling the thrum of its potency. It wrapped around him, giving him a golden form. He watched as his new image was created, turning the gilded hands and moving the fingers, light like fire dripping from the tips. He felt the force, *the old magic*. It filled him until he was bursting with its power, tingling with its potential.

He was suddenly aware of another presence, a flickering, spluttering form, fighting to survive. It was being smothered by a darker, much stronger force. He swung to its aid, the magic surging, erupting from his newly formed limbs, a blade of flame growing from his clenched fist. The weaker presence had almost expired, a fluttering match head. Dave swung the force, the arc of its course immense and frightening in its intensity. The dark form released its victim, but Dave felt little improvement in its life-force. He swung again and the other flinched and he could feel its frustration and confusion as it just managed to parry the blow. Dave threw all the magic he could muster behind the next blow and the dark form disappeared before his blade could destroy it.

He reached the feeble form of the dying force and gathered it up, using his own power to revive it. It began to glow as it absorbed the energy, and he knew it would survive. He detached himself and let himself drift towards the light that was beckoning him. He saw the boxes containing his thoughts and knew it was fine to open them again. He opened his eyes, the force still running through his veins. The others were crouched around Seth, their anxiety obvious. He went to join them knowing that Seth would be fine. The man's face was pained and pale, his breathing shallow. Dave reached between Phil and Jack and laid his hand on Seth's shoulder. Seth's eyes fluttered open and the colour began to return to his cheeks.

"Thank you," he croaked.

Phil looked from Seth to Dave and back again, her mouth open, her face a mask of confusion. "Can someone tell me, what the hell is going on here?"

Seth pushed himself up and took in a deep breath. His hands were shaking, and he looked frail. "It would appear that the force is not with me," he said softly.

"Oh, bloody marvellous," Phil said. "What do we do now?"

"Try to be more patient, Phil," Seth continued, unable to hide the irritation in his voice. He raised his right hand, the shaking subsiding, and pointed to Dave.

"Dave, however, seems to have absorbed enough to further our cause."

Phil looked at Dave, her mouth wide once more. "You? How the fuck......?"

Dave shrugged. "I have no idea. I just thought I'd try a bit of this meditating stuff and see what happened." He grinned. "I have to say though, I feel on top of the world. I can feel it – sort of coursing through my veins."

"You saved my life," said Seth. "He was feeding on what little power I'd managed to access, which wasn't much. I could feel myself drifting towards The Grid, all hope of joining with The Machine

69

gone. You shared enough of the old magic to bring me back but, most of all, you managed to chase off our friend and cause him a great deal of consternation."

Jack slapped Dave on the back. "I always knew you had it in you, Dave."

Dave gave his arm a friendly punch and nearly knocked him off his feet. "I have now," he said. "Sorry man, I think I need to adjust my settings a bit."

Jack was rubbing his bicep. "Bloody right you do. You nearly took my pissing arm off."

It was like Phil had been put on pause. She stood and gaped at him; total disbelief etched into her features.

"Say something then," he prompted her.

She closed her mouth, licked her lips and couldn't stop shaking her head. Dave waited until she'd processed the information. It took a while. Dave thought part of the problem was that she'd always seen him as some sort of buffoon and now she had to totally reassess the situation.

"Soo," she began. "Let's get this straight. Seth tried to tap into this old magic shit and failed. You just nodded off, got a huge dose of the stuff, chased off tosspot over there and saved him." She jerked a thumb at Seth, who was looking much better now.

"In a nutshell, yes," said Seth. "I have misjudged this young man from day one." He looked at Dave and held out his hand. "What can I say? I am so sorry, Dave. You are a dark horse, indeed."

Dave was about to slap him on the back but refrained. "No sweat. I thought you were a pompous twat."

Seth chuckled. "I think you may have been right."

Dave held out his hand and Seth shook it. Dave made a conscious effort not to squeeze.

"We're in this shit together," he said. "I suggest we take a breather, regroup, and then go and get those kids."

Phil took him to one side. "What's the plan?" she asked him eagerly.

Dave shrugged, grinned and said. "We go down there, and I kick his ass."

"Don't underestimate him."

Dave looked around and Seth was behind them, appearing to be fully recovered. "Don't forget, you've only just tapped into the old magic, he's been using it for eons."

"But Dave chased him away, when he saved your arse," Phil pointed out, a little too forcefully.

"Indeed," Seth agreed. "But you have to remember that he had been using his power all day to control his little army. Dave had just received his initial charge, so to speak. When we go down there, he will have had time to recharge; he won't be running away with his tail between his legs, believe me. I understand your desire to get this over and done as quickly as possible, but I'm afraid, our attack still has to be planned."

"You tell me what to do and I'll do it," Dave said. "But we need to get those kids out ASAP."

"That's exactly why we have to have some sort of strategy," said Seth. "Focus on releasing the children and not on revenge against their captor. No disrespect, Dave, but you're new to the game. He's not."

"I've been trained by the best, Seth. Okay, I know I need to get a better handle on my newly acquired power, but I'm a fast learner. I know I can beat him," He was becoming a little frustrated. He could feel the old magic bubbling up inside him, burning to be released. "I don't see how standing here talking about it is going to help; and no disrespect to you Seth, but you didn't see those poor kids."

Seth put his hand on Dave's arm. "I know I didn't, but I've lived a long and testing life. I've witnessed depravity and cruelty at its worst and, with what you told me, I think I have a clear picture of the situation. What I'm trying to stress to you is this — we have one chance, if we blow it, those children are as good as dead. I know the power is urging you on. Don't let it make you reckless. You must learn to control it and not let it control you. You now have a massive responsibility. The old magic can be used in many ways and can consume its wielder. You have a good heart and a desire to use it wisely. A few minutes now could save those children from a fate worse than death. Learn patience and wisdom, I beg you."

Dave sighed. He knew Seth was right. This was not the time to go off half-cocked. They were those kids' only hope. He closed his eyes and imagined a jar of bubbling liquid, about to flow, lava-like over the sides. He took a lid and sealed the jar, unable to stem a feeling of regret. Seth was spot on. If he didn't learn to control this thing, it would devour him, and he'd end up like the last of the exiles. He smiled. "Okay, big man, let's get some planning done."

They formed a tight circle, and all Dave could think of was going down there and doing the dance with old LOTE. He'd always been impetuous – act first, regret it later, most of the time. He guessed that's why people like Seth existed, to rein in the likes of him. They all waited to hear what the great man had to say.

"Feel free to offer any ideas you may have," Seth said. "This is a democracy we have here, you know."

"You already know what I think," Phil said. "We now have a secret weapon. Let's use it."

"If Dave were, indeed, our secret weapon, I would agree. As it is, the last of the exiles knows about him and is expecting him. That's about as far away from secret as you can get, I'm afraid."

"Come on then Seth," Dave said. "It seems pretty obvious that the rest of us can't get past, going in hard and taking the dude out. I think it's time for you to show us the error of our ways."

"Alright, if no-one else has anything to add," he said. "I think the best course of action is for you – Dave, to stay back a bit. The rest of us go in there from as many directions as possible, try as much as we can to confuse him. He'll be looking for you and won't want to waste any of his attention on us mere mortals. We're no threat to him; he can dispose of us at his leisure."

"When you say – stay back a bit – what do you actually mean?"

He looked at me and grinned. "How are your climbing skills, now you're in possession of the old magic?"

The penny was starting to drop. "I could climb the Empire State Building and not break a sweat," Dave replied. "I like your style, Seth, my man. He's about to learn what a ton of bricks feels like."

Jack was looking confused, but by their expressions, Phil and Garrow were cottoning on.

"I'm going to jump on the fucker's head, Jack, my old mate. You lot distract him at ground level, I climb up and over his little tower down there, and then – kapow. He won't know what's hit him."

Seth cringed at his profanity, but Dave didn't really care. He might have accessed the old magic, but he wasn't about to change into a choir boy. Phil and he 'high-fived'.

"Make the bastard suffer, Davey boy," she said, grabbing his shoulders. "Make him suffer, real bad."

"In my mind, he's a paedophile, and there's nothing worse. I'm going to teach him a valuable lesson. Unfortunately, it will be his last chance at education." Dave grinned and could feel the pure aggression in his expression. Soon there would be no exiles.

"We must not let emotions cloud our judgement and make us reckless," Seth warned, concern etched into his features. "I realise that Dave has the power, but I beg you all to follow my instructions. I do, after all, have a great deal more experience than any of you."

"Would you be saying the same thing, if you'd managed to soak up this magic shit?" Phil asked him. "Or is it just a bit of sour grapes – you just trying to keep a handle on things?"

"Come on Phil," Dave said. "Stop being a twat. We all know Seth's the man. You've got to try and knock that chip off your shoulder."

Anger flashed in her eyes and he waited for her to fly at him. Instead, she looked down at her feet and shuffled away.

"For Christ's sake Phil," he said. Seth laid his hand on Dave's arm and when Dave looked at him, Seth shook his head. "Leave her," he mouthed.

Dave was anxious to get things moving, to get those kids back to their mums and dads. He was in no mood for stroppy bitches. "Shall we get this show on the road?" He asked Seth.

"Ready when you are," Seth replied.

"Okay, folks. Let's do it." Dave looked over at Phil. "Are you coming, or are you going to stay here with a face like a slapped arse?" She was starting to piss him off. This was no time for egos. "Or don't those kids warrant your attention?"

"Fuck off, I'm coming," she said." Just 'cos you're some sort of Jedi knight – you don't frighten me."

He'd had enough. "Just fucking grow up, will you?"

"Please," Seth said. "Can we try and keep calm. We need to be focused when we go down there. We all have our parts to play, if we're going to get those children back to their parents."

Jack and Garrow looked on, not wanting to get involved, Garrow eager to get going.

"Phil?" Dave said softly. "Are you with us?"

She glared at him, and then nodded her head. "You don't think I'm going to let you cock everything up, do you?"

"I hope not," Dave said.

She punched his shoulder – hard. He found it odd that he felt nothing. He nodded to Seth. Seth nodded back. "Let's go," he said. "Keep any noise to a minimum. When we get closer, I'll direct you. Do as I ask, and we may well return those children to a normal and healthy life."

"And send that bastard to hell," Dave added. He saw Seth about to educate him in the ways of The Grid, but then thought better of it.

"Let's rock'n'roll," said Phil.

As they climbed to the top of the ridge – again, Dave was buzzing. He was keeping the old magic harnessed but it was raring to go, and he was keen to let it fly in the exile's direction. He had never felt so full of life. He remembered an old mate of his, Rich Dawkins, explaining his emergence from depression to him, once. He'd sunk as low as it was possible to go, gone down the anti-depressants route, visits to the psychiatrist, even gone to see a hypnotherapist and none of it had made a blind bit of difference. He ended up trying to top himself. He'd driven to a secluded spot one Monday night in January, thrown a load of tranquillisers down his neck, washed down by a bottle of Jack Daniels. The sad bastard was married with a couple of kids and he'd convinced himself they'd be better off without him. He'd drifted off into oblivion, or so he thought, but woke up the following morning on the sofa at home, the sour taste of whisky mixed with the unmistakable tang of vomit in his throat. He broke down and wept, telling his poor wife, what he'd tried to do. She immediately rang his doctor and the following day; he was in a psychiatric hospital. Months of treatment followed, more anti-depressants, more psychiatric bollocks with ward rounds, where three or four of the fuckers sat staring at him as though he was some kind of weird exhibit. He was even subjected to electro-convulsive therapy, where an electric current was passed through the poor sod's brain. This went on for months with no effect, the darkness still consuming him. Then one morning he woke up and the clouds had parted, the sun was shining inside and out. He stuck his headphones on, listening to a mix tape his missus had done for him and walked to breakfast, head held high. The reason he remembered this little story is because of what Rich said to him about that morning. He told Dave that he felt as if a strange power was flooding through his veins. That was exactly how Dave felt as they reached the top of the ridge. He was on fire.

Seth put his arm around Dave's shoulder before they began their descent. "Can I just give you a little bit of advice, Dave?" He asked.

"Go for it, big man."

"Surprise is our greatest ally here. He mustn't know you're there before you hit him. We'll do our best to draw his attention away from you. I suppose what I'm saying is – no Geronimo moments, do you know what I mean?"

Dave smiled. "Don't do or say anything to announce my arrival?"

Seth nodded. "It's just." He paused and waved his hands in a – I'm not trying to tell my Grandmother how to suck eggs – motion. "You get it now but, when you see him and the power's surging, you may find it hard to keep yourself in check."

"Don't sweat it," Dave said. "I've got this."

Seth gave his shoulder a squeeze. "I hope so. Just bear it in mind when the time comes, yes?"

"Don't worry Seth, I know what I'm doing. Really."

PART TWO
NEW ALLIANCES

ONE

To say they were shocked was an understatement. Danny had expected to be standing in a small bedroom with the queen of the 'blue people' maybe propped up in bed against a mound of pillows. Instead he, along with the others, looked out across a blue, rippling ocean, where, just offshore, a strange looking vessel bobbed up and down on the incoming tide. He looked behind and, strangely, was not surprised to see towering, sandstone cliffs where the queen's house had been. He was surprised to see the cliffs but not surprised that the house had gone.

"Where's Dave and the others?" asked Harry, looking left and right, scanning the shoreline.

"I believe we may have just passed through yet another portal," said Sebastian.

"That's as maybe, but where are the others?" Harry insisted. "Why aren't they here?"

Sebastian shrugged. "If I had to guess; I'd say that whatever force is controlling our lives now has different plans for them. I feel reasonably confident we'll be reunited in the not too distant future."

"Reasonably?" Harry said. "Fucking reasonably?"

"Calm down Harry, it's not his fault," Ringo said. "And he can't see into the future, any more than we can."

"Indeed," was all Sebastian said.

It didn't take Einstein to see that their choices were limited. The cliffs behind them were sheer and, as Danny gazed up at them, small rivers of sand and pebble trickled down to the ground. There was no way of climbing them, that was a certainty. The ocean stretched out before them, the beach, endless.

"Who's up for a paddle?" He suggested, taking off his boots.

"I think the choice has been made for us," Sebastian agreed, removing his shoes.

Ringo shrugged. "What the fuck."

Harry still wasn't happy but wasn't about to stay behind either. "Shit," he said. Pete shrugged and followed suit. They waded out to the boat, Blue gambolling in the water and tossing up spray with her muzzle. The sea was warm, the sand soft. If he could have put all that had happened up 'til now to the back of his mind, Danny could have imagined this to be the first day of a holiday on some remote, Greek island. By the time they reached the strange looking craft, the water was almost up to their armpits. A rope ladder hung from the boat into the sea.

"Are we sure this is a good idea?" asked Harry.

"I believe our options are limited," Sebastian said. Pete had surged forward and was halfway up the ladder.

Ringo shrugged. "What's good enough for Pete," he said.

Danny looked up. If he were forced to describe the vessel, he would call it a mini galleon. It was about sixty feet long, one tall, wide main sail, dormant in the stillness. He climbed up after Ringo. The deck was a sea of polished wooden planks, the helm at the rear, home to, what Danny thought they called the tiller. Forward was a wooden cabin-like structure. They all piled in and found a galley area. Although there were no 'mod cons', as in cooking equipment, there were small barrels against one wall. Sebastian wandered over and opened a couple.

"Well, we appear to have food," he said. "It may be simple fare, but it'll keep us going."

A closer inspection revealed casks of salted meats and others containing pickled vegetables, potatoes, carrots, onions etc. There were also kegs of fresh water.

"I thought there'd be rum, at least," said Ringo mournfully.

"I think this must be a tee-totaller's boat," Danny said. "By the way, has anyone done any sailing?"

"I've been on the ferry across the Mersey, if that helps," Ringo said with a grin.

"How hard can it be?" Harry asked.

"If I'm not mistaken," Sebastian said. "We have a sail, requiring a certain amount of wind to give us motion, a tiller, which connects to a rudder underneath the ship that allows us to steer and an anchor, which acts as a kind of hand brake. I believe they are the rudiments. We are, to a large extent, at the mercy of the elements."

Harry shrugged. "As I said – how hard can it be?"

They explored the rest of the boat. A wooden ladder led down from the galley to sleeping quarters, where five bunks were bolted in place. Ringo laughed. "Where's the dog bed?"

It was apparent that their particular group had been expected and catered for. After Seth's explanation of how everything is controlled by The Machine, Danny found this all a little disconcerting. They were being controlled by something – or someone. From what Seth had said, The Machine kept the world turning, so to speak. It didn't play silly games.

He looked at Sebastian. "What is going on here?"

Sebastian returned his gaze. "I wish I could tell you," he said. "My mother told me everything she knew about The Machine and The Grid. What is happening now has never happened before. We are, literally, in uncharted waters."

"I think we ought to eat," said Pete.

They all looked at him, expecting some psychic reason why they should fill their bellies.

"I mean," he said, with a sort of apologetic smile. "I'm famished, I don't know about you lot."

"Crack open the barrels, my son," Ringo agreed. "I'm feeling the salted beef vibe already. As for the pickled veg, bring it on."

"It is a while since we last ate," Sebastian said, looking at Danny.

Danny gave him a nod. "I'm ready to try anything. Anything's got to be better than my dad's 'chicken vindaloo'"

"I love vindaloo," Harry said enthusiastically.

"Not my dad's you wouldn't," Danny assured him. "It was a cross between paint stripper, charcoal and pot pourri. I always wondered how anyone could take a piece of chicken and make it inedible. Yet, once a month, he would insist on cooking his 'speciality' and we would, dutifully, force it down. Mum eased it down with gin but me and the kids had to suffer in silence. Bless him; my dad lost his sense of smell and taste when he was about thirty, although he wouldn't admit it".

Pete was taking metal plates from the shelves above the barrels and placing them on the wooden table.

"Metal plates?" Harry said, with a puzzled expression.

"I think if the water gets a little…er…choppy," suggested Sebastian.

Harry shrugged. "What?"

"The bastards are going to be flying about, all over the place," explained Ringo, hands indicating the motion. "Come on man, think about it."

The lightbulb above Harry's noggin went on. "Oh yeah," he said.

Danny went over and helped Pete and Sebastian dish up their first maritime meal. It might have looked insipid but, by God, it hit the spot. As for the water, the last time he'd drunk water was to wash down paracetamol when he'd run out of gin. This was cool and sweet, the best he'd ever tasted. It doesn't take long to get used to the lack of artery clogging substances, he thought. He'd never tried salt beef with pickled spuds and cabbage before, but he was impressed. Mind, given the choice he didn't think he'd choose it over a meat-feast pizza.

"I didn't realize how hungry I was," Ringo said, wiping his mouth with the back of his hand.

"I guess we've been a little distracted," Sebastian said.

Blue whined and put her paw on Sebastian's leg. He picked up a piece of beef from his plate and dropped it into her open jaws. "Typical Labrador," he said. "She's had a plate of her own but it's never enough."

"My mother had a Labrador, a chocolate one," said Ringo. "She used to make up a plate of his own from our dinner, on top of the huge bowls of dog food she gave him. He died of a heart attack. She was devastated. So was I, come to that. I loved old Roly."

"Obviously not enough to stop your mother killing him," Sebastian said sharply.

Ringo held up his hands. "Hold up, my old mate. He wasn't my dog."

Sebastian glared at him, hugged Blue and shook his head. "No-one wants to take responsibility anymore," he said.

They lapsed into silence. No-one knew what to say. Ringo looked both hurt and guilty, Sebastian's face still full of anger as he chewed, cheeks flushed. Danny looked at Pete and Harry and raised his shoulders in a –what can we do – motion.

Sebastian swallowed, coughed and swallowed again.

"I apologise," he said, in a tone lacking remorse. "I'm afraid there are more ways to mistreat animals other than beating them. Obesity in dogs is just as harmful as it is in humans. Yet stupid people feed their pets until they practically burst. A certain percentage of dogs, especially Labradors have a gene preventing them from being satisfied. Therefore, the more people feed them, the more they will eat. The more they eat, the fatter they become, and the more strain is put on the heart. I realize your parents' dog was not your responsibility and their over-feeding may have been an amusement to you. Treatment like that does not amuse me, I'm afraid."

Danny looked over to Ringo, wondering how he would respond.

Ringo stared at Sebastian for a minute or so, then he said. "You are a dog owner. My parents were dog owners. I was only the son of dog owners. Roly was a happy dog and lived to a ripe old age of fourteen years. Whether, had they not fed him so much, he would have lived any longer, I can't say. All I can say, in truth, is that dog had a happy life."

Sebastian looked down at his empty plate. "I'm sorry," he mumbled. "I didn't mean to offend you."

Ringo reached over and patted him on the shoulder." Hey, no sweat man. I can see Blue means the world to you."

Sebastian looked up and smiled. "She does."

"Right I'm going to catch a few rays, if we've got to wait for elemental assistance."

Danny followed him out. "Did your Mum's dog really live to fourteen?" he asked him, impressed. "Nah," he whispered. "He died aged nine from heart failure. But I wasn't going to let him know that. I'd have been the biggest bastard in the world." He winked. "He's happier thinking Roly had a long and happy life. Sometimes, to maintain the status quo, you have to give people what they want, even if it requires a little white lie. Maybe I'll tell him the truth, later – maybe not."

Danny shook his head. "He's right though." The conversation had taken him back to the days when his Dad used to stuff his face constantly. Look how that had ended. Not only did he kill himself, but he also took Danny's brother and sister with him.

"You're just a lying bastard," he said. "Stick that up your status fucking quo."

"Come on Danny," Ringo said. "He wasn't my dog, after all."

Danny turned away from him and stepped up to the tiller. He sat with his back against the side of the boat, memories flooding back with a vengeance. Ringo could see he'd pissed him off, more than he'd done with Sebastian, so gave him a wide berth. In his defence, Danny's past life was still a mystery to him, as Ringo's was to him. He needed some time to himself.

He sat gazing out across the water, the sun, a huge, pink grapefruit in a cloudless sky. There was no breeze to speak of and it didn't look as though their new 'house-boat' would be moving anytime soon. He'd been there for about ten minutes when Blue joined him, nuzzling his hand. He lifted his arm and she snuggled down at the side of him, her head on his lap. He stroked her back and smiled. It's incredible how affection from our four-legged friends can alter our moods so drastically, he thought. He was, suddenly, more peaceful than he'd been in a long time. Blue groaned in satisfaction and he joined her. "Good girl," he said softly.

Sebastian joined them. "I think she likes you," he said with a grin.

"She's a lovely girl," Danny said. "You must be very proud of her."

"I don't know what I'd do without her," Sebastian said.

"He lied to you," Danny said. "Ringo, I mean. He lied about Roly."

Sebastian nodded. "I thought so. He's a bit of a wide boy but he's not a bad sort, really. Don't let it bother you."

Danny told him about his dad and Sebastian flopped down by his side. "I'm sorry Danny, I didn't know. But neither did he, you know. I'm certain he wouldn't have said what he did if he had."

Blue inched herself further onto Danny's lap and he rubbed her ears. "I know he wouldn't. It just brings it all back, that's all."

Sebastian put his hand on his shoulder. "Try and remember some of the good times," he said. "You must have some wonderful memories."

Danny wiped a tear from his cheek. "I do, but they make me sad as well – sad that he's not here anymore. I miss him so much."

"I know, I miss my mother too." Sebastian stood. "Blue will help you; she helps me – all the time." He left Danny hugging his dog and joined Harry at the stern. Ringo looked up at Danny, shrugged and mouthed a 'sorry'. Danny nodded to him and carried on stroking Blue, gazing out over the still water. He laid his head back and closed his eyes, memories of his dad, when he was still relatively slim, playing football with him in the garden, then running behind him, his hand on the saddle of Danny's bike, newly de-stabilised, as he learnt to ride. Blue let out another satisfied, doggy sigh and Danny smiled. Sebastian was right, she did help. His reverie was interrupted by Pete.

"Come and give us a hand," he called. He was trying to bring up the anchor. He was struggling with a handle, attached to the cog holding the anchor chain. The chain itself disappeared through an aperture in the stern into the water. Ringo joined him and, between them they began hauling up the anchor. The slight breeze Danny had felt earlier became stronger. The sail began to flap a little. The chain wound around the cog and with every revolution the wind increased in strength. By the time Ringo and Pete had hauled the anchor onto the deck, the sail was filled, and the craft started to glide through the water.

"Off we go," Sebastian said with a broad grin. Blue looked up, sniffed the air and whined.

"What's the matter, girl," Danny asked, hugging her tighter. At first, she snuggled up to him more, then she was up and off, back to Sebastian.

Ringo came up to Danny. "That's pretty freaky, right. We pull up the anchor and suddenly we have wind. Wow." He paused and shuffled his feet. "Look, I'm really sorry, man. I'm a complete arsehole sometimes, you know?"

Danny nodded. "Yeah, you are, "he said. "I think you need to apologise to Sebastian; after all, it was him you lied to."

"I just have, he's cool."

Danny shrugged. "I guess I am too, then." He held out his hand and Ringo shook it, gratefully.

"Honesty is always the best policy, you know."

"I know," he sighed. "It's just that he gets really fucking pious at times. I just wanted to bring him down a peg, that's all."

Danny grinned. "Kind of backfired, eh?"

Ringo let out a short laugh. "Too right. I promise, from now on, no more lies."

He sat down by Danny's side and they watched the boat slide through the water.

"Any ideas," he asked. "About what's happening now, I mean."

"Considering this was like a mill pond a few minutes ago, without the hint of a breeze. Then you and Pete haul up the anchor and, instantly, wind fills the sail and we're on our way. I'd say that someone or something is directing our every move, wouldn't you?"

Ringo looked at him. "Life used to be so simple," he said. "Go to the job centre every couple of weeks, give 'em a load of bollocks about all the jobs you'd applied for, get your dole and spend it down the pub – sweet. Now it's all this........." He held up his hands. ".... whatever this is."

"Mmm," was all Danny could manage.

"How did you get into this fucking mess, anyway," Ringo asked him.

Danny realized Ringo knew little of Seth and nothing of The Grid and The Machine. He was about to blow his mind even further. He gave him the highlights, not the whole feature. When he'd finished, Ringo's mouth was wide open. He clamped it shut, swallowed, let out a deep breath and massaged his temple.

"What – and you believe all that?" He asked. Danny gave a shrug. "It makes as much sense as anything else. Plus, Sebastian corroborates his story, his mother having been a guardian, as well. Seth's seen The Machine, for Christ's sake."

"According to you, He, definitely, never existed," he pointed up to the sky. "So, all of this is down to a fucking machine?"

"Not exactly," Danny said. "According to Sebastian, this is something else. Either that or The Machine's blown a gasket."

"So, where does that leave us?"

"Completely in the dark," Danny said. "All we have is speculation, and that doesn't help, one bit."

"This is mental, man, totally mental." Ringo gazed into the blue, his eyes wide. "I mean, whenever I was asked, I always said I was an atheist, but, I suppose, in the back of my mind, I sort of wished, maybe really believed, there was a God."

"Well, the way things are going, I wouldn't give up on your beliefs," Danny said. "As far as I see it, at the moment, we are in the lap of something that may still be the Gods. To be honest, I haven't a clue what to believe anymore."

They sat and watched the sail billow under a cloudless sky. Danny licked his finger and held it up to feel the direction of the wind. There was no wind.

Sebastian re-joined them, Blue at his side. "I'm afraid we are at the mercy of …." He held his hands in the air. "Whatever force is controlling us." He stuck out his bottom lip. "We've just got to go with it."

"Yeah, rock 'n' roll," said Ringo.

TWO

The three of them watched the non-existent wind fill the sail of their custom-made vessel and propel them to – who knew where.

"Land ahoy," yelled Pete, slipping into the nautical theme.

They followed the direction of his pointing finger and, sure enough, a certain amount of land was 'ahoy'. This was beginning to feel more and more like an island skipping holiday. The only difference was that, on holiday, you're not expecting anyone or anything to try and rip your throat out. This was more of an 'adventure' vacation.

"Well, that was a short trip," said Harry, and he was right. They'd been sailing for about thirty minutes. Whoever or whatever was directing them didn't want to hang about.

As the mysterious force steered them nearer to the land mass, all any of them could see, was a golden, sandy beach reaching up into a thick forest of oak, ash and beech.

"Where are the palm trees?" Ringo asked, unable to hide his disappointment.

"I have to admit, they would be more in keeping," said Sebastian, a confused expression on his face.

"Just got to go with it, right?" Ringo said.

"Indeed," agreed Sebastian, with a nod.

As they neared shore the wind that wasn't ceased to fill their sail and they glided to a halt in the soft sand. Blue was over the side first, frolicking in the shallows. The rest of them followed, holding back on the frolicking.

"What now?" Danny asked the nearest they had to an oracle.

"I guess we follow the footprints," Sebastian replied, pointing toward the trees.

There were several prints, bare footed with a couple of lines, indicating the dragging of another being. That was Danny's 'Hercule Poirot' assessment of the situation. As they made their way up the beach, it became apparent that the person being dragged had been struggling, the way the sand was churned up.

Blue was back and forth, sniffing the indentations, barking continually.

Ringo fingered his bow. "I've got a bad feeling about this," he said.

"You've only just started having bad feelings?" Danny asked him.

"I mean – a really bad feeling," he replied.

"We're, obviously, being led," said Sebastian. "And the bad feeling Ringo has, is probably justified."

Pete was already halfway up the beach.

"Hold up feller," shouted Ringo. "It's not a fucking race."

"No point in wasting time," Pete yelled back.

"Does he know what he's doing?" Harry asked.

"He seems more certain than the rest of us," Sebastian said, hands on hips, gazing up towards the trees.

"That's not difficult," Danny said.

There was a lot of shrugging, nodding, a bottom lip or two pushed out in agreement.

"Onwards and upwards, I guess," said Sebastian. They trailed after Pete, all looking at the tracks with trepidation.

"I wonder if that was a thing or a person they were dragging," pondered Ringo.

"Maybe we'll soon find out," Danny said.

"I don't like it, either way," said Harry. "I mean, this place looks like the ideal holiday destination, golden beaches, blue sea, shady trees. You, sort of, expect plush log cabins nestled amongst the foliage."

"You never know your luck," Ringo said.

"Somehow, I think I do," said Harry.

Pete was about ten yards from the trees and Danny had a vision of him, literally, disappearing.

"Hang on Pete," he called. "Don't go in there on your own."

Pete turned impatiently. "Well get a bloody move on then."

"We're coming, keep your hair on, man," Ringo said. He turned to Danny. "What is the matter with him these days? He's like something possessed."

"He does seem to be a trifle animated, I must confess," said Sebastian.

"Maybe he wants first dibs on the log cabins," Harry said with a grin.

They caught up and just before Pete could plunge headlong into the unknown, Danny grabbed his arm.

"You haven't had any more weird feelings, have you?" He asked him.

"No, not as such," Pete answered. "Other than an overwhelming one of urgency."

Danny was about to ask him to explain himself when Pete held up his hand and said, "Don't ask me why, 'cos I haven't got a clue."

They stood, looking at each other, Pete, itching to be on his way, the rest of them concerned about their immediate future.

"There's no going back, I suppose," Sebastian said.

"Ah, come on. What the fuck," said Ringo.

There was a definite path through the wood and the tracks continued along it. The sun created a delicate dappling effect through the trees as the whisper of a breeze nudged their leaves. The ground turned gradually from sand to hard-packed soil as they went deeper.

"These trees are getting thicker," said Harry.

"Steady on," said Ringo. "You'll hurt their feelings."

Harry gave him a 'piss off' type smile.

"Come head, Harry," Danny said. "That was slightly amusing."

"Like the scouse," Ringo said. "You could go far."

"My dad loved 'A Hard Day's Night'," Danny said wistfully.

"Oh Christ, don't start him off on the bloody Beatles again," Pete pleaded.

"They revolutionised music," said Sebastian.

"Their songs are timeless. It doesn't matter what

your musical preferences are, that cannot be disputed."

"Jesus in a fucking hamper, I'm surrounded by people who just can't leave the past in the past. Come on, guys; move on, for God's sake." At least the banter was taking Pete's mind off the urgency of them, possibly, getting killed.

"I firmly believe, that in hundreds of years' time, people will still be listening to the Beatles, in the same way as they listen to Mozart and Beethoven," said Sebastian.

Ringo nodded vigorously. "This man knows what he's talking about."

"I guess it's four to one," said Harry.

"Give me Oasis anytime," Pete said adamantly.

"Ah, come on, Pete," Danny said. "Even Noel admits he nicked shit off the Beatles, the Stones, the Kinks and no end of others."

"A recycler," said Sebastian, with a nod.

"A fucking thief," Ringo said with a sneer.

Harry shrugged. "I'm with Ringo."

Pete looked at them with disgust. "The Beatles were shit," he said, with serious venom. He increased his speed, as if he would be glad to separate himself from the rest of them.

"Don't be a twat," said Ringo. "Hold up, don't go off like a spoilt kid."

Danny was about to chase after him when Sebastian put his hand on his arm.

"Let him go," he said softly.

"He might get himself killed, the daft sod," said Ringo.

"I think this is the way it's supposed to be," Sebastian said.

"What? Him, getting himself killed?"

"No – something is driving him." He looked from Danny, to Ringo, to Harry. "I think we've just got to go with the…. flow."

"Do we have a choice?" Danny asked.

"I think we lost the option of choice a while back," Harry said.

"A-fucking-men to that," said Ringo.

Once again, they followed in the footsteps of Pete – literally. Harry had been right, the wood was becoming denser, the sunlight having greater difficulty finding ways through. Away from the water, the air grew heavier, an unpleasant aroma beginning to emanate from the foliage.

"Smells like rotting cabbage," said Harry, turning up his nose.

"I can't say that I've ever had a whiff of rotten cabbage," Ringo said. "But whatever it is, it, sure as hell, stinks."

"We had a pleasant boat ride," Sebastian said. "Landed on a beautiful, sandy beach. I guess, we've got to pay for it now." He paused. "That smell is getting worse."

Up until now, they had managed to keep Pete in view but, as they moved deeper into the forest, the path became narrower, the trees crowding in more and more, Danny lost sight of him.

"Pete. Wait," he called. The words seemed to die as they fell from his mouth. The atmosphere was becoming oppressive.

"If this is payback for a nice boat trip, it's over the fucking top, man," Ringo said, through gritted teeth. "That stench is getting unbearable. It's getting into my fucking head."

Danny had thought it was him, overreacting. He was starting to feel faint, having trouble breathing. "Maybe....we...ought....to...turn.... back," gasped Harry.

"I....don't...think...it'll....do...any...good," Sebastian croaked.

"We're....going....to...lose…consciousn…."

He collapsed on the path, Blue by his side, panting slowly. Her eyes were starting to glaze over. Danny stopped and put his hands on his knees, trying to catch a breath. He knew that trying to speak would be the worst thing he could do. He was trying to expend as little energy as possible. He watched as Harry stumbled and fell. Ringo had the same idea as Danny. They faced each other, bent double, sucking in what little air was available. Danny now knew what it must be like to be smothered. He thought about saying a mental prayer but decided there was no point in praying to a God that didn't exist. Instead, he readied himself for the nothingness that must be death. After everything Seth had said and Sebastian's conviction that they were destined for a higher purpose, it seemed rather amusing that they were about to breath their last breath in the middle of a putrid forest. He almost laughed. He took a last look to see if he could spot Pete; he couldn't. He wondered how he'd managed to forge ahead through the airlessness, when the rest of them were about to expire. For all he knew, Sebastian, Blue and Harry were already dead. Ringo looked at him, panic in his eyes, then he dropped to the floor. His feet twitched slightly in the dirt and he was still. Danny's legs could no longer support him, and he slumped down onto his backside.

It was as if another thick pillow had been pushed over his face. His last thought was – please let there be something – let me see my dad again.

THREE

He was convinced he was in Heaven. He was floating. Billowy white clouds drifted dreamily by, one supporting Frank Zappa, in white, playing 'Peaches En Regalia'. Danny was waiting for the dancing girls, hoping it wouldn't be ballet. Darcy Bussell, complete with lisp, rocked along with the sixties vibe, her and Frank morphing into a grotesque version of Toyah. He was a spectator to a spectacle, never to be seen again. After all, Frank was dead and had been for years. Suddenly John Peel stuck his thumbs up and said – how's about that then? He stood back and with a flourish, pulled back an imaginary curtain revealing John Lennon, walking hunched through Central Park holding his son, Sean's hand. Danny's dad was running towards them, waving his arms. And then the park faded, and five gunshots rang out and Danny crumpled to the floor, knowing that the music had died. Tears ran down the cheeks that were being slapped. He moaned, wanting to live and die at the same time.

"Danny, Danny, come on man, wake up."

His eyes were glued shut – he was dying, wondering if the pennies on his eyes had been declared, thinking, maybe, he'd finally got one over on the taxman. He began to laugh uncontrollably, and then he was coughing, retching. Gradually the glue dissolved, and he forced his eyes open. Pete was slapping his face and it was becoming irritating. He waved his hand in front of Pete's. "Lif i'" he mumbled. "Am a'righ."

"I think you can stop slapping him now," said a voice Danny recognized. It was followed by a sharp bark.

"C'm 'ere Blue," Danny muttered and was rewarded by a course tongue, lapping at his nose and mouth.

He tried to turn away. "You're smothering me baby."

"Leave him, girl," said Sebastian.

Lucidity was returning. He sat up and looked around. Pete and Sebastian were standing, appraising him, Blue sat by his side, wagging her tail.

"Come here girl," he said to her. She pounced on him, pushing him flat, continuing her licking. Danny laughed, between catching his breath. "Steady, now."

He eased her back and sat up again. Apparently, he wasn't dead, unless the rest of them were as well. He looked to where he'd last seen Ringo. He was still laying on the floor.

"Is he all right?"

"Well, he's still breathing," Sebastian replied.

"They haven't been able to bring him round," said Pete.

"They?"

"You won't see them for a few minutes," Harry said. "And when you do, it's a bit of a mind fuck."

Danny looked at him, looked at Sebastian, then Pete, back down at Ringo.

"Has anyone tried the kiss of life?"

Ringo's eyes flickered. "You...can...fuck...off," he managed.

Danny helped him to sit up. Whatever had hit them seemed to have cracked Ringo a good one.

"Who was the rhythm guitarist in the Beatles?" Danny asked him.

"Are you taking the piss?" Ringo's eyes were suddenly bright, his speech back to normal. He pulled himself up and shivered. "The thought is bad enough."

"What?" Pete asked.

"One of you bastards…. you know?"

Harry blew him a kiss.

Ringo grimaced and shivered again. "I'd rather die," he said, grimacing.

"You'd rather die than have a male give you the kiss of life?" Sebastian said. "That's preposterous."

"Yeah, well, each to his own. It's a kind of phobia I have." He shivered once more. "I mean, I've got nothing against gays. I just ain't one of 'em, know what I mean?"

"A paramedic gives CPR as a part of their job, probably three or four times a week, to males and females alike. Men to men, men to women, women to women. It's a medical procedure, not a sexual deviance, "said Sebastian, shaking his head in disgust.

"I know," said Ringo. "I'm not stupid – just – oh, I don't fucking know. Can't we just let it drop?"

Harry was nodding his head slowly. "I think you need to talk to a shrink, man. It probably goes back to some traumatic experience in your childhood."

"Fuck off, the lot of you," said Ringo. "I don't like blokes kissing me, that's all there is to it. Okay?"

"Yes, but......" Harry started.

"Leave it Harry," Danny said. "We've got more important issues to address."

For the first time since regaining consciousness, he realised they were in a clearing. The stifling forest was surrounding them but no longer smothering them. They were in a shallow valley, small cave mouths in the inclines.

"Who are 'they'?" He asked Pete.

"They're here to help us," Pete replied.

"I repeat – who are they?"

"There," said Sebastian, pointing to one of the caves. As if on cue, our new hosts emerged and slid gracefully down to our level. Soon we were surrounded by tall, slender beings, naked but for brightly coloured, loose fitting garments, covering their dignity. Most had prolific facial hair but none covering their heads. They all appeared to be male. Their chatter was soft and soothing. They crowded around them, the chatter becoming a chant, a throbbing hum. As it increased in volume, four more appeared dragging a man-size figure.

"I don't believe this," said Ringo.

"Is he dead," Harry asked.

"I don't think this is what it appears to be," said Sebastian.

Blue didn't seem to notice the body they lay before them. And she knew Seth.

Pete knelt and touched Seth's face.

"Fuck." Ringo gasped, as they all watched Seth crumble and disintegrate like Christopher Lee in one of the old Hammer 'Dracula' films, when he was skewered by a wooden stake or exposed to a severe dose of sunlight.

Danny was still trying to evaluate their present situation, but Ringo was full of Liverpudlian fire, up on his feet, face to face with the nearest of their latest acquaintances.

"What have you done, you scrawny bastards?" He screamed. The creature receiving the brunt of his emotion looked back at him, expressionless. Ringo lashed out and his clenched fist connected with its cheek. As with Seth, it fell in a pile of sand. From the caves above them, a keening arose. One by one, the figures in front of them crumbled into the ground, until they were left with a dusty stillness. The keening ceased and, just as they were about to try and assess the situation, it came back tenfold, causing all of them to fall to their knees, hands over their ears.

"For Christ's sake," yelled Harry.

And then it was gone. It still rang in their ears, but the excruciating, high pitched monotone had faded.

They all looked at each other and at their surroundings, unsure of their next move. None of them had planned any of their recent moves so this was nothing new.

"What now?" Harry was keen on driving the point home. Ringo looked at him out of the corner of his eye.

"I tell you what, man. You fucking decide," he said.

"There is nothing to be gained by bickering," said Sebastian. As if to qualify his statement, Blue sidled over and licked Ringo's hand. He rubbed her ears and sighed. "I can see why they take you fellers around hospices and dementia wards. You calm the bollocks out of me, that's for sure."

"Humankind can learn a lot from their animal counterparts," said Sebastian. Blue wagged her tail to enforce the statement.

"Has anybody got a clue what's going on here?" Harry asked.

"We have to go up there," said Pete, starting to climb up the sandy wall of the valley, the loose earth slipping beneath his feet.

Ringo sighed and shook his head. "He's off again. Can't any fucker rein him in?"

"I think he may be our guide," said Sebastian.

"I think we may be fucked, then," Ringo said.

"Oh, ye of little faith," said Harry, following in Pete's showery footsteps.

Danny looked at Ringo, then Sebastian, even Blue. "Does anyone have a previous engagement?" Sebastian smiled; Ringo shook his head. "In for a fucking penny," he said.

"Eloquent profanity, it rolls right off his tongue," said Sebastian.

Danny smiled. His dad had a few CDs by Little Feat, and he recognised the line from one of their songs, but the title evaded him. Sebastian could see the cogs working overtime.

"Roll 'Um Easy," he said. "From 'Dixie Chicken'. Lowell George at his best."

Danny nodded in agreement. "Good songwriter and excellent slide guitarist," he said.

"Come on, keep up," Harry said.

"I think he's become Pete's second in remand," Ringo said, with a wink. "And, by the way, I heard all that Little Feat shit." He stuck his bottom lip out and nodded his head. "Good band, not as good, obviously as...."

"Do not say it," Harry and Danny said in unison. "The whole world knows they were the greatest band ever," Danny continued. "But to have to compare every other group with them is tedious, to say the least."

"I think we might need to concentrate on the matter in hand," said Sebastian, as they watched Pete disappear into one of the caves.

"He thinks he's Butch Cassidy," said Ringo, as Harry followed Pete into the great, narrow, beyond. Ringo scrambled after them, Sebastian and Danny and Blue, not far behind.

"It's been a bit too easy, of late," Sebastian pointed out.

Danny had to agree. Since their tussle with the giant in the model village, their path, although strange, had not thrown up any real challenges.

"I have a feeling we're going to pay for it in the not-too-distant future," he said. "Best go and see if we can keep 'Beatle-head' from getting himself killed."

Sebastian gave a nod and rubbed Blue's ears. "Come on girl. Time to rock 'n' roll."

Danny chuckled. "You want to be careful man, you'll be too cool for school, if you don't watch out."

"I was always too cool for that place, Danny. I just didn't know it." He grinned. "Let's do this, whatever this is."

They climbed up after the others and reached the mouth of the cave.

"Now I know how Alice felt," said Sebastian. He crawled over the edge, Blue by his side. Danny heard 'Jes…' and they were gone. He echoed Ringo's last statement - in for a penny - and threw himself in. He was in total darkness, no sign of the rest. He shouted, but the words were swallowed by the blackness. He began to panic. He tried to scramble back into the light but found himself in a terrifying envelope of pitch. There was no going back. He took a deep breath, tried to calm himself and crawled forward. He kept thinking about what Sebastian had said, about having it too easy, and thanking whatever, that he wasn't claustrophobic. He reached above his head, expecting to feel the roof of the cave, but his hand waved in space. He knelt, then stood slowly. He waved again but his hand touched nothing but the stillness. He began to walk into the unknown. His dad would have told him to count his blessings. He was struggling to get past zero.

He walked as a sightless person, hands stretched out in front, the darkness, a heavy cape. He had never known such blackness. It was stifling. He started to sing but the melody was drowned in the treacle of desolation. His heart thumped in his throat and, although he could breathe, he felt smothered. His thoughts were jumbled, rolling round his brain like clothes on a fast spin. He knew he was suffering a panic attack. He tried to calm himself, regulate his breathing but, the more he tried, the more air he sucked in. He stumbled on, his body on automatic pilot, one foot placed mechanically in front of the other, the only sound, the rasp of his erratic breath as it rattled in his throat. His heart rate increased, until the organ was practically bursting out of his chest. And then he felt it – a chill breeze. Somewhere, up ahead, was an opening. He scrambled forward and, slowly, the soup that was the darkness became less dense. He held his hand in front of his face and could see the outline. He realised how it must feel to be buried alive. As the gloom slowly lifted, he wept. Relief flooded through his body, slowing his pulse rate, his heart deciding to stay put. He had never been so terrified. He could now see the light at the end of the tunnel. An oval of brightness, the size of a large egg, beckoned him on. He picked up the pace, almost running, not thinking what the light may signify, only wanting to be out of this grave of black asphyxiation. The shadows receded with every pace he took, his breathing back to almost normal. For the first time since he was plunged into blindness, he started to think about the others. Where were they? He shouted their names, even Blue, and the sound of his voice rang out unimpaired. There was no answering cry, however. He carried on towards the light, hoping he'd meet up with them there. After all, he had been last into the 'rabbit hole'. He could now see the smoothness of the cavern floor, a strange, silver beetle scuttling across his path. It was sort of comforting to know there were other living creatures here, even if they were only beetles. Something in the back of his mind told him that the Beatles had once called themselves the Silver Beetles, but he could have been wrong. Ringo would know and he prayed that they'd be reunited so he could ask him. He hurried on, trying not to think negative thoughts. They'd all be fine. They were in this together and they'd see it through together. Another silver beetle rushed past him and he almost said, 'Hi John' but stopped himself. The light was becoming brighter, the breeze refreshing, drying his tears into icy pearls on his cheeks. He could see blue sky through the widening opening. He shouted Ringo's name again and, this time, was rewarded by a faint – 'Danny?' He rushed forward, his heart beating faster again. He covered the remaining ground in double quick time and almost fell to his death. He just managed to stop himself plunging headlong down the sheer cliff, by wind milling his arms.

"For fuck's sake man," he heard Ringo yell. "Steady on."

He looked towards the sound of Ringo's voice and saw him gazing at him from another hole in the cliff wall. Beyond him, in their own separate apertures, were Sebastian and Blue and, further on, Pete.

"Where's Harry?" He called.

Ringo pointed and Danny followed the direction of his finger. "Oh no," he said.

About fifty metres below their little windows, Harry writhed in pale, slowly engulfing quicksand. The more he struggled the quicker he sank.

"For fuck's sake, keep still mate," cried Ringo. "We'll get you out."

Danny looked at Ringo and Ringo looked back. His face mirrored Danny's despair and he shrugged, as if to say – what else can I say?

Harry was up to his armpits. He stopped struggling, looked up and gave us a sickly, resigned grin. "Just for the record," he said. "John Lennon was the man."

Danny could see tears rolling down Ringo's cheeks. "No Harry, you're the man, you ugly fucker. Now shut your gob and keep still you stupid bastard. We're going to get you out of this."

Even though he'd stopped moving, he was still sinking slowly. Like Ringo and Sebastian, Danny felt helpless. He couldn't remember a time when he wished that God existed, more than then. "For Christ's sake, help him," he yelled to the sky. As if there was a supreme being and he was taking the piss, he heard Sebastian scream, "Nnnooo."

Danny couldn't believe his eyes. Blue had leapt into the air and was falling like a stone towards Harry, her legs twitching like wings. The four of them watched in horror as she plummeted. Sebastian was on his knees, hysterical. For a split second, Danny thought, we all have our breaking point.

"This is getting severely fucked, man," cried Ringo. Danny remembered thinking, this is not real, before he closed his eyes and stepped forward.

He heard Ringo cry, "Oh Jesus on a stick," as he dropped. He didn't even have to bend his knees as his feet hit solid ground, about three feet below his 'window'.

Harry was standing next to him, looking confused, whilst Blue jumped up at both of them, wagging her tail. Seconds later, Ringo and Sebastian were beside them, Ringo confused as a tooth fairy at a dentist.

He shook his head and drew his sword. "I'll fight the biggest, meanest, ugliest motherfucker on the planet," he said. "But I can't be doing with this shit." He looked at Danny. "How did you know?"

Danny shrugged. "Dogs aren't stupid, contrary to what cat lovers and dog haters believe. When Blue jumped, she was showing us what we couldn't see. All she saw was our distress and the object of that distress. She was just doing her best to maintain the status quo. Please, no silly jokes."

Sebastian was still shaking. "Why didn't I see it?"

Danny gripped his shoulder. "You're too close, that's all. Your soul mate leapt to, what you believed to be, her death. In a situation like that, no-one can be objective."

"I'm not stupid, Danny," he said.

"I know you're not. But we can all be blinded by love. Believe me, I know that more than most."

"What are you all talking about," asked Harry.

Ringo slung his arm around Harry's shoulders. "We just thought you were being sucked down into the ground, that's all. Just another normal day in this weird, fucking.......whatever it is," he explained.

Harry appeared relieved. "Thank God for that," he said. "For a minute I thought you'd started batting for the other side."

"If that ever happens, you'll be the first to know, Harry my boy," Ringo said with an exaggerated wink.

"Piss off," said Harry.

"Does anyone have any ideas?" Sebastian asked. The cliff with its man-sized holes was at their back and before them was a complete wasteland, stretching as far as the eye could see.

FOUR

"I'm fresh out," Ringo said.

"Not a clue," Danny added. Harry shrugged. Pete was looking around as if expecting to see something that wasn't there.

"What is it, Pete?" Danny asked him.

He looked at Danny with a puzzled expression. "I don't really know," he said. "Just another weird feeling, as if we're missing something, you know?"

Ringo sighed. "Moses up a drainpipe. Brace yourselves."

They all started to look around, having no idea what they were supposed to be looking for. Then they felt it. It was how Danny would imagine the beginning of an earthquake to feel. The ground began to tremble, and sand began to fall from the cliff behind them.

"Run – that way," said Sebastian, pointing into the wasteland. They didn't need telling twice.

As they ran the tremble became a shudder and they increased their speed.

"Wait," Pete called. "Look!"

They followed his gaze and stopped in their tracks. The cliff-face was crumbling away, revealing a huge, slate-grey, craggy monolith. Pete looked satisfied, Sebastian looked intrigued and Ringo looked totally pissed off.

"When are we going to see some fucking action, instead of all this mind-bending bollocks. We're getting nowhere fast here. We're just going from one piece of ridiculous shit to another."

"Maybe our resolve is being tested", said Harry with a grin.

"The way I see it," Danny said. "It's as if someone or something is playing games with us. Moving us here and there like toy soldiers."

"And the trouble is," Sebastian said. "We have no option but to comply. It isn't as though we're given choices. We're being ushered in a particular direction."

"Well, I'm right, royally pissed off with it all," Ringo said morosely.

"Nothing we can do about it, mate," Danny told him.

"Here we go," said Pete enthusiastically.

A great slab of slate creaked open at the base of the monolith. Ringo looked up at the sky. "Can we stop playing games?" He asked the sky, then added "Please?"

Pete was on his way, discretion, obviously not a word he was familiar with.

Ringo shook his head. "I'm done worrying about him," he said. "It'll put me into an early grave."

"We stand here or we follow him," said Sebastian. "Once again, we have little choice."

Harry grabbed the hilt of his sword. "I'm with Ringo. This crap is starting to get me down." Then with a manic expression, he continued. "I want to see blood and gore and guts and veins in my teeth, I wanna kill."

Ringo laughed. "Classic, man."

Sebastian looked mentally constipated, as if
something were there but wouldn't come.

"Arlo Guthrie," Danny said, "Alice's Restaurant."
Sebastian smiled and nodded. "I used to love that
– officer Obie and the garbage – brilliant."

Danny suddenly realised for people who were born
in the eighties, they had a more than reasonable
knowledge of sixties' music. Danny's dad, who was
a teenager in the seventies, used to play more
sixties than seventies. The fact that they all
remembered the stuff, must say something, Danny
thought. Even now, if someone asked him to name
half a dozen Beatles albums and the same amount
by Oasis; he'd have no problem with the Fab Four
but struggle with their counterfeiters. In truth,
there was so much music created in the sixties and
seventies that transcended time. A simple fact,
which is why so-called artistes of today regurgitate
past classics, unable to come up with anything
better. Those were his dad's words, but he agreed
wholeheartedly, no two ways about it.

"I think we need to concentrate," Sebastian said.

"Why?" said Ringo. "It's just going to be more....
fucking......" he trailed off, shaking his head.

As Danny watched Pete close in on the monolith,
it occurred to him that Pete had been chosen by
whatever was controlling them to urge them on.
He was almost at the doorway and Danny knew he
had to stop him. He rushed forward, yelling his
name, nearly falling over Sebastian, who had the
same idea. They fell in a heap and looked up,
screaming, as Pete stomped on to the entrance.

Suddenly Blue leapt forward and took the legs from under him, rolling like a bowling ball. Pete fell to the ground, frustrated, shouting and cursing. "What're you doing, dog?" He wailed.

"Probably saving your life," said Sebastian, as the door slammed shut.

"More mind games," Ringo said with a sigh.

"I think it's ceased to be a game," said Sebastian. "This is the real deal now. Pete could have been chopped in half there. Like I said, we have to concentrate from now on."

"So – what now?" Harry asked no-one in particular.

"We stop whoever or whatever is pissing about with us," said Ringo helpfully.

"We're being tested," Sebastian said. "When I say we must concentrate, I mean – we stop with the smart-arse remarks and the stupid banter and *concentrate.* It really could be a matter of life and death. If anyone doesn't understand, can he please raise his hand?"

"You think you're so much better than the rest of us, don't you?" said Ringo. "Just because we didn't go to private, fucking school, and bleeding university, doesn't mean we're thick, you know."

Sebastian looked at him with an expression that combined frustration, anger and pity.

"I attended a boarding school and never went to university," he said. "I did, however, concentrate at the school I frequented and came away more knowledgeable, due to that fact. I'm assuming that was not the outcome in your case."

Danny held up his hands. "Whoa, what's going on here? Squabbling amongst ourselves is not doing any of us any good." He glared at Sebastian, expecting better from him.

Sebastian returned his gaze and shrugged. "Even members of Mensa are allowed to become irritated now and then," he said.

"What, you're in Mensa?" asked Harry.

"It's no big deal," said Sebastian.

"My dad was a member of Mensa," Danny said. "He used to tell me it wasn't a measure of intelligence; it was just the ability to look at things a certain way. He went to a couple of gatherings and came back saying that half the people there had about as much common sense as most candidates on 'The Apprentice'. Sure, they could solve problems a bit quicker than the rest of us, but they weren't the mental heavyweights they were made out to be. So, Sebastian's right – it's no big deal."

Ringo looked about to gloat, then thought better of it. Sebastian was about to protest but shrugged and nodded.

"We are all unique," said Pete.

"Yeah, but some of us are more un…." Ringo began to brag. Four sets of eyes sent out the message – stop being a twat. He complied.

"Good," Danny said. "Can we get back to trying to figure out what's going on here, using *all* of the brainpower on hand?"

"The way I see it is, we're stuffed until whatever is shifting us about decides to do something," said Harry.

"I disagree," Sebastian said. "We need to be proactive. We're not sheep."

"What do you suggest?" Ringo tried hard but could not disguise the acid in his tone.

"I suggest we decipher the code for the door. Maybe a member of Mensa might come in handy." He pointed to a metal panel that Danny hadn't noticed before.

There were four lines with a series of five numbers in each on the left and ten numbered buttons on the right. Sebastian stared at it for about a minute and then emitted a 'mmm' sound, followed quickly by a 'yes, I see'. He pressed two of the buttons, paused, nodded and pressed another two. He did this three more times, there was a sharp click, and the door began to swing outward.

"How did you do that?" Harry asked him.

"It was the same simple sequence on each line," Sebastian explained. "The first and third numbers equal the second, so, therefore the fourth and sixth equal the fifth, so all I had to do was subtract the fourth from the fifth to find the sixth. Extremely simple for a Mensan."

"Fair play," said Ringo, humble for a change. "Now we'll see what further bollocks are in store for us."

They all peered into the gap; even Pete was a little reticent about crossing the threshold, after nearly having his legs separated from his torso. A flight of stone steps led upward, dimly lit.

"How do we know it's not going to slam shut again, when we're going through," Harry asked.

"We don't – for certain," replied Sebastian. "But, as we have just been required to figure out a pass code, I think we'll probably be fine."

"Probably?" said Ringo.

"I'm afraid that's the best I can do," Sebastian said with a shrug.

Danny was tired of the whole thing. He was with Ringo, pissed off with the manipulation. It appeared all that Seth had told him about The Machine and The Grid had gone out of the window. He walked through the door and started to climb the stairs, not really bothered if anyone joined him or not.

"Hold on, sunshine," called Ringo, and was soon by his side. The rest followed and, as Sebastian had surmised, no-one was sliced in two.

They reached the top of the steps quickly and stopped just in time to avoid plunging headfirst into a lake that spread out across a large, low ceilinged chamber. The same subtle lighting, provided by sconces in the walls, revealed another doorway on the other side of the low-ceilinged cavern.

"I guess it's time for a dip," said Harry. He bent down and put his hand in, to feel the temperature. "Get your hand out," yelled Ringo. "Quick, for fuck's sake."

Harry snatched his hand back as a shark's fin glided past. "What the f….," he mumbled, looking at his hand, as if it had already been bitten off.

"I think swimming may be out of the question," Sebastian pointed out.

"There are no flies on you," said Ringo. "So, come on Mensa Micky, how do we get across?"

"There has to be a way," Sebastian replied. "We just have to figure it out."

They looked at each other, around the chamber and all returned their gaze to Sebastian.

"If anyone mentions Mensa again," he warned, waving a pointed finger around the group. "Maybe it's time you started using your brains a bit more and stopped relying on others to do your thinking for you."

"Keep your wig on," said Ringo. "It's you who thinks you're better than the rest of us."

Sebastian appeared genuinely hurt. "I do not," he said sharply.

"He's winding you up," Harry said.

"You spoil everything," Ringo told him. "I was only having a laugh."

"At someone else's expense, as usual," said Sebastian.

"What's this?" asked Pete, kicking something with his foot. He bent down and when he straightened up, he was holding the end of a thick rope. The rest of it disappeared into the water.

"Maybe this is our way across?" Danny said, wondering how a rope laying in the lake was any help at all.

"There must be a reason why it's there," said Sebastian, moving over to where Pete was standing. He passed Pete and went to the far side of the chamber, squinting into the feebly lit gloom. "Danny, can you come here please."

Danny shuffled behind Pete and joined him. "What is it?"

"Are those hooks in the wall?" Sebastian pointed from the doorway on the other side of the lake and slowly brought his hand over to their side. Danny followed his example and squinted too and, sure enough, he could just make out black metal hooks, the first one, a metre from the water level. They crept upwards, at roughly two metre intervals until they were about two feet from the roof of the chamber. Then, they came back down to a similar level on their side. By this time, everyone was peering up at the wall of the chamber.

"They're too far apart to swing from one to the other without risking an early bath with old Jaws," Ringo said.

Pete lifted the rope and started to pull it out of the water.

"You've got it," Sebastian congratulated him.

"Got what?" Harry asked.

The penny had just dropped with Danny and he could see the lights go on with Ringo. "How heavy is that rope, Pete?"

Pete shrugged. "Not too bad. It's swingable, put it that way."

Harry started to nod. "Ah, yeah. I get it now."

Sebastian turned to Ringo. "You're probably the strongest," he said. "Plus, I think this may be in your skill set. Do you fancy trying it?"

"Is Garibaldi a biscuit?" he said with a chuckle. "Give it here, Pete. Let the master show you how it's done."

Ringo lifted the rope, letting the water drip from its fibres, swinging it slowly.

"Come on then, hotshot," said Harry.

"Hold your water, Coach. This sort of thing takes time and concentration."

Ringo closed his eyes for a couple of minutes and started to breathe deeply. Danny smiled and shook his head; there was nothing like milking it. Even Blue began to whine.

"Everyone's a fucking critic," Ringo said. He started to swing the rope with a little more intensity, eyeing the hooks. "Here goes," he said, hurling the rope up towards the roof of the chamber. It came down and settled into the first two hooks on the opposite side. "Who's the Daddy?" He said with gusto, throwing up his arms. In doing so, he nearly let the rope slide back into the water.

"When you said it needs concentration, you weren't wrong," Sebastian said. "I suggest you concentrate more and try to show off a little less before you lose the rope altogether."

"Okay Einstein, who's doing this? Me or you?"

"You," Sebastian replied. "But, at the moment, not very well. If you don't think you're up to it, I'm sure Danny or Pete or Harry will give it a go. I think Blue could even give you a run for your money."

Ringo looked at him, not trying to hide the venom in his gaze. "Look and learn, Mensa man." He swung again and the rope dropped into two more of the hooks. Only another six remained. He eased off on the power and added a little more finesse. Within seconds the rope was draped across the chamber, a crude but serviceable route from one side to the other.

"Well done," said Sebastian. "I knew you could do it."

"I think there may be a small problem," Danny said.

"What now?" snapped Ringo.

Danny held up his hands. "Nothing to do with you, mate," he assured him. "I just can't see anywhere to anchor this end of the rope."

They all searched the chamber wall and floor for a hook or ring to tie off the rope. There was nothing.

"That's a lot of pissing good then," said Harry. "Probably two of us could get over there with the others holding the rope, but, what then?"

Sebastian was shaking his head. "Blue could never get over this way anyway. Not even Ringo could climb over with her under his arm." He looked up, with a glint in his eye. "Only one of us needs to cross. Obviously."

Ringo massaged his forehead. "It may be obvious to you, but I'm sure I'm not the only one finding it not so fucking apparent." His voice rose quite considerably at the end of the statement.

"I'll go across and show you," Sebastian said. "I'm probably the lightest anyway."

They all stood and waited. Sebastian sighed and shook his head. "Grab hold of the rope and pull it tight, and, whatever you do, don't let go. I don't fancy being that thing's dinner." He pointed at the fin that was gliding slowly around the lake.

Danny picked up the rope, Ringo and Pete joined him, and they pulled until it was taut against the hooks.

"I hope whoever put those bastards in knew what he was doing," said Ringo, eyeing the hooks suspiciously. "Mensa meat might be a bit too rich for our friend." He winked at Sebastian. "Come on, hot shot, show us your moves."

Sebastian looked at them, looked at the rope, took a deep breath and was off. Danny was surprised at the ease with which he swung across the rope. A chimp couldn't have done better. He reached the far side, where the rope began its descent to the ledge. He turned and gave them the thumbs up. It was almost the last thing he did. He was holding on with his left hand, the thumb of his right extended in triumph. Suddenly the fin, that had been meandering lazily back and forth, made a dart towards him. He lifted his right hand back up to grab the rope but missed and nearly dropped into the water. His second attempt was successful, and he pulled his feet up, just in case. The shark swam beneath him and swung back towards the other side of the pool.

"That'll teach you to be a smart arse," Ringo called, unable to stifle a smug grin.

Sebastian looked shaken and suitably embarrassed and climbed down to the ledge, keeping his feet well away from the water. He disappeared into the tunnel on the other side of the lake and returned seconds later, dragging a rowing boat. He was looking slightly perplexed.

"What's wrong?" Danny called across.

"There don't appear to be any oars," he replied.

"Maybe, just put it in the water and get in?" suggested Pete.

Sebastian shrugged and eased the craft onto the lake. He stepped in carefully and, as soon as he sat down, the boat began to move through the water towards the other side.

"I suppose it saves getting the oars chewed to fuck by his nibs," Ringo said.

A couple of minutes later their latest mode of transport bumped into the rocky ledge on their side. Ringo held it whilst Pete, Harry and Danny boarded. Blue was sniffing the boat and barking.

"Come on girl," urged Sebastian. "It's fine. Come on, jump Blue."

Blue looked at him, sniffed the boat again and jumped. She landed between Pete and Sebastian, her claws trying to gain purchase on the bare boards. Sebastian hugged her and whispered soothingly in her ear until she calmed down.

"Your turn," Danny said to Ringo.

"I'm waiting 'til that fucker goes back over there," he said, watching the shark's fin. Seconds later, he was in and the boat began to move backwards to the other side of the lake.

None of them took their eyes off the fin as they moved slowly across the water. Danny was replaying scenes from 'Jaws' in his mind's eye, waiting for the thing to take a big bite out of the boat and, maybe, one or two of their legs. The relief, when they reached the other side, was palpable. Ringo was up and off the boat in a flash, followed milliseconds later by Harry.

"You go next," Danny said to Sebastian. "Make sure Blue's okay getting out of the boat." He glared at Ringo and shook his head.

"Come on mate," Ringo said, reaching out to Sebastian. "Let me give you a hand."

Sebastian waved him away. "I'm sure we'll manage, won't we girl?"

Blue was off the boat in a flash, wagging her tail, obviously happy to be back on terra firma. Sebastian stepped after her, then Pete, with Danny bringing up the rear. As soon as he had both feet on the ledge, the shark raced through the water, like a torpedo. Its head lurched out of the lake and smashed down on the boat, shattering it into firewood. It dove back into the water and disappeared. What was left of the boat dissolved until all that was left of both were vague ripples.

"Was any of that real?" asked Harry.

"The boat was real enough when it got us over here," Danny said.

"Maybe all of this shit is in our heads," said Ringo. "Like some kind of group hallucination, or weird hypnosis bollocks."

They all, automatically, looked to Sebastian for an explanation.

"Will you stop doing that," he said, his irritation clear. "I'm not a bloody oracle. I don't know any more than the rest of you."

"But you're a member of M..." Harry began.

"Don't say it," Sebastian said. "I wish I'd never mentioned it in the first place."

"But do you have any ideas?" Danny asked him, trying to make his expression as apologetic as he could.

"As I've said before – we have no choice but to follow the rules of whatever game we're having to play. To do otherwise would *not* be wise. That is my opinion. If anyone has better advice, I'm all ears."

"Are all Mensans so highly strung?" Ringo asked him, smirking. Danny loved a good joke, but, as his dad used to say – bugger a pantomime.

"Give it a rest," he said. "Just accept it that he has more brain cells than you and stop being so jealous."

"Jealous? More brain cells......What the f....."

"Shut up Ringo," said Pete and Harry and in unison. "And stop being a twat," Danny added.

"Are we ready to continue?" Sebastian asked.

"Let's do it," Danny replied. "Ringo?"

He shrugged. "I guess so." He paused, looked at Danny. "I can't believe you called me a twat."

"If the cap fits," Danny said, giving him a wink.

FIVE

They set off along a perfectly structured, stone walled corridor, about three metres across, the roof about a metre above their heads. The floor was smooth and even. It was obviously man-made or created by some sentient beings.

"I wonder what's waiting for us next," Harry mused.

"Well, so far, our intellect has been tested. I see no reason why that should change," said Sebastian.

"It could become more physical," said Ringo.

"Yeah, I think your intellect's been tested enough, mate," Danny said to him, with a grin.

"Fuck off," Ringo replied. "I thought you were my mate. Stop taking the piss, will you?"

"I'll stop if you do," Danny said. "Now you know how Sebastian feels, with all this Mensa crap, you keep dishing out."

"Alright, alright," he said. He looked at Sebastian, "Truce?"

"Truce," Sebastian agreed. Blue barked and wagged her tail, as if she were glad that Ringo had stopped being a pain in the arse to the leader of her pack. She even padded over and licked his hand. Ringo bent down and massaged her ears. "Hey brave girl. Do you want Uncle Ringo to stop being a twat?" He looked at Danny as he finished the question. Blue barked twice in agreement. Danny stroked her head.

"We'll hope for the best, eh girl. Don't hold your breath though."

"Okay, enough. Alright?"

"If you give it, you've got to be able to take it," Pete said.

"Never mind," said Sebastian. "I think we're about to face our next test. Look."

About twenty yards ahead, the tunnel seemed to angle to the left, a faint, reddish hue bleeding into the dim light. They all slowed their pace automatically, moving to the right to get the best view around the corner, as they approached. As they moved closer, Danny could feel the temperature rising.

"I think our trials may be to do with the elements," said Sebastian, as they rounded the bend. For once, Ringo didn't feel the inclination to make some flippant remark. Instead, he said. "I hate fire." The look on his face told a different story. He was terrified.

Up ahead, flames rose from the floor of the passage, a wall of fiery sentries.

Danny scrutinised the floor, walls and ceiling, looking for some way of overcoming the blaze, but saw nothing. By now, Ringo was visibly shaking.

"What is it mate?" Danny asked him.

"I hate fire," he repeated, pushing himself against the wall, as if he thought he could pass through it, like a ghost. By the look in his eyes, he was close to panic.

"Calm down, mate," Pete said soothingly. "We'll get through it........somehow."

133

Ringo started shaking his head violently. "Not me," he blurted. "Not me, not me, not me." He was clawing at the stone wall and Danny could see the blood on his fingers.

He slapped Ringo across the face. "Stop," he yelled into his face. "What is the matter with you?"

Ringo stared, wide eyed at the flames, sunk to the floor and buried his head in his hands. "I'm sorry Stan, I couldn't do anything," he mumbled. "It was too hot, just too fucking hot." He began to weep.

Danny sat down and put his arm around him. "Talk to me," he whispered. Ringo did.

He looked back at the flames and the fear remained in his eyes.

"I couldn't save him Danny, I couldn't save Stan," he said quietly.

He was leaning into Danny and Danny hugged him closer. "I'm sure you would have, if you could," he said. "Was Stan a friend of yours?"

Still gazing into the fire, Ringo shook his head. "My brother," he said, the firelight turning his tears into jewels. "He was two years older than me."

Danny glanced at the others and with a simple flicker of his eyes indicated that they should leave them be. They moved back around the bend.

"Do you want to talk about it?" He asked Ringo. Ringo didn't reply, just sat there staring into the flames, remembering. Danny had no intention of pushing him. If he wanted to tell him about his brother – he would, if he wanted to keep it bottled up, there was nothing Danny could do about it. They sat side by side for a good ten minutes before

he said. "It was a red-hot summer's day. You know when we used to have proper summers. Stan was ten and I was eight. Old farmer Jessop's wheat field had been harvested and bailed up. The day before, Stan had won a bet with his mate, Ralph Barlow and pocketed his Swiss army knife. He took it out and cut the ties on one of the bails. We made a den out of the straw. It was good, even if I do say so myself. We were sat in there, getting our breath back, really pleased with ourselves."
Danny felt him shiver but he continued.
"Stan reached into his pocket and brought out a bent fag and a box of matches. 'I nicked it out of Dad's box yesterday,' he told me. I asked him why. He said that all grown-ups smoked and if we wanted to be grown-up, we had to do it as well. I didn't want to; I hated the smell when the old man lit up; but Stan insisted. He stuck the fag in his mouth and took a match out of the box. I still remember how he winked at me as he struck it. He lit the fag, took a drag and blew out the match. I could tell he wasn't enjoying it, but he carried on regardless; Stan was never a quitter. I had shuffled nearer to the opening of our den to get as far away from the stink as I could, without actually leaving. Stan was pretending to be Dad, puffing away and I was laughing. Then he tapped the fag to knock off the ash."
He paused and his voice started to crack. It was obvious what had happened next, but he had to get it out. The tears were rolling freely down his cheeks now and he wiped his nose with the back of

his hand. "It went up like a b... bastard," he stuttered. "I scurried out and watched as my brother was engulfed in flame. It took me five minutes to run to the farmhouse. Stan had no chance anyway. Jessop rang for the Fire Brigade and the Ambulance, but I still remember that look on his face. Even aged eight, I could tell a –serves you right – expression when I saw one."

Ringo broke down and sobbed and Danny wondered if this was the first time he'd talked about the death of his brother. "It wasn't your fault," he told him quietly. "It was an accident, a terrible accident, that's all. There was nothing you could have done."

"That's easy for you to say," Ringo muttered, and he was right.

They sat for another five minutes and then Ringo wiped his eyes and nose with the back of his hand. "I suppose we've got to do this?"

Danny nodded. "I don't think we have a choice, mate," he said apologetically.

Ringo stood up. "I guess you'd better get Mensa man then. See if he can find a way through this." He gestured towards the flames and grimaced.

Danny was about to call for the others, but they appeared from around the corner.

"I'm so sorry man," said Pete, going in for the man hug.

"You touch me, and I'll drop you," Ringo warned him. "I mean it Pete. I can't be doing with all of that shit."

Pete held up his hands. "No sweat mate." He paused. "But it's like Danny says, it ain't your fault."

Ringo glared at everyone. "Can we just leave this the fuck alone. Yeah?"

They all nodded, Blue lay down and whined, inching nearer to Ringo. He sat down and patted his leg. Blue sat on his lap and licked his face. "I love this dog," he said.

Sebastian smiled. "I don't know what I'd do without her," he said. "She's a part of me."

Ringo looked at him. "You're lucky, man. Now stop pissing about and use your superior brain to sort this out. If you can find some way of putting out the fire, I'd really appreciate it."

Sebastian walked towards the flames, stroking his chin. When he was as near as he could get without scorching himself, he knelt, his arm shielding his eyes and peered at the base of the conflagration. "It's as I thought," he called back. "There are jets producing gas or some type of fuel. It's like a massive gas fire. That means there's got to be some way of turning it off. I just can't see it at the moment. Maybe another pair of eyes might help. Danny?"

Danny gave the others an apologetic smile. It seemed that whenever Sebastian wanted assistance, he always asked him. Pete shrugged and grinned. "Go for it man, I'm hot enough as it is."

"In your dreams," Harry said with a laugh. He turned to Danny. "Go on Dan the man. You might not be top of the pops, as far as brain power's

137

concerned, but you're in the top ten. We're just bubbling under."

"Damned right," Ringo said. "Now fuck off and be Robin to his Batman."

Danny gave them the thumbs up and went to join Sebastian at the wall of flame.

"Come on Boy Wonder," Sebastian chuckled. "Help me sort out this fiery conundrum.

Danny hunkered down beside him and there they were, two hunched up figures watching the credits for 'Tales of the Unexpected' without the dancing girls. After about five minutes, Danny was stumped. "There's nothing," he said to Sebastian. "Save walking through the fire, we're stuck."

Sebastian leant forward until Danny could practically smell his hair singeing. "You're a genius, Danny. Do you know that?"

Danny was lost. "I think an explanation might be in order," he said.

"Look." Sebastian pointed. "Through the flames."

Danny followed the direction of his finger and immediately saw the lever beyond the flames.

"We're stuffed," was all he could think of to say.

Sebastian looked at him and grinned. "I expected more from you Danny."

Danny looked from him to the giant gas oven and shook his head. "I'm obviously missing something, but, for the life of me, I can't see what. Correct me if I'm wrong," he continued. "Are we to assume that the lever on the other side of the raging fire, switches it off?"

Sebastian nodded.

"But it's on the other side," he said. "We'd have to walk through the flames to get to it."

Sebastian nodded again but said nothing. The silly, expectant grin on his face was starting to irritate Danny slightly.

"Well, unless you have an asbestos suit secreted about your person, as I said before – we're stuffed."

"Oh Danny, come on. What puts out fire?"

"Water," he replied.

"And what have we just sailed across?"

"I didn't see any buckets laying around though," said Harry. He and Pete had joined them. Ringo was staying put.

"That would be much too easy, don't you think?" Sebastian said, enjoying this little game.

"If we can't bring the water here and we can't take the fire there, I don't see that it's much good," Pete said.

Sebastian sighed and shook his head. "Don't any of you possess any imagination?"

"He wants one of us to chuck ourselves in that lake," Ringo called. "Am I right?" He asked Sebastian.

"I don't want anyone to throw themselves in," Sebastian said. "Submerge themselves – yes."

"There's just one small problem there," Danny pointed out.

"You need glasses, if you think it's fucking small," said Ringo. "I think we're talking about Jaws' slightly smaller brother, the emphasis on 'slightly'."

"I admit, it won't be as simple as I would like," said Sebastian. "But with a little diversionary tactic and a lot of care, it's easily doable."

"So, are you going to be the shark's dinner then?" Ringo asked him.

"Erm, I thought, maybe, we'd see if anyone wanted to – sort of – volunteer?" Sebastian said expectantly.

"I'll do it," Danny said. "If he says it's doable, I trust him. Let's face it, without him, we really would be stuffed."

Ringo looked at Danny and smiled. "You never fail to surprise me, Danny. I think I've seen the limit of your stupidity, but then, you raise it another notch. Come on man, this is ridiculous. Plus – I really like you."

"Have you got any better ideas?" Danny asked him. Ringo shook his head sadly. "Let's get on with it then," Danny said.

"It's time to revisit our fishy friend, I'm afraid," said Sebastian.

"Is this really the only way?" Harry asked.

"Unless you can think of another?" Danny said.

"I'm afraid it's simple," Sebastian explained. "We need to get past the flames. The only way to put them out is to reach the lever beyond the flames. As Danny mentioned – an asbestos suit would be extremely advantageous. Unfortunately, we don't have one. So, we have to use what's available to us and make the best of it."

"What diversionary tactic are you going to be using with 'Jaws'?" Ringo enquired. "Are you going to tell him a bedtime story?"

Sebastian looked at him and shook his head in despair.

"Let's just work as a team, here," Danny said. "Unless anyone has anything sensible to add to the mix, it's probably better not to take the piss. What do you say?" He stared at Ringo.

Ringo held up his hands. "Okay. I'll try. But you ought to know – I was born a piss-taker. It's in my blood."

Despite himself, Danny had to smile. "Well, if you could try and curb your natural urges, it would be appreciated."

"Yeah. Just hit pause and stop being a twat for an hour or so. Or at least until we're the other side of that pissing fire," said Pete.

Ringo made a zipping motion across his lips and winked at Danny.

He could be infuriating but deep down, Ringo was a decent sort who would lay his life on the line for his mates. Danny winked back.

"I hate to interrupt the bromance," said Sebastian. "But we've got things to do."

"You mean, Danny's got things...."

Danny held up his hand and stopped Ringo mid flow. "Let's just get on with it,"

They made their way back to the lake and Danny didn't think he was the only one to hope that the dreaded fin would be nowhere to be seen. As soon as the water came back into view, however, so did

141

'Jaws', gliding back and forth, as if he was expecting them.

It was Sebastian's turn to hold up his hand. "Keep as quiet as you can," he whispered. "It hasn't been proven but it's possible that sharks' hearing is almost as good as their olfactory sense. Best to be on the safe side."

They crept into the cavern and stood silently, watching, as the fin swung from left to right. It swung nearer to the bank and they glimpsed those dead, black eyes just below the surface.

"It knows we're back," said Harry.

"Maybe, maybe not," Sebastian said softly. "Just remember, as far as brain power is concerned, we are superior."

"That's easy for you to say," Pete said.

"It is," Sebastian agreed.

Ringo took his knife out of its sheath and held it against the palm of his hand. "Ready when you are, hot shot," he said quietly.

Sebastian looked shocked. "I wasn't thinking of that," he said with a disgusted shake of the head. "I thought we'd just shake the rope around a bit. Get his attention."

"Shake the rope around a bit," Ringo repeated. "Shake the bloody rope." He suddenly stopped. "That's it – we combine your idea with mine."

Sebastian was still looking slightly squeamish. "You mean to smear your blood all over the rope?" He asked Ringo.

"Oh no," Ringo replied. "Not just my blood. I was all right dripping some into the water, but if that rope's going to be covered in it, well – it'd be getting on for an armful, to paraphrase Tony Hancock. No, let's give the fucker a bit of a cocktail, really tantalize his bloodlust. What do you say chaps?"

"I'm game," Danny said.

Ringo shook his head. "Not you, firewalker. You must be squeaky clean. We can't have the faintest whiff of blood from your corner. Pete, Harry?"

Pete nodded. "It's a good idea, mate."

Harry looked down at his hand and at the knife on his belt. "I guess we don't have a lot of choice," he said reluctantly.

"Hotshot?"

Sebastian looked uncomfortable but realised refusal was not an option. "Yes, I suppose so. It is a good idea. I would appreciate it, though, if you could call me by my name and cut out the 'hotshot, Mensa man' stuff. Deal?"

Ringo shrugged. "Whatever."

They stood, waiting for someone to take the initiative. Ringo sighed, yanked the rope out of the hooks and drew the blade of his knife across his palm. "Come on you pussies, let's see some blood." He made a fist, until the blood was dripping from the base of his hand, onto the rope. He ran his hand back and forth, his blood sinking into the fibres.

"Here goes," said Pete, taking his own knife out and following suit. Ringo stepped aside and let Pete take his place.

Harry had his knife in his hand but was hesitating. "Go for it Harry," Ringo urged. "It doesn't hurt that much, honest."

Harry drew the blade across with a grimace. "Fucking liar," he said. He went up to Pete and shoved him aside. Danny could see the blood glistening on the rope.

"Your turn, Hot......sorry.......Sebastian," said Ringo, with a grin.

"I haven't got a knife," Sebastian said apologetically, hoping that this omission might let him off. Ringo wiped his on his breeches and held it out to Sebastian.

"You'll be alright, I ain't got aids or anything." Sebastian took the knife gingerly, bent down, gave it a swill in the lake and wiped it on his own jeans. "Just to be on the safe side," he said. He held it against his palm, closed his eyes and yanked it down. "Bloody hell," he said. He added his blood to the existing cocktail, and they were set.

"Okay, let's get this shit done," said Ringo. "I suggest that Harry and Pete help Danny get suitably dowsed, and we lure old toothy to the cocktail bar. What do you say, Sebbie, my old mucker?"

Sebastian winced and dropped his head. "It seems like a reasonable idea," he said.

"For God's sake, stop being such a girl," Ringo said. "What's a bit of micky taking amongst friends? Stop taking things so personally."

"He's right," Pete added apologetically. "He takes the piss out of everybody – not just you. You've got to let yourself drop a few levels; you do tend to come across a bit high and mighty. Sorry."

Sebastian looked shocked and was about to respond, but then let his gaze fall. "I suppose Blue and I have been on our own for so long now, I've lost the ability to interact with morons."

"Now that's more like it, Hotspot," said Harry, clapping. "Get down and dirty."

"I hate to interrupt the bonding process," Danny said, smiling. "But I imagine fresh blood is more enticing to our fishy friend than dried up leftovers."

"Indeed," Sebastian agreed. "Ringo – lets shake it up baby."

Ringo grinned. "Now you're talking my language; let's twist and shout my man."

"One of you will have to take off your shirt and soak that as well," Sebastian said to Pete and Harry. "Danny will need to put it over his head when he goes through the flames. All of his flesh must be covered with sodden clothing."

Pete was pulling his shirt over his head before Sebastian could finish.

Ringo was really getting into it. "Once we start shaking this baby and you see the fin racing in for the feast, you two lower him in slowly, causing as little disturbance as possible. Got it?"

145

Danny thought Ringo was enjoying being back at the forefront of the action. "Ready, Seb?" Sebastian nodded, and they dropped the blood smeared rope into the water and started to swing it to and fro. The shark, that had been drifting aimlessly, suddenly found a new purpose. The fin sliced through the water at a rate of knots. As it passed Danny, Harry and Pete, Ringo gave the nod. Harry and Pete lowered Danny gently into the water, Pete's shirt clutched to his chest. He held his breath until they pulled him clear. The shark was savaging the rope, never realising that fresh meat was only yards away.

Ringo gave the rope a final yank. "Chew on that, you thick fucker," he said.

"Speed is of the essence," Sebastian urged. "He has to stay as wet as possible."

They raced back to the fire, Danny pulled Pete's shirt over his head, hid his hands in his sodden cuffs and ran through the fire before he could have second thoughts. Even with the wet clothing, he could smell his hair singeing, the heat intense. He rolled on the floor to smother any flames that may have gained purchase.

"Are you all right Danny?" Ringo called.

Danny pushed the lever down, the flames disappeared. "Cool man – cool."

The others joined him, stepping gingerly across the hot floor.

"Jeez, you can still feel the heat through the soles of your boots," said Ringo.

"I suppose it'd been burning for a while," Harry said. "It'll take a time to cool down."

"What's that?" Pete asked, pointing behind Danny. They all followed the direction of his finger and saw a crack in the cavern wall. A soft, yellow glow seeped from it.

"Only one way to find out," Danny said, walking towards the gap. Ringo sprinted to his side.

"Let me go first, Robin," he said with a wink. "You've faced enough danger for one day and I've got some making up to do."

Danny stood aside. "Be my guest, my friend, I'm knackered. Rolling through massive gas ovens tires you out, you know."

"Not to mention being potential shark bait," Harry added.

"Indeed." Danny glanced at Sebastian. "You're quiet."

"I was just thinking that whoever or whatever is creating these little problems for us should be rewarding us for solving them. I don't know about anyone else, but I'm starving."

"I didn't like to say anything," said Pete. "In case old Beatle-head over there called me a wimp."

"The grumbles in my belly are having baby grumbles," Harry confessed.

"I guess I've been a bit preoccupied," Danny said. "But now the adrenalin's settling down, the old gastric juices are starting to flow, I have to admit."

Ringo let out a shriek of delight. "Oh, you fucking beauty," he yelled.

"I think he might have found a box-set of original Beatles albums," said Pete.

Ringo popped his head back into the passage. "Not quite," he said. "Nearly as good though. Who's hungry?"

SIX

They almost fell over each other in their haste.
Hunger can do strange things to a man.
They tumbled in after Ringo and let out a
communal gasp. The cave was small but big
enough to contain a stone slab of a table, piled
high with a reasonable variety of food. There were
cooked meats, fruits, vegetables, hunks of floured
bread and jugs of water. They fell on it as if they
hadn't eaten for months. That is, except for
Sebastian. He took some meat, some veg and
broke up a chunk of bread, mixed it in a bowl and
put it down for Blue. He placed a bowl of water by
its side. She didn't need to sniff it, she was straight
in. Danny suddenly felt so selfish and it must have
showed in his expression.
"Eat," Sebastian said. "She's my responsibility, not
yours."
"But I didn't even think about her," he said.
Sebastian smiled. "Like I said Danny, she's not
your responsibility."
Danny shook his head. "No, we should be like the
musketeers – all for one and one for all. Blue is
one of us."
Sebastian's smile widened. "You're a good man,
Danny, a true friend – to both me and Blue. Now,
for God's sake – eat."

Danny nodded and did as he was told. They sat on
the floor in silence, filling their bellies. Although it

was simple fair, it was very tasty. Blue soon polished off her bowlful and looked at Sebastian expectantly.

"Let me," Danny said. Sebastian carried on chewing and gave him a 'go ahead' sign with his free hand. The other held a roughly fashioned smoked ham sandwich.

Danny put more meat, veg and bread in Blue's bowl and she dived in immediately. So far, the water had been ignored. She wolfed down her second helping and let out a loud belch. They fell about. Before Blue, Danny hadn't had that much experience of dogs and he had certainly never heard one burp before. By the way the others were reacting, they hadn't either. Blue took no notice of their hilarity and decided it was time to wash the food down. She lapped away at the water for a good minute before lying on the floor at Sebastian's side, apparently sated.

Ringo followed Blue's lead and let out a good old rip snorter. "This is not bad scran," he said, reaching for another chunk of cheese. "It's a shame there's no ale to wash it down, though. I've never been a fan of water."

"Water's good for you," Sebastian said.

"Yeah, but I'd rather have all the things that are bad for me," Ringo said with a grin. "They always taste better."

"Or get you pissed," Harry said.

"Indeed," agreed Ringo. "A good slap-up meal full of cholesterol, followed by eight or ten pints of the falling down water. What could be better?"

Since they'd embarked on this strange journey, Danny hadn't thought about booze once. Now, however, he was craving a few pints of lager too, to wash his dinner down. He was thankful that there was only water on the table; he didn't want to revert to the arsehole he'd become, prior to Seth's and Phil's intervention.

Sebastian was shaking his head. "I don't see the point of spending a fortune so that you can fall in the road or vomit all over your shoes – or both. Not to mention the beer belly. How about you Danny?"

Danny thought he was expecting him to agree and wished that he could.

"Before all of this," he said, waving his hands around. "I was drinking myself into a stupor every day. Before Seth found me, I was on course for total self-destruction. I'd had enough of the shit that life covers you with. I wanted out. Sorry to disappoint you, Sebastian."

They all stared at him as if he'd grown another head. Good, old Danny had been a pissed-up waste of space with a death wish. Ringo gained his composure first.

"You must have been through some heavy shit, man," he said softly. "You're a good bloke, Danny and, unfortunately, most of the detritus in life gets heaped on good blokes and not the fuckers that deserve it. The main thing is – you came through it, yeah?"

"Without Seth, I wouldn't have done," he said flatly.

"It doesn't matter what happened to change things," Sebastian said firmly. "All that matters is that it did happen. As Ringo inferred, you must have suffered a great deal to hit rock bottom. If you ever need to talk........."

"Same goes for me, man," said Ringo. The other two nodded and Blue licked his hand. Maybe now, he had a new family.

He was close to tears, and he couldn't have that. The situation needed lightening a touch.

"And why would I want to talk to you load sad sacks?" He asked light heartedly.

Ringo laughed. "You never know, you might get desperate one day."

"He'd have to be bloody desperate to want to chew the fat with you," said Pete, with a sly grin. "You'd just bore him with bollocks about the bleeding mop-heads."

"Mop-tops, you moron. Haven't you learnt anything?" Ringo asked indignantly.

"Nah, I tend to switch off when you go into Beatle mode."

"That's because you're a Philistine."

They were, apparently back to normal, and a potentially embarrassing situation had been averted.

"I'm stuffed," said Harry, rubbing his belly.

"Me too," Ringo agreed. "I think I'd struggle getting any beer down me, as it happens."

"I'm sure you'd give it a shot though," Danny said.

"Well, if ale were present, it would be rude not to. As it is, the problem doesn't arise."

Blue started to twitch and let out funny little yipping sounds. She was fast asleep, her head in Sebastian's lap.

"I think she may have the right idea," Sebastian whispered.

As if Blue's canine sleep antics had been a trigger, one by one, they began to yawn and stretch.

"I think we might have earnt a bit of a kip," said Ringo, between yawns. "Especially you, firewalker." He nodded in Danny's direction before sliding down the wall a tad and closing his eyes.

"For once, I think he may be right," Sebastian said, following suit.

Danny glanced over to Pete and Harry; they both shrugged and settled themselves down. Danny was wondering if the food had been drugged but realised, if he really tried, he could stay awake. No – this was just tiredness, combined with a full belly and a release of pent-up stress. He closed his eyes and fell asleep, listening to a cave-full of steady breathing and Blue's soft, contented cries.

Although their beds weren't the most comfortable, they slept like the dead. Danny was dreaming of Beth and his previous life when Blue's excited yaps woke him with a start.

She was standing barking at a steady stream of earth that was falling from the roof of the cave above where the entrance used to be. Instead, it was as if someone had sealed it silently while they slept. There was no hint of where the opening used to be, just solid stone.

"This is taking things too bloody far," Ringo said, rubbing his eyes.

Sebastian was staring at the falling earth, as it piled up on the floor of the cave, the sides creeping towards where they sat. "Earth," he said softly. "We're having to conquer the elements. We've faced water and fire, and now it seems as though we're about to be buried alive."

PART THREE
LAST OF THE EXILES

ONE

"Are we going to do this, or what?" Phil asked.

"Just do what Seth tells you to do, okay?" Dave said.

"Oohh, Mr. Fucking Sensible, all of a sudden," she said, waving her hands in the air.

"You okay man?" Dave asked Garrow. He was totally spaced out with the whole thing. It was probably like introducing E.T. to Henry the Eighth. He started to nod, then shook his head.

"All I want is those kids back," he said. "How it happens – I don't care. Tell me what to do and I'll do it."

"Good man," Dave said. "By the end of tomorrow, they'll be back with their parents, I promise."

"I hope you're right Mister," he said. "'Cos if you're not, I ain't going back there, I'd rather die."

"Nobody's going to die," Dave told him. "At least, none of us, and – none of those kids." He looked at Seth and could tell by his expression, he wasn't convinced.

"Are we going to stop talking and get on with it?" Phil asked impatiently.

"This time," Seth said. "We don't creep down – we swarm, except for Dave. He'll be looking out for us, waiting."

Jack looked puzzled. "Dave'll be looking out for us?"

Phil let out a gasp of frustration. "The exile dude," she said. "For fuck's sake, keep up, will you."

Dave put his arm around Jack. "Don't worry about the wicked witch of the west, mate. She's all mouth and trousers."

Jack looked at Phil's cut-off jeans and let his gaze follow her shapely legs down to her Doc Martens.

"You looking for a fat lip?" she asked him.

He averted his gaze and mumbled something that sounded like 'piss off' to Dave. Luckily, Phil didn't catch it.

"Can we get back to the problem in hand?" Seth asked forcefully. "There are children down there needing our help. It would be beneficial if we could stop bickering amongst ourselves."

"What he means is," Dave said. "Stop fucking about and do as you're told. Are we good to go?"

"I've been good to go since yesterday," Phil said angrily.

"Then – let's swarm," Seth said with a smile. He looked at Dave. "Wait."

"I'm all over it Seth, don't worry," Dave said. "Just direct the others – I'm good."

Seth nodded. "Okay, as I said – swarm."

Dave watched as they ran down into the valley, hoping that Seth was right, and the exile would be looking for him and leave them alone. He let them get to the bottom and then started to creep down himself, intent on the tower.

Within seconds, with his new abilities he was down the slope and at the base of the tower. As he started to climb, his hands and feet finding purchase easily, he heard Phil's less than dulcet tones shouting, 'over here you motherfucker'. This was followed by Seth, Garrow and Jack shouting, their input not as impressive as Phil's, he had to admit. He wondered why Seth found the 'F' word so offensive. It was, after all, a slang term for copulate and so much shorter. People get so hung up about words. Come on, life's too fucking short. As he neared the top of the tower, he heard Garrow yell out in pain and Seth's exasperation. He increased his speed and, in seconds, was looking down on the scene below. Garrow had apparently charged the exile and was lying on the ground, his arm bleeding. Seth was bent over him. He could see Phil getting ready to try some of her Kung Fu shit. Don't these people listen, he thought? He could see the exile, looking around for him, but keeping an eye on the rest of them. Jack was wandering about like a lost sheep, but that was fine – he wouldn't get hurt. Before he leapt, he saw Phil going in for a roundhouse that would leave her with a broken leg, at least. He dropped between her and the exile, his arm sweeping her back.

"I'm fucking Spartacus," he yelled. "Come on you spineless paedophile."

He didn't know what he was expecting, but the exile just stood there smiling.

"Spartacus?" He said with a mildly bemused expression. "You'll need to be more than some washed-up gladiator to defeat me, young man."

"Will I now," Dave said. He hurled himself at the man and caught Seth shaking his head as he was propelled backwards into the tower.

"Channel your anger," Seth yelled. "Channel the fucker."

Dave thought it was Seth's sudden and unexpected use of profanity that brought him back down to earth. He'd been telling the rest to do as Seth told them and he'd just gone off half cocked.

He walked slowly forward, feeling the pressure pushing against his chest. He took a deep breath, closed his eyes and focused. He imagined an acorn and directed all his power into that seed, feeling the roots of the old magic spread and sink into the soil. He waited, as the roots became his trunk and filled his head and limbs. He opened his eyes.

"Now let's see who's a washed-up gladiator," he said. His voice ricocheted off the tower. He could see the fear in the exile's eyes as he hurled himself at Dave. Dave batted him away, like a fly. He was beginning to enjoy himself when the exile grabbed Phil and ran for the tower. She was screaming and kicking and swearing like a trouper. Dave rushed after them and just reached the tower as the capsule sped past him, down the tracks. It must have been going at 180 miles per hour. He threw himself after it but fell short.

"I'm coming after you Phil," he shouted, unable to stop the tears.

"We'll get her back," Seth said. "Look."

The robotic structures were wide open, and the kids were pushing them over.

"We did what we came to do," he said.

Dave shook his head. "No, we didn't."

The kids came running over to their reduced group, laughing and crying. Many of them threw their arms around Garrow. His arm had been gashed on a piece of slate when the exile had hurled him to the ground like a rag doll. He held it above the children's heads and managed not to wince too much when one of them knocked it. As they clamoured around him, Dave could see him pointing towards him, his face stern yet kindly. Two young lads came over to him and gazed up at him with something that bordered on hero worship.

"Mr. Garrow says it was you who saved us," said the shortest of the two. His ginger hair was plastered to his skull with sweat, his blue eyes wide and earnest.

"We all did mate," Dave said, ruffling his moist hair. "Time to go back to your mum and dad, yeah?"

"I'm sorry he took your friend," the other one muttered, his head bent. Dave put his hand under the boy's chin and lifted his face gently. His dark eyes were full of genuine sorrow and a tear was creeping over his grimy face.

"We saved you, didn't we?"

They both nodded. "Well, we'll save my friend as well," Dave said and managed a smile.

"Will you beat the shit out of him?" Ginger asked him. Dave could see the hope in those pools of blue.

"Not only that," Dave told him. "I intend to rip his head from his shoulders. How's that?"

That seemed to satisfy him, and he nodded. The other lad, however, wasn't so easily pleased. "Cut his bollocks off first," he said. "Make him suffer."

Dave put his hands on his shoulders, bent down and looked into his troubled, brown eyes. "Believe me, son – he'll suffer, I'll make sure of that."

"And then you'll kill him?"

It was Dave's turn to nod. "Now go with Mr. Garrow and let him take you back to your parents."

They stood, staring at him for a few more seconds and seemed convinced that he would do as requested. They turned and went to join the others. Seth came up to him and Dave glared at him.

"How could you let that happen?" He said.

"I'm sorry Dave," Seth said.

"Fuck off, it's not your fault, it's mine," Dave said, massaging his temples. "I'm the one with the fucking power. Sorry."

For the first time since he'd met him, Seth appeared to be lost for words.

"Why did he take her?" Dave asked him. "Why didn't he stay and fight like a man, the piece of shit?"

"I think you've just answered your own question," Seth said.

Dave looked into his eyes. "Tell me honestly – can we get her back?"

Seth held his gaze. "Honestly? I don't know. If, however, I was a betting man, which I'm not, I'd put my money on you. Delve deeper into the well, trust in the old magic and yourself."

Garrow prized himself away from the kids and came over to join them; he'd ripped off his shirt sleeve and tied it around the cut in his arm. "I can't thank you enough," he said. "Will you be coming back? All the parents will want to thank you personally. I'm sorry about Phil, but you did say there might have to be sacrifices."

It took all of Dave's self-control, not to rip his head off. "You were supposed to be the sacrifice," he said. "They're your kids after all."

Seth put his hand on Dave's arm. "It's not his fault, Dave."

Garrow sighed and shook his head. "I would gladly have sacrificed my life for theirs," he said. "And I'm terribly sorry about your friend. But I think the one you call the exile may find he's got a tiger by the tail. Phil can look after herself."

"You know nothing about it," Dave said impatiently. "Take that lot back and leave us to get on with the rest."

"But......"

Seth put his arm around Garrow's shoulders and led him back towards the children. Dave was grateful for the peace. He rubbed his forehead, trying to focus. Garrow had been right about Phil, and that was what worried him. She wouldn't take any shit and would probably end up injured – if not dead. He punched the side of the tower and felt the vibrations under his feet. It was then that Jack came up to him with a steaming mug of coffee.

"There's a load of supplies in there," he said, nodding towards the tower. "I thought, maybe, you could use this." He paused. "We'll get her back, Dave. You know we will."

"And when we do, I'm going to rip that bastard limb from limb," Dave said through gritted teeth.

"I don't think anyone would try and defer you from that course of action," Jack said. "If you need any help........."

"Cheers Jack, you're a mate," Dave said. "My head's all over the place, at the moment, know what I mean?"

"Well, being as Seth is concentrating on PR, I think you need to get inside that place and see if there's any way to do what he's just done." He jerked his thumb towards the tower.

"Come on," Dave said, realising that he'd been wallowing in self-pity. "From now on, if I get like this again, I want you to punch me in the face – hard. Deal?"

"Just as long as you don't hit me back," Jack said. "I might bloody your nose, but now, with this magic shit, you'll knock me into the middle of next week."

"Don't worry, I won't retaliate. I just need someone to keep me grounded."

Jack smiled. "In that case, I'm your man."

Dave winked at him. "Let's see what we can find in there, then, eh?"

By this time Seth had sent Garrow and the children on their way and joined them as they were about to enter the tower.

"Be careful," he warned. "He might have left some booby traps."

"You'd better go first," Dave said to him. "I'm not in the frame of mind to be searching for the bollocks he might have left. I'll probably get us all blown to fuck."

Seth patted him on the back, gave him some weird sort of sympathetic grimace and entered the building slowly. "Wait 'til I've checked things out," he called back over his shoulder.

Dave slumped to the ground, back against the tower, his mind racing, the old magic burning to be released. "I'm going to kill him," he growled. "Rip his miserable head off and force it down his fucking throat."

"Man, I think you got to calm down a bit," Jack said. "Once we find them, you can let as much of that shit loose on him as you want. Until then, me and Seth are going to need you focused."

Dave glared at him, punched the ground and let out an exasperated sigh. "I know," he said. "But it's hard. I've got all of this anger fuelling things, you know?"

Jack nodded. "I know, Dave. I liked Phil – a lot, but you guys had something kind of special. Severely strange but, definitely special."

Dave laughed. "You're not wrong there, mate. Talk about love, hate relationships. I think we took it a mile or two further. I've never met anyone like her before."

"You can say that again," Jack said, with a grin. "Feisty ain't the word."

"Yeah, she could either break your heart or rip it out with her bare hands," Dave said with a chuckle.

"Seriously though, Dave. We will get her back."

"Yeah, 'course we will." Dave wished he felt as confident as he sounded.

Seth popped his head outside the tower. "All clear, I think. And there's a second pod."

"What?" Dave said. "What are we waiting for?"

"I don't think it's going to be as easy as that," Seth said. "You'd better come in and see for yourself."

Dave and Jack entered the exile's tower. The rails ended at the back, where, indeed, a second pod sat. What looked like various mechanical bits and pieces were strewn about the place. There was an untidy kitchen/dining area where he'd obviously tucked into a variety of interesting looking grub, whilst feeding the poor kids that pigswill, a huge tub of which, rested against the wall. A staircase led upwards to the left. Seth saw Dave looking up. "There are three more floors, the first contains more supplies, the rest are totally empty. I'd be interested to know what he intended to use this place for."

"I don't give a shit," Dave said. "Let's get in that pod and get after him."

"Ah, that's the problem. I think that, maybe, he's the only one able to pilot the thing."

Dave walked over and looked in, expecting to find some ignition mechanism, gear stick or something. There was nothing, apart from a long seat. The rest of it was a smooth Perspex looking material. His heart sank.

TWO

"There must be a way," he said. "Come on Seth, help me out here, man. You know about all this shit. There's got to be something we can do to get this fucking thing moving."

Seth looked at him and looked at the pod. He scratched his head. "He obviously used the old magic, but in situations like this, it's sort of personal."

"What does that mean – personal?"

Seth screwed up his face, trying to think of a way of explaining. Suddenly a light seemed to go on. "When you've got a secure building where access to certain localities is restricted. A select few have pass keys that are programmed to admit them to particular high security areas."

Dave wasn't getting the analogy. "What has that got to do with this bloody thing?" he asked impatiently, flicking the pod with the back of his hand. It hummed for a few seconds. "What the...."

"Place both of your hands on it," Seth said quickly. Dave laid both of his palms on the pod's roof. It hummed again and shook beneath his hands.

"Forget everything I just said," Seth said with a shake of his head. "All that is required, it appears, is someone who has access to the old magic. I assumed he would have customised it."

"You know what happens if you assume," said Jack.

"Yeah, Jack, we do. Now be quiet." Dave turned back to Seth. "So, what are we waiting for?"

"Well, before we go any further, may I suggest we collect some supplies to take along. We have no idea what's ahead or when we'll see anything resembling food again," he said.

Dave sighed. "Can't we just get moving?"

"It'll take a couple of minutes."

"He's right," Jack agreed.

"Okay, let's be quick about it then."

They gathered some dried meat, cheese and strange looking, hard biscuits and small barrels of water. They dumped it all in the pod, behind the seat. Dave was itching to get after the kidnapping bastard.

"Before you touch anything inside, let all three of us get in, okay?" Seth said.

Dave nodded. "Fair enough. I don't have a clue what I have to do to get the thing moving, anyway."

"No," said Seth. "It will be a bit of trial and error, I dare say."

Jack got in first, Dave followed, and Seth brought up the rear. Dave sat with his hands in the air. "What now?"

The Perspex was a little darker in colour below what would probably be classed as the windscreen.

"Try touching it there," Seth said pointing. "Gently though."

Dave reached out and placed his hands on the darker strip. The pod shot forward. He pulled back his hands and they stopped dead.

"Right," he said. "Hold on to your fucking hats."
He rammed his hands against the strip, and they
were off. A bat out of hell didn't come close.
Whatever scenery, good or bad, flashed by in a
monotonous blur.

"Can't you slow it down a bit, Dave?" pleaded
Jack. "I think I'm getting travel sick."

"Try and hold on to it feller, there are no sick bags
in here," Dave told him. He was on a mission, and
no-one was going to stop him. He was focused.

"Maybe he's right," said Seth. "You are, after all, a
bit of a novice with all of this. We don't want to fly
off the rails."

Dave glanced at him and he was almost as green
around the gills as Jack. "Try and relax boys, I've
got this, trust me."

They groaned in unison but, unfortunately, not in
harmony. Harmonious groaning can be a beautiful
thing, when performed with finesse. He realised
slowly that his thoughts were becoming muddled
and bizarre. He began seeing little pigs flying along
by the sides of the pod, one playing a bugle, one, a
bassoon and another stuffing his face with cheese
and crackers. He shook his head, and the pigs
shook his hands.

"You.......have......to.......slow...........down," he heard
Seth moan. He turned to look at him and laughed.
"You look like Quasimodo,"

"Dave.......you're.... going....to.... kill....us," Jack
croaked. Dave turned to tell him not to be so
stupid and was horrified to see a face he didn't
recognise. The skin was stretched so much that

169

Jack's nose was being flattened against the rest of his distorted face. He blinked and the action seemed to take an age, the lids of his eyes moving towards each other in super, slow motion. He tried to tell them both that everything was fine but all that came out was a formless dirge. He watched as Seth's hand crept forward and tediously clamped itself around his wrist. He grinned and allowed him to pull his hand back, nodding like a father does to his son, when the boy has received his first gold star at primary school.

The pod began to slow. Dave shook his head, nausea building as they dropped from around 250 miles per hour to 70. He was about to put his hand back when Seth added his other hand to the mix.

"Dave, we aren't going to be much good to Phil if our brains are spilling out of our ears. To get there slower is much better than not getting there at all, wouldn't you agree?"

Dave looked from him to Jack to the slowly disappearing pigs, his brain struggling to make any sense of the last few minutes. He was still trying to pull his arm away from Seth's vice-like grip.

"Let me go," he protested. "I'm the fucking pilot." Out of the corner of his eye he saw the fist becoming larger until it connected with his jaw.

"For Christ's sake, pull yourself together," Jack yelled.

Dave let go with his other hand and rubbed his eyes. "Shit," was all he managed to say.

"I'm sorry mate," Jack said. "But you'd lost control. My brain was about to explode."

Dave patted his shoulder. "No need for apologies, Jack." He grinned. "Mind you, I'll miss those pigs."

"Pigs?"

"I guess that's why they call it speed," he added.

"I have no clue what you're talking about," said Jack, a bemused expression plastered on his chops.

"I've heard it said that speed is a drug," said Seth. "Maybe it's true."

Jack looked from Dave to Seth and back again and shook his head. "The pair of you are talking in riddles."

"Ringo would have loved that," Dave said. "'Lucy in the Sky', 'Strawberry Fields' and 'I am the Walrus' all in one, complete with pigs."

Dave could see he'd lost Seth as well and just yearned to see Ringo's ugly mug again. He and the scouser had always had the craic. Sort of kindred spirits. He wondered where he was now, where Pete and Harry were. This ridiculous journey started out as unbelievable and quickly became fictitious. He sniggered – you couldn't write this; it was too ludicrous. He just hoped they were okay.

"You all right, Dave?"

He turned to Jack. "I haven't been all right for a time now, mate. I don't know why. Any suggestions?"

"No need to take the piss, I was just asking."

He increased the pressure on the dashboard a little and their speed rose to around 150 m.p.h., a manageable rate of knots. Although not able to observe the details of the landscape, it was obvious

171

that the lush, greenery was giving way to dirty, brown scrubland.

"Jesus, what a stench," Jack said, wrinkling his nose.

Seth and Dave both grimaced. "You're not wrong there, man," Dave said. Waves of putridity washed over them, the reek of decay and hopelessness. Until then, if someone had told him that hopelessness had a smell, he would have laughed in their face. Not now.

"You'd better slow down," Seth advised. "I have a bad feeling."

"I'm not surprised," said Jack, retching.

Dave eased off a little, Seth's bad feeling nudging his elbow and whispering in his ear. "If this was a book, these would be the 'Wastelands'," he said. The stink was intense, its ammonia content making their eyes water.

"I used to smell something like this when my mum and dad took me on holiday in Somerset, years ago," said Jack. "It didn't make my eyes water, though."

"I'll bet there wasn't one of them in Somerset, either," Dave said. He slowed down to a roll, his hand on the hilt of his blade.

Up ahead, the scene became even more unpleasant. A waterfall, like a mini-Niagara in its magnitude but reversing its savage beauty into an intoxicating, abhorrent deluge gushed over the rails. Enormous, sightless creatures flapped massive fins attempting to leap, salmon-like, against the repulsive torrent.

The odour was suffocating, filling their nostrils and throat with its decay. But, in the centre of this vitriolic vista hunkered a gigantic, parody of a whale crossed with a rhino, a huge foot covering the rails. The thing's scabby skin erupted in angry, malignant pustules from which oozed maggots the size of ferrets.

"What is that?" Jack whispered, unable to hide the terror in his voice, eyes still watering from the stink.

"That is some big, ugly fucker," Dave said. They were stationary, gazing up at the scabrous leviathan, its black, soulless eyes fixed on the pod.

"Any suggestions?" Dave asked Seth.

"It could be a hologram," he said.

"Could be?"

Seth shook his head. "I don't know Dave. I'm afraid I'm as much out of my depth as you are."

Dave looked into his eyes. "What would you do, if you were me?"

Seth thought for a few seconds. "Hit the bastard with all you've got." He held up his hands. "What other choice do you have?"

Dave nodded. "My thoughts, exactly. Jack?"

Jack looked startled. "Don't ask me, you're the one who's magic, and he's, supposedly, the main man."

"I'd just like the decision to be unanimous, that's all," Dave said, with a grin.

"Go for it, anything to get away from this fucking stench."

"Good enough."

He gave Goliath the finger and jammed his hands on the dashboard. They hurtled forward and Dave closed his eyes waiting for the impact.

"Bloody hell." Jack's tone was bordering on the wondrous. Dave opened his eyes and was close to speechless.

"That's an improvement," said Seth. "I think you can take it down a bit now, Dave."

"This place does your head in."

The 'Wastelands' had become 'Utopia'. For as far as the eye could see, lush greenery prevailed, even the occasional rabbit hopped past. It was a different world.

"My old dear used to take me to the Cotswolds and we'd stay in a cottage on a farm," Jack said.

"All we're missing is the sheep."

The pod hummed as they sat admiring the scenery, the sun, a balloon in a clear, blue sky. Dave revved her up. "I don't like to spoil the moment," he said. "But we still have unfinished business."

"Maybe, all is not as it seems," said Seth.

"As in?" Dave asked him.

He shrugged. "To go from that to – this," he waved his arms, indicating the beautiful, urban landscape. "With no difficulty." He shook his head. "It feels like a....."

"Trap," Jack interrupted, nodding his head.

"Indeed," said Seth.

Dave looked from one to the other and held up his hands. "So?" Severe irritation was building again.

"The way I see it is – we stay put or we carry on. If

either of you has some other cunning plan, I'm all ears."

"I'm just advising caution, that's all," Seth said softly. "Don't go haring off into the sunset like a mad thing."

"I'm done with caution," Dave said. "If I'd have gone in, all, fucking guns blazing back there, he wouldn't have taken Phil."

"You don't know that," said Seth.

"Don't I?" He glared at Seth, gritting his teeth.

"Just do as he says, Dave, eh?" Jack implored. "Slowly, slowly catchy........."

Dave turned the death stare on him. "Don't - say - it," he warned him.

"I'm just asking you to be bloody careful," said Seth. "You want to get her back, don't you?"

This was becoming tedious. "You know I do," Dave said. "What I don't want, is to sit here all fucking day talking about it. That's not helping Phil, is it?"

Seth sighed. "Just keep the speed to a level, where we can see what's coming before it hits us between the eyes. For me?"

"Please listen to him, Dave," said Jack.

"All right," Dave said. "Stop wetting your knickers, the pair of you."

He hit the ignition and they shot forward like a bullet from a gun. Before the two of them could start whining again, he eased off and they were cruising at a reasonable speed. Although he would have preferred to gun it a bit more, Seth was right, it was no good shooting hell for leather into some trap or other; they'd be no use to Phil then. He'd never been the most patient person in the world, and, at that moment, he was having trouble holding onto what little he had. He scanned the horizon for any sign of trouble. The rails ran into the sun, glistening like snails' trails. He was finding it hard to believe that anything evil could be lurking in this wonderful landscape. It was like the best of the British countryside, without the patchwork of farmland and the sheep and cattle that went with it. It was, literally, a sea of green, clumps of trees and bushes, rising like rocks from the luxurious ocean of grass. He increased the speed a tad. He could feel Seth's eyes boring into his skull, but he didn't care. His acquisition of the old magic had also increased the power of his senses. He could see all around quite clearly. Nothing was going to catch him unawares.

THREE

For a time, they cruised along in silence, the three of them keeping their eyes peeled for any anomalies. Although the scenery and smell were much improved, its continuance was frustrating. Dave was up for a fight, not a drive in the country. He nudged the speed a little.

"Dave," Seth said sharply. "I thought we'd sorted this out."

"Come on Seth, we're hardly moving," he complained. "Get with the fucking programme, will you?"

"What?"

Suddenly he was talking like a yuppie. He was beginning to irritate himself.

"Sorry." He massaged his temples. "I just feel so helpless." He gestured to the emerald landscape. "And this ain't helping matters. I need to do something."

"I think you might want to rethink your policy on speed," said Jack, looking behind. "'Cos, I think, at the moment, that's going faster than we are."

Dave and Seth followed his gaze. The land behind them was crumbling away into a steaming hole, the rails buckling and melting. Dave hit the dashboard. "Any objections?" He asked Seth.

Seth looked at him, back to the devastation behind, then back at him. "As far as I'm concerned, you can hit light speed," he said.

They hurtled on, the ground holding the rails disappearing behind them. The faster they sped, the quicker the quake followed them. The G force was stretching the skin across their faces and Dave's head felt as if it were about to explode. He saw their fate before the other two. It was as if the world they were now inhabiting was like earlier thoughts about the earth. They appeared to be about to fall off the edge of the world. He looked back and swore. They were well and truly fucked. Seth grabbed his arm and squeezed. "Use the old magic," he said.

Jack's face was a contorted mass, the terror in his eyes evident.

Strangely, Dave felt calm. As they charged to their doom, he was at peace with himself. He was tired of this shit, He was ready to shuffle off this mortal coil, one way or another. He suddenly felt exhausted. He closed his eyes and waited for the end.

Seth was shaking him. "Use the magic, Dave," he urged. "He'll destroy Phil and the rest of this sorry planet. You can't give in."

Dreamlike, Dave smiled at him. "It's over," he whispered.

He vaguely remembered Jack screaming as they began to plummet to oblivion. He smiled and tried to console him, tell him that this was how it had to be.

"Use the m..a..g..i..c," he heard, in the distance.

The darkness was closing in and he welcomed it. All he wanted was sleep.

They dropped like an anvil, Dave's hands resting in his lap.

"Do something Dave," yelled Seth. "You're going to hit her."

He looked lazily out of the front screen and saw Phil. Their capsule was about to crush her.

He jammed his foot on an imaginary break. Needless to say, they hurtled on. He could see the terror on Phil's face. Instead of rescuing her, he was about to kill her. Panic gripped him as he searched the capsule for some means of stopping it.

"You have to believe," he heard Seth say, through gritted teeth. "Her life is in your hands. For God's sake man, use the magic."

Dave's mind was racing, thoughts tumbling over each other in a melee of desperation. The fact that Seth had used the 'G' word, however, didn't escape his notice. He closed his eyes and sank into himself, mentally gathering all his resources. He was either going to blow them all to hell, if such a place existed, or become the hero of the hour. Seth had told him to believe and, although he found it difficult, he'd run out of other options. In his mind he saw a wide blue band of nothingness and guided the capsule into it. He lifted his hands and touched the capsule's roof. He even prayed to anything out there that might be listening. He needed all the help he could get.

In the distance he heard Jack say, "Jesus Christ, he's doing it." He felt a brush of a hand and then him crying out. "Bloody Hell, I just got a shock off him. Look he burnt me."

Dave focused on the blue, his belief growing by the second. Nobody was dying on his watch.

"You've done it, Dave," Seth said. "She's safe."

He opened his eyes, and the capsule was on the ground next to Phil. He leapt out and sliced through the ties that held her to a crude, yet effective framework, weighted with huge hunks of stone. He pulled her to her feet; she was shaking.

"I thought you were hard," he said, with a wink.

"I thought you were going to kill me, you mad fucker," she said.

"There's only one person I'm going to kill," he said. "Where is the bastard?"

She waved her hand. "Out there somewhere," she replied. "He disappeared into the blue – literally."

His focus had been solely on saving Phil's life. He now looked at the bigger picture. The landscape before them was varying shades of blue. "Didn't some artist have a blue period?" He asked, knowing who would respond.

"Picasso," said Seth. "But he didn't paint this. This was here a long time before he graced your world." He wasn't trying to hide the smile lighting up his features.

"What? Is blue your favourite colour?" Dave shrugged. "It's weird; that's what it is."

Seth let out a satisfied sigh. "We're back on track," he said softly.

"That bastard's still out there," Dave said.

Seth put his hands on Dave's shoulders. "Don't worry, Dave. He's going where we're going. You'll soon have your gunfight at the O.K. coral and, from what I've just witnessed, my money's on you."

"I thought I was lost before," mumbled Jack. "Now I *know* I am. Why has everything turned blue?"

"We're getting closer to The Machine," Dave said, surprising himself with the statement. "Aren't we?" He looked at Seth.

Seth gave a nod. "Yes, Dave, we are. I think this may be the final leg of our journey."

"That's easy for you to say," Jack said.

"What's his game," Phil asked, waving her hand over the blueness.

"To put an end to it all," Seth said simply.

"If he's been here since the beginning," Phil continued. "Why hasn't he done it before?"

"When The Machine was initialised, any opposition to its primary function was deposited as far away from it as possible. A force field, like a locked door, was put in place, to prevent any future intervention," Seth explained.

"So how is he here?" Dave asked.

"Unfortunately, over the years, The Machine has experienced fluctuations in its power, mainly down to the tardiness of the guardians, but, also, unforeseen magnetism of this planet." He shrugged. "I imagine that, as the power has subsided, it has allowed the exile to increase his grip on the old magic."

"What do you mean – tardiness of the guardians?" Dave asked.

Seth was in his face. "I've made this journey three times before," he said. "As you've seen for yourself – it's not a walk in the park. Plus – it changes every time. Nothing is ever the same."

"Okay, keep your hair on," Dave said. "Which way do we go?"

Seth took out an electronic looking gadget and held it above his head. The top of it glowed blue – what else?

"That way," he pointed in a northerly direction. As far as Dave was concerned it could have been southerly, easterly, westerly; he really didn't have a clue. He was just trying to appear knowledgeable. He chuckled.

"What are you laughing at?" Phil asked.

"For the first time in a while, I've actually found something funny." He held up his hand. "Don't worry, the moment's gone."

"Shall we go?" Seth said.

"You lead the way, big man, the sooner we get this over, the sooner we can get back to......" He stopped. "What actually happens, when this is all done and dusted?"

Seth gave him a sickly smile. "As far as you're concerned – I don't know, I'm afraid. Once I go into The Machine, Phil and Danny will temporarily return to their lives, whilst Sebastian will be tasked with locating the next guardian." He shrugged. "Then it starts all over again. You, and your other friends are, how shall I put it, a bit of a mystery."

Dave had been called some things in his time, but mystery wasn't one of them.

"What does that mean?" Jack asked. "Do we just disappear into thin air? What?"

"We could be trapped here," Dave said flatly. He looked at Seth. "Is that a possibility?"

"I really wouldn't want to speculate," Seth replied. "But from the two options offered, I would pick the latter. You may be flung back to your previous lives. In all honesty, I couldn't say. It's never happened before."

"Thrown back to the twenty first century or the pissing twelfth, which?" Jack said.

Dave flung his arm around him. "He doesn't know, mate, and it's not his fault we're in this situation. If anybody's to blame, it's that fucker, Christian. I tell you, if we get back there and I've still got a handle on the old magic, he's severely dead." He squeezed Jack's shoulder. "Don't worry, my man, I'll look after you."

Seth was hiding his impatience quite well, allowing them to mourn their unknown fate, but Dave could tell he was itching to be on his way.

"Come on," he said. "Let's follow Seth's gizmo and get this over with as soon as we can. I've still got a gunfight to get to."

Seth laid a hand on his arm. "I ought to warn you before we set off," he said. "It won't be plain sailing. We will meet resistance – quite a lot of it."

"What sort of resistance?" Jack was near the end of his tether, Dave could tell.

"The sort that wants to stop us completing our task," Seth explained. "And the best way to do that is to kill us, I'm afraid."

"Bring it on," Dave said. He was yearning for a fight, to let the old magic fly, to destroy anyone and anything that got in his way.

"That's easy for you to say," Jack said. He clearly needed a bit of geeing up.

"I've told you, I've got your back," Dave said forcefully. "Come on, Jack, you're a trained man. Trained by the meanest mothers around, who, incidentally, are also dead, if we get back. Pull yourself together – we'll get through this, right?"

Jack nodded and sighed. "Okay, let's get this show on the road."

"More like it mate." Dave went to punch him on the shoulder but thought better of it. He glanced over to Phil. "You're quiet." He suddenly realised he hadn't asked her about her abduction. "He didn't hurt you, did he?"

She shook her head. "Just strapped me in that capsule thing and sped off." She rubbed her wrists. "Strong bastard, though. When we got here, I tried to knock his fucking head off." Her expression was one of disgust. "He threw me about as if I was a rag doll, I couldn't do anything." He could see the tears welling up in her eyes. "I haven't felt so helpless in years."

He took her by the shoulders. "*I'll* knock his fucking head off." He kissed her forehead. "Then I'll stuff it up his arse."

She grinned." I bet you say that to all the girls."

Dave was about to treat her to a bit more of his witty repartee when he felt his muscles bulge and his eyes try to escape from his skull. He staggered and if Phil hadn't supported him, he'd have ended up in a heap on the ground. He was dizzy, on the verge of a panic attack. He shook his head. "What the fuck?"

Seth turned to him. "As you get nearer to The Machine," he explained. "The stronger the power – or so the stories go." He put his hands on Dave's shoulders and immediately drew back, as if burnt. "They appear to be true," he said, rubbing his hands.

Dave had to blink repeatedly before he could focus again. "Just when I think I'm sorted."

"Believe me, the more you can tap into the old magic, the better," Seth said. "What you're experiencing now is akin to a rechargeable battery being plugged into the mains." He shrugged. "That's the best analogy I can come up with."

Dave managed to focus on his frock coat, his silver hair and piercing blue eyes. He took a deep breath and could feel the heat when he exhaled. Shit, he thought, I'm turning into a dragon. He walked over to one of the strange, blue, poplar trees and punched the trunk. His fist, with one punch, did what an axe would have taken a few strokes to accomplish.

"You'll stuff it right up there, won't you?" Phil said.

Dave tried to turn his attention to her, but he was still struggling with the lack of control he had over his own body. "Yeah," he said. "You bet."

FOUR

They all scanned the cave for possible means of escape. They looked at each other, hoping someone else had spotted something miraculous. "Come on Seb," said Ringo. "Not to put too fine a fucking point on it, we don't have much time here."

"In that case, I suggest you start using that previously redundant muscle in your skull and stop constantly relying on others to get you out of the shit. Try and stop acting like a child and more like a responsible adult – can you do that?"

"Okay," Ringo said. "I can see I've touched a nerve here. I'll leave you to work your magic." Sebastian spared him a momentary glare, before returning his attention to the matter in hand. The problem was – Danny could see his own despair mirrored in Sebastian's confused expression – the man wasn't super-human, after all.

The earth continued to fill the cave at an alarming rate and, they were all preparing themselves for a pitiful and meaningless death. Danny watched a couple of tiny stones roll over the cavern floor and disappear beneath the table support. He scurried forward and felt a breeze on his face.

"Sebastian – come here," he said. Sebastian joined him on the floor and then leapt onto his feet.

"Come on, we have to move this table," he yelled. They all pushed and pulled, but to no avail. The table wouldn't budge.

"I don't mind dying, having my head chopped off by some fifteen-foot super villain," Ringo said solemnly. "But not buried under a pile of rubble. That's no end for anyone."

"There has to be a way out," Sebastian said, scanning the table.

"Oh, fuck you," Harry snarled, sweeping his arm across the table, knocking plates and bowls to the floor. "We're done and, literally, fucking dusted. Time to meet our maker – if he exists." He shrugged. "Who gives a monkey's, really?"

"Wait!" Sebastian said. He bent down, until his chin was almost level with the top of the table. He moved the plates and bowls that remained on the table, inching them back and forth.

"What are..........?" Ringo was about to ask.

"Ssshhh," Sebastian hissed, picking up a few of the dishes, including the one that had contained Blue's water. He moved them slowly and silently across the table, still bent over.

The others could only watch as the earth filled the cave, already, almost up to their waists.

"Come on," Sebastian urged. He moved one of the dishes a millimetre to the left and all the dishes and bowls on the table began to sink into the stone. The table itself slid backwards, revealing a steep staircase. He pushed Blue towards the opening and looked up at Ringo. "Get your scouse backside down there."

Ringo stuck out his bottom lip, nodded and saluted. "You're the fucking man," he said, following Blue down the stairs, earth and stones tumbling after.

They all piled after, escaping an early burial; once again, thanks to Sebastian. Danny wondered what it must be like to have such an imaginative, yet incredibly perceptive mind. Sebastian was the nearest living being to the fictional Sherlock Holmes that he had ever met, or, indeed, heard of. He brought up the rear, and as soon as he was clear of the opening, they all heard a scraping sound, as the table swung back into place.

"Do you think this is some weird, team building exercise?" Ringo asked.

"What, d'you mean, there's a load of blokes up there sweeping all the shit away, ready for the next unsuspecting clients?" Harry said.

Ringo shrugged. "Anything is possible. We think we're the only ones going through this..........madness. Maybe we're not. Maybe, all is not as it seems."

"And what does it seem?" Danny asked him.

"Fucked if I know." He paused and looked at Sebastian. "What I do know is this – if it wasn't for this geezer, we'd all have soil clogging our orifices now, slowly suffocating."

"I doubt it would have been that slow," said Sebastian. "But thanks for the kind words, anyway."

"Just don't get used to it," Ringo said, with a grin.

"I wonder what's in store next?" Pete said, as if he was looking forward to it.

"I would imagine – something to do with air," Sebastian replied.

"Yeah, you're going to have to get your wings on, old parsnip," said Ringo.

"I think I've just reached the bottom of the steps, by the way."

"Considering we're underground, it's nowhere near as dark as it should be," Harry said. "It should be bloody pitch black."

He was right, the lighting was dim, but Danny could see where he was walking, even a few steps ahead. There was no visible means of illumination, just a strange greyness.

"At least we don't have to trundle to our next trial, blind as bats," he said. "I guess you have to be grateful for small mercies."

"Oh yeah, I'm overflowing with gratitude," said Ringo. "I never knew I had so much of the stuff inside of me."

"I don't like to sound negative, but we don't really seem to be getting anywhere," Harry pointed out. "When you take away the trials, what are we achieving?" There was quite a lot of positive nodding going on.

"I apologise if I'm repeating myself," said Sebastian. "But what choice do we have?"

The nodding continued.

"You seem to have lost your second sight, as well, Peter, my boy," Ringo said.

Pete shrugged. "Since we entered this place, I'm not getting any..........feelings at all. It's weird."

"I think that's one thing on which we are all agreed," Danny said. "Still, onwards and upwards, eh?"

"I think downwards may be more appropriate," Sebastian said.

"I stand corrected," Danny said with a grin. "Anything up front, Ringo?"

"I guess that should be down front, if we're being pedantic," Ringo replied. "Either way – no. Just more dimly lit cave-work. Tedium is beginning to set in, to be honest."

"What's tedium?" Pete asked.

"It's a Latin term for boredom," Sebastian explained. "Although the Latin word has an A before the E."

"What's the Latin for – smartarse," Ringo asked him.

"There is nothing wrong with education," Sebastian said haughtily. "You should try it sometime."

"I was educated at the university of life, my man. I know everything I need to. I even knew what tedium meant, with or without the fucking A. So, stick that up your smart arse."

"Now children, come on, play nicely," Danny said. "It becomes tedious when you bicker."

"Is that with the A?" Harry asked.

Danny didn't know if it was the constant stress, coupled with their increasing camaraderie, but they couldn't help themselves. They were in fits, even Sebastian was sniggering.

"I love you really, you little Mensa man, you," Ringo managed between snorts.

"I think 'love' may be a little strong, don't you?" Sebastian said, causing even more hilarity.

"Hold up," Ringo said, raising his right hand to reinforce the point. "This cavern is starting to open up. I think we're about to see what 'air' has in store for us."

They picked up their pace. Sure enough, the passage began to widen, the light changing too. An orange hue started to seep into the atmosphere, their shadows weird in its strange radiance.

"Got your wings on, Pete?" Ringo said. "'Cos, I think you're going to need 'em."

They were suddenly on another wide ledge, in another chamber. Danny walked to the edge. Hundreds of metres below lay stagnant looking water, the occasional craggy rock breaking the surface. He glanced across to the opposite side of the chamber, where a similar ledge resided, another passage leading off, like a mirror view. It only took a quick perusal to see there was no way to cross.

"Okay, Brains, do your stuff," said Ringo.

Danny watched Sebastian as he walked back and forth across the ledge, peering down to the putrid pool far below and then over to the other side. After a few minutes, he shook his head. "There has to be a way," he said. "But, at the moment, I can't, for the life of me, see how."

"You're a failure, Mensa man," said Ringo, in his best John Lennon voice.

Sebastian looked at him and held out his hands. "Be my guest," he said sarcastically. "You've already told us you know all you need to know. Carry on."

"You're just way too touchy, Seb, old chap," said Ringo. "You need to learn to lighten up a bit, before you give yourself a heart attack, man."

Sebastian glared at him but said nothing. It was obvious to Danny that he hated to be defeated. He was merely taking out his frustration on Ringo.

"We could always turn around and go back," Harry offered.

Ringo looked at him and held up his hands in mock surprise. "My God, Harry's turned into a fucking mole."

"We were nearly buried alive, mate," Danny said softly. "Remember?"

Harry sniggered. "Oh yeah, I was forgetting that."

"Understandable," said Ringo, with a vigorous nod of his head. "After all, it was such a fucking long time ago, wasn't it?"

"Cool it Ringo," said Pete. "We're all stressed. The main thing is finding a way across this shit, yeah?"

Ringo shrugged. "Yeah, right." He turned to Harry. "Sorry, man, I shouldn't have snapped at you. But then, on the other hand, you shouldn't be so bloody stupid, know what I mean?"

"Ringo!" Danny said sharply. "Leave him be. You want to pick on somebody, pick on me."

"So, you're the big, hard man, are you?"

Danny held out his arms. "Why don't you find out?"

They were about to square up to each other when Sebastian called out.

"Blue – get away from the edge."

Blue was sniffing the ground and was an inch away from falling into the putrescence below. Then, she was walking on air. Sebastian's expression changed from blind panic to sudden realization. He dropped to the ground and laid his head on the floor, looking out across the void. By this time Blue appeared to be suspended in mid-air about a third of the way across the gap. They all followed Sebastian's lead and fell to the floor of the cavern.

"Well, bugger me," Danny said. "That is beyond devious."

A walkway, coloured exactly as the stagnant water below, stretched across the gap. It was about two foot across, and Blue was now halfway to the other side.

"Jeez, is she a member of Mensa, as well?" Ringo asked.

"She's got more chance of becoming one, than you have," Sebastian said – then he winked.

"Maybe you've got a sense of humour after all," said Ringo. He turned to Danny. "Look, Danny, I'm really sorry. What can I say – I'm an arsehole."

"Finally – the truth." Sebastian was on a roll.

They all laughed, except Harry, who was gazing at Blue, abject fear oozing from his every pore.

"What is it Harry," Danny asked him, putting his arm around the man's shoulders.

"I – hate – heights," he said. "Especially when there's nothing to hold on to. I don't think I can do this."

Ringo came up to them and patted Harry on the shoulder. Harry drew away and glared at him. "Leave me alone," he said.

"Harry, man. I'm sorry. I didn't mean to be such a twat."

"Maybe, if you thought, before you opened your great, scouse gob," Danny pointed out. "You wouldn't need to keep apologising."

Ringo held up his hands and nodded. "I know," he said softly. "I just wanted to say, I know how Harry feels. Remember the fire?" He squeezed Harry's shoulder. "I'm just saying, I know what you're going through."

Harry looked at him warily, as if waiting for the punchline.

"I think he's being genuine, for once," Danny said to him.

By this time, Sebastian had followed Blue across the chasm and both stood on the opposite ledge.

"You lot go," said Harry. "Leave me here, I'll be fine."

"How are you going to be fine?" Pete asked him softly. "You can't go back. You'll starve to death."

"I'll be all right," Harry insisted, nodding his head vigorously.

Ringo grabbed his head and turned it so that they were eye to eye. "Listen to me, you ugly bastard. We've come a long way – you, me and Pete, and there is no way we're leaving you here. Even if we have to carry you over there, kicking and screaming – you're going. Understand?"

Harry looked from Ringo to Pete, the terror never leaving his eyes. "I can't," he said.

"Look, mate," said Ringo. "We'll take it steady. You hold on to me, Pete will hold you and we'll shuffle across slowly. You can even close your eyes if you need to. Between us, we'll get you over there. Come on, mate, we have to do this. It's the only way."

"They're right, Harry," Danny said. "There aren't any choices. It's, literally, do or die."

He couldn't remember the last time he'd felt so sorry for someone. Harry was starting to shake.

"You can do this," said Ringo. "It's going to be fucking hard, but you can do it."

"We're all here for you, mate," Pete said.

"Yeah," Danny said. "Just grab hold and off we go – slowly, of course."

Harry took a few deep breaths, nodding as he did, his eyes darting between us and Sebastian and Blue on the other side.

"Grab on," said Ringo, lifting his arms. Harry dug his hands into Ringo's sides.

"Not so tight, mate," Ringo said with a groan. "If that's possible."

Harry eased his grip a notch and Pete laid his own hands on Harry's hips.

"Let's go," he said.

It was slow going but they were getting there. If sweating were an Olympic sport, Harry would have won gold several times over. The poor sod trembled and dripped all the way across. It must have taken about five minutes to cover the same distance Sebastian and Blue had managed in thirty seconds. They all urged him on quietly, even Ringo. In fact, he was the driving force, insistent but compassionate.

By the time they collapsed in a panting heap on the other side, they were all drained.

Harry looked around the group, tears in his eyes. "Thank you," he said. "I couldn't have done that on my own."

"Sorry son didn't hear you," said Ringo cupping a hand around his ear.

"Piss off," said Harry, flinging his arms around the Liverpudlian. Ringo hugged him back. "Behave yourself, you soft get," he said light heartedly.

"I hate to spoil a bonding session," Sebastian said. "But I think we should get on. This is probably the last of the elements tests, but we shouldn't rest on our laurels."

"For Christ's sake, man, let the man have a breather," said Ringo.

Danny nodded. "Let's just take a minute, mate," he said to Sebastian.

Sebastian shrugged, sat down and rubbed Blue's ears. Danny wondered when he'd become so pragmatic and limited emotionally. In their present situation, it was beneficial, but, now and then, it was frustrating and harsh. But, as is often said – you can't have everything. Considering what they had been through and still had to go through, they weren't doing so badly. Danny slumped down, next to Sebastian.

"Some people don't have your mental strength, you know," he said to him.

Sebastian looked him in the eye. "They do," he said flatly. "They just don't believe they have."

"But we all get scared."

"Fear, eighty per cent of the time, is conjured up by a fertile mind, and not warranted. Too many people live foolish, fear fuelled lives, meeting pitfalls before they occur, worrying about what's going to happen tomorrow. Shit happens, it always will. The trick is to cope with it and don't let it grind you down." He looked at Blue. "She's fearless - puts me to shame."

Danny put his arm around the Labrador, and she licked his cheek. He chuckled. "She is something special, that's for sure."

Suddenly Sebastian grabbed his arm. "If anything happens to me, you'll look after her, won't you, Danny?"

Danny sat back and looked at him. "Of course, I will. But nothing's going to happen to you. We'll get through this together – all of us."

"Maybe," he said, nodding slowly.

Danny punched him on the arm. "Come on, you're starting to freak me out."

"I know I have my part to play and it's Seth's time not mine," he said. "But, nevertheless, I have a weird feeling."

"You'll be fine," Danny said.

"Just promise me, Danny. You'll take care of her."

"For God's sake, you don't have to ask. What do you take me for?"

He took in a deep breath. "A good bloke," he said. Danny slung his arms around him, and Sebastian reciprocated. It appeared to be man hug time within their little group, and why not? Blue nuzzled her way between them, licking both of their faces, clearly not wanting to be left out. They both hugged her and, as Danny looked into her brown eyes, he realised how fond he'd become of her. He knew that dogs had been called 'man's best friend' for decades, maybe even centuries and, he believed the statement was truer now than it ever had been. They are consistent in their love and loyalty, never wavering. He was sure Blue would lay her life on the line for Sebastian, maybe even him and the rest, as well. They were her pack now. He rubbed her ears, and she buried her nose into his neck, moaning with pleasure.

"You're a very special girl," he whispered in her ear. He leaned back against the cavern wall, Sebastian's dog laying against his chest, feeling guilty that she wasn't snuggling up to him. He glanced at him and he was smiling.

"She really likes you, Danny," he said. "But then, she's always been a good judge of character."

It was Danny's turn to smile. "I envy what you two have," he said. "Maybe when we get out of this madness, I'll get myself a new, best friend."

"What would you call her.... or him?"

It didn't take much thinking about. "If it was a bitch, I'd call her 'Tara', and if it was a male, I'd call him 'Sam'." It was the first time he'd thought about his brother and sister since he'd sunk into the depths of self-pity, prior to Seth intervening and, once again, as tears filled his eyes, he felt guilty. Sebastian laid his hand on his arm.

"I don't know what to say, it must have been terrible," he said. "I'm so sorry."

Danny shrugged and sniffed. "Water under the bridge," he said. "Like you said – shit happens."

"I didn't mean...."

Danny cut him off with a wave of his hand. "I know, I know. Just rather not talk about it, you know?"

"Sometimes it helps," Sebastian said quietly.

"Nah, that's bollocks," Danny said harshly. "That's the shit peddled by so called councillors, to justify their existence. When people are dead, they're dead, and no amount of talking about it will change that. Let's leave it at that, shall we?"

"No problem," said Sebastian. "But you know – if you ever want to talk?"

Danny nodded and carried on stroking Blue. He'd lost both of his parents to different excesses, and one of them had, indirectly, taken his kid brother and sister too. Left to his devices he'd have followed them. Maybe, one day, he'd sit down and work through the pain he'd locked away. All he knew was - now wasn't the time.

"When you two have stopped bonding, I think you'd better come, look at this," said Ringo, interrupting Danny's reverie. He gave Blue a last rub of the ears, eased her off his chest and stood up. Sebastian was already following Ringo down the passage. Before Danny caught up, he heard Sebastian take a sharp intake of breath. He rushed forward and looked over his shoulder. "Jesus," was all he could manage.

FIVE

A short passageway through the rock had brought them to level ground. But it was like nothing Danny had ever seen before. The landscape wasn't particularly unusual in its layout, but it was like a 'paint by numbers' picture where the only colours available were blue – different shades of blue.

Sebastian was nodding, a weird grin on his face.

"Maybe this is where the 'Blue Meanies' came from before they invaded 'Pepperland'," said Ringo.

"I have no clue what you're talking about," said Harry. "But then, that's nothing new, really."

"Yellow Submarine," Danny filled him in. "Beatles cartoon film, done with very little input from the group itself."

"Yeah, they donated a few mediocre songs, apart from Lennon's 'Hey Bulldog'. That's a classic," said Ringo, joining Sebastian in the nodding competition.

"Why do you look so pleased?" He asked the Mensa man.

Sebastian didn't take his eyes away from the azure pools, the petrol fields and navy trees.

"It's just how my mother described it," he replied.

"And what, exactly, is it?" Harry enquired.

"I have a very strong feeling we're getting close," said Pete.

Sebastian slapped him on the back. "This, my friends, is the beginning of the end."

Ringo nodded more vigorously. "Oh right, the beginning of the end." His nodding turned swiftly to shaking. "Why the fuck, do you have to talk in riddles?"

"This is where Seth's forefathers began construction of The Machine – well, not that far away from here anyway."

"There's only one problem," Danny said. "Seth isn't here."

The other three were looking at them with utter confusion. It was then that Danny realised they knew nothing about the Guardians role in maintaining The Machine. Sebastian gave them an abridged version.

"So, let me get this straight," said Ringo, rubbing his forehead. "You two, Seth and Phil are guardians, yeah?"

They both nodded.

"And it's Seth's turn to...." He waved his hands around. "Do whatever has to be done with this Machine, to keep things on an even keel?"

"That's it, in a nutshell," Danny replied.

"Can't either of you do it?"

Sebastian shook his head. "No, it has to be Seth, otherwise it could destroy everything. It would be like putting a twelve-volt battery into something that required a one point five."

"Nice analogy," said Pete.

"So where does that leave us?" Ringo asked.

"To use another analogy," Danny said. "Up shit creek, without a paddle."

"I think," Sebastian said slowly. "We have to believe that Seth and the others are striving for The Machine, as well."

Ringo glared at him, unable to hide the contempt he was feeling. "And why do we have to do that, Brains? As far as we know, they could be as dead as six-inch nails."

Sebastian shrugged. "If you want to kill yourself," he said. "I don't see a queue trying to stop you. As for me – if there is still a glimmer of hope, I'll keep going. The choice is yours."

"Who said anything about topping myself?"

Sebastian looked him up and down. "It was just a thought," he said.

"Come on, chaps," Danny said wearily. "Let's not start this again. It is becoming tedious."

"So, you're the mediator now, are you?" Ringo snapped.

"Somebody has to be," Pete said. "You're acting like a proper arsehole, just lately."

"Hear, hear," Harry agreed.

"Maybe I'm the only one seeing the bigger picture," Ringo said defiantly.

Sebastian let out a heavy sigh, his boredom and frustration apparent. "I'm sure we'd all like you to show us the 'big picture'," he said, sighing again.

"This isn't Pepperland and there aren't any Blue Meanies," Danny told him.

Sebastian grabbed his arm. "Not strictly true," he said.

"See?" Ringo blurted. "He's not telling us everything."

Sebastian's eyes flashed in anger. "If you shut your stupid mouth, I'll tell you what my mother told me."

Ringo held up his hands in a 'get on with it then' way. He was starting to get on Danny's tits as well as Sebastian's, which was a shame. Ringo and he had hit it off earlier – he'd seemed like a decent bloke. A bit near the mark with his jokes, to be sure, but someone Danny could relate to. Lately, he had become irritating, to say the least.

"Come on then, Mensa man – spill," Ringo continued.

They all looked at him and indulged in various speed, head shaking. Harry was swiftest, followed by Pete, then Danny and bringing up the rear, Sebastian.

"You've got to cut out the shit," Danny said to him. "We're in this together, remember?"

Ringo stared into his eyes, then looked over to Sebastian and Blue.

"All of my life, I've been told I was an idiot." He scratched the top of his head. "Until we got into all this," he said, waving his arms around. "I'd begun to believe they were right."

"Nobody's calling you an idiot," Danny said. "You're being a bit of a twat, that's all."

"Twat, eh? That hurts, Danny. I thought me and you had some sort of connection. Obviously not." With that, he turned and walked off into the blue. Danny called after him, but his words died as they fell from his lips.

"C'mon Ringo," Pete called after him. "It's only a bit of banter."

"Let him go," said Sebastian. "He's more trouble than he's worth."

Danny looked at him, hoping to see he was joking. He wasn't.

"Hey, we're in this together, aren't we?" he said. "This is not like you."

Sebastian shrugged. "Isn't it? Maybe I'm tired of being the butt of his ridiculous jokes."

"Like Pete says – it's only banter. He never means anything by it. You know that, right?"

"Trouble with you, Danny, you see the good in everyone."

Danny was flabbergasted, this wasn't the Sebastian he knew and respected. "I thought you did too."

"You can only see good if it's there," Sebastian said with a sneer. "He's an arsehole."

Danny looked at Pete and Harry. They were obviously as confused as he was. Even Blue sidled to his side and sat, leaning against his leg, her ears back. Harry gazed in the direction Ringo had stormed off in. "Where's he gone?"

Pete turned and looked. "He was there a second ago," he said. "He's just disappeared into thin air."

"Good riddance to bad rubbish," said Sebastian with a sneer.

"What's the matter with you, man. Are you feeling okay?" Danny asked him.

"Oh, I'm just fine and dandy," he said. "Just tired of baby-sitting you and your, so-called, friends. You haven't got a brain cell between you."

"You're going too far now," Danny said, clenching his fists.

"Where's he gone?" Harry asked. "He was there."

Danny looked to where Ringo had been stomping forcefully on and, as Harry had stated, he was nowhere to be seen.

"What's going on here?" Pete asked Sebastian.

"What's going on here?" Sebastian mimicked. "Pathetic – the lot of you."

With that he strode off. "See you soon," he called over his shoulder. "By the way, you can keep the dog."

Danny watched him walk away, feeling deserted and lost. Why did everyone he got close to leave or betray him. Blue nudged his leg and he looked down into her brown eyes. He rubbed her ears.

"It's all right girl, I'll look after you."

"Why didn't she go with him?" Pete asked.

Danny shrugged. "I guess she didn't like the new Sebastian, and, from what he said, he didn't want her anyway. I don't know, Pete."

"Can someone tell me what just happened?" Harry asked.

"And then there were three," said Pete.

"Four," Danny corrected him.

"Oh yeah, sorry Blue."

"What do we do now?" Harry levelled the question at Danny. It seemed that the role of leader had been passed on and he was the recipient.

"I have as much idea as you, Harry. We appear to have lost the experienced one amongst us." He was missing Ringo already. For all his caustic wit, he had a good head on his shoulders. Sebastian had turned from Dr. Jekyll into Mr. Hyde and he didn't know why. He'd seemed so glad when everything went blue. Now, there they were, Danny, Pete and Harry – the lost boys.

Sebastian was still visible, although travelling at a fair rate of knots.

"I suppose we follow him," Danny said with a shrug.

He was beginning to wonder whether anything they were doing was worth a gnat's bollock. Sebastian was supposed to be next in line, after Seth. Then it was either Phil or himself – no-one had specified the order. Seth was – who knows where, and Sebastian had, apparently, relieved himself of any iota of responsibility to the rest of the guardians, i.e., in this case – him. As they trudged along, he wondered how much and how many more people he'd lose before this was all over, whatever this really was.

"Shit the bed," Harry's dulcet tones roused him from his reverie. "Look out, Danny."

Danny jumped to the left as the ground erupted to his right, spewing a noxious substance. A spot landed on his wrist and he realised it was red hot.

"Bastard," he yelled.

From then on, the three of them were dancing like marionettes, whose operators were trying to avoid being shot by a machine gun.

"This....is.... not.....fun," Pete spluttered as he did a poor imitation of 'Riverdance'. If it hadn't been so life threatening, Danny would have pissed himself.

As it was, he was part of Michael Flatley's production, as well, leaping this way and that. Suddenly Pete yelled – "Stay still, don't move." When someone is instructing a body to stay still when something akin to lava is shooting up that body's trouser leg, it's difficult to take their advice. Having said that, the more Danny leapt about, the more eruptions there were and the nearer they came to his nether regions.

"They follow your movements," Pete added helpfully.

"So – what are you saying? We stay here, like statues, for the rest of our lives?"

"At the moment," said Harry. "Unless you want your bollocks roasted."

Danny sighed. "Where's Sebastian, when you need him."

"Forget him," said Pete. "Look."

Blue was shuffling along on her belly. The eruptions had ceased. Danny stamped on the ground and it erupted as he yanked his foot away.

"All I can say is – I'm *glad* he didn't take her with him," he said gratefully.

The three of them lowered themselves gingerly to the ground and followed Blue's lead. Danny almost burst out laughing at that. All they needed was a copper to make a 'collar'.

"What's the matter with you?" Harry asked him. Danny shook his head. "Nothing."

For a good five minutes they crawled after Blue, until she sniffed the ground, lifted her head and sniffed the air. She pushed herself up, sniffed again and placed a paw gently on the ground. She shook herself and barked.

"I think we're through the volcanic shit," Danny said, rubbing his arm. "Here girl," he said softly to Blue, tapping his knee. She came over to him, sat and licked his hand.

He couldn't help grinning. "It seems you're stuck with me now, girl," he said to her. She leaned against his leg and nuzzled his hand again. It seemed they had an understanding.

"That is some dog," said Harry, his admiration apparent.

Danny still couldn't get his head around how Sebastian had suddenly changed. Blue had meant the world to him, and yet he'd walked away from her without a backward glance. He'd thought they were friends, they seemed to get on so well, sharing a moment or two along the way. It was as if all that had gone before meant nothing.

"Penny for 'em," Pete said.

Danny shrugged and shook his head. "Just thinking about Sebastian. It's weird."

"Maybe he's schizophrenic," said Harry. "You know – a bit of a Jekyll and Hyde character."

Danny wondered if he'd been reading his mind.

"Or the colour blue affects him," Pete suggested.

Danny thought about it. When they first emerged from the cavern and he saw the landscape, he was so pleased. It wasn't until Ringo started to dig at him that he began to change. Normally it would have been like water off a duck's back. This time he'd bitten back and, from then, he'd morphed into Mr Hyde. When Ringo had stormed off, it seemed like the 'nasty dial' had been turned up to full. He just couldn't believe that Sebastian had meant all the offensive things he'd said before he left. Maybe he was right – he always did see the good in people, even when it wasn't there.

"I'm going to miss him," said Pete.

"I'm going to miss his brain," Harry said. "After all, we haven't got a brain cell between us, apparently."

"He was very harsh there," said Pete. "I mean, you've got at least three."

"Maybe he was just talking about you," Harry said, giving Pete the finger.

Danny smiled. At least the banter was still there.

"Well chaps, I think it's onward and upward," he said. "What do you say, Blue?"

She wagged her tail and let out a yap of agreement.

"Do you think we'll ever see the others again?" Pete asked him. "I'm including Ringo in that, by the way."

"I'm sure of it, mate," Danny replied. He just wished that he were as confident as he sounded.

"I hope so" Pete continued. "I really miss Dave, he's a laugh."

SIX

Dave was finally getting a handle on managing the old magic overload. He breathed deeply and controlled its flow. He was thinking about the exile and squinting into the sun.

"Can anyone see that?" He asked.

A figure was stumbling towards them and Dave drew his sword. As it came closer, he began to smile. It had only been days, but it seemed like years. Ringo was almost back in their midst. He dropped to one knee, grinned like a dozen Cheshire cats and let out a tired and croaky welcome.

"Ringo, you old bastard," Dave said happily. "I've missed you, man."

Ringo looked from Dave to Phil, to Jack, to Seth and collapsed in a heap.

Dave rushed forward, followed by Phil and Jack. Seth stood back, trying, unsuccessfully, to hide his irritation.

Dave was cradling Ringo's head in his lap, making sure he was still breathing. Suddenly he could feel the old magic trickling from him and seeping into his old friend. He expected this to be the time when Ringo's eyes sprung open, like in any weird story. Not this time – his Liverpudlian friend slept like a baby.

"Where did he come from?" Jack asked.

Dave looked up at Jack. "Stop asking questions that no-one can answer, mate."

Jack shrugged. "I thought you," he nodded to Seth. "Or he, might know. Is he all right?"

"He seems to be," Dave replied. "He just needs a bit of time, that's all."

Seth was about to complain but Dave gave him the look. Seth shook his head but kept schtum.

"I wonder where the others are," Phil muttered. "I hope they're not.........."

She let the rest of her plea hang in the air, maybe thinking to articulate it would make it true. Seth shook his head. "If something had happened to Sebastian or Danny, I would know."

"What about Harry and Pete?" Dave asked him. Seth shrugged.

"Well, if those two are okay," Jack said. "Harry and Pete should be, surely?"

"I'm afraid we'll have to wait until your friend here wakes from his beauty sleep," said Seth, not even trying to conceal the distaste he felt.

"Has anybody ever told you, you're a snob?" Phil said to him.

"I'm not a snob," he said. "I just have certain standards, that's all."

"I have to admit, Seth," Dave added. "You do act like you've got a broomstick stuck up your arse, half the time. Plus – you do look down on most of us."

"I....I....do not," he protested, his cheeks flushing with embarrassment.

"So, why are you blushing?" Phil asked.

"Hold on," Jack said. "I think he's coming round."

214

Dave turned his attention back to the head in his lap and, sure enough, Ringo's eyelids were beginning to flutter. Slowly his eyes opened, and he blinked, trying to focus.

"Easy mate," Dave told him softly. "Take your time."

"F... fuck me, Dave, is that you?"

"It certainly is my old Beatle-headed mucker. It's good to see you."

"You got any water mate? My throat's as dry as nun's twat."

Seth grimaced but handed Dave a bottle. He placed it against Ringo's bottom lip and tipped gently. Ringo gulped it down and let out a hearty belch. "That's better," he said. "What happened?"

"We were hoping you'd be able to tell us,"

He rolled off Dave's lap and sat up, gesturing for Dave to hand over the water. After practically draining it, he belched again.

"Do you have to do that?" Seth said with a face like a squashed frog.

Ringo looked at him, then back at Dave. "He ain't changed then," he said. "Still got that broomstick up his arse."

"See," Phil said with a grin.

Seth ignored her. "Where are the others?" He asked Ringo.

Ringo shrugged. "I'd just about had enough of that tit, Sebastian." He grabbed Dave's arm. "Just like him, thinks he's better than everyone else. It got to the stage; I couldn't stand it anymore." He paused for a few seconds. "Not just that though," he

215

continued. "He'd changed. If I'm honest, I didn't trust the fucker."

"He probably didn't trust you either," Seth said.

"Never mind that," Dave said to Seth. He turned back to Ringo. "Where are they, though?"

He shrugged. "I stormed off, suddenly felt really weird, and the next thing I know, I'm staring up at your ugly mug."

Dave looked up at Seth. "Any thoughts?"

"There is obviously, at least, one fragile partition in this particular part of The Grid - as we knew before. Your friend here, has apparently managed to barge his way through from Sebastian's and Danny's side to ours."

Ringo eyed Seth with a mixture of suspicion and dislike. "How long have you known Mensa man?" He asked him.

"Who?"

"Sorry – Sebastian." He made a throw away gesture. "The other thing's just a nickname."

"I met him when Phil, Danny and I pitched up at his flat, before beginning our quest," Seth replied. "Why?"

Ringo nodded. "So, you don't know him well then."

"I suppose not, but I knew his mother very well. A fine woman and dedicated Guardian."

"Well, maybe the apple fell a long way from the tree, in his case," said Ringo.

Before Seth could respond Dave jumped in. "Come on mate, in the short time I knew him, he always seemed to be a straight up bloke. Are you sure you're not imagining things?"

Suddenly Ringo stumbled. "Whoa," he said, grabbing hold of Dave's arm. "I think I'm still feeling some aftereffects." He took a few deep breaths, closed his eyes for a few seconds and continued. "He seemed all right to me for a while," he admitted. "A smart arse, like, but okay." He shook his head. "I can't put my finger on it, but he's got a side to him." He paused, searching for the words to describe his feelings. "It's like.......like, I don't know.......like, he's got some sort of secret."

Seth had heard enough. "I'm sure you're a wonderful judge of character," he said. "Being such an upright citizen yourself."

Ringo glared at him. "Maybe the two of you are in cahoots," he said.

Seth threw up his arms. "For goodness sake, Dave, can't you do something with him," he said, clearly exasperated.

"Why don't you try," said Ringo, clenching his fists.

"Right," Dave said. "That is enough. The pair of you are behaving like kids. Now cut it out, this is getting us nowhere."

Phil clapped her hands. "Bravo. A bit of sense, at last." She looked at Ringo. "You – stop acting like an arsehole – and you." She turned to Seth. "Stop acting like a fucked-up schoolteacher."

Dave smiled and nodded. "I couldn't have put it better myself." He placed one hand on Ringo's shoulder and the other on Seth's. "Now, you two –

shake hands and let's get back to the matter in hand."

Seth was the first to hold out his hand, clearly reluctantly.

"Ringo?" Dave said.

Ringo grabbed Seth's hand and pumped it vigorously, as if trying to yank it off.

Dave slapped him on the back and sent him sprawling, forgetting the old magic.

"Jesus Dave, what the fuck?" Ringo gasped.

"Sorry mate, I forget my own strength sometimes." He held out his hand and pulled Ringo to his feet. "Right, time to decide on our next move."

"We go that way," Seth said sharply, pointing in, what appeared to be, a southerly direction.

"Why?" Ringo challenged.

"No, mate, leave it," Dave said, feeling tired and wanting to tear his hair out. "He's got this gizmo, like Doctor Who's sonic screwdriver. It picks things up – sometimes. If it says that way, I'm happy."

"Trouble with you, Dave, you're too easily pleased. You don't question things enough."

Dave was beginning to think poor old Ringo was suffering from paranoia. He loved the man to death, but he didn't need him and Seth at each other's throats for the duration, however long that may be.

"C'mon man, he's cool, really. He might be a bit of a stuffed shirt, but he's the salt of the earth."

The suspicion in Ringo's tone didn't diminish. "If you say so." He didn't sound convinced.

"Are we going to make a move?" Seth asked impatiently.

"Keep your hair on, old man," said Ringo. "You'll give yourself a heart attack."

"Time is of the essence," insisted Seth, his teeth gritted. He looked at Ringo as if he were an unsinkable turd. Dave sighed. He couldn't help thinking about when Christian first sent them all back in time, and the camaraderie. It was, literally, all for one and one for all. He knew Seth was an okay geezer, but, for some reason, Ringo had a problem with him. He wasn't cut out for all this shit. It was hard enough coping with this fantasy world, without having to referee stupid skirmishes. It was time to put the old foot down.

"You two have got to put this to bed – now. If you don't, I'll knock your heads together; and believe me – you're not going to like that – one bit."

"Do it anyway," said Phil, with a mischievous grin. "I could do with a laugh."

"You're not helping here," Dave told her, unable to suppress a grin.

"Come on, possessor of the old magic, show them a trick. Saw them both in half – or, at least, chop their fucking tongues out. This is like watching an episode of EastEnders."

Ringo beamed. "I like her," he said. Dave thought – oh no.

Phil smiled at him, winked and caught him square on the nose with a left jab. As he blinked away the tears, she hooked her ankle around his calf and sat him on his arse. "Never do that again. If you have something to say, say it to me," she said. "The next time, I'll take your head off, understand?"

Ringo nodded, whilst massaging his nose. If anything, his smile had broadened.

"I like you," he said.

"I'm afraid the feeling is not mutual," said Phil. "Arseholes piss me off."

Jack was sat on a rock, observing, trying not to chuckle.

"Are we done with the tantrums?" Dave asked.

It was apparent that Seth was not accustomed to dealing with the young and uncouth, and his patience was being well and truly tested. Dave admired his restraint. Although he kept his composure, his eyes betrayed his true feelings. Dave could almost see the thoughts that tumbled irritatingly through his frustrated mind. When he was the main man and everybody did as he suggested, without question, a certain status quo was maintained. Since Dave's acquisition of the old magic, all of that had changed – the king was dead, long live the king – so to speak. To be honest, Dave had preferred being the dog shit he'd just stepped in. He was more comfortable in that role. Having those roles reversed, everyone revering the old magic and its possessor, brought a multitude of problems. He was, normally, driven by lust and desire, the most basic of emotions. Now he had added revenge, and mediation was not something he'd ever dabbled in. Yet, here he was, trying to keep the peace between his best mate and the geezer he had come to hold in such high esteem. Life is mental, sometimes.

Like a schoolteacher he pushed for a response. "Are we done?"

Seth looked him in the eye. "All I want to do is fulfil my destiny and get the rest of you through this, the best I can. That's all I've ever wanted."

Dave looked at Ringo, who was staring at Seth. "What about you, man?"

Ringo shrugged. "To be honest, Dave, I ain't got a clue. Before we met him and boy fucking wonder, I'd managed to get a handle on the time travel shit – in fact, I was quite enjoying it. Then along comes Ratman and Bobbin and it all goes shit-faced."

Phil punched his arm. "And who am I in your stupid Marvel comics analogy?"

"Oh babe, you're something else," Ringo said, practically drooling. Now, at this point Dave was becoming a little irritated. His best mate was coming on to the first girl he'd had real feelings for in years. Admittedly, she wasn't indulging in any form of reciprocation, and to be fair to him, Ringo didn't know how he felt.

"Leave her be, mate, yeah?" He said, tipping him the wink. Ringo looked at him, then at Phil and let out a heavy sigh.

"Fucking story of my life," he said.

Seth was watching the interchange with little interest. If there had been a desk in front of him, he'd have been tapping his fingers. Meanwhile Phil was not happy. She grabbed Dave's collar and spun him round.

"First," she began. "I'm not your property. So, don't go telling blokes to leave me alone, as if I was, right? Second," she turned to Ringo. "I hope you have a good imagination, because you're going to need it – wanker."

Seth shook his head. "For pity's sake, can we stop this soap opera rubbish and get on with the job in hand? Dave – please?"

Dave nodded. "Yeah, sure. I'm sorry Phil, I'm a dick. Now can we get on with it?"

He suddenly had a flashback, sitting in his bedsit, eating cold beans from the can. How he yearned for those simple days.

"Are you okay to walk, mate?" He asked Ringo. "Yeah, I think it's passed now. I should be fine," Ringo replied. "Even if I am broken hearted." He grinned at Phil and winked at Dave. "Methinks the lady protesteth too much," he said.

"Do you want me to sit you on your arse again?" Phil asked, trying to suppress a smile. Dave thought she liked the idea of Ringo and him fighting for her affections.

"Okay, into the blue," Dave said striding off in the direction indicated by Seth's sonic thingamajig. He was itching for some action, especially with that exile bastard. He wanted to rip his lungs out and wrap them around his throat like a scarf – and he would – soon. He started mulling over what Ringo had said about Sebastian, wondering if he was right. The bloke had always seemed fine to Dave, a bit up his own arse, maybe, but a decent enough sort. Ringo's Batman and Robin analogy wasn't too far off the mark. Sebastian had always appeared to be Seth's sidekick. Suddenly Seth was tugging on his arm, panting.

"Slow down Dave, the rest of us are struggling to keep up."

Dave stopped. "Sorry, I guess this old magic shit is like a turbo boost. I was in a world of my own." Ringo and Phil joined them, followed by Jack.

"If I smoked, I'd give it up," Ringo said, breathing heavily. "Man, you'd give Usain Bolt a run for his money. You ain't got any of that stuff to spare, have you?"

"'Fraid, it doesn't work like that, mate. If it did, we'd all have our fair share."

Ringo looked at Seth. "How come you're not full of this 'magic' bollocks?"

"That's a bit of a sore point," said Phil.

Seth sighed. "I do wish you'd stop acting like children," he said. He turned to Ringo. "I tried to gain the old magic but, unfortunately, could not. It nearly killed me. Dave, however, absorbed it without difficulty and saved my life in the process – for which, may I add, I'm incredibly grateful. It is not a sore point. Are we clear?"

Ringo stared at him for a few seconds, then turned to Phil, who said. "See what I mean."

Seth shook his head. "I give up."

Dave felt sorry for the old chap. He was, obviously, not used to banter. He had gone through his life being respected and revered. Now he had been thrust into a situation where he was surrounded by jibes and jests and he couldn't handle it.

"Just ignore them," Dave told him. "If you let them wind you up, they'll do it even more. It's the nature of the beast."

"He shouldn't make it so easy," Ringo said, grinning.

"Yeah, you are a bit of a push over," Phil agreed.

"You should both respect your elders," said Jack.

Ringo spun around. "Jesus, man. I thought you were asleep."

"Piss off, you scouse gargoyle," Jack said.

"See," said Ringo. "Banter. You gotta get with the programme Seth, my man."

Dave had to smile. It was good to have Ringo back in the fold. Unfortunately, Seth wasn't of a similar opinion. Maybe it was an age thing. The rest of them were only a few years apart, God knew how old Seth was. Dave grinned – he'd forgotten, apparently there was no God. It would explain why there were so many versions of the same supreme being – He's just a manufactured figure head, to be adapted as required in order to commit genocide. Dave liked Seth's explanation a lot more. The question needed to be asked – if there really is a God, what fucking use is he?

"You're very pensive," said Seth, interrupting his reverie.

"Just mulling over your theory about The Machine," Dave replied. "If that really is the case, why do so many people believe in some God or other?"

"Because they want to think that when they die on this planet, they have a soul that is whisked off to a better place, where all of their dreams come true. They don't want to think that death is the end of their existence. Most people, basically, want to live forever, in some form. Wouldn't you like to think that Heaven is real and that, when you shuffle off this mortal coil, you have angels attending to your every need?"

Dave nodded. "I must admit, the idea does have a certain appeal."

"There is a God," Ringo butted in. "When he was on this earth, he was known by another name and we crucified him; only this time we used fucking bullets, not nails."

Jack sighed. "He's off again," he said.

Ringo pointed both of his index fingers at him as if they were guns. "Just you wait and see, Jacko, my old scrotum. When you pop your clogs, if you're lucky enough to go up there, he'll be there at the gates, sat in front of that white piano. Imagine."

Dave laughed. "It's so good to have you back, mate."

"What? I'm fucking serious. John Lennon is God. Don't you get it? He led us out of the darkness that was Bill Haley and Lonnie Donegan and showed us the light. With the help of his disciples, Paul, George and Richard, he did more for this world than Jesus did. I just don't understand why you can't see it. Mark Chapman was Judas and Pontius Pilate rolled into one."

"And in centuries to come, if we achieve our goal, and future guardians do the same, maybe he will be elevated to the role. It's not unthinkable and, I guess, he's as good a choice as any. The fact still remains, however, that there is no God, no matter who you might want him to be," Seth said.

"Okay," Ringo continued. "So, you're saying that your lot came here and set up this.........Machine, started our population and did whatever else you did, it don't really matter. Where did you come from?"

"I've told you; we came from another planet."

226

"No, I mean, who made you?"

Seth was about to answer when Dave stopped him.

"What is that?"

Seth squinted and said, "This is the start."

In the distance, small specks, like a flock of small birds, were increasing in size by the second.

"Get behind Dave," Seth said to the group.

"What?" Dave looked around as Phil, Ringo and Jack slipped behind him.

"Use the magic," Seth whispered in his ear, as he joined the end of the line.

Dave turned his attention back to the skylarks that were rushing towards them, only now, they had lost their bird-like qualities. He'd heard about a swarm of locusts, from somewhere in the Bible, and as these specks drew closer and larger, he shivered. He'd always hated creepy crawlies of any description and, with his enhanced visual powers, he could see the tiny wings and beetley legs, even the antennae.

"Christ on horseback," he said, grimacing.

He closed his eyes, extended his arms, like the 'Angel of the North' and waited. The first thing was the stench, a mixture of sewage and death, there was no other way to describe it. He gagged and could hear Phil retching behind him. The air these things were displacing battered him with its force and putrescence.

"You're a wall," yelled Seth, above the din of myriad insect wings. "They can't hurt you."

That's easy for you to say, Dave would have said. As it was, he dared not open his mouth. He took a quick peek just before they hit him. There were millions of the filthy little beggars, oversized flying cockroaches. They swarmed over and around him, their mandibles ripping his flesh as they flew by, many using his chest and arms as docking stations. He could hear Phil, Ringo and Jack flapping their arms and cursing behind him.

"The magic, Dave," Seth pleaded. "Use the old magic."

One of the little bastards flew up Dave's leg and nipped his scrotum. He snarled, clenched his fists and let fly. He could feel the air around them shatter and crumble as if it were solid. His body felt aflame as he released his anger. He glimpsed Phil covering her ears as he bellowed, the magic flowing through him. A small group of their insect friends headed for the hills as the rest turned to ash around them.

"You've got to get quicker with this shit," Phil complained, wiping blood from her face and arms.

"I hate fucking bugs," Ringo said, shivering. "Are you sure you can't share some of that 'electric' stuff?"

Dave watched as his skin resealed itself over the wounds inflicted by the stinking insects, thinking, that's handy.

"I'm afraid, that's just the start," said Seth, "Sorry."

"Are we going to come up against something we can actually fight?" Ringo asked him, still looking at his arms and frowning.

"Yeah," Phil added. "This ain't 'I'm a celebrity, get me out of here'."

"Be careful what you wish for," Seth said solemnly.

Dave had to admit, he was with Ringo. He was pissed off with this surreal shit. He wanted to get stuck in. The old magic was bubbling away, and its recent, restrained release seemed to have put even more fire in him.

"Come on, Seth, what's the worst that can happen?" Dave asked him. "You've been here before." He was about to say that they were all big boys here, but sucked back, just in time. Instead, he said. "We're all grown-ups here."

"Yeah, man, don't keep us in the dark," said Ringo.

Seth sighed. "I've told you – it's different every time." He looked at Ringo. "Whatever happens, it won't be pleasant. I will say this, however, it's unlikely you'll get a dozen or so incompetent bodies waving swords like children."

Ringo curled his lip, turned back to Dave. "What *is* his problem?"

Dave was getting tired of this 'in house' bickering, and, in this instance, was on Ringo's side.

"If it comes to a fair scrap," he said. "He's already proved himself, more than once."

Seth laughed. "A fair scrap?" He shook his head. "After all that you've seen, do you think we're going to be presented with that option?"

"All I'm saying is – he can look after himself," Dave said, feeling a little irritated.

"We can all take out a few drunks – even me."

"You're starting to get on my tits," Ringo said to Seth.

"And what are you going to do about that?" Seth asked him, sticking his face and inch from Ringo's. Ringo pulled his fist back and Dave shook his head. You were trained much better than that, he thought.

Seth swerved away from the blow, planted a palm in Ringo's chest and sent him sprawling. Dave was disappointed.

Ringo scrambled back to his feet. "If that's the way you want to play it," he said.

"Enough," Dave shouted. "We've got enough problems, without fighting amongst ourselves."

"I don't know, I was quite enjoying watching 'Liverpool' getting his arse kicked," Phil said, with a grin.

"It wasn't a fair fight," Ringo said weakly. "He fucks with your head."

Phil stared at him. "If you were trying to impress me – you failed. Tosser."

Ringo was crestfallen and Dave felt for him. Both Phil and Seth were sneering at him. They didn't know him. Dave wasn't aware of the old magic when he growled 'Leave him alone'. They both fell on their arses.

"I can fight my own battles," Ringo said sharply. "I don't need any of your fucking mumbo-jumbo."

You can't do right for doing wrong, Dave thought.

"I expected better from you two," he said.

"Especially you, Seth. I thought you were above this sort of thing."

"If you can't beat them, join them," Seth said sulkily.

When did I become the sensible one, Dave asked himself? It was only five minutes ago that he was something that Seth wouldn't even consider stepping in. Now, here he was, telling the big man to get his act together.

"You've changed," Phil said moodily.

"And maybe it's time you did too," Dave said. He was nearing the end of his tether. "Banter is one thing. This is getting very personal and very nasty. I thought we were all supposed to be on the same side. Maybe I was wrong."

Phil gave him a pouty sort of look and Dave remembered his mother saying, 'beauty is only skin deep'. He had never really understood the expression before. Phil was stunning, but underneath, she could be ugly, a nasty, vindictive piece of work.

"I would like you all to shake hands and put this shit behind us," he said.

"And what if we don't want to?" Phil asked, pouting even more.

Dave shrugged. "It's up to you. I can't make you."

Ringo held out his hand. "Actually, you probably could," he said. "But I'm prepared to be the bigger man." There was a mischievous glint in his eye.

One thing Dave did know – he was tired of being in the middle of other folks' hang-ups. At that moment, he was ready to piss off and leave the bastards to their bickering; but he knew he couldn't. Not until he knew they were all safe. For the first time in his life, he stood there wondering what the point of it all was. It didn't matter what happened in this life, someone would always be fucked off with somebody else. And when those people were kings or presidents, the rest suffered. When they weren't, friends and family went to hell in a hand cart. That's how it had been for hundreds of years and will be for hundreds more. Human nature – it's a bitch. He brought his mind to the matter in immediate question.

"Seth, Phil?"

Seth shook Ringo's hand. "I'm sorry," he said. "I'm not normally like this."

"What, a twat?"

"Ringo – leave it," Dave said sharply.

Jack, who had not been involved in any of this, grabbed Dave's arm and pointed. "I hate to spoil the 'bonding process' but, what....is.... that?

EIGHT

Danny hadn't really had time to get to know Dave but, from what he'd seen and heard, he seemed like a decent bloke. What he wanted most was, for the whole thing to be over, one way or another. He was tired of being a plaything for whomever or whatever was controlling this charade.

"I wonder how far it is to this Machine," Harry pondered.

"Sebastian seemed to think we were close," Danny said. "The sooner we get there, the sooner whatever's going to happen, happens, I guess."

"I betcha a load more shit'll happen before then," Harry said, with a nod.

"Careful," Pete said, his expression one of concern. "You'll wear out them brain cells."

Harry laughed. "Piss off, parsnip head."

Once again, they were off into the unknown, feeling more apprehensive, now they didn't have Sebastian's knowledge and intellect to rely on.

"We'll be fine," Danny said out loud, surprising himself.

"'Course we will," Pete agreed, his facial expression not completely in line with his statement. "Why wouldn't we be?"

"What? Do you want a list?" Harry asked, twiddling his finger against the side of his head and pointing at Danny and Pete, in a – you're both mental – gesture. "We'd probably all be dead if it weren't for old Mensa man. If things are going to be as bad as they have been, and I was a betting man, I'd put our chances of staying alive at 10 – 1, at best."

"You always were a pessimist," Pete said.

"Realist," said Harry.

"At least we've still got Blue," Danny said. "She just saved our bacon, back there."

"So, now we're relying on a dog to get us through this, are we?" Harry asked. He turned to Blue. "No offence, girl."

Blue looked up at him, wagged her tail and barked twice, as if saying – none taken.

"You know what?" Pete looked from Danny to Harry and back again. "I have a feeling she's integral to all of this, whatever this is."

"What, do you mean a real feeling, like a feeling, feeling," Danny asked him.

"It's not as strong as the feelings I was having before," Pete admitted. "But it's definitely more than a, sort of, notion type thing, if you know what I mean."

"You do talk some shit," said Harry.

"Well, whatever, we aren't exactly surrounded by options," Danny said. "We go on and face what we have to face. If we live, we live – if we die, so be it."

Blue had been sitting by his feet. As if she was tired of their tedious procrastinations, which was all they were. She stood and began to trot along in the direction that Sebastian had taken.

"I guess we'd better follow our new leader," said Harry.

The three of them fell in behind their 'guide dog' and Danny couldn't help smiling. Three grown men were following a Labrador into, what could be the jaws of hell. None of them had the faintest perception of what was to come. At least Blue seemed to have some idea of what she was doing. Whether that was the truth or just wishful thinking, none of them, at that time, could know. They were following Sebastian's trail; what else could they do?

"I wonder if Ringo is with the others," Pete mused.

"Let's hope so, Pete," Danny said. "I miss the cantankerous sod, I have to admit."

"He's a good bloke, just a bit of a twat at times," said Pete wistfully. "Maybe, we should have listened to him more. Especially after what happened with Sebastian."

Danny nodded. "Hmmm, maybe."

He was sinking. He was so tired. When Seth and Phil had pulled him out of that pub and made him feel a part of something important, it had given him a new lease of life. Now, they were both gone, and he was sick of the psychedelia that life had become. All he saw before him was more of the same and, although Sebastian had indicated that the end was in sight, he was gone. He stared at the landscape and found no consolation. His mood matched the colour of the grass and trees. From nowhere, a song came into his mind from his dad's collection. It was by the Bonzo Dog Doo Dah Band – 'Can Blue Men Sing the Whites'. Despite his mood, he chuckled.

"What's so funny?" Harry asked.

"*Can* blue men sing the whites?" Danny said, still laughing.

"The Bonzos were brilliant," said Pete, nodding as if to drive home the point. "Viv Stanshall was something else."

Danny wondered if any thought process he had would be explained away or understood by the people around him. Was he going insane, or becoming paranoid, or both? Whatever it was, he was starting to lose the plot.

"Are you alright, Danny?" Pete asked him.

"Not really," he answered honestly. He slumped to the floor, his laughter becoming tears. Blue stopped in her tracks, rushed back to his side. She licked his face and whined. Danny hugged her. Although he didn't want to drag her into the sea of desolation he was drowning in, he held onto her as if she was the last of the lifebelts.

"For Christ's sake, Danny, what's the matter?" Pete's concern was genuine.

"I don't see the point of it anymore," Danny said, stroking Blue.

Pete shrugged. "I've never seen the fucking point to most things," he said. "But that's life. Most of it seems pointless." He took a breath. "You can't bail out on us now, mate. At least you're supposed to be destined for greater things. Me and him are just.......misplaced fuck-ups."

"Oy," said Harry. "Who are you calling misplaced?"

Danny couldn't help himself, he laughed, a real belly laugh. He couldn't remember the last time

he'd laughed like that. The moment had arrived and, thankfully, gone. He realised how much his own depressive tendencies were personal, solitary, dark tentacles that wrapped themselves around him, pulling him to the heart of his own despair.
"I think we've still got things to do," Pete said softly.

Danny took a deep breath, rubbed Blue's ears and looked at him. "We'd better get on with it then."

Pete and Harry both slapped him on the back and Blue resumed her guide duties, trotting ahead.

"When you're in deep shit, don't bend down to tie your shoelace," said Harry.

"What does that mean?" Pete asked.

Harry shrugged. "Dunno, it just sounded good."

Whatever happened from now on, Danny didn't really care – he realised he was with friends. His temporary lapse into total self-pity had come and gone and, for the first time since the early days with Joey, he felt a connection, warmth, a part of something. Whether that something turned out to be the end of this crazy paraphernalia and resulted in his death didn't concern him. He was tired of being hung up on life and its twists and turns. From now on he would take everything The Grid had to throw at them and deal with it the best he could. If his best wasn't good enough – fuck it.

"I'd just like to say," he said, choking back the emotion. "I love you ugly bastards." He slapped his knees and whistled. Blue stopped in her tracks, turned and ran back to him. "But I love you best, gorgeous girl," he said as she jumped up and licked his face.

"That's favouritism," said Harry.

"You bet," Danny replied with a wink. He looked back into Blue's brown eyes. "Show us the way girl."

He was sure she smiled before she dropped, sniffed the ground, and was off again, head down, tail wagging.

"That is some dog," Harry said again.

"I just hope she doesn't turn weird, like he did," said Pete, jerking his thumb in no particular direction, but leaving them with no doubt of its intended recipient.

"Nah, dogs are loyal," said Harry. "You can be a bastard to 'em, but they'll still follow you to the ends of the earth."

"How come she didn't follow Sebastian then?" Pete asked him.

Harry thought for a few seconds. "Fucked if I know."

"Maybe she's not as gullible as you think she is," Danny said.

"I said loyal, not gullible," Harry said.

"But surely," Danny said. "There are times when loyalty, if unquestioned, becomes gullibility."

Harry looked at him, his brow furrowed. He turned to Pete. "What's he talking about?"

"He's just saying that Blue was loyal to Sebastian until she realised he wasn't what she thought he was – making her loyal but not gullible."

"So now she's loyal to him." He pointed to Danny.

"Yeah," replied Pete.

Harry thought for a moment. "That's fickle, if you ask me."

"No. Look Harry......." Pete continued, before Danny cut him short.

"She's a dog, Harry," he explained. "She has more brain cells than me, you and Pete put together – plus an amazing sense of smell."

Harry nodded. "And, for that, I'll be eternally grateful, believe me."

Suddenly Blue stopped and began whining. She started to dart back and forth, sniffing the ground. Then she started to dig.

"What is she doing now?" Harry asked.

"Digging, old chap," Pete replied.

"Well, I can see that. I mean, what's she digging for?"

Pete put his index fingers to his temples and shook his head. "No, sorry, still haven't mastered it."

"Mastered what?"

Danny watched the exchange with amusement. Harry was truly a decent bloke, but so easy to wind up.

"Telepathy," said Pete. "I'm nearly there."

Harry pulled a face. "Oh, very fucking funny, I'm sure."

Danny patted Harry on the back. "Take no notice, mate."

Blue had dug down about two feet and stopped. Now, she was circling the hole, barking.

"What's wrong with her now?" Harry mumbled, then to Pete. "Don't you dare."

Danny looked into the hole she'd made and could just make out an iron-coloured ring, peeking through the sand.

"What's this?" he said.

"Don't you start," Harry said.

"No – look."

The three of them stood looking at the ring, whilst Blue ran around them barking.

"She wants us to pull it," Danny said.

Harry looked at him and shook his head. "So now, we are actually taking orders from a dog?"

Blue was very insistent, her yaps becoming more frequent and higher in pitch.

Pete looked at me. "Do you trust her?"

Danny nodded. "With my life." He bent down and gripped the ring.

"Whoa – wait," said Harry. "We *are* talking about a dog here."

Danny smiled at him. "Man's best friend." He yanked on the ring.

He didn't know what he'd expected, but it wasn't what happened next. The landscape shimmered, the blueness fading, a sad sigh becoming an aching silence.

"I could never get used to blue grass," said Harry. "It just ain't right."

The trees were green leafed again, their trunks a lustrous brown.

"I don't know," said Pete. "I think I'm going to miss it."

"I think Blue's happier about it," Danny said, watching her squatting and peeing in the grass.

"That dog's smiling," said Harry.

Danny looked at her face and he was right. As she urinated, a smile of contentment crinkled her nose and muzzle. He looked to the horizon and wondered what was next on the agenda for them. Blue finished her ablutions and kicked up some grass. Danny patted his leg, and she came over, wagging her tail. If he could have died there and then, he would have died happy.

"I've just noticed something," Harry said. He was on a roll.

"What?" Pete asked, humouring him.

"There's no sun."

As a unit, they looked to the sky.

"You're not wrong, my friend," Pete agreed.

"So, where is our light source?"

"And our warmth," Danny added.

As a unit, they shrugged. Blue leant against Danny's leg, her tail swishing against the grass in a non-committal sort of way.

"It is what it is," he said. "I'm guessing, we're going to have bigger fish to fry."

"Fish and chips." Harry drooled. "With lashings of salt and vinegar."

Danny smiled. Even the weirdest, baddest shit can be forgotten, when you're in the company of friends. Although he'd only known Harry and Pete for a short time, it felt like they'd been mates for a lifetime. As for Blue, she was the daughter he never had. Looking into her soft, brown eyes was like sinking into warm chocolate. He knew the other two were missing Sebastian; he wasn't. Only dog owners will know how he felt. Blue and he had bonded, although he wasn't sure which of them was the pack leader. At the moment, his money was on Blue.

"So, what's it like being a guardian of this green, stroke blue, pleasant land?" Pete asked.

Danny considered the question seriously before giving his reply. "I feel like a square peg in a round hole," he said. "And since we lost Seth, and now Sebastian, I have no clue what I'm supposed to do."

"Well, I hope you soon find out," said Harry, pointing to the horizon. "'Cos I think we might soon have guests." He drew his sword.

Danny followed his finger and saw the dust cloud created by, as yet unknown forces.

"You always look on the black side," said Pete, lifting his blade. It was only seeing the pair of them with the weapons outstretched that Danny realised he didn't have one.

"I'm feeling a bit naked here, chaps," he admitted. Harry glanced at him. "Here – catch," he said, tossing him a dagger. "Sorry, that's the best I can do."

Danny caught the knife by the handle and felt comfort as he clenched the leather covered hilt. He nodded. "That's great, mate. I wouldn't be much use with one of those, anyway," he said, pointing to their swords. "I haven't been on the course." Blue started to whine, and he patted her. "I'll look after you, girl," he said softly, not knowing if he would be able to look after himself. One thing he did know, he would sacrifice his own life for hers. All four of them squinted into the dust covered vista, trying to make out the source of the agitation.

"All for one and one for all," said Harry.

Pete looked at him and shook his head. "Which one are you? Porthos, Aramis........"

He didn't get the opportunity to complete the trio. "I'm 'Comehereandhaveadoseofthis," he said, hefting his blade.

They stood in a semi-circle, if three people and a dog can fashion a semi-circle. Danny was at the back, knife at the ready. Blue was by his side growling, the hackles on her back raised. Pete and Harry were either side in battle stance. If it weren't so serious, it would have been funny. Hell, no – it was funny. It started as a snigger, turned into a giggle and became a full, belly laugh. Pete and Harry looked at Danny, looked at each other, looked at Blue and fell into fits.

"What are we laughing at?" Harry managed to ask, between guffaws.

"Fucked if I know," Pete replied. "He started it." He jerked his thumb in Danny's direction.

Danny shrugged. "I don't know, I just couldn't help it."

"Well, I hope *they* see the funny side of it," said Harry, still chuckling.

"There are only two of them," Pete said, squinting. "It looks like they're dragging something behind them."

"They're either big bastards, or they're on horseback," Harry said.

"Definitely horses," Danny said, a smile still on his face.

"Horses or not, if there's only two of 'em, this should be a piece of piss," Harry said.

Somehow, Danny didn't think that would be the case. Nothing was as it seemed in this place. "Expect the unexpected," he said.

"I've always thought that was a stupid expression," said Harry. "I mean, if it's unexpected, it's something you didn't know was coming. So, how can you expect it? You don't know what it is."

"I think what it means, Harold, my old chum, is don't expect this to be a walk over. It won't be the 'Chuckle Brothers' riding along with a ladder between them," Pete said.

"It could be," Harry replied. "Because I definitely wouldn't be expecting that."

That was it – Danny was off again, howling like a banshee.

Although he couldn't help sniggering, Pete said. "I think we ought to focus on the matter in hand, Chuckle Brothers or not. Whoever they are, they're not that far away."

He was right. The two riders were easily recognisable as such now, although what they were dragging was still a mystery.

Pete and Harry resumed their stance and Blue seemed happier that they'd started to take the situation seriously again. She sniffed the air and started to whine.

"What is it girl," Danny said softly. The whine became more guttural as it slowly became a growl, which increased in volume, the nearer the riders came.

"Is that......?" Pete began.

Harry cut him off, mid-sentence. "That twat, Sebastian," he said. "And he don't look like he's wanting a reconciliation, by the way he's swinging that fucking axe about."

He was right; the one on the right was Sebastian. The other bloke had long, black hair and a black beard. Both wielded axes and didn't look as though they were on a tree felling expedition.

By this time Blue was baring her teeth, her growl insistent and aggressive. She was down on her haunches, as if ready to pounce. After becoming close enough for the three of them to recognise their features, everything seemed to slip into slow motion. Pete and Harry stood their ground, and Danny could tell by their weight placement, they were ready to leap to one side or the other at a second's notice. He, on the other hand, felt a little like a spare part, with his inadequate weapon. He wasn't a trained man, but even he could see that a man, on foot, with a dagger was no match for someone on horseback swinging a bloody, great axe. The horses themselves could trample them into the ground. He waved his dagger at their attackers and burst out laughing again. Maybe I'm having a breakdown, he thought. Surely this can't be the way a man in full charge of his faculties reacts in a situation like this.

"Will you shut the fuck up, Danny," Harry said through gritted teeth. "This ain't funny anymore." Danny shrugged; have it your own way, he thought. Suddenly he felt a sharp pain in his calf. He looked down to see Blue looking up at him. She had nipped him, and had she been able to speak, he was sure she'd have been saying – pull yourself together.

The smile left his face and he felt ashamed. He'd told her that he'd look after her and here he was acting like a complete imbecile. He patted her on the head.

"Don't fret, girl. We'll get through this." He stopped flipping the knife about and took a deep breath. Focus, man, he said to himself, for Christ's sake focus.

He put on his game face, the one he'd used in the ring. Get the face on and the rest follows. Well, it used to.

"Come on you bastards," he yelled.

Pete glanced back and nodded. "More like it, man."

Somebody must have pressed the fast-forward button, because from that point everything happened at break-neck speed. Sebastian and the man in black were upon them. What they had thought was something they were dragging was a dense, grey mist. It surrounded them. Pete leapt to the left, avoiding Black beard's horse's hooves by centimetres. Harry wasn't so lucky. Sebastian's horse caught his shoulder, spun him round and knocked him to the floor. Danny vaguely saw Sebastian bring his axe down. He grabbed the dagger by the blade and was just about to launch it when he saw a black flash from the corner of his eye. Blue flew through the air, snarling like a wolf. Sebastian pulled his hand back as she hurtled past him snapping at his axe hand. Danny rolled out of the way of Sebastian's horse and was at Harry's side.

"I'm alright man," Harry said, rubbing his shoulder. "Nothing broken." He coughed. "That stuff stinks."

Their attackers gone past them and were reeling around for a second run.

"Come on then Chuckle Brothers," growled Harry. Danny admired his pluck.

"While they're on those fucking horses, we've got no chance," said Pete, trying not to gag.

"We'll have to go for the horses then," Harry said. His regret was almost tangible.

The pair of them took up their stance again and Danny got ready to throw the knife. Let's face it, he thought, I won't be able to do anything else with it.

As the horses thundered towards them, the light changed, the air crackled and exploded.

It was as if someone had decided to rip holes into a painting he was looking at. The filthy mist remained, but the landscape behind it was torn away. Suddenly Dave was there, arms outstretched, floating metres above the ground, Seth, Phil, Jack and Ringo were to his side, suspended in mid-air.

NINE

Dave followed the direction of his finger and shivered. He had never felt this way before. It was as if energy was leaking from his body, dribbling away through his fingertips, through his pores. A weird mist raced towards them, clinging to the ground. As it swirled around them, Dave took a deep breath and released the old magic. The ground shook, the sky wept, and shadows chased fire through his mind. He held out his arms, the wildness exploding around him. He was floating above the ground, the power around him snarling and hissing. "Come on," he screamed.

The old magic flowed inward and outward, the atmosphere rabid under its force.

He felt like a giant in the midst of a hurricane. He caught a glimpse of Jack spinning wildly in the melee. He directed the magic, creating a shimmering hammock, depositing Jack and the others into its safety. He was Atlas, about to hurl the world into the abyss; he was God almighty about to destroy his flawed creation.

He was the culmination of every storm, tornado, tsunami, hurricane to ever savage the earth. He was all these things and more. He was pure power, unassailable, uncompromising – complete.

Or so it felt.

The sky cracked, the earth rumbled, rents appearing in the horizon. He felt a niggle of resistance and smacked it away. Within seconds it was back, stronger. Dave increased the force and it disintegrated. The tears in their world peeled away, like old wallpaper and two worlds became one. Now he felt the other's power. It was no longer a niggle but an insistent, piercing pain. He pushed and it pushed back.

"It's them," he heard Ringo shout.

As he fought against the increasing force, he saw Harry, Pete, Danny and the black Labrador. They were almost under the heels of two huge horses, carrying the exile and Sebastian. The riders' intent was obvious.

"Let us down," yelled Ringo. "They need some help over there. While you're playing with your new toy, they're about to get wasted."

Dave let the force field drop and turned all his attention to the matter in hand. Their power was twofold. Suddenly he was no longer the Supreme Being. He was the underdog. He drew his sword, the blade radiant with old magic. He charged, watching the others running, weapons in hand, to the aid of Danny and the others.

The exile leapt from his mount to face him and they clashed in mid-air, Dave's sword parrying the blow from the exile's axe. His power shocked Dave.

He landed, roaring, waiting for him to attack, summoning every ounce of the old magic he could access. He saw Sebastian running circles around the others, a sadistic grin on his face. They don't have a chance without the old magic, he thought; he's just playing with them. The dog was knocked aside and howled in pain. He couldn't just turn away and fight his own fight while they were slaughtered.

"Danny – catch," he called, throwing his sword. "And concentrate on the blade." He hoped that the connection he'd felt before, between Danny and himself, went deeper. He saw Danny catch the sword by the hilt, as he dodged another blow from the exile's axe. Come on, Danny, come on, he muttered. He was now unarmed against his opponent, but he still turned to face him.

"Come on, you piece of shit, let's see what you've got," He roared in his face.

The exile stared at him with eyes so dark they were almost black, and then laughed. It was a harsh sound, devoid of any joy or happiness.

"You are a mere bug," he snarled, showing small, sharp teeth. "You think you are powerful, full of the old magic. You are about to realise the truth."

Dave held his gaze. "Have you never heard the phrase – never underestimate an opponent?"

TEN

Seth and the other two fell to the ground in a heap. Ringo was up first, racing towards Danny, Harry and Pete, blade aloft. Phil and Jack were right behind him. The cavalry had arrived – just in the nick of time.

Pete, who had been concentrating on black beard's horse, turned his attention to Sebastian. They were all there – Danny, Ringo, Pete, Harry, Jack, Phil, Seth and Blue.

"Come on, you fucking traitor," yelled Ringo, both hands on the hilt of his sword, swinging it slowly from left to right. "You're a dead man."

Sebastian didn't even slow his pace. He thundered towards them, a maniacal grin, revealing his teeth. He laughed. "I wish I could say you're going to meet your hero, but you're not," he jeered. "Your miserable. Liverpudlian bones will just become nothing. You will become nothing. No God, No John Lennon – just nothing."

He raised his axe again and Danny saw the haze surrounding it. Flashes of fire rippled up the shaft. Sebastian pulled his horse up and it reared, towering above them.

"Go for the horse," Ringo screamed. He'd already weighed up the situation. It only took him seconds to assess their chances and decide on the best course of action. Danny felt a strange flush of pride. He didn't know why, he just did.

Pete slid under Sebastian's mount; sword ready to hack at its back legs. The horse danced like a ballerina, avoiding the blade easily. Danny could hear Sebastian howling with glee.

Harry and Jack went for the other leg. Harry missed by a mile and Jack went sprawling, almost trampled under-foot. Blue was growling and barking wildly, running around the horse, trying to spook it. Even though the horse couldn't see what was happening, it was as if she had sensors all over her body. Her front feet landed back on the ground. Even with four to go for, seven of them couldn't get anywhere near damaging the bloody thing. It skipped, hopped, just dancing around them. There was no way they could win this fight. They couldn't get to Sebastian and his horse was something else. In fact, Danny thought the bastard was enjoying the situation as much as Sebastian was.

Blue ceased her worrying tactics and pulled back. Just before she leapt Danny saw her intention. "No Blue, don't," he cried.

She flew at Sebastian and he batted her away with the shaft of his axe. She howled in pain and fell to the ground. It was then he heard Dave shout, "Danny – catch."

He turned just in time to catch the blazing sword by the hilt. Immediately, he felt the surge. It felt like he was on fire. He looked up and saw fear in Sebastian's eyes. Danny closed his eyes and allowed the power from the sword to flow through him. He felt it pulling, drawing more power. From where, he didn't know. He didn't care.

He opened his eyes and saw Blue lying on her side, panting. If that bastard had damaged her, he would rip him apart. The others were still hacking away at the prancing horse, missing every time. Danny looked into Sebastian's eyes and saw the fear and uncertainty. The bloke with the beard was screaming for him to believe.

Danny knelt by Blue and lay his hand on her back, allowing a little of the force that now filled him to pass into her. She shuddered, whined and licked his hand.

"Come on girl, I told you I'd look after you," he said, tears in his eyes. He pushed a little more and he could feel her pain. When he had flung her aside, Sebastian had broken her left, back leg. He let the force increase, probing, finding the break. She howled as he fused the bone. Her panting eased and she moved the leg backwards and forwards.

"Lie there and rest, girl," he told her. "I've got this."

He stood and faced Sebastian. He felt about ten feet tall. He absorbed the force, feeling it flooding through his veins, turning his muscles to steel. Suddenly Ringo was at his side, gasping for breath. "It's no good," he rasped. "That bloody thing is like Muhammad Ali on steroids." He looked at Danny. "Man – you're rippling. Where did you get that fucking thing from?" He said, pointing at the flaming blade.

"Leave it chaps," Danny said. "This is my fight."
They all turned and looked at him.
"It's the old magic," said Phil. "He's full of it, just like Dave." She stood aside. "Let him kick the bastard's arse."
"He's all – sort of – fuzzy," said Harry.
"That's the magic, numb nuts," Phil said, a wild grin on her face. "Go, Danny."
"Are you coming down, or am I coming up to get you," Danny asked Sebastian.
Sebastian looked from him to the sword, the fear beginning to overwhelm the uncertainty.
"What's wrong shit head," Danny continued. "Having trouble believing?"
It was obvious he had no intention of dismounting and that made Danny feel good. The bastard was scared. Sebastian yanked on the reins and the horse reared again, the hooves of its front legs above Danny's head. He could see no reason the hurt the beast. He was only doing what Sebastian forced him to do. He rolled under the horse's belly, leapt and grabbed Sebastian's arm, the one holding the axe. He felt the resistance as he pulled downward. He could see the terror in Sebastian's eyes now. He closed his own eyes again and directed the old magic. He heaved and pulled Sebastian to the ground. The coward managed to wrench his arm from Danny's grip. He faced Danny, axe at the ready. He was beaten already. Danny had seen that look so many times from opponents in the ring. He smiled. "Are we going to do this?"

Sebastian was in two minds. He glanced around, weighing up his chances, if he did a runner.

"Kill him," yelled black beard. "You – are – my – son."

Danny grinned as he swung the blade above his head. "Are you a dutiful son?"

There was absolute terror in Sebastian's eyes now. Danny could feel the rest of them watching, waiting for one of them to make a move. Danny took a step forward and Sebastian took a step back.

Just then Danny heard Dave yell "Oi, come back here."

He looked over to see black beard leap back onto his horse and thunder away. That was the last straw for Sebastian. It only took him seconds to realise that Danny would cut him down before he could remount. He turned and fled. The old magic gave his legs extra power, and he ran like an Olympian. Danny contemplated letting him go, but this had gone too far. He leapt up on the horse and spurred him forward. Within seconds they were galloping alongside their prey.

Danny had to know why Sebastian had turned against them, or whether it was his plan all along. "One question," he said. "Why?"

Sebastian looked up, his expression now, one of resignation, tinged with hatred.

"My father and I were going to ruin your ridiculous world. By destroying the rest of the guardians, we would have infinite power. The Machine's defence system would not cope. We could override the programme, install new parameters. We would destroy your stupid earth and every weak individual in it."

They had reduced their speed to a trot. "Well, it looks like we've scuppered your plans," Danny said to him.

Sebastian laughed. "My father can do it alone; he doesn't need me. And you will be the first of those he slaughters."

"So, he doesn't need you, we don't want you. I guess you're surplus to requirements."

Sebastian stopped, held his axe in a battle stance, ready for his last stand. Despite his demeanour, his eyes still betrayed him. Danny thought about how he had batted away Blue, as if she were an annoying fly, after all the loyalty she'd shown him. The man before him, once a friend and a person he respected, disgusted him. He was just another power-crazy maniac. Any feelings of mercy Danny may have felt were gone, and he was back in the playground with Lawrence Carter. He'd merely exchanged one bully for another.

He dropped to the ground and faced Sebastian, the old magic torrential in his veins.

"Will The Grid absorb your miserable corpse, once I've killed you?" He asked.

Sebastian hefted the axe in a false show of bravado. "No, but it will, yours."

He feinted to the left. He brought his axe through thin air as Danny leaned to the right, swinging his blade with all the force he could muster. It smashed into Sebastian's collar bone, the fire consuming the whole of his body in an instant. Danny watched in amazement as Mensa man became a staggering inferno. It was as if he had spontaneously combusted. Within moments, there was nothing left. Even the axe had gone. The Grid had done its job. Danny almost expected the ground to let out a satisfied belch. The blazing sword that Dave had thrown to him was now a normal, tempered steel blade. He could still feel the old magic, but it was bubbling beneath the surface. He stuck the sword through his belt, jumped back onto the horse and steered him back to the others.

ELEVEN

If he'd expected a hero's welcome, he'd have been disappointed. The exile had screamed off, to fight another day, he realised that, but a bit of a smile wouldn't have gone amiss. He pulled up his horse and jumped down.

"Why the long faces?" He asked. "We'll catch up with him."

"You shouldn't have killed him," Seth said softly. Danny looked at him in astonishment. "What was I supposed to do – stand there and let him lop off my head? What do you mean – I shouldn't have killed him. I wasn't overwhelmed with choices."

This was about as far away from a hero's welcome as was possible. He was being chastised for taking out one of the bad guys.

"Apparently, one guardian shalt not kill another," said Dave with a wry grin.

Danny's astonishment had morphed into utter confusion. "What?" He looked at Seth. "What does he mean?"

"It was the first rule to be made," Seth explained. "Under no circumstances shall one guardian take the life of another."

"It's a bit late now. I take it there will be consequences then."

"Yes."

"So, why didn't you feel the need to share this information?" Danny asked him, the anger building. "This is just like you. You love playing the big man, being in control, keeping everything to yourself. Well, congratulations, whatever happens now is all down to you, for not trusting your friends." He was livid.

"That's a good point, well put," Phil agreed.

"He's always had his head up his arse," Ringo said, obviously enjoying Seth's lambasting.

"Come on people, bickering amongst ourselves isn't going to get us anywhere," said Dave. "Anyway, nothing's happened yet. Maybe this ultimate 'commandment' is just a load of hot air."

"Well, whatever happens or doesn't happen," said Pete. "We're still in this together."

"And at least we are all back together again," Harry said.

Seth laid his hand on Danny's arm. "I'm sorry Danny; it's something I'd almost forgotten. It wasn't until I saw you chasing after Sebastian, it all came back to me. By then, it was too late. I wasn't trying to keep things from any of you. As Pete said – we're all in this together. I'm sorry."

"So, what's likely to happen, and why hasn't it happened already?" Danny asked him with a sigh.

"There's no telling how long it will take for the information to filter back to The Machine. At a guess, I'd say a few hours at most. As to what it will be, I don't know, but as we've broken a fundamental law, I believe it will be significant."

"We've been over this shit already," said Ringo. "We can't just sit here and wait for Armageddon to launch itself at us. I vote we get after that other bastard."

"He's right," said Dave. "Whatever this bloody Machine has to throw at us, we'll deal with it, when the time comes. In the meantime, let's get on with the job in hand."

Which, they did. Danny was glad to see that Blue had made a full recovery. She ambled along at his side, occasionally looking up. If a dog can smile, she did.

Sebastian's horse seemed to have taken a shine to him as well.

"We'll have to start calling you, Johnny Morris," Harry said.

"Who's Johnny Morris?" Jack asked.

Harry looked at him and shrugged. "Not a clue. It's a name my old man bandied about whenever there was a programme about animals on the box."

"He used to pretend to be the animals," explained Pete. "Silly little voices and such. To be honest, I found it irritating. What about you, Danny?"

Danny remembered his dad sitting on the sofa, a bowl of crisps perched on the top of his considerable belly. This didn't resemble those days, at all. In fact, these days were like nothing he'd ever experienced before. Although the old magic coursed through his veins, he was tired, mentally and physically. Blue nudged his hand with her nose. He looked down and smiled. There seemed to be no aftereffects from her broken leg. The old magic had done its job well. She whined and wagged her tail. He bent down and rubbed her ears. She leant against his leg, sighing contentedly.

They were a team, the two of them. He would gladly lay down his life to save hers.

He heard a snort and then felt Sebastian's horse's nose in the middle of his back, the nag's teeth nibbling at his shirt.

It seemed they had a new member. Danny stroked his nose with one hand, rubbing Blue's ears with the other. Why couldn't people be as loyal and loving as animals?

"You appear to have an affinity with our four-legged friends," said Seth, his smile still apologetic. Danny looked at him and rubbed his temples. He had a headache. "When will this end?" He asked Seth.

The concern was clear in the big man's expression. "I wish we could change places," Seth said. "But with all that has happened, and yours and Dave's recent acquisition, I'm afraid it is what it is."

"You still have your part to play though, don't you?

He shrugged. "I don't know, Danny. I really don't know."

Sebastian's horse nuzzled him again.

"You need to give him a name," said Harry. "He loves you, man."

Danny put his cheek against the horse's head and stroked his neck, wondering why people couldn't be as simple as our animal friends. "There's no hurry," he said. In all honesty, he wanted to be left alone – him, Blue and his new equine buddy. Once again, he was becoming tired of the whole thing. Apparently, if Seth was right, and he had no reason to doubt him, the guardians were absorbed by The Machine. What that meant, he hadn't clarified. Danny hoped it meant oblivion. He could see Dave bristling with the old magic, on fire. He was jealous. It had served him when he needed it, but now, it grumbled like an ulcer. He felt so tired, confused. He stroked Charlie's cheek.

"Charlie," he said. "His name is Charlie."

It was like he was disappearing, losing his flimsy grip on this ridiculous reality. Without Blue and Charlie to anchor him, he would have drifted away. He realised how stupid that sounded, but it was how he felt. The three of them were in their own little bubble. He'd had it with humans. They let you down, they betray you. The worst feeling of all was the shame. He'd let his parents and siblings down. If he'd done something to prevent his dad eating himself into an early grave, taking his brother and sister with him, stopped his mum becoming a 'falling down drunk', his family would still be alive. Instead, here he was, lost and alone. He listened to the banter going back and forth, and he was envious. They always tried to include him, especially Dave, but his heart wasn't in it. When Seth had first entered Danny's life, he'd given him a purpose. Now, after all that had passed, coupled with the whole business with Sebastian, he was done with it all. He wanted out. To be honest, he wanted out of life altogether. To live years, in this state, would be purgatory. The black dog of depression was nipping at his heels again. He began to reminisce. That first meeting with Joey –

their wonderful collaboration, both musically and profitably. Then, along came Beth. He'd never known such happiness. He could still see the two of them in bed together, and it still hurt.

He kissed Charlie's cheek and rubbed Blue's ears. If they all got out of this alive, Charlie. Blue and he would be setting up home together and bollocks to everyone else.

As they walked on, Danny bookended by Blue and Charlie, Dave began to reflect, for the first time, on the events that had brought him here. Even the weirdest fantasy novel didn't come close. Less than twelve months ago, he had been living off the state, no more than a tenner in his pocket, no future, but reasonably content, nevertheless. There was something to be said for monotony. For one thing, you knew where you were, every week the same as the last, not much in the way of surprises. Did he miss those days? Did he fuck. He had never felt so alive. He was surrounded by good friends, the banter was good, most of the time. Don't get me a kong (as they say, apparently, in Lennonesque circles), he thought, we all have our moments, especially Ringo. For all his faults though, Dave loved the bastard like a brother. Danny was a different kettle of fish. They had a connection, that was apparent, and he really liked the bloke. There was always something lurking in the shadows, something unresolved or waiting to blossom, he didn't know what. He'd never been particularly good with words. He just felt that they would be more than the casual mates, they were, at present. He could think of no other way to explain it. It was like there was something waiting for the two of them. Something that only they could deal with. Wow, he thought, I'm getting kind of deep here, ain't I?

He looked over at Phil and smiled. He loved the jut of her chin, the way it said – don't fuck with me. He'd never been in love and he didn't know if, what he felt for her, was the big deal. He just knew she meant the world to him. He had never met a girl, so feisty, so self-assured, so bloody minded. She was special, no doubt about that. She must have felt his gaze. She turned, grinned and winked.

"You alright, Davey boy?"

He nodded. "Fine and dandy. You?"

"Apart from having a severe need to kick some fucker's arse, yeah, I'm good."

"You certainly look good," he told her, grinning. He could tell she loved the compliment, even though her verbal response was a little contradictory.

"Didn't your mummy ever tell you not to look at things you couldn't afford?"

"You love me really."

She snorted. "Keep on dreaming, sunshine, keep on dreaming."

She turned away but he could still see that satisfied smirk, even though she was trying to hide it. Once all of this was over, they would be together. It was what he wanted, and, despite her derogatory comments, she did too.

"Hey, mate, fancy a bit of a sing-song?" Ringo was by his side.

"You getting withdrawal symptoms?" Dave asked him.

"Yeah, I'm missing the old days."

"You talk as if it were years ago, it was only a couple of weeks at most. I must admit, I lose track of time in this place."

Ringo nodded. "Me too – anyway you up for it?"

"Go on then, you start, I'll come in on the chorus."

So, old Beatle head launched into a reasonable rendition of 'Please Please Me' and, one by one, they all joined in. Even Danny couldn't resist. He was back in the pub, with Joey doing his licks and him singing his heart out. Happy days – short, but happy.

He joined in, loving singing those timeless classics. As he sang, the shit that had been eating away at him took a back seat. He closed his eyes and let it flow.

Even Seth started to hum along. Ringo attacked the Fab Four's back catalogue with gusto. Dave had to admit, walking along with a bunch of mates, belting out Lennon and McCartney's greatest hits, kind of lifted the spirits. Danny seemed transformed. He never knew he had such a good voice. Ringo could hold a tune well, and the rest of them were passable, except Jack, who was flat as a pool of piss; but Danny put them all to shame. By the look on his mug, he was in a different place – a better place. Dave was happy for him. If he wasn't mistaken, Dan was a troubled soul.

Ringo got out his air guitar and hit the opening chord to 'A Hard Day's Night' and they were away again. Phil had found her harmonising button and was an octave above the rest of.

Danny heard the hum first but ignored it.

Whatever will be, will be, he thought.

The hum increased and the ground began to shake.

"I think we may be about to find out what happens when one guardian offs another," Dave said.

The hum became louder and the vibration grew into a shake. Their legs trembled in time with the undulating.

"Shit, we aren't going to have an earthquake, are we?" Jack asked anyone who was willing to listen.

No-one answered, they all stood, like quivering statues, waiting for the earth to open up and swallow them.

Dave could feel the old magic rushing around his body like it was trying to find an escape route. He looked over to Danny and could tell, he was feeling the same. Dave knelt and made his hands into a double fist above his head.

Danny felt the old magic started to churn and boil and he knew what had to be done.

Dave was on his knees as Danny opened his eyes. He nodded and Danny nodded back.

"Let's do this," he said.

They both slammed their fists into the ground, the magic flowing between them. The heaviness in the air had become lighter and tighter. For a second or two, the quivering ceased, and all was calm – the quiet before the storm. The others looked from Danny to Dave, looking for assurance that nothing else was about to happen. Danny watched the sky darken.

Harry muttered something about an earthquake. Danny could feel its power growing as it sucked up the trees and earth.

"Don't fight it," he said.

Dave said, "Get ready to do the twist."

Danny hugged Blue with one arm and Charlie with the other. Whatever happened, he wouldn't allow them to be separated. He let out the old magic, forming a shield over the three of them. Maybe he should have felt guilty, but he didn't. The rest would be up to Dave. He was perfectly capable.

"I don't like things I can't fight," said Ringo, shaking his head.

"I bet this is going to hurt," added Jack.

Dave looked over to Danny. He had his arms around his animals, kind of like Noah, when the floods came, only there was one horse and one dog. So, nothing like Noah, really – wrong analogy.

"We'll do everything we can," he said to Jack, nodding towards Dan the man. "It's only a bit of a storm, after all."

"That looks like a lot more than 'a bit of a storm'," said Harry, his hair being blown back, the wind rippling his tunic and breeches.

Seth stood, stock still, arms folded, eyes closed.

Dave shrugged - each to his own.

"You'd better have plenty of that magic shit in the tank," said Phil, the wind cold enough to urge her nipples to stand proud. Unfortunately, she turned her attention from the oncoming twister before Dave could avert his gaze.

"Jesus up a drainpipe," she said with venom. "You're all the fucking same." There was disappointment in her eyes. "I actually thought you might be different."

"I...I...am," Dave blustered. "But I am a red-blooded male, as well. And you are awesome looking," he added quietly, with a sheepish grin.

"You're just a dirty old man," she said.

"Aw, come on, he's not old," said Ringo, obviously enjoying Dave's humiliation.

"Time to refrain from banter and concentrate, I believe," said Seth, placing similar emphasis on 'banter' as he probably would on 'excrement'.

Dave readied himself, drawing in the old magic. He could feel Danny doing the same. They would kick this mother's ass.

He yelled, "Are you ready, mate?" His words were torn from his mouth and absorbed by the introductory nuances of the tornado. Nevertheless, he felt confident.

Then, it hit. Its power was immense, much stronger than he'd expected. He delved deeper into the well again, feeling Danny doing the same. It wasn't until they were twisting and turning, everyone shouting and screaming, that he realised that Danny and he were pulling in opposite directions. He saw him in a huddle with Blue and

Charlie, channelling the magic like a pro. In fact, so much so, he was beginning to feel his own power diminishing. He threw everything he could, to protect his mates but the twister dragged them up, like rag dolls.

Danny closed his eyes and waited. Charlie whinnied and Blue whined. He shushed them both and hugged them tighter, his new family.
The force was incredible. It crashed into the defence barrier he'd conjured up and he had to summon up every ounce of power he could muster. He could vaguely hear the others screaming and yelling as the three of them hunkered down, Blue now howling, Charlie shaking uncontrollably, his bladder letting go with fear. Danny lifted his head and stuck his chin into the heart of the storm, growling with the effort. Within seconds they were in the eye, the wind shrieking around them. He took a minute to regroup.
"Don't worry kids," he said to Blue and Charlie. "We'll get through this. I won't let anything hurt you." He braced himself for the next onslaught. Strangely, his friends' cries seemed distant. Time for any more thought disappeared as he turned his shoulder into the other side of the twister, holding his 'kids' to him, like a second skin. He had never felt so determined in his entire life. He felt like he had been given a second chance. He was now the patriarch and his job was to protect. He gritted his teeth and sucked up the old magic, throwing it

around them like castle walls. The storm raged and wailed, its frustration showing as it battered against his formidable defences.

Danny grinned. He felt invincible – a giant. Then, they were through, and he howled with relief and joy as the tornado left empty handed. Blue was panting, Charlie snorting. He eased his hold on them.

"It's all over," he said softly. He checked them both out; they were fine, not a mark on them. He looked around for the others. The three of them were alone, the storm racing away behind them.

TWELVE

Dave cursed Danny and pushed with all his might. He was left with enough power to prevent his friends being torn apart, but only just. He could feel all his muscles straining, almost tearing apart from the exertion, as they span around and around, going higher and higher. He recalled reading, somewhere, how tornados are connected to the ground below and some sort of cloud formation above. He knew there was no way he could prevent them from reaching the top. He just hoped that he'd be able to manage some sort of control over their landing once they were spewed out.

It was like the worst fairground ride he'd ever been on. He was not normally a sufferer of motion sickness, but the incredible speed of the twister, coupled with the exertion of keeping the group safe, was taking its toll. His stomach was doing back flips and he was struggling to keep what little was left down there in its rightful place. Suddenly Phil slid around to his side.

"What the fuck's going on man?" She asked. "Can't you do something with that magic bollocks?"

"I'm saving you from being battered to a pulp," he replied through gritted teeth. "Danny made a sizeable withdrawal. Funds are a little low, I'm afraid."

"I didn't realise that was how it worked," she said, looking him in the eye. "You're all red and your neck's all sort of stretched." She turned her top lip up in disgust.

"Thanks."

"Is there anything I can do?"

She appeared to be genuinely concerned and he batted away the lustful thoughts that had popped into his head.

"I need to concentrate," he said. "Unless you want to become the filling in a Ringo and Harry sandwich."

"That's fucking gross," she said with a shudder, her top lip curling even more. She made a zipping motion across her mouth and winked at him.

He was straining even more, every muscle and tendon in his body as taut as a guitar string. Why was Danny taking so much? Surely, he was aware of the situation. He wouldn't do this to them, would he? Then he realised – the higher they were drawn the weaker the old magic became. They were both drawing it from the earth. He'd misread this whole thing. Phil started to drift away from him again.

He dug deeper and deeper, trying to suck up everything he possibly could.

"What's happening?" She yelled.

The pain was becoming unbearable. He was about to be ripped apart.

"Dave – do something," he heard her plead.

He almost passed out, his eyes practically on stalks. Then they were flying, spinning and falling. He imagined a huge blanket and slid it underneath them all. As they dropped, the power increased, and he slowed their descent. By the time they reached the ground, he'd managed to reduce their speed to a gentle, feather-like sway.

"Shit," Ringo said. "That was scary."

"I think we all need to thank Dave for getting us back to terra firma in one piece," said Seth.

Dave was flat on his back, feeling like he'd gone six hundred rounds with the Hulk. His body was one huge, excruciating slab of agony.

"This is doing my head in," Jack groaned.

Dave lifted his head and let it drop again. "For fuck's sake," he muttered.

He lay there letting the old magic seep into his ravaged muscles and bones. He was in no hurry to do anything else. One look at their new situation was enough. The noxious, methane-type smell that hung over them was sickening.

"Aw, come on man," Ringo said to no-one in particular. "What is this shit, now?"

"Smells like a cesspit," said Harry, wrinkling his nose.

"Can't you do something about it, Dave?" Phil asked sharply.

That was it; everyone has a breaking point and Dave had just reached his. He leapt up.

"Who the fuck do you think I am - Environmental Health?" He snapped. "Why is it down to me to sort every fucking thing out? Have none of you got any bollocks anymore?"

"Steady on, tiger," Ringo said. "You're the only one of us with the......" He moved his hands in circles. "Crazy shit. I think she was only asking if there was anything that could be done about the smell, that's all. If not – eh, no sweat." He patted Dave on the back. "We're all really grateful for getting us through that tornado, mate – really."

Dave looked at his ugly mug and the anger fizzled out. He hugged him. "I'm just getting so tired of this," he said. He looked at Seth. "Is it always like this?"

Seth shook his head. "Like I told you before; it's different every time."

"Yeah, I get that, but *is* it normally this hard."

Seth's expression was one of apology, although he couldn't be blamed for any of this. "It isn't normally quite this arduous, I have to admit. Plus, we've never had to deal with the exile before."

"How much longer?" Dave asked him, knowing the answer.

"I wish I could tell you; I really do."

Dave waved a hand. "Ah well, here we go again." They all stood looking at the road ahead for a few minutes. The term road was a little complimentary; it was actually a nebulous path meandering through filthy, stinking swamp land.

"At least this reek subdues the old hunger pangs," Harry said.

"Small mercies, eh," said Phil.

Morale was at an all-time low, that was clear. They all wanted this endurance test to be over. Just when they thought they were getting near the finish line, something else came along to throw a spanner in the works.

Seth was the first to move. "Make sure you keep to the path," he said. "There's no telling what's in that mire."

It seemed they let out a communal sigh, before following his lead. Phil was, suddenly, by Dave's side.

"Soz, Davey boy," she said, with a grin. "I'm a bitch, ain't I?"

He looked into her beautiful, brown eyes and smiled. "Just a bit."

She gave a sort of 'that's the kind of girl I am' shrug and punched him playfully on the arm.

"What can I tell you – I'm a puzzle wrapped up in a conundrum, rolled in an enigma – or something like that."

Dave laughed. "Yeah – something like that."

The path narrowed, forcing them to walk in single file. Seth was in front of Dave, then Phil and the others.

"One thing I don't understand," Dave said to Seth. "If this Machine stops functioning if the guardians don't manage to reach it on time, why make it so difficult to get there?"

"Originally," Seth replied, not looking back. "It was set up with certain safeguards in place. Trials that could, because of the knowledge they possessed, only be survived by guardians. Unfortunately, over time, due to a lack of insight by the old ones who put the system in place, those trials have become magnified and corrupted. As each guardian reaches The Machine and becomes one with it, the power generated, not only reinforces The Grid, it also feeds the nefarious aspect of it. Hence, each time we return, the tribulations we must face are expanded, more surreal, more menacing, more......."

He appeared to be searching for a suitable word. Dave felt it was his duty to help the big man out.

"Shitty," he said, toning it down a notch or two.

"Indeed," Seth said. For the first time, Dave didn't detect any distaste in his intonation.

"So, this is your fourth time, right?"

"Yes."

"Have there been any close shaves? You know, occasions when you nearly didn't make it."

Seth sighed. "Are you just making conversation, Dave, or are you really interested?"

It was then that Dave realised, they had never really conversed before. He'd asked Seth questions and Seth had given him answers when he could. They'd never talked; but then, Seth had never made it easy. Dave had always felt like the turd he'd inadvertently put the sole of his new brogues in. Since his acquisition of the old magic and Seth's failure to do the same, he had noticed, however, a change in Seth's attitude towards him. If he wasn't mistaken, it bordered on respect.

"Seth," he said softly. "I have the power and you have the knowledge. If I could pass on some of that power, I would, you know that. Similarly, I would appreciate you sharing your experience and understanding of this mad, twilight world. So, in answer to your question – I'm really interested."

"Each time has been perilous, that goes without saying; each worse than the previous one, obviously. Last time there were only two of us, myself and my fellow guardian, a man of great courage and resourcefulness. We had almost reached The Machine and were, perhaps, a little complacent. Mark my words, Dave; I will never make that mistake again."

If he wasn't interested before, Dave was now. He'd never really understood the term – bated breath but he thought it probably applied to this moment. If his breath had ever been bated, it was now. He waited for the man to qualify the statement he had just made. He had never been the most patient person, it had to be said.

"So, what happened?" He prompted Seth.

Seth seemed to scrutinise his face, maybe trying to detect his true feelings before opening up. It was clear he was not in the habit of sharing – emotionally, that is. Dave felt a little more encouragement was in order.

"Come on, Seth, spit it out, man."

Seth still looked forward and Dave had to strain to hear. "My colleague's name was 'Chuck' Spencer, Chuck being a strange substitute for Charles amongst our American friends. Why, I don't know."

"Yeah, I know," Dave said impatiently. "Chuck Norris, Chuck Connors...."

"Quite," Seth said.

This was worse than pulling teeth. Dave could feel the old magic building again and he was itching to get out of this swamp and set up a rematch with the bearded one. Either that or return to the twelfth century. It was strange; at that time Dave saw no way of getting back to his own time, he didn't know why. Although Seth couldn't see, he made 'get on with it' gestures with his hands.

"What happened with you and Chuck?" He asked him, trying to keep the irritation out of his voice.

"We came upon a horse drinking from a pool," Seth said.

"Go on," Dave urged, his mind replaying how easily Sebastian's horse had changed alliance.

"Chuck was a real animal lover," Seth said. "His daughter had two ponies."

He had, apparently, come across a problematic molar. Dave took a deep breath. "Just tell me what happened," he said softly.

"Just be aware," Seth said. "Not everything is as it seems."

After all that they'd been through, this went without saying.

"I think we're all aware of that now," Dave said. "I believe you brought Sebastian along."

Seth didn't even flinch. "He was – a guardian. This has never happened before."

"You're not such a hotshot, are you Seth?" Phil said, sticking her head on Dave's shoulder.

"This is not the time, Phil," Dave said, breathing in her aroma. "Let the man speak."

To have a conversation with a man's back is not easy, but the width of the path prevented anything else.

"Go on Seth."

The big man continued. "We were nearing the end of an extremely arduous journey, or so we thought. We were both tired, hungry, but, most of all – thirsty. The sight of the pool coupled with the appearance of the horse was more than a breath of fresh air as far as Chuck was concerned. Although he had made one more trip than I had, and was, generally, very wary; he couldn't hold himself back. I called out for him to be careful, but it was too late, he was almost at the water's edge."

He stopped and let out a heavy sigh.

Years ago, Dave knew a kid who used to pause in the middle of sentences and, kind of drift off. It always seemed to be at the moment when whatever it was he was going to say was at the 'punchline' stage. An example would be – so, Jimmy told this big geezer to piss off and this big bastard turned around and..............It used to be so infuriating. The kid's name was Bernie Clayton, but Dave and his mates used to call him – 'Pause for Thought'. At this particular time, Seth was reminding him of young Clayton and annoying him as much.

"And?" Phil asked forcefully. She was obviously feeling the same.

"He reached the pool and dropped to his knees by the side of the horse. He began scooping up handfuls of water. For a minute or two all was well, and I relaxed. I quickened my pace and was about five yards from Chuck when it happened."

Old Bernie was in on it again and it was Dave's turn to gee him along. He was getting a severe dose of Deja Vu.

"What happened?" He urged.

"Chuck turned to the horse, making comforting sounds. He stood and reached out to stroke the animal's nose. I don't know why, but just then, I had a terrible feeling that something was wrong. Chuck must have had a similar foreboding, but it was too late to do anything about it."

Dave was about to spur him on again, but Seth stopped and turned, facing the two of them. Dave held out a hand to the others and they all came to a halt.

"What was a beautiful chestnut mare became a cannibalistic beast. He whipped his head around and nearly took Chuck's hand off. Chuck fell into the water and was scrabbling about whilst the beast hovered over him, I ran at the bloody thing, I didn't know what else to do. I had no weapon – nor did Chuck. Its jaws opened like a crocodile's, the teeth nothing like those of a horse. They were huge and jagged, drool dripped from the thing in anticipation. I hit it in the flank with my shoulder, putting all of my weight behind the blow."

Dave could see the fear in Seth's eyes as he relived the moment. This was not the time to urge him on. They all waited until he was ready to continue.

Seth swallowed and took a deep breath.

"The thing howled and turned its jaws towards me. I had fallen to the ground and only just managed to dodge out of the way, those teeth snapping like a bear trap."

Since first meeting Seth, Dave had never known him to show fear. He seemed to take most things in his stride. He guessed, after three previous trips to The Grid, he had experienced a great deal. As he described his encounter with the horse turned dinosaur, however, his composure was lacking its usual calm, to say the least.

"Why didn't you have any weapons?" Harry asked. Seth looked at Harry, happy with the interruption. "The guardians are not allowed to bring weapons into The Grid. Everything required to reach The Machine each time can be found within The Grid, itself. That is how it has always been.

"Well, obviously Red Rum didn't gobble you up," said Phil. "So, you, obviously, came up with something."

"Not before the horse took the lower half of Chuck's right arm, I didn't," he said.

They all wore the same expression. Imagining having your arm bitten off at the elbow makes it hard to smile.

"I thought the thing was about to get its laughing gear round your head," Dave said.

Seth nodded. "It was. I was shuffling about, trying to get to my feet, but trying to put some distance between us at the same time. It was impossible. I was at its mercy, and, it was apparent, it didn't possess any of that."

"So, what happened?" Ringo asked.

Seth took another deep breath, before continuing. "Chuck punched it on the side of its head. I've never seen anything move so fast. It spun around and snapped those awful jaws together before Chuck could move. I just remember the blood."

By this time, they were all watching the scene in their mind's eye. No-one said a word.

"I dug my hands into the sand, to gain purchase. My hand closed around something and my whole body came alive. I yanked, and pulled out a long, curved dagger. Luckily, the horse was still intent on finishing Chuck; I think it was, probably, bloodlust. In a flash, I was on my feet. I swung that blade with all the strength I could muster. It sliced through the beast's neck like butter. The jaws were still snapping as the head fell, nearly took a chunk out of my thigh."

He paused, visibly shaking, put pushed on.

"I had to tie a tourniquet around Chuck's upper arm and make a fire quickly."

"A fire?" Jack was puzzled.

"He had to cauterize the wound," Ringo explained.

"Shit," said Jack.

There were tears in Seth's eyes. "He was a very brave man. I will never forget him."

Phil was looking at Seth intently. She took in a sharp breath and let it out slowly.

"I've always looked at this," she waved her hands around, "as a bit of a game. I mean, I know there have been some hairy moments, but, somehow, I never thought any of us could be seriously injured."

283

Seth looked at her. "When have I given you the impression that it's a game?" He asked angrily. "I thought I'd made it crystal clear how important and dangerous our mission is. 'A bit of a game – a bit of a game'?" His voice rose and he began to shake with fury.

Dave put a hand on his shoulder. "Calm down, man. It's probably just her way of dealing with all of this shit."

Phil shook her head. "No," she said. "I'm sorry Seth but......" She held her hands in front of her. "I just thought you were playing the bogeyman – trying to scare us into doing what you wanted us to. This thing about Chuck – well – it changes everything."

He glared at her. "I thought you were an intelligent woman, Philomena," he said. "Now, here you are talking about the bogeyman. I don't know what to say." He shook his head. "I despair."

"I've said I'm sorry," she muttered.

Seth turned and walked away. "Let's just get on with it, shall we?" He called back over his shoulder.

Dave looked at Phil, smiled and shook his head. "I'll give you this – you never fail to surprise me. Just when I think I've got you pegged; you go off at a tangent again. Did you really think this was some game, devised by Seth for your entertainment? Like, a weird sort of ghost train?"

She shrugged. "That's how it seemed to me. I thought, maybe, we were in some Xbox game, you know, virtual reality, and I was the only one who could see it."

"If that's the case, why didn't you say anything?"

"Well, I didn't want to spoil it for everybody else, did I?" She looked hurt that Dave would think otherwise. At that precise moment, he didn't know what to think. If there had been a biscuit about, she would have taken it.

"You are something else," he said.

"So, this is all real," she said.

"I think it's as real as we're going to get for the time being," he said. "Reality, as we knew it, went out of the window a while back. What you have to remember is — you can get hurt — even killed, and I wouldn't want that to happen."

"Now I know this is the real deal," she said," whoever or whatever wants to fuck with me, better think twice. You know what I mean, Davey boy." She winked at him.

"Sure, you're a real badass."

THIRTEEN

The path widened and the stink became less intoxicating. Once more, in situations like this, one must be thankful for small mercies. The fact that Dave accepted situations like this was a testament to his adaptability. Once you've got your head around time travel, anything else is small spuds. "She's weird, man." Ringo said, drawing level with them. He looked at Phil. "I don't believe you." "Piss off scouser," Phil said. "Stay out of my face." Dave felt the spittle fly as Ringo let out a forceful exhalation. "I have no intention of getting anywhere near your face," he said. "I'm not your man's biggest fan," he said, pointing to Seth's back, "but, for all of his faults, he's straight up. What you see is what you get. I mean, come on, what the fuck?"

Phil turned to face him; fists clenched. Dave was glad for the extra manoeuvrability. He positioned himself between the two of them, facing Ringo. "Leave it mate," he said quietly. "It's not worth the hassle."

"I'm sure he can fight his own battles," Phil said through gritted teeth.

"No problem there girl," Ringo replied.

"Unfortunately, I was brought up to never hit a woman."

"Well, this'll be easier than I thought then,"

"In your case, maybe I'll make an exception."

Dave grabbed them both by the shoulders, his fingers digging into the muscle. "This stops now," he said shortly. "We're all on the same side here. Am I clear?"

The pair of them stared at him. He detected a hint of respect in Ringo's gaze, and, if he wasn't mistaken, admiration in Phil's.

"Am I clear?" He repeated.

Ringo looked at Phil, his lip still curled. "Suppose so," he said.

"Phil?"

"Yeah, whatever. Just keep him away from me."

"Don't worry darling, he won't have to."

"Call me darling again and I'll rip your...."

"Stop – now," Dave said sharply. He looked at Ringo – he was grinning. "Come on mate. Stop winding her up. Please." He made sure Phil didn't hear this particular exchange. Ringo winked at him. "She makes it so easy though," he said.

Dave nodded. From being a freewheeling tosser to becoming a custodian of the old magic was starting to take its toll. He was not used to being responsible for anyone but himself.

"I don't know why you like him," Phil said, looking as if someone was holding a three-month-old kipper under her nose, "he's a complete knobhead."

Dave was trying to think of a way of resolving their apparent differences when Ringo let out a shout and yanked his sword from its sheath. From the corner of his eye, Dave saw the tentacle burst from the swamp.

He turned and saw a thick, black, sinuous arm wrapping itself around Ringo's leg. The suction pads latched on quickly and Ringo stumbled, fighting the strength of the pull. He brought his sword down in a shallow arc, the keen blade slicing through the tentacle. The rest of the limb disappeared quickly.

"What the fuck was that?" Ringo said, rubbing his leg. "Have we entered 'Lord of the Rings' territory?"

"I can't be sure," said Pete, "but I think it was 'The Hobbit', mate. Are you alright?"

Ringo looked at him aghast. "Oh yeah, I'm just tickety-fucking-boo, mate. I've just had the thing from the swamp try to take me down to its watery lair, but, other than that, I'm simply fine and dandy."

"I meant, is your leg alright. Them suckers looked nasty."

Ringo had already pulled up his pant leg, revealing a circle of red suction marks. Luckily, the skin wasn't broken.

"I dare say I'll live," he said.

"I'm surprised at you," Dave said, "I thought you'd have dived in there after it."

Ringo looked at him and winked. "If we weren't so pressed for time – well – you know me."

"That's what I love about you, man. Always looking at the bigger picture."

Ringo shrugged. "That's just the kind of guy I am."

"I told you to keep your wits about you," Seth said.

Ringo shook his head. "Don't be a stuck-up twat all your life, Seth. Take a day off, will you. If I hadn't got my wits about me, I'd be down in old Davy Jones' locker. Or this swamps version of it." He looked at Dave. "He's really getting on my tits, mate. Can't you do something about him? Zap him or something?"

"Come on Seth, he's right. You're not being helpful."

Seth shrugged and moved off. Dave was beginning to know how a primary school teacher felt. Ringo held out his hands in a 'see what I mean' gesture.

"I know, mate," Dave said. "I think the stress is getting to him. Cut him a bit of slack?"

"He's already been given enough slack to make a sizeable fire," he replied. "He's just a pompous arsehole. You know me mate, I always call a spade a digging implement."

"Indeed, you do. You, however, aren't fighting to give your life to some weird and wonderful Machine."

"I thought it was his destiny – taking him to a higher plane, or something."

"Yeah, maybe; but things are not going according to plan, are they?"

Ringo shrugged. "Whatever. Just keep the miserable bastard away from me, will you. I've got enough of my own hang ups, without taking on his."

Dave clapped him on the back. "I'll do my best."

Phil grabbed Dave's arm. "I don't suppose you've got any idea how much longer this doomer is going on for. I mean, with this magic shit you've got."

"If I did, you'd be the first to know," Dave said. "I'm afraid we're all in the same boat."

"Only tensions are getting a lot more – tense, I guess."

"Really? I hadn't noticed."

She punched his arm yet again. "Don't be a patronising dick," she said, "I was only asking."

"I know, and I wish I could tell you what you want to know, but I can't."

"If it goes on much longer, Seth and Ringo are going to be at each other's throats." She looked him in the eye. "I mean – literally."

"Don't worry, whatever happens, I'll sort it."

Looking into her eyes was intoxicating. He wanted to take her in his arms. She could, obviously, see it in his eyes.

"If we get through this," she said softly. "And you don't piss me off. Who knows?"

That was as close as he was going to get to a little verbal foreplay. "I'll look forward to it. And I'll try not to. Piss you off, that is."

She patted his cheek. "Good boy – you're learning."

"Can we all concentrate," Seth said sharply. "Contrary to popular belief, I would like all of us to get through this. Whatever's in there," he pointed at the putrid swamp water, "is probably going to be a bit miffed at having one of its tentacles lopped off."

"For Christ's sake," Ringo said through gritted teeth. "Was I supposed to let it drag me in? Is that what you're saying? Like some kind of sacrifice?"

Seth sighed. "Of course, that's not what I'm saying. I'm merely pointing out that it isn't going to be very happy, and, maybe, looking for revenge."

"Mate," Dave said to Ringo. "What are you doing? You know Seth doesn't wish you any harm."

"Yeah, even if he thinks you're a donkey," Jack said, grinning.

Dave turned in time to see the tentacle curl itself around Jack's upper body, pinning his arms to his sides. Ringo's blade flashed again, but, this time, it missed its mark. Jack was lifted off his feet and disappeared beneath the surface. Ringo was about to dive in after him. Dave grabbed his arm.

"You can't save him, man," he said, tears trickling down his cheeks.

"Fuck, fuck, fuck," Ringo yelled, his own tears flowing freely. He glared at Seth. "You say one word and I'll cut your fucking head off."

"I'm sorry, he was a good man," was all Seth said.

Dave hugged Ringo and they both held out their arms to take in Pete and Harry. They'd just lost their brother.

FOURTEEN

Dave didn't know how long they stood like that. Time didn't matter anymore. Although they'd only been together for a relatively short period of time, they had been through a lot. They'd fought side by side, took the piss out of each other but, it was a given – they'd do anything for each other. If Dave hadn't stopped him, Ringo would have dived into that mire after Jack; no question, and no thought for himself. But then, there would have been only three of them left. To lose Jack was bad enough but losing Ringo would have devastated Dave. He had never met anyone like him, he loved the man. He and Ringo were more than brothers, it went deeper than that.

He felt a hand on his neck. "I'm so sorry, guys," Phil said softly. Despite what she meant to him; her condolence felt like an intrusion. They were a band of brothers, a gang of wonderful misfits, a force to be reckoned with – a unit.

Ringo broke away. He wiped the snot and tears away with the back of his hand.

"One of us should say something," he said, more tears replacing those he'd smeared across his face. Dave nodded. "Do you want to do it, or do you want me to?" He asked him.

"I think it should be you," Ringo said. "You're the main man."

Dave was about to protest when Pete and Harry said together. "It should be you, Dave."

Dave looked at the faces of his comrades and knew they were right. He wiped away his own tears with both palms and took a deep, ragged breath. If someone had asked him to do something like this twelve months ago, he would have coughed, spluttered and mumbled something incoherent. That was then.

"We stood together, brothers in adversity, but we never let the bastards get us down. It was us against the world, and we welcomed the fight. We were a five-pointed star. Now, one of those points has been taken from us and we mourn the loss. We say goodbye to our friend and brother, Jack and vow to complete this mission and kick ass, in his name. For Jack." He made a fist and held up his right hand. Ringo, Pete and Harry placed their palms over his knuckles. "For Jack," they said together. They hugged each other one last time, then Ringo snorted, hawked up a greeny and spat into the water. He looked up at Seth.

"Let's get this show on the fucking road, big man," he said, the emotion still evident in his voice. "This ain't going to get the donkey a new hat."

"Take as long as you need," Seth said. "I'm not rushing you. You've just lost a good friend."

Dave coughed. "No, he's right. The sooner we get going, the sooner we're out of this quagmire."

Seth shrugged. "If you're sure?"

Pete and Harry nodded. "We've said our goodbyes," said Pete. "I, for one, want all this shit over and done with."

As expected, under the circumstances, they trudged on in silence. Phil stroked Dave's arm. He looked at her; she mouthed 'I'm so sorry'. He nodded and looked away. The four of them needed to be alone with their thoughts and memories. Dave felt as though they'd been forged in steel, an impenetrable entity. Stupid, he thought, but when you've been through the amount they'd been through in such a short time and survived everything; you think, as a group, you're invincible. They hadn't just lost Jack, they'd lost their invincibility. They were only human, skin and bone, blood and muscle – living on their wits. Ringo had kept his about him and thwarted the thing in the swamp, and, to be fair, had nearly saved Jack. If he had been a fraction of a second quicker, that filthy monstrosity would have lost another tentacle. Dave was sure he was thinking the same thing and blaming himself. He glanced over and saw his friend clenching his jaw, shaking his head slowly, the tears still in his eyes. Dave squeezed his shoulder.

"It's not your fault, man" he said softly.

Ringo looked him in the eye. "Isn't it? If I'd been a bit quicker, he'd still be here."

"Yeah, and if he'd been as diligent as you, he would have taken care of himself, like you did. You can't be everyone's carer. We're all responsible for our own safety." He paused. "At least you tried – what did I do? I'm full of this mumbo jumbo and I did nothing."

"Man, you've got enough on your plate, keeping all this shit together, and I ain't been helping, keep kicking off with him," he gestured to Seth.

"Yeah, but that's six of one and half a dozen of the other. He's not the easiest geezer to get along with, I should know. Until I managed to tap into the old magic when he couldn't, he treated me like dog shit. You've just taken my place, that's all. Just don't let him wind you up."

Ringo nodded. "Easier said than done," he said. "I'll try though, I promise. Now, fuck off and leave me alone. I need to grieve, man."

Dave gave his shoulder another squeeze and let him be. They all needed to grieve.

For the next half hour or so, they kept their own counsel, although Dave knew they were all watching for the slightest movement on the surface of the water. Once bitten, twice shy is a true statement. Mistakes like that, you do learn by. When a good friend loses his life, it focuses the mind. He felt Phil's arm snake around his waist. She leant her head into him, and he put his arm around her. They walked like that, comfortable in silence. After his short conversation with Ringo, Dave didn't want to talk to anyone. She understood that. He was grateful for the comfort but felt guilty for it, as well.

They began to see patches of grass invading the dried mud underfoot. It seemed they might be emerging from the swampland. It was just a pity; their group wasn't intact. He wondered how much more they'd have to face, and how many more they might lose before they reached Seth's precious Machine.

Gradually, the filthy water became more like deep puddles than the putrid lakes they'd grown accustomed to. The stench was less offensive and, had they not lost Jack, Dave was sure all their spirits would have lifted slightly. As it was, there was no discernible change to their mood.

"I'm not sure, but I think we may be approaching the final leg of our journey," said Seth.

Ringo glared at the back of his head and was about to speak. Dave gave him a nudge. Ringo looked at him and Dave shook his head. Ringo sighed and made a zipping motion across his lips.

"What makes you think that?" Dave asked Seth.

"They don't fly too far from The Machine," he said, pointing upwards.

Dave looked in the direction of Seth's finger but couldn't see a thing. "I can't see anything,"

"I can," said Phil. "A tiny dot." She pointed as well. "Over there."

Dave squinted and could just make out a speck. "Bloody hell, that is tiny. How big is it when you're close to it?"

"The size of an eagle," said Seth.

"Well, that's fucking miles away then," Ringo said sharply.

"But, at least, it might be our first glimpse of the light at the end of the tunnel," Pete suggested.

Ringo snorted. "And it might be something totally different to what he thinks it is," he said. "Am I right?" He asked Seth.

Seth turned and faced Ringo and Dave could see the guilt and remorse in his expression. "It could be, yes. Maybe it's wrong of me to get anyone's hopes up."

"Damned right it is," Ringo said with a sneer.

Dave put his hand on Ringo's shoulder again. "Come on mate, I know you're hurting, we all are, but Seth's not to blame. He didn't bring us into this, it just happened. We've got to look after each other from now on, yeah?"

"I suppose so," Ringo replied. "Let's just get on with it."

Dave looked at Seth and shrugged. Seth nodded, gave him a half-smile and turned back to the path. Onwards and upwards, Dave thought.

"I wonder where Danny is," said Phil. "He should be there, at the end. He may be stuck in some other dimension."

"Well, if he is, there's not a lot we can do about it. All we can do is hope that he finds his own way back."

"I hope nothing's happened to Blue," Harry said. "I really like that dog."

"I'm sure they'll all be fine," Dave said, trying to sound convincing. "Danny's a resourceful sort, and he can tap into the old magic, let's not forget that."

"Yeah, don't forget that," Ringo said. "That's how we landed up in this shithole in the first place."

Pete, Harry and Dave exchanged looks. Ringo was hurting more than the rest of them. No matter how hard anyone tried to convince him that Jack's death was not down to him, the more he needed to take responsibility for it. Because of that, he needed to lash out. A half decent psychologist could probably come up with a syndrome for it. Poor old Ringo would replay Jack's final moments over and over in his head for some time yet, and any attempt at exonerating him was futile. He had to work through it in his own time. Eventually, he would realise that he could have done no more. Dave thought, in that way, he was like his idol, Lennon. In the early days of the Beatles, John had been the driving force – the leader. Unfortunately, Ringo couldn't help trying to emulate him.

"He couldn't save Stuart," Dave said softly.

"What?"

"Your man couldn't save his best mate. Neither of you are God. Shit happens, it always will."

"That was different," he said. "He had an aneurysm."

"It's no different. It's life. You tried your best, and that's all anyone can do. You're not fucking Superman."

He looked at Dave and the tears were in his eyes again. "There are times when a seven stone woman can lift a car off her Labrador. All I needed to be was quick enough to lop another tentacle of the swamp monster. Is that too much to ask?"

Dave hugged him. "Ah, man, Jack wouldn't want this, you know he wouldn't. "

"Before he became magical," Harry said, jerking a thumb in Dave's direction. "You were always my Lennon."

Ringo rubbed his eyes. "So, a bit of mumbo-jumbo and I'm relegated to Pete Best, is that it?"

"What can I say – I'm fickle."

"You can get cream for that," Pete said, with a wink.

"I think a group hug is required," Dave said.

"I've never hugged another geezer, and I ain't about to start now," said Ringo. He looked from Pete, to Harry, to Dave "Ah, fuck it." He held out his arms. "I love you bastards. Come here."

They stood for a minute or so, sharing their pain and their friendship. Seth and Phil gave them the time they needed. Suddenly, Ringo started to sing 'In My Life' and, within seconds they were with him, their vocals croaky but sincere. Dave was sure Jack would have approved.

"Okay, I'm good," said Ringo, after the final chorus. "Well, as good as I'm going to be. Let's get this old bugger to his 'destiny'." He made parenthesis signs either side of his head.

Phil stepped forward and gave him a hug. He squeezed her bum cheek and she slapped him.

Normal service has been resumed, Dave thought.

She glared at him. "Under normal circumstances I'd have knocked your fucking head off for that. I'm making allowances. Is that clear?"

Ringo held up his hands and tried to look suitably ashamed. "It was a kind of reflex action," he said, managing to suppress a grin. "I beg madam's forgiveness."

Phil was not a million miles from a smirk herself. "Just try it again, sunshine and you'll feel the full force of 'madam's' wrath. Got it?"

That's how people like them got through shit – banter. It's a coping mechanism. Everybody has their own way, and this had always been theirs.

"I can't see that bird anymore," said Pete.

They all scanned the heavens, looking for the slightest blemish in the greyness.

"Well, it may or may not have been anything of significance," said Seth. "As Ringo so rightfully pointed out. I suggest we forget about it for the time being and....just keep going."

The puddles had disappeared, and the ground was firm and dotted with clumps of tired looking grass. It was as if it had been baked by the sun and had had no rain to refresh it. It was good to be out of the swamp, but this was not a whole lot better in the 'lifting the spirits' department. Dave thought back to how they'd been on their way to the coast, when they were unceremoniously slung into the middle of Seth's quest. They were looking forward to dipping their toes in the sea. Jack had been like a little kid going on his holidays. It would have been nice if they could have made it there before they were dragged away, but, hey ho, life's a bastard most of the time. Dave supposed the existence of a Machine and the non-existence of God would answer all the 'Why would God let this happen?' questions. He still couldn't get his head around a

Machine that needed to be fed people every so often, being responsible for keeping the world as they knew it – operational.

"You're doing that thinking thing again, aren't you?" Phil said, tapping him on the arm.

"More philosophising, I'd say."

"Jesus, get you, Socrates."

"I'm not just a pretty face," Dave said, with a grin.

"You can say that again."

He stuck his tongue out at her.

"Yuk, put it away," she said, with a grimace.

"What do you think of all this?" He asked her. "I mean, do you go along with this Machine stuff?"

She shrugged. "Well, Seth's seen it, seen his mates gobbled up by it. He seems to know what he's talking about."

Dave shook his head. "I don't know, it just seems a bit like an Asimov novel."

"And believing in a supreme being with no evidence to support such a belief is better?"

He smiled. "I suppose, when you put it like that."

"I didn't realise you did 'deep', Dave," said Ringo.

"Like I said, I'm not just a pretty face, mate."

"That, I did know."

Dave gave him the finger. "What's your take on it?"

"I've already told you. There is a God, and his name is John Lennon."

"No, but seriously – God or Machine?"

"Fucked if I know. I always thought you lived and then you died – end of story. Always been a bit of an atheist, I suppose. As far as this Machine bollocks is concerned – I'll believe it when I see it swallow the big man, know what I mean?"

"So, you're keeping an open mind?"

"I'm not troubling my mind with it at all," he said with a shake of his head. "My mind is busy elsewhere, just reminiscing about a young Japanese girl who thought I was Lennon's illegitimate son. Very attentive she was."

"Why did she think you were his son?" Phil asked.

Dave looked at her and shook his head. "Why do you think?"

The penny dropped immediately. "You dirty bastard," she said to Ringo, her nostrils flaring.

"She was happy, I was happy, where's the harm?"

"You pretended to be the son of a legend, just to get your leg over?"

Ringo stuck out his bottom lip and nodded. "That's about the size of it, yeah."

Phil was about to lay into him again, but he held his hand up. "I did give her a signed Lennon photo as well."

"They're worth thousands, aren't they?" Dave said.

"Well, they are, if they're signed by the man himself."

Phil punched his arm. "You disgust me."

Ringo rubbed his bicep. "It's been said before."

"You need to get some better friends," Phil said to Dave and, with that, she waltzed off after Seth.

"Now, see what you've done with your grubby, little anecdotes," Dave said with a grin. "I bet she wasn't the first."

"Or the last. I had that autograph off to a tee." He winked and, although Dave knew he shouldn't be seen to be condoning such behaviour, he couldn't help but admire Ringo's entrepreneurial flair.

PART FOUR
THE MACHINE

ONE

This would have been the time in a B movie when the hero would have called out his friends' names, a bemused expression on his face. Danny watched the twister move away, and then the guilt kicked in. He had been so intent on protecting Blue and Charlie, he had left everyone else in Dave's care. To begin with, he had struggled to keep the two of them by his side. Dave had himself and six others to contend with. He had let them all down. He slumped to the ground, ashamed of the person he'd become. Blue whined and licked his face, Charlie nuzzled his ear. He stroked them both. "Looks like it's just the three of us now," he said, the sense of loss joining the guilt. He was now in a situation, where he had no clue what to do. His overwhelming urge to protect a dog and a horse had left him directionless and condemned his friends to a fate, he didn't even want to contemplate. Whether, between them, Dave and he could have brought everyone through the twister would, now, never be known.

There he was – one man and his dog – and his horse. They moved off in the direction they'd been heading before the tornado struck. Where they were going and what he was going to do when they got there, if they ever did, Danny didn't know. For all he knew, they could wander through this wilderness until they dropped down dead. His throat was already dry, and his stomach was growling. The thought of collapsing, starved and dehydrated, waiting for oblivion was comforting. The idea of the same thing happening to his two companions, however, was unthinkable. He used the old magic to ascertain their condition. After his terror within the twister, Charlie needed water more than Blue.

"Come on, boys and girls," he said. "Let's go and find some water."

They must have appeared a strange trio to anyone watching, Charlie trotting slowly to Danny's left, Blue padding along to his right. His mind turned its attention back to the others. He'd managed to draw enough of the old magic to get the three of them through the tornado. He was hoping that Dave had managed to pull enough to save the others from serious harm. He hadn't been able to drag them through, that much was clear. Danny had to hope they'd survived and were trying to get back on track. He conjured up a picture of their reunion and locked it in the forefront of his mind. Like a criminal in prison would have a photograph of his family by his bed. He hoped that, and his concern for Blue and Charlie, would be enough to keep him going. He closed his eyes and took a deep breath and exhaled, allowing the force to flow slowly and seep back into the earth. He found he had a built-in water diviner. As he probed, he was aware of how the composition of the soil was altering. He detected traces of moisture to begin with, traces becoming trickles. He drew the magic in carefully, his brain collating all the information.

He estimated they would find some kind of watering hole in about a mile or so. He relaxed a little and sent out soothing thoughts to Charlie and Blue. It seemed the old magic could be utilised for more things than kicking ass. He hoped Dave had explored its facets and not just directed it towards destroying the exile. He was savvy – there wouldn't be a problem. It occurred to Danny then, that when one's only companions are a horse and a dog, conversations with oneself become more frequent. He decided to concentrate on finding water and, maybe, some form of sustenance for the three of them. Although his newly acquired power afforded him a basic sort of human/animal maintenance package, it wouldn't take the place of food and drink. If it came to it, he could probably ease the pain of death for Blue and Charlie, but that wasn't an option he wanted to consider.

"We're going to stay positive, eh kids?"

Blue looked up and wagged her tail, Charlie nuzzled his ear. Despite their situation and his concerns for Dave and the rest of the gang, Danny had to smile.

"It'll all turn out fine, don't you worry," he said, wondering who he was trying to convince.

There are times when too much thought is detrimental to health. As he wandered this wasteland with his two lovely, but verbally restricted companions, he realised this was one of those times. He believed that many people think themselves into anxiety and depression. Both, after all, are ailments of the mind. To switch off that dangerous organ, however, is no mean feat. He found himself going back over the car crash that had been his life up to this point. There had been good points, especially throughout his childhood and, although his parents had their problems, they loved their kids unconditionally. His dad had been his hero and he still missed him, his mum, before she became more dependent on the demon drink, had been one massive safety blanket, always ready to soothe his pain with her love. His brother and sister had been.........well.... his brother and sister, and he'd loved them with all his heart.

This was one of those times when there were no arguments or any banter to distract the mind. He had started to consider himself a solitary person but, now he realised, it wasn't solitude – it was loneliness. He was afraid to get too close to anyone, although he had thought that Sebastian and he could have become good friends. For a time, they had seemed to be on a similar wavelength; and look how that had turned out. He was becoming maudlin, diving in and wallowing in that pool of self-pity – again.

"Come on, Danny," he muttered. "There's always someone much worse off than yourself, remember that."

Blue looked up at him, as if she were confirming the statement.

He was just wondering if he was going mad, when Charlie snorted, scraped the ground with his front, right hoof and increased his speed. Blue sniffed the air and Danny could have sworn she smiled. She began wagging her tail and whining.

It was obvious she wanted to follow Charlie.

"Go on girl," Danny urged. They were nearing water; he could feel it. His friends, it seemed, could smell it. Blue trotted off after her new friend. Danny put his mawkish thoughts on hold and quickened his pace. One moment, the landscape was stretching out before him, unhampered by any alteration of any description, the next he was entering a full-blown oasis. Water trickled from a spring, below a copse of palm trees, into a clear, blue pool. There was a patch of lush, green grass that Charlie was munching on happily. Blue was lapping away at the pool, her tail still wagging. Bushes grew on the other side of the pool, the reds and blacks of raspberries and blackberries resplendent in their abundance. Coconuts had fallen from the trees and lay on the grass.

Danny dropped to the ground beside Blue and started to scoop up water in his cupped hands. It tasted so sweet and fresh; it was like nectar. After they'd slaked their thirst, he picked handfuls of berries and shared them out between the three of them. He smashed coconuts and it appeared that dogs and horses liked coconut as well. These two did, anyway. Initially, he'd thought that berries and coconut would not be enough to sustain them, but, after about ten minutes he was stuffed, Charlie was back to the grass and Blue was curled up by his side, her eyes closing. Danny put his arm across her flank, leant back against a tree trunk and followed suit.

He was tired, the feel of Blue's fur under his hand comforting. The idea of going to sleep and never waking again was appealing, but, unfortunately, wasn't going to happen. His body begged for rest, but his mind was a mess. Thoughts banged around his skull, the old magic highlighting the guilt he felt for depriving Dave of his fair share, and the responsibility for Blue and Charlie. He just wanted to clear his mind and sleep. It wasn't going to happen.

Charlie had clearly filled his belly. He glanced at Blue and himself, snorted and lowered himself to the ground. He rolled onto his side, snorted again and settled into equine slumber. Danny felt as if he was at a party when everyone's pissed, and he was the designated driver.

He realised that ever since Seth and Phil had entered his life, he really hadn't had time to think. It had all been such a rollercoaster of madness. For the first time, he had time to himself. Time to try and put things into perspective.

Seth had told him categorically there was no such thing as God. A machine, of some description, kept the world as he had known it, prior to this dubious expedition, rolling along in the sad, sadistic manner it appeared to favour. It struck him that, just as he had been brought up to believe in God, sent to Sunday school and made to attend R.E. classes, so Seth had been indoctrinated in his own particular beliefs. He didn't know, for a fact, that God did not exist, and he didn't know he did. Seth's beliefs had been passed down to him, the same as Danny's had. Looking back over the events, since being drugged and being dragged into this weirdness, The Machine scenario seemed more likely. But, when a different story line has been forced down your throat for years, it's difficult to disregard it without question. It wasn't inconceivable to believe Seth to be some sort of 'Manson' character.

Then, there was all this time travel stuff with Dave and his gang. The whole thing was mind bending, to say the least. If Danny hadn't pinched himself numerous times, he would put this down to some booze induced dream – the product of a lost weekend.

He looked down at Blue, as if he thought she might disappear into thin air any moment.

"Get a grip," he said to himself. "You're in danger of losing it."

He yearned for a guitar, or an iPod – to hear Lennon screaming 'Twist and Shout' or Clapton's solo in 'Crossroads'. He needed normality.

Then another thought occurred to him. If you're alone, how do you know if you're mad? You can't get a second opinion. Can you drive yourself mad? Blue rolled onto her back, legs in the air and broke wind.

Danny laughed like a drain, even though he didn't really think drains could laugh.

The first couple of drops of rain brought him back to his current situation. Blue twitched and Charlie snorted again. A man of few words, he thought, still giggling.

A slight drizzle became rain and, soon, they were sat in a full-bodied downpour.

"This is more like it," he said to his buddies.

The rain was clean and refreshing. He sat with his face skyward, his confused tears at one with the cloudburst – except there wasn't a cloud in the sky. Under normal circumstances this would have been more than strange, but, after everything he'd experienced since entering this weird world, it was just another bizarre occurrence.

Blue shifted, sneezed and sat up with a start.

"It's just a shower, girl," he said to her.

She looked past him and whined. He turned his head and saw the landscape disappearing beneath the rivulets of water. It was as if the horizon had been painted on a sheet of glass and the rain was washing it off. Behind the sprawling greenery and blue sky emerged a different picture. As the rain eased and the last of the grass dissolved, they were looking at dense woodland.

"Plenty of places to cock your leg there Blue, if you were a boy, eh?" he said. He was finding it difficult to place his thoughts in any sort of sensible order. His stomach was bilious and his mouth dry. He began to hyperventilate, the panic rising.

He had never suffered a panic attack before joining this crazy adventure, but he'd seen kids at school having them. His heart was beating like a hammer, his vision beginning to blur slightly. As if it were happening to another person, he felt Blue licking his face. He tried to stroke her, but he couldn't move. He remembered teachers bringing out paper bags and getting the kids to breathe slowly into them until it had passed. Shame he didn't have one in his back pocket. Pictures flashed through his mind – Seth, Phil, Dave, Ringo, Sebastian. These were replaced by his mum and dad, his brother and sister, Lawrence Carter and Billy Arnold. He reached out mentally and held Billy's face in his mind's eye. He focused on everything Billy had been to him, mentor, friend, maybe even a second dad and he started to control his breathing, remembering his training, Billy pushing him, as he always did, past the pain barrier. Slowly Danny's vision cleared, his heart rate lowered, and his stomach stopped doing forward rolls. He was able to move again. He hugged Blue and kissed the top of her head.

"I'm alright, girl," he said soothingly. "It's okay."

He felt exhausted. If that was how a panic attack felt, he didn't want to go there again.

The rain had stopped, and Charlie was back on his feet, looking at the two of them, his head cocked to one side.

"Hey Charlie," Danny said. "We're all good, yeah?"

Charlie snorted and followed it up with a neigh of, what Danny took for, agreement. For a minute there, he had totally lost control. He was shocked. He was glad the oasis hadn't been washed away by the rain. He drank more water and stocked his pockets with berries. He wished he had some sort of container to fill, for there was no knowing when they would see water again. He tried to get Blue and Charlie to drink some more before they set off again. He picked up Blue and stood her at the water's edge. She took a sip or two, but Charlie wasn't having any. As the saying goes – you can lead a horse to water...

They turned and faced the lush greenery. Blue and Charlie seemed as reticent about entering the forest as Danny was. The only other choice was to stay put at the oasis, but the way things went in this place, that could disappear at any minute. He'd come to realise that the rule of thumb was to keep following the signs, however weird or perilous they appeared.

"Into the deep, dark woods," he said. He looked at Blue. "Be handy if we had Gandalf with us, eh girl?"

She looked up and wagged her tail. He turned to Charlie and patted his neck. "What about you, mate, you ready for the next leg of this wonderful journey?"

Charlie swayed his head up and down and from side to side, snorting. Danny hugged him, bent down and rubbed Blue's ears.

"Onwards," he said.

The first thing he noticed as they left the brightness of the oasis for the shade of the trees was the silence. Whenever he had walked through woods before, the sound of birds was prominent.

As they walked, the quiet became oppressive and Danny was on edge – waiting for the next surrealistic apparition. To ease the tension, he started to sing 'You've Got to Hide Your Love Away', his mind unable to prevent itself returning to the early days of 'Danjo' before everything went to shit. He was happy in those days, his family was well, he'd dealt with his tormentors and he was being paid for doing something he loved to do. Best of all, he was doing it with a good friend; or so he thought. He stopped himself before he started the whole depressing cycle again. Life, for a lot of people, is a tired montage of deception, realisation and loss. That was certainly his life. Add to that, the knowledge that you're a guardian of some strange Machine that, apparently, keeps the planet the human race call home functioning. He longed for the days when they'd all be sat in the lounge watching 'Coronation Street', even though he detested the programme. It was normality. The sunlight, if that was what it was, was filtered by the trees, creating a dappled effect. That, coupled with the silence, was soothing. As much as he loved Blue and Charlie, he longed for some human company. Someone who would react if he made a statement or asked a question. Again, a lot of people yearn for peace and quiet, wanting to be left to their own devices. This, however, does not normally mean no outside stimulation at all. No books, music, art, TV – nothing. He felt like Robinson Crusoe, with a dog and a horse standing in for Man Friday. All he had were his memories, some good, some bad, but he couldn't separate the two. They came as a package, the bad, definitely, outweighing the good. It was strange, the more he tried not to think, the more thoughts flooded his mind. First, he thought the buzzing was a remnant of some memory.

It began faintly, a bee on its way to a nearby source of nectar. As it became louder, Danny recognized the sound, from a few years back. His dad had hired a local company to tidy up the back garden. There were a few Leylandii at the bottom that had grown, as they do. The neighbours had been complaining about how they had started to block out their light. His dad, ever the responsible citizen, immediately took appropriate action and hired someone to take care of it. That was how he recognized the sound – it was a chainsaw. His next thought, after the decapitation of the Leylandii, was of the horror film, 'The Texas Chainsaw Massacre'.

"Slowly does it, kids," he said to his two chums, readying the old magic. Part of him was grateful for signs of another being, even if it turned out to be a psychotic killer.

He slowed his pace, nevertheless, Blue and Charlie following suit. Blue whined and Charlie shook his head. Neither was keen on the sound, that was obvious. Whether or not they detected anything else, Danny couldn't say.

By now he could see the trees moving, up ahead, to the right of the path.

"Stay behind me," he told them, holding out his arms. They dropped back dutifully.

He crept towards the sound, the magic bubbling away. If a would-be 'Leatherface' was lurking amongst the trees, he was about to get a taste of his own medicine. Danny's nerve endings were tingling. He was ready.

"Hello son, how's it going kiddo?"

In a small clearing, stood Danny's dad, an array of felled trees around his feet. Only this wasn't his dad as he had last seen him, the overweight, thinning couch potato. This was Dad as he had appeared in photos of him and Mum before they were married – a slim, muscular hunk of a man. He stood there, topless, the sweat glistening on his biceps and pecs.

Danny gaped at him, mouth open.

His dad switched off the chainsaw. "I don't think there's any flies around," he said. "But close your mouth, Danny. It makes you look simple, son."

"Dad?" Danny managed to say.

"Yes, son?"

He had seen some things since meeting Seth and Phil, but this was something else. He had been questioning his sanity earlier, now, he was seriously worried that he was completely losing it.

"You're......." he started to say.

"Dead," his dad said, nodding. "I am aware of that, son. I had thought I might have gone to heaven. After all, I wasn't that bad, was I?"

Danny shook his head. "You were great."

His dad shrugged. "If this is hell – I suppose it's not so bad. I work hard but get fed well." He dropped the saw and pointed to his torso. "Not looking too shabby, eh?"

"You're looking great Dad."

He held out his arms. "Come and give your old dad a hug, then."

Danny practically ran into his arms, unable to stop the tears running down his cheeks. His vision blurred as he went to hug his dead father.

He fell to his knees, tears streaming down his face. His dad had disappeared into thin air and it was just him, Blue and Charlie again. Blue could see he was upset and lay beside him licking his face. He put his arm around her.

"I don't know what I'd do without you girl," he said, burying his face in her fur. "This was bad enough before, without having to suffer hallucinations of my dad."

Unless he was truly trapped inside The Grid. That was something Danny didn't really want to contemplate, even though he had appeared, reasonably content.

"Am I losing my mind?" He asked himself. He ran his fingers through his hair and sobbed uncontrollably. He needed a drink and a pot full of tranquillizers. If he'd thought he was at his lowest ebb before Seth found him, he was mistaken. He was at the end of his tether – he'd had enough. Blue nuzzled closer and laid her head on his shoulder, her brown eyes staring up into his.

Charlie came over and nudged his cheek with his nose. Danny raised his other hand and stroked Charlie's neck. He'd been brought up to face his responsibilities and do everything he could to look after those who depended on him.

"You guys," he said, remembering a film called 'The Goonies', he'd watched repeatedly in his youth. "Come on, let's carry on, before I self-combust."

He'd never been gregarious but the longer this went on, the more he missed the interaction of another human being.

"Those animals depend on you, Danny."

He groaned as he looked round. His mum was picking berries from an adjacent tree.

She popped a couple into her mouth. "You can't have any," she said with a shake of her head," they're poisonous."

"Why are you doing this to me?" He pleaded.

"I'm proud you were chosen," she said, smiling.

"You're not real Mum."

"And what is real, Danny?"

He covered his face with his hands and rubbed his eyes. He didn't know how much more of this he could take.

He looked at his mum's smiling, drink free face and memories of his early childhood came flooding back. Times before drink became his mother's primary need and his dad could take a few crisps out of a jumbo pack and put the rest back in the cupboard.

"I know you won't let us down."

The voice began as that of his mother but crumbled and became a buzz in his head. He closed his eyes, searching for her dulcet tones once more. He lay on his back and allowed all the anguish, guilt and sadness free reign. He wept as he had never wept before. A quote from Oscar Wilde came to mind – we are all in the gutter but some of us are looking at the stars. Poetic bullshit, he thought, wishing this would end – he would end.

Many people go through life, never facing their lowest ebb. Some, probably, never having a clue what desperation is. They become so involved in their materialistic existences, working overtime to afford themselves more overseas holidays, memory foam mattresses, sixty-inch TVs, emotion an inconvenience.

Shit, however, happens to all. At some point, reality kicks in. From experience, Danny thought, it's rarely pleasant. Reality at that precise moment, however, seemed a million miles away. Here he was, in the middle of the magic forest with a horse and a dog, hobnobbing with his dead parents. It doesn't come much more surreal than that.

He just hoped Sam and Tara weren't behind the next mighty oak – that would destroy him completely.

He pushed himself up and made himself move forwards. Fortunately, the hallucinatory aspect of the wood took a back seat for a while and they walked in silence. Had the situation been different, it would be classed as a pleasant ramble. He tried to pretend that they were out for an afternoon stroll, after a sumptuous lunch and would be returning to the bosom of a loving family. Imagination, however, had never been one of his strengths, at the best of times – so he failed miserably. He was hovering between clinical depression and insanity, or that was how it felt. If he could have switched off his mind for a time, it would have helped. He wondered if there was a part of the brain, unused so far, that was able to clear away all the nasty stuff. A kind of disc clean-up for the old grey matter. It would be handy.

Blue began to bark, her hackles up. Danny looked in the direction that seemed to be concerning her but could see nothing untoward.

"There's nothing there, girl," he said to her.

She was growling now. All he could see were trees, but she could either smell or sense something else, that was clear. He stepped off the path and walked towards the area that was causing her distress. She slunk along by his side, her growl low and menacing.

He suddenly felt a tug at the old magic. They were not alone.

"I warn you, I'm in no mood for games," he said. "Whoever you are, you'd better show yourself." He let the power seep out.

An old man stepped from behind a clump of bushes, his eyes bright, hair dishevelled, dressed in rags. A wispy, white beard covered his chin and cheeks.

"Who are you?" Danny asked him.

"You have the old magic," the old man said, a demented grin showing off extremely white teeth. "It's strong."

My God, Danny thought, I'm re-imagining Yoda.

"Who is Yoda?" He asked, frowning.

"He was a Jedi from........." Danny began, before realising the stranger had just read his mind. "How do you do that?"

"Do what?"

He was grinning again. He looks madder than I feel, Danny thought.

"Madness is underrated," the Yoda sound-alike said with a nod.

TWO

If Danny had thought he was in a surrealistic enclosure before, he was mistaken. This new development put a whole new slant on the whole situation. He was now in the presence of a weird, little man, who could read his mind. He didn't know why he had made the Yoda reference. The little feller before him did not resemble the great Jedi at all. His face was white and, although wrinkled, completely human. Whenever he spoke, it was Danny that imagined the 'Yoda' inflections.

"Confusion is detrimental," the man said, with a nod.

Even in his already maxed out emotional state, Danny couldn't help laughing. When he'd managed to control himself, he looked at the stranger. The little man immediately averted his eyes, looking to the left, not wanting to meet Danny's gaze.

"You won't turn to stone," Danny said.

"Ah, the myth of the gorgon," the man said with a satisfied nod of his head. "Fictitious and hardly representative of this particular situation."

"You don't appear to want to look me in the eye," Danny said.

"Indeed."

"It is conventional to look at the person you are speaking to."

"Convention is a word invented by the unimaginative," the stranger said.

Danny chuckled again. "Do you have a name?"

"Probably many."

"I'm Danny, pleased to meet you." he held out his hand. The man looked at it with distaste.

"I know who you are," he said.

"Well then, you have me at a disadvantage."

"Why does your race place so much importance on labels? You must name everyone and everything. It is so unnecessary, and so restrictive."

Danny shrugged. "I suppose it just makes life easier."

"And you believe that to be a good thing?"

"I do," Danny said. "Don't you?"

"I believe that trying to control the uncontrollable is a waste of effort. Has the possession of the old magic taught you nothing?"

"It lost me my friends," Danny said, wanting to grab the stranger's head and force him to make eye contact.

"I wouldn't do that, if I were you," the little man said, looking over Danny's left shoulder. "As for your present situation, all blame lies at your feet. The old magic is a power at your disposal. How you utilise it is your choice. If you decide to deprive your, so called friends, of their share, the onus sits squarely on your shoulders."

"So, you're here to make me feel even worse than I did already. Is that it?"

"I'm here to aid you," he said, lowering his gaze, to take in Danny's kneecaps.

"And how do you intend to do that?"

The stranger glanced at Danny's face for a second. "That, person who needs to be called Danny, is up to you."

"I don't need to be called Danny," Danny said, unable to hide the irritation. "My parents christened me Danny." He was about to explain why but realised that would be as pointless as the statement he'd already made. He was sure his new acquaintance hadn't a clue what christenings were. To him, names were unimportant, that was evident.

"Where did you come from?" Danny asked him, instead.

He furrowed his brow. "I didn't come from anywhere."

Danny tried a different approach; this wasn't going to be easy. "You say you're here to help me?"

His gaze didn't waiver. His eyes were finally meeting Danny's, which was a start.

"Were you sent?"

"I am here because I am needed," he said.

Although it was stimulating to talk to someone who could reply, it was also infuriating to receive such emotionless and uninformative responses. Danny thought he had been a little unfair to the Jedi when he had made the Yoda comparison. Talking to this little fellow was akin to sucking up rice pudding through a straw.

"How did you know you were needed?"

The furrows in his brow deepened. "I don't understand the question."

"How did you know I needed you," Danny said slowly, as if he were talking to a foreigner with a limited knowledge of English.

The stranger looked away to his left, dealing with the tedium of answering Danny's questions, clear. "Why do you need to know?" He asked.

"Just call me curious," Danny replied.

"I was under the impression you needed to be referred to as Danny," the man said.

Danny nearly laughed and would have if he were joking. He wasn't.

He waved his hand. "Yeah, I do. Forget it. Just tell me how you're going to help me before I lose the urge to live."

"You have just answered your own question," he said.

Danny stopped and looked down at the weird, little man. "You thought I was going to top myself?"

It was obvious his use of slang drifted way above the little man's head.

"You are needed. No chances could be taken," he said solemnly.

"You know what – I'm tired of being needed." Danny bent down until they were eyeball to eyeball. "You've got the wrong man, my friend. Seth's the next sacrifice to this ludicrous nightmare. To be honest, I'm close to the end of my tether."

The furrowed brow smoothed, and Danny saw something in those strange eyes. He had always thought of himself as another guardian, one who would take his place when required.

"I am not just another guardian – am I ?"

"No," the little man said.

"So, what's so special about me?"

He looked confused. "I didn't know there was anything special about you. If you don't know either; it would seem reasonable to conclude that there is nothing special about you."

Danny sighed. "But you just said, I was not just another guardian."

"I believe you said that."

"Yes," Danny said, through gritted teeth. "But you agreed, did you not?"

"I did."

Danny decided to take a minute or two to think about things before continuing their conversation. It was apparent that he had to choose his words carefully.

"Very wise," the little man said.

"Can you stop doing that – please?" Danny asked him. "It is most disconcerting."

"That is like asking someone like you to stop listening. It's impossible."

"Well, can you, at least, not make it so obvious. I would appreciate it, if you could only answer or comment on my verbal questions and keep your responses to my thoughts to yourself. Would that be possible?"

The stranger thought for a moment. "Yes, it would."

"Good. Now can I think for a while without any interruptions?"

"Yes."

Danny wanted to know why the man had turned up in the first place, and why he was so......... weird. His new friend had already made it clear that he would only answer Danny's questions and not indulge in any form of elaboration. If the questions weren't the right questions, he would be no further forward, just more frustrated with the man's stunted replies. He'd indicated that his appearance had something to do with Danny's present state of mind, and that he wasn't the same as Seth and Phil. Finding out why that was, didn't appear to be that easy. Blue was sitting by his side, looking at the little man, her head moving from side to side, as if she couldn't decide whether he was friend or foe. Danny rubbed her ears. "It's alright, girl. He's here to help us – allegedly."

The man was about to speak but Danny held up his hand to stop him. He closed his mouth and waited.

"We've ascertained that I'm not just another guardian," Danny said. "And, that I'm not special. If you had to choose a word to describe my part in all of this, what would it be?"

"Integral," the man said, without hesitation.

It was the first time Danny had been integral to anything. What he really wanted to know, however, was why.

"Do you know why I'm integral?" He asked.

"I do not have that information," the little man said.

"So, you're here to help me because I'm integral, but you don't know why?"

"That is correct," he said, with a nod.

Danny looked him up and down again. He didn't look as though he could knock the skin off a rice pudding.

"What is a rice pudding?" The man asked.

"I told you not to do that," Danny said.

"I know you did, but if I read something in your mind that I don't understand, I must ask for an explanation."

"Don't tell me, it's your duty."

He looked at Danny.

"Well, is it?"

"You told me not to tell you," he said, his voice and face expressionless.

Danny shook his head and sniggered. "I did, didn't I?"

"What is a rice pudding?" He asked again.

"It will be easier if I imagine it and you read my mind," Danny said. "I think trying to explain it may be difficult and take more time than it's worth. Ready?"

The stranger nodded. Danny thought back to school lunches, rice pudding was a frequent item on the menu. He pictured the dish, before it was served, the skin brown and still intact.

"Why would I want to knock the skin off it?" His little friend inquired, a slight frown wrinkling his brow.

329

"It's just an expression," Danny said. "It sort of indicates a lack of strength and fighting ability," he said, hoping that would do. Surprisingly, the man nodded.

"I see. I believe you have another expression – appearances can be deceptive?"

"We do indeed and, just recently, it has proved to be true on a number of occasions."

"Just so, the one who needs to be called Danny."

"Please, just call me Danny. Can you manage that?"

"I can."

"Well, if we're going to be together for a while, I need to call you something."

"I don't see why, but something is fine."

Danny sighed. "No, I mean I need a name for you. I'm Danny – you're ....?"

Danny was not sure if he detected a glint in the stranger's eye – probably not.

"I do not have a name," he said, "If you need me to have one, you must choose one."

"Okay," Danny thought for a minute or two.

"How about Bobby?" Years ago, their neighbours had owned a Yorkshire terrier called Bobby and it used to run up to Danny every time it saw him.

"Bobby is fine, although I'm nothing like your other friend. You seem to have a lot of friends with four legs."

"Yeah well, they're better than most of the two-legged ones, believe me."

"Bobby, Bobby, Bobby," he said, as if he were trying it on for size.

"Do you like it?"

He nodded. "It will suffice."

Not for the first time, Danny felt as if he was in the middle of some badly written fantasy novel. It was weird enough to be travelling through this mad world with a dog and a horse. Now, an extremely strange, little man, who could read his mind, had joined their unusual troupe. To have to censor your own thoughts is unnatural and restrictive; not to mention intrusive.

"I don't suppose you can switch off this mind reading stuff," Danny said, "It is disconcerting, to say the least."

Bobby looked up at him. "You are able to do the same," he said bluntly.

"I don't think so."

Something resembling a smile flashed across Bobby's features. "That is the trouble with most human beings; they live their lives in cages, denying the mental capacity they possess. Instead of developing simple skills, they choose to destroy each other. It is not how it was supposed to be."

"Are you one of the elders that Seth spoke of?"

"Sadly, the elders perished long ago."

"So, who – or what – are you?"

"I'm Bobby," he said simply.

"But that's just a name I gave you," Danny said, unable to hide his frustration. "What is your purpose?"

"To aid you, I have already told you that."

Danny let out a heavy sigh. "Well, you're not doing a great job. If I was considering killing myself before, I'm still in two minds. The only thing that's different is – I feel like throttling you first."

"That would be inadvisable."

Danny bent down, until they were eye to eye. "Would it?"

Bobby cocked his head to one side, as if listening. After a few moments, he said, "You need to be unlocked."

"Unlocked?" Danny managed to say, before Bobby grabbed his wrist.

His eyes must have bulged. His mind felt like a bud bursting into bloom. Blue's thoughts were simple and monochrome – I'm hungry. Danny laughed – a typical Labrador. Charlie was reminiscing about past conquests.

His little friend, however, wasn't giving anything away.

"Why can't I read your mind?" Danny asked him.

"Because there is nothing to read," Bobby said. "Too much thought can be detrimental."

"You can say that again."

Bobby was about to repeat himself when Danny stopped him with his mind. He nodded. "This is a lot better."

From then on, Bobby would read his thoughts, but he would read his reactions to them and stem any irritating responses. He was still no nearer to ascertaining who the little man was and where he had come from, however.

After short mental conversations, Danny became bored with such exchange and resorted to more conventional methods.

"Do you know where we are going?"

Bobby looked at him in bewilderment. Danny felt him probing his mind and found there were defences he could use. It was like closing a door.

"You learn quickly," Bobby said, with a half-smile.

"It's been said before. Now, answer my question."

"Of course, I know where we're going." He paused, his feelers knocking at the door Danny had closed. "You are a guardian, you know where you're going, don't you?"

Danny could see the irritation in Bobby's eyes. Before he closed his own mental door, he was able to read his regret for 'unlocking' him. Danny smiled.

"When we started this ridiculous journey, the four of us, and Blue, of course, we were bound for Seth's Machine," he said. "To be honest – now, I don't know what I'm doing. It feels as though I'm drifting aimlessly."

"First of all, it is not Seth's Machine," Bobby said indignantly. "You are still a guardian and you must witness your friend's joining. It is how it must be."

"So, where is my friend?"

"Within The Grid, situations can be misleading, certain tests may be employed. I can say no more than that."

"Can't or won't?" Danny asked harshly.

"Cannot," he said. "I do not possess that knowledge."

"But we're still on course for The Machine?"

"You will always be on course for The Machine."

"What about Seth and the others?"

"They are also on course for The Machine."

"Are there different dimensions in The Grid?"

"Not different dimensions, no."

"So, where are my friends." This was returning to the pulling teeth scenario.

"Sometimes, it may be necessary to make certain temporary alterations."

"As in splitting up groups of guardians?"

"This is a unique situation, in more ways than one," Bobby said. "There are strangers with the guardians. That has not happened before. One of the guardians was not as he seemed. That has not happened before. Why you have been separated, I cannot say, but there must be a reason. There is always a reason."

Danny shook his head. "You haven't told me anything, I didn't already know. You're as much in the dark as I am, aren't you?"

"All either of us need to know, is that we are heading for The Machine. At some point you will be reunited with your friends. I have no doubt of that."

"In that case, we'd better get on with it, I guess."

"That is a good idea," Bobby said with an exaggerated nod.

THREE

Blue nuzzled Danny's hand and whined. After being his main companion for a time, Danny thought she was jealous of Bobby.

"Hey girl, how are you doing?" He said, bending down and letting her lick his face.

"If I may say so," Bobby started to say.

"Oh, be quiet," Danny said. "You know nothing about the relationship between a man and his dog."

"I was about to say how much that animal means to you and vice versa," he said. "I have never experienced such an overwhelming feeling of devotion before."

"Have you never heard the phrase – a dog is man's best friend?" He sighed as Bobby looked at him quizzically. "Of course, you haven't."

"No, but, like you, I learn quickly. There is an intensity between you – a warmth." He closed his eyes and smiled. "It is nice."

Danny was shocked. "I didn't realise you could feel emotion."

"Nor did I." Bobby's expression was a mixture of surprise and wonder. "May I stroke her?"

Danny rubbed Blue's ears. "What d'you say girl?" She licked his hand and wagged her tail.

"Go for it," he said to Bobby. "Gently though. Let her sniff your hand first."

Bobby held out his hand. Blue sniffed it and looked up at Danny. He nodded to her and she licked Bobby's fingers. He giggled like a girl. "That tickles," he said.

For the first time since he'd thrust himself upon him, Danny saw a human being and not some kind of artificial intelligence.

"I take it you've never met a dog before," he said to him.

Bobby glanced up at him, his eyes wild with excitement. "I have known of them but, yes, Blue is the first I've come into contact with." He paused. "She is lovely – is that the right word?"

Danny grinned. "Yeah, I'm sure Blue would agree with that. Eh girl?"

Blue wagged her tail faster, happy with the extra attention. Danny was chuckling when Charlie butted him in the small of his back. He turned around and rubbed her nose.

"You feeling left out, mate?" He said. Bobby was still stroking Blue with his right hand but started to rub Charlie's neck with his left. He was in his element, as were Blue and Charlie.

Danny stood back and watched Bobby discover himself. He wondered how old he was and how many other lost guardians he'd had to nudge back onto the right path.

"Animals are better than most people," Danny said to him.

Without looking up, Bobby said. "They are certainly better than those I have met."

"What you see is what you get, my friend. Once you have a bond with an animal, they will lay down their life for you – and, in most cases, you'll do the same for them. You know they won't piss off with your woman."

For the first time in a while, he thought about Joey and Beth. It was a fleeting thought.

Bobby looked at him with a confused expression.

"Don't worry about it," Danny said to him. "That is definitely not important. Just another reason why animals are better than humans."

Bobby nodded to Blue. "Her mind is filled with aromas and odours, some of them quite disgusting."

"Dogs have an amazing sense of smell, thousands of times better than any man or woman, and Labradors, which is Blue's breed, are in the top five of all dogs. A lot of the time, something that smells repulsive to us, is very enticing to a dog – even excrement." He decided not to say 'shit', not wanting to go into any detail over bodily waste. He figured Bobby had a basic vocabulary programme which would include excrement but not necessarily include slang terms. It seemed he was right. His little friend screwed up his nose.

"Knowledge is important to me," he said, "but some information is unpleasant."

"Just like life," Danny said. "I'm afraid you've led a very sheltered one – not coming into contact with much of the excrement that goes with it."

He looked even more confused.

"Metaphorical, not physical."

Bobby suddenly beamed and nodded. "I think I understand that. You losing your friends is metaphorical excrement? Is that correct?"

"Bob on."

The confusion was back again.

"Look, Bobby, there are so many phrases and nuances in our language that you won't understand, and to be honest, most of them, you don't need to. If I say something you don't understand and it's important – I'll explain – I promise."

"It would be much easier if I could see your thoughts again," he said, hopefully.

Danny shook his head. "No. There are some thoughts I wish to keep private."

"But you could........."

"No," Danny said firmly. "Now, leave it, please."

Bobby went back to stroking Blue and Charlie and, Danny was sure, he was sulking.

"What's that?"

In the sky, flashes of silver were appearing. They were like lightning but less aggressive, they almost caressed the horizon.

"I think," said Bobby, "that you will be reunited with your friends soon."

He seemed to be afraid.

"That's good, yeah?"

For the first time since Danny had met the funny, little fellow, he detected a reluctance to speak truthfully.

"What is it, Bobby?"

"I don't know."

Danny could tell he was lying.

"Something's going to happen, isn't it?"

Bobby looked at him and then the sky, his expression revealing his extreme consternation. Danny felt a shift in the old magic, but, strangely, became calmer than he'd been in ages. Blue was whining and Charlie pawing the ground. Danny put a hand on each of them. "Steady, girls and boys, you're safe with me." He turned his attention to Bobby, ignoring the flashes in the sky. "Come on, sunshine, what's going on?"

"I like you, one who likes to be called Danny, and I like your animals. I was enjoying our time together."

"Do I get the impression, you're about to leave us?"

"My services are no longer required," he said sadly.

"What do you mean, you've only been here five minutes?" Danny was about to explain his meaning, but Bobby held up a hand.

"I've served my purpose," he said, his sorrow almost tangible.

Blue jumped up, licked his face and sat down. Charlie laid her head on his shoulder. There were tears in Bobby's eyes.

"Be careful, Danny, and remember – all is not as it appears, sometimes people are not as they seem."

"What do you mean by that? I wish you'd stop talking in bloody riddles."

"You think he's your friend," Bobby said, "but he's.............."

Bobby started to fade in front of Danny's eyes.

"Wait, who are you talking about? Bobby?"

It was too late. Bobby had slipped away just as quickly as he had appeared. Maybe he had served his purpose. Danny was feeling strangely serene. He looked up, mesmerised by the silver streaks, as they danced with each other, meandering gracefully across a darkened sky.

FOUR

Pete stuck his head between Dave and Ringo. "Is it getting colder, or is it me?"

Phil turned around and Ringo and Dave said in unison. "No. It's not you, it's definitely getting colder."

Luckily, they averted their gaze before she could see the relevance. She was rubbing her arms. "It's bloody freezing."

Unfortunately, Harry's eyes were locked on and going nowhere. That was, until Phil changed their direction with a rather forceful left hook.

As the temperature dropped, a cold breeze began to caress them with its icy fingers. They were all rubbing their arms with their hands as the breeze slowly increased in intensity until it was a sharp wind.

"I hate the cold," said Harry, shivering, whilst rubbing his chin. "Especially when I haven't got a bloody coat."

Even though they were freezing their taters off, all, except Seth, kept sneaking peeks at Phil's chest. She put her arms over her breasts, hugging herself. "Will you perverts cut it out?" She said angrily. "I expected better from you, especially you – Dave."

"Sorry," Dave said, trying to look contrite.

"Get over yourself," said Ringo. "Men ogle attractive women, it's a fact. You'd hate it more if none of us gave you a second glance."

Phil turned on him, her cheeks flushed with a combination of anger and cold.

"Would I now? Let me tell you, I've spent a lifetime dealing with dirty bastards like you lot. Do you think I've enjoyed that – feeling like a piece of meat hanging in a butcher's window. Well, do you?"

She was in his face now, her fists clenched by her sides. "Answer me, cretin."

Ringo looked into her eyes and then lowered his gaze. "I guess, maybe you're the exception that proves the rule."

Phil's expression was one of complete disgust. "You're a typical male chauvinist pig," she said, "think you know everything about women, when really, you know fuck all." She waved her finger around the four of them. "If I catch any of you leering again, I'll knock your teeth down your throat, understand?"

They all nodded. "I really am sorry," Dave said, "truly."

"Leave me alone, Dave. I'm severely pissed off at the moment, yeah?"

Dave held up his hands. "Sure."

"Why has he got a bleeding coat?" Harry asked, pointing at Seth. "Probably knew this was going to happen."

"It belonged to my predecessor," said Seth. "I can assure you, I have as much idea as you, as to what's going to happen next. You can borrow the coat if you want."

Harry scowled at him. "Nah, I'll be all right."

"This is getting serious man," said Pete. "That wind is turning into a bloody gale. It's like pissing Siberia here."

"And, if I'm not mistaken, that sky looks full of snow," Ringo said.

As if on cue, flakes started to float down, gently and sparse at first; before long, they were in a full-blown blizzard.

"Jesus," said Ringo. "We'll all die of fucking hyperthermia, at this rate. This is getting beyond a joke."

"Just keep going," Seth said.

"That's easy for you to say," said Phil.

Seth took off his frock coat and gave it to Phil. "Here, put this on."

Phil looked at it and then back at Seth. Dave could tell she was wrestling between wanting to be warmer and cover herself up and appearing a weak woman. In the end the former won. She grabbed the coat and wrapped it around herself.

"Just to stop these warped bastards leering at me."

Harry was looking at her with envy. He was regretting turning down Seth's offer earlier.

"I've never known wind like this before," said Pete, "It cuts right through you."

"You can say that again," said Harry.

"Stop winging and get on with it," said Ringo, visibly shivering.

The snow was thick and heavy. It made them look like snowmen or should that be 'snowpersons'. Dave thought Phil would like that better, the mood she was in. Ringo hadn't been wrong when he'd stated that most men looked, appreciatively, at attractive women, especially if something not normally visible was on show. There are some women who like the attention and those that don't. Considering Phil's background, it was obvious to see why she reacted the way she had. Ringo, unfortunately, tended to speak his mind, without any thought for other people's feelings or, indeed, the consequences. That was one of the things Dave liked about him – what you saw was what you got. Ringo possessed no airs or graces. In fact, he and Phil were fairly similar, which was probably why, they rubbed each other up the wrong way.

"I don't know about hyperthermia," said Harry, spluttering. "We'll choke to death on the bloody stuff."

The snow was becoming more prolific, to be sure. They were wading through about six inches of it already. The wind had increased in intensity and dropped by several degrees. If this weather continued, it would become a major problem to their survival.

"Can't you do something, man?" Ringo asked Dave. "Zap the fucker, or something?"

Dave thought about it for a minute. He hadn't considered the option until Ringo mentioned it. "I don't know, mate, I guess I could try."

"Sooner rather than later would be good."

Dave closed his eyes and let the power seep into the atmosphere, probing for anything that could be influenced by the old magic. The coldness retreated from him, as he let the force extend. Tendrils of some opposing power shrank back. He discovered they originated from one source. As he pushed on, the heat he was generating destroyed those icy fingers. He was higher than a kite. He was consumed by his own power. He raged at the insolence of his opponent. His blade was in his hand and he was on fire. "Fight me," he yelled. Everything shrank back, retreating from his fury. He'd begun to give chase when he felt the constant tugging at his arms.

"Dave....Dave.... let it go man, it's all stopped, it's over mate."

Ringo's words were, at first, a vague irritation.

"For Pete's sake, wake up, you silly sod."

Dave was so absorbed with the madness of vengeance; it took time to calm the magic. Ringo's voice, combined with the hefty slap he administered, brought him back to the group. The sun was shining, and the wind had disappeared completely, as had the snow. It was as if it had never been there. Much like the British weather, they had gone from winter to summer in the space of minutes.

"Man, you were out of it," said Ringo. "Raving like a fucking madman."

Pete grinned. "Mind you, he got rid of that bloody blizzard."

Ringo glared at him and shook his head. "Moron." He looked back at Dave. "I thought you were going to explode. Really mate, you were pissing nuclear, all blazing and shit. I was scared to touch you to start with." He paused and then said quietly. "But I wasn't about to lose anybody else, especially you."

Dave hugged him; he couldn't help himself.

"I'm sorry, mate, I think I got a bit carried away."

"You can say that again," Phil said, trying to hide the concern she was feeling.

"I'm fine, never felt better – and, as Pete said, I did manage to bring the sun out."

Ringo slapped him on the back. "Next time, I'll just put up with the snow,"

"Hey, you lot, are we stuck in a balloon, or is it me?" Harry asked.

There seemed to be some sort of membrane around them.

Ringo drew his sword. "Balloons, I can handle."

"Wait," Seth said, "you don't know what will happen."

Ringo didn't even turn around. "If it's a choice of spending the rest of my days stuck in a party decoration or facing whatever's outside it, I'll take my chances."

"Perhaps it was a snow globe," Pete said. "And now the snow's gone......"

"It's just a globe?" Harry said. "Anything's possible. We could be stood in a bubble floating on the water, and when Ringo hacks at it, we all drown."

"As you say, Harry, my old son, anything's possible." Ringo swung his sword and the blade cut through the membrane, like butter. No water flooded in, so they all piled through the hole.

FIVE

The silver streaks dived and soared, gaining brightness. The brighter they became, the more oppressive the atmosphere seemed. Danny began to sweat, the serenity short lived. He was on the verge of another panic attack, his breathing course and erratic, his heart rate soaring. He tried to take a deep breath and hold it.

"Come on," he said to himself, "get a grip, get a frigging grip."

He tried to imagine breathing into a paper bag and failed miserably. He suddenly realised that facing the unknown with a peer is much easier than having to do so with two dependents. He panted for a time until the black specks swirling before his eyes subsided and he could focus again. He tried to take a really deep breath but couldn't. It was as if they were nearing the summit of Everest, the air much thinner. The edges and sides of his present world pulsed, and he was about to pass out. He dropped to his knees, hugging Blue. She was panting. He fell onto his back, the silver threads drifting closer. The one thing he knew for certain, before he closed his eyes was, they were here to help him. It was suddenly like being sedated, a dreamy, welcome sleep. He let himself drift into clouds of oblivion, happy, if this was the end. He felt Blue lift his arm with her nose and lay her head on his chest. He smiled and let himself fall.

He floated amongst the silver ribbons, their caress soothing and comforting. His mind was de-cluttered, his heart salved. If there was a heaven, this is how it would be – peaceful, free of worry or stress – a blanket of ultimate salvation, a mattress of serenity. There wouldn't be the underlying nag, the insistent aggravation. No matter how much he enjoyed the tranquillity, he couldn't deny its temporary nature.

He had responsibilities, dependants and, much as he wanted to drift in this cotton wool world, he knew he couldn't.

Bobby's words came back to him – "You think he's your friend." In his present state, the phrase seemed like a vague whisper.

In his previous life, he'd been drunk, trying to fight his way to some form of sobriety. This was the opposite, he wanted to sink deeper, to leave Seth and the others to do their thing and let him be. This seemed to be the oblivion he'd been wishing for but, no matter how hard he tried to sink deeper and disappear, his duty wouldn't allow him to. He felt Blue lift her head and lick his face. Charlie snorted and pawed the ground by his head. Reluctantly, he opened his eyes, "S'alright," he said sleepily. "I'm here."

Blue moved until she was laying on his chest, practically smothering him with her licks.

"Steady girl," he said, gasping. "I can't breathe." Charlie started to chip in, nudging him with his nose. He was in danger of being asphyxiated by love.

He sat up and looked to the sky. The silver ribbons had disappeared, and the darkness was fading. The light was a cross between tomato soup and marshmallow. His eyelids were still heavy. He pushed himself to his feet and took a deep breath. The air smelled fresher than it had since he entered this mad world.

"You okay kids?" He asked Blue and Charlie. Blue sat by his side, her tail brushing the dusty ground. Charlie stuck his nose in his ear and neighed.

The atmosphere seemed to have taken on a moon-like feel. Danny was sure, if he jumped, gravity would have left the building. He felt as though they were in a weird limbo world.

"I suppose that's how I've felt for a long time," he said aloud. "Brace yourselves girls and boys." The old magic surged through his body. His legs cramped, suddenly replaced by pins and needles. His surroundings were becoming elastic, the horizon bending and undulating. He closed his eyes and breathed in. At first, there was nothing but shadows, but, gradually, images emerged.

SIX

Dave couldn't believe it. Straight in front of them stood Danny, Blue and Charlie. This was becoming tedious. They came together, they were separated, came together again, separated again. He hoped this was the last reunion they'd have.

"Good to see you, man," he said shaking Danny's hand. Danny looked genuinely shocked and pleased in equal measure.

"I didn't think I'd see you lot again," Danny said, grinning. "Bobby told me I would, but I thought he was telling me what I wanted to hear."

Ringo looked at him as if he'd got a screw loose. "Who the fuck's Bobby?"

"Well, he was a bit like Yoda, but - nothing like him really. He just, sort of appeared. He thought I was going to top myself."

"You haven't found some booze somewhere, have you?" Harry asked him.

Now, they were all looking at him with a similar expression, that is, except Seth.

"I take it you named him Bobby?"

"Yeah, he didn't seem to have a name and, I had to call him something. He taught me how to read minds." Danny looked at Ringo. "I can assure you, I'm not a 'fucking picnic, short of a sandwich'." He turned his attention to Phil. "Nor am I 'ready for the funny farm'. Do you want me to continue Harry?"

Harry blushed and looked at his feet. "I didn't mean it."

"What were you thinking, mate?" Ringo asked him.

"It doesn't matter," Danny said.

Seth rubbed his chin and nodded. "I've heard tell of such a being. Tell me – was he irritating?"

Danny chuckled. "Yes, at first, he was extremely irritating, but, when he disappeared, we all missed the little fellow. I think he and Blue had formed quite a bond."

Dave grabbed him by the shoulders. "You weren't really going to top yourself, were you?"

Danny looked him in the eye and thought for a minute or two. "If I'm honest, I don't know, maybe. I was in a pretty bad place. I'd been through this forest and bumped into my dead mother and father." He glanced at Phil. "At that time, I really thought I was ready for the funny farm. If it hadn't been for Blue and Charlie, perhaps I would have thrown in the towel. I love the pair of them to death, they're my responsibility." He put his hands on Dave's. "I needed someone to talk to, man. I think I might have been on the verge of a nervous breakdown."

"So, this 'Bobby' helped you through it?" Pete asked.

"Definitely."

Ringo punched Dave on the shoulder. "He's got one up on you, mate. Not only can he use the magic shit, but he can also read fucking minds."

Danny winked at him. "Yeah, I'd try and moderate your thoughts, mate." He dropped his voice to a whisper. "Especially where Phil's concerned."

"Eh, come on, man, I've already had a bollocking for saying the wrong thing, don't start censoring my thoughts, as well."

"Only joking. I can switch it off, you know. Anyway, it's bloody wonderful to see you all again."

"This shit just gets madder and madder," said Phil.

"Have you turned it off now, man?" Ringo asked Danny.

"Yeah, don't worry your lewd thoughts are safe."

"Thank fuck for that. I was starting to feel paranoid, you know, like everyone was out to get me."

"That is paranoia, dickhead," said Phil.

"That's what I said, didn't I? Jeez, I'm starting to feel like a leper."

Phil was obviously still stewing about his sexist remarks. Dave was starting to feel sorry for the great lump.

"You've just got to put your brain into gear, before opening the old trap door," he said to him, with a grin.

Ringo winked at him. "Where's the fun in that?"

"It'd save you a lot of grief," said Pete.

"I like a bit of grief, breaks up the monotony."

Dave was about to ask Danny if he was okay. He was looking around their merry, little band with a concerned expression.

"You all right, mate?" He asked him, anyway. He had, obviously, interrupted some thought process. Danny looked at him, his expression a bit vague to begin with.

"Er, yeah, I'm good. You?"

"Apart from being stuck in some badly written fantasy novel – yeah, I'm ticketyboo. You just looked a bit thoughtful, that's all."

Danny paused for a minute, and Dave could swear he was getting ready to tell him something. Instead, he waved a hand.

"Just thinking about my family, you know?"

"Yeah, sorry mate. It must have been awful, you know, seeing your..........." He thought it better not to complete the sentence.

"It was and it wasn't. It was sort of good to see them again, before they sunk into obesity and alcoholism, even if it was a cruel illusion. Like I said, my mind was getting more messed up by the hour."

"But you're all right now?"

Danny gave him an expression that appeared to be a cross between a smile and a grimace. "I'll just be glad to get all this over and done with."

"Amen to that, mate."

"I think it's about time we got moving again," said Seth.

"I'm champing at the bit," said Ringo.

"Time and tide wait for no man," said Harry.

They all looked at him with a 'what the...?' sort of expression.

He looked embarrassed. "Just something my dad always used to say."

"You are a donkey," said Ringo.

"That was something else my dad used to say." Dave looked at Ringo and they both cracked up. Harry was a natural comic, even if he didn't realize it. His timing was immaculate.

Danny listened to the banter and thought about Sebastian, and how much he'd admired him. He had considered the two of them friends and look how that had turned out. He looked around the group, all of whom he regarded as friends. They hadn't been together long but, it had been an intense experience and they had bonded. To think that any of them could be his enemy was unimaginable.

Dave had noticed his perusal of them all and asked if he was okay. Danny thought of taking him to one side and relaying what Bobby had told him. A little voice in his head said, 'it could be him' and, although the idea seemed preposterous, it was a possibility. He reiterated he just wanted it to be all over. Their explosive reunion had been such a shock, he hadn't realised that Jack wasn't with them.

"Where's Jack?"

"Gone," said Ringo, tears moistening his eyes.

"Some bloody octopus-thing got him in the swamp," Harry said.

"It was my fault," Ringo said.

Dave shook his head and let out a heavy sigh. "Come on, man, let's not have this again. You did a whole lot more than any of us. You tried to save him. It wasn't your fault."

This was the first Danny had heard about a swamp. He realised, since they'd parted company, he knew nothing of what had happened to them.

He put his hand on Ringo's shoulder. "If there is one thing I do know, you would have done all that is humanly possible to save him."

"Yeah well, this time it wasn't enough, was it?"

In time, he would realise that no-one could have done any more but, at that moment, it was all too raw. Danny felt guilty, not noticing Jack's absence as soon as they had been reunited. He felt even guiltier for causing their situation, in the first place. "If anyone's to blame it's........."

"No-one," Dave said quickly, catching his eye and shaking his head. "It was tragic, and it could have happened to any of us. I don't mean to sound callous but, no amount of self-recrimination is going to bring him back. We just have to try and put it behind us."

Ringo stared at him. "Considering you don't mean to sound callous, you're doing a pretty good job of it."

"I'm sorry mate, I miss him as much as you but, we have to get our shit together."

Ringo shook his head and trudged after Seth.

"I don't know how to stop him from feeling responsible," Dave said to Danny.

357

"You won't. He has to sort it out himself. Once he's got his head around it, he'll see there was nothing else he could have done. In the meantime, let him be."

"I'd say something," said Phil. "But he'd get the wrong idea."

"Leave him to get it out of his system," Danny said. "He'll realise he's not Superman."

Phil put her arm through his. "It's good to have you back, Danny."

Danny looked at her and raised his eyebrows. "Have you had a knock on the head or something?"

"I'm afraid we're all in the bad books," said Dave, "You're the only gentleman around, that is, apart from Seth."

"Well, tell me all. I'm intrigued."

Phil told him all about the blizzard and the 'disgusting' behaviour of Dave, Ringo and the other two, especially Ringo.

Danny shook his head. "I thought you were badass. You let a bit of leching get to you? This is not the Philomena, I've come to know and love."

She took her arm back and punched his shoulder. "I've told you not to call me that. You're as bad as the rest of them."

Danny laughed. "You're just so easy to wind up, mate. As some of our less intelligent peers say – take a chill pill."

"I shouldn't have to put up with it though, especially not from, so called, friends." She shot Dave a harsh glance.

"Look, Phil, you're an extremely attractive, young lady. Why don't you just take it as a compliment? Nobody's tried to molest you for Christ's sake."

"If they know what's good for them, they'd better not, either."

Danny sighed. "Just let it go." He wondered how heavy the chip on her shoulder was. "I'm sure they all apologised?"

She nodded slowly. "I suppose so."

"Well then, forget it."

He wanted her to be quiet because he wanted to think. He couldn't get Bobby's words out of his head. He could only have meant either Dave or Seth, maybe Ringo at a push. Pete and Harry were sort of along for the ride, always waiting for others to make the decisions. Dave seemed such a nice bloke and he valued his friendship, Seth was.... well....Seth, the trusted leader of their group. He couldn't find any reason to doubt either of them. But then, before he showed his true colours, that had applied to Sebastian, as well. He was tired, mentally and physically.

"You all right, mate?"

Dave looked concerned, and it appeared to be genuine.

Danny's initial happiness at their reunion seemed to have abated considerably. He appeared to be troubled. Dave had asked him if he was all right and he'd said he was tired. He was lying. There was something troubling him, that was clear, even to Dave. He shrugged, he would tell him in his own time – or he wouldn't – his choice. Dave had had his fill of baby-sitting. In fact, he was pissed off with the whole kit and caboodle. Having said that, he still felt for Danny. He was a decent sort, salt of the earth.

He was beginning to wonder if there was any future for him and Phil. She was, if he was honest, starting to irritate him. There was no denying her beauty, her exquisite figure, but looks weren't everything. She had severe issues – that went without saying. The trouble was, she seemed to tar every male with the same brush. Okay, Ringo was a bit of a male chauvinist but the rest of them were only common or garden, red blooded blokes. None of them were dirty, old men and he, for one, was getting ragged off with the accusations and insinuations. He yearned for some sort of normality. His life on benefits seemed a lifetime away, and he missed it. Everything used to be so simple – if you didn't have money, you stayed in bed or mooched about a bit in the summer, enjoying the rays. When the opportunity had arisen to change that, he'd grabbed it with both hands. Now, although he'd made some good friends, the rest of this shit was getting him down.

He caught up with Seth. "Is this nearly done?" Seth looked at him and he was sure there was sympathy in his gaze. "I don't think it will be much longer."

"Think?"

"Sorry, that's the best I can do."

He dropped back to walk beside Ringo. "This is becoming a ball ache, ain't it?"

Ringo nodded. "I can think of better things I'd rather be doing. What's the big man say?"

"Not much."

"You know what I miss?"

"Liverpool?"

"Getting bladdered. Man, I'd kill for a night on the piss."

"When we get out of this, we'll bathe in the fucker."

SEVEN

Danny was becoming pensive as well. Most of the things you encounter in life, he thought, are finite. You go to work, you know when you're going to knock off, you drive to somewhere, you have a rough idea how long it will take to get there. The only thing you cannot assess is how long you're going to live. This journey was akin to life, none of them, including Seth, who had made the trip before, had a clue when it would end. That, in itself, was frustrating. To walk mile after mile, not knowing what would be around the next bend, or drop from the sky, or shoot up from the ground and unable to see a conclusion became soul destroying. Add to that, the fact that someone you trust may be about to stab you in the back increased the desperation and paranoia. It seemed, if Bobby's words were true, the only person he could really rely on was Phil. He wished the little man had kept his mouth shut.

"You're really quiet," Phil said, bringing him out of his reverie.

"I don't see anyone else singing and dancing."

"There's no need to be like that. I'm worried, that's all. I don't know why I bother."

"I'm sorry." Danny sighed. "I value your friendship and am touched by your concern."

She looked at him, a wary expression on her face.

"Are you taking the piss?"

He tried to smile. It probably resembled a baby with wind. "No, I mean it. You might be a bolshy cow but you're the business, a real friend. I'm just tired of this whole..." He waved his hands around. "Whatever it is?" He was finding it tiring and tedious holding a conversation. He was in some kind of limbo world. His mind was starting to turn in on itself. He was struggling to cope. He knew Phil meant well, but he was in no mood for small talk, in fact, any talk at all. He wanted to sink into the abyss, to implode. He didn't just want this farce to be over, he wanted his life to be over. He yearned for the oblivion of death. He envied Seth becoming part of his Machine and having nothing more to do with this sad, unsavoury world.

"You don't look well," Phil said.

He tried the smile again. "I'll be okay," he lied. "I just need to be left alone for a while. I'm still dealing with things, you know?"

"Well, if you need to talk, you know where I am."

He nodded. "Cheers, Phil, you're a diamond."

He re-joined his inner turmoil, sure that he was on the verge of some kind of breakdown. He pictured his brain as a black, cancerous tumour devouring everything it encountered. Suddenly, he felt a strange probing sensation, a light amongst the detritus. Dave was using the old magic. The words floated in on a wispy cloud.

'Man, you're a mess.'

Danny tried to bat him away, but he didn't have the strength. 'Leave me be.'

363

'I can't, you need help.' Dave grabbed his arm. "Christ Danny, what's happened to you?"

Danny shook off his hand. "Life – too much fucking life."

Danny could feel him in his mind, probing. He brought the walls down.

"How come you can do that?"

Dave shrugged. "I suppose it must be transferable or something. You know – over the old magic. I didn't know I could do it until I felt your utter misery. This is not like you, mate. Come on, you can talk to me, you know that, right?"

Danny could still feel him trying to get in. "You're wasting your time."

"I'm sorry, mate, it just seems to be happening. I guess I haven't got a handle on it yet. Anyway, I can't see anything now."

"That's what I said – you're wasting your time."

"Look Danny, I only want to help."

Danny looked him in the eye. "Do you? Do you really?" He started to do his own bit of probing.

Dave held his arms out. "Help yourself. I'm an open book. What you see is what you get. Like I said, I just want to help you."

It was as if he'd opened the door of his house and said – go on, have a good old nosey around, I'll be waiting in the garden. He was right, his mind was like a huge room with all these feelings sitting there - guilt over Jack, worry over Danny, himself but, most of all, affection for his friends, especially Phil. There were no barriers, no walls. Unless he was capable of some serious mental gymnastics, Dave wasn't the one, he really did want to be Danny's friend, and help. Danny felt guilty for doubting him. He crawled from his mind, his cerebral tail between his legs.

"I'm sorry, Dave."

"There's no need to apologise. Something is, obviously, bothering you. If you want to talk, I'm here. A problem shared, and all that?"

Danny nodded. "I'll bear that in mind, and – thanks. At the moment, I need to sort a few things out in my own head, you know what I mean?"

Dave looked at him, his bottom lip sticking out. "Just don't bottle things up, man, it ain't healthy."

Danny clapped him on the shoulder. "I'll be alright, just need a bit of time, that's all."

Dave patted his hand. "I get it, I'll leave you be."

Danny smiled. "Cheers, mate, and thanks again for your concern."

"Hey, we're all in this fucker together."

Danny looked at the back of Seth's head and wondered. It was akin to doubting your own dad. He was solid. He turned his attention to Ringo. He was strolling along whistling 'Ticket to Ride'. He kept glancing at Phil's rear end, not even attempting to hide the lust he was feeling. Ringo was more – what you see is what you get – than anyone. He was one of the lads, pure and simple. The more Danny thought about it, the more confused he became. He decided to let it go for the time being before it sent him round the bend. He joined Ringo, whistling in harmony. Ringo grinned and gave him the thumbs up.

Dave was enjoying listening to Ringo and Danny whistling their way through the Beatles song book. He had to admit, he'd never heard harmonised whistling before, it was quite something. Unable to compete – he'd never been a good whistler –he began to sing. Within seconds, Harry and Pete added their voices to the mix. Dave wasn't an expert, but it sounded pretty good to him.

Seth stomped on, ignoring the lot of them, whilst Phil had an expression on her face which seemed to be a cross between constipation and appreciation. Not an easy look to pull off.

For a few minutes, music united them and put the bad stuff on the back burner. Even Danny's frown was bordering on a smile.

Dave hadn't lived through the Beatles' heyday, but he'd enjoyed their legacy, mostly due to Ringo. He couldn't help thinking how different the world would be if every country had a Beatles song for their national anthem and they all 'gave peace a chance'. Of course, it would never happen, men would always find a reason to kill each other. Probably, like the difference in religions, the more weeks the song stayed at number one would come into play. Man would always be a bomb waiting to explode.

They finished 'Nowhere Man', Ringo and Danny doing a fine job on the guitar fade out. If it weren't for the darkness behind Danny's eyes, he would have seemed like the rest of them, pissed off but getting on with it.

Ringo was on a roll, he dispensed with the whistle and launched into a raucous version of 'Come Together'. This time, even Phil joined in.

Seth still ignored them, tramping on, shoulders hunched.

"You must know the Beatles," Dave said, tapping him on the arm.

He didn't even turn around. "Do you know Mozart, Beethoven, Delius, Wagner?"

"I've heard of them, yeah, but they're not exactly sing-along material, are they?"

"Indeed, they are not."

He increased his speed, leaving them to their non-classical renditions.

"That bloke is a miserable twat," said Ringo, leaving the rest of them to bumble their way through 'walrus gumboot and Ono sideboard'.

"Who gives a toss," Harry said. "We might as well make the most of this shit. Am I right?"

Ringo slapped him on the back. "Damned right my man. Boredom is a killer."

He bumped into Seth's back.

"Prepare yourselves," Seth said.

"For what?" Danny asked him.

"For the final hurdle," Seth said, pointing ahead. "Look."

It began as a smudge in the sky, difficult to discern with tired eyes. Danny squinted, the sun not helping matters.

"What is it?"

"A clamouring," Seth said, with a certain amount of satisfaction.

"And what, exactly, is a clamouring?" Ringo asked him.

"The bird I thought I saw earlier?" He looked to Ringo for confirmation.

"Thought being the operative word," said Ringo, with a sneer.

"It was a Barrarhawk."

"A what?"

"They nest in and around The Machine. It's said that they are as important as the guardians. They are integral to its continuance. Without the Barrarhawks, The Machine would lose its focus and malfunction."

Ringo was looking at him with an – are you fucking serious – expression.

"So is this – clamouring – a good thing or a bad thing," Danny asked him, not really bothered either way.

"A bad thing," Seth said. "They clamour to attract the guardians' attention. I suspect, the exile has beaten us to the finish line. We have little time." He looked at Danny and then at Dave. "Your power is needed now, more than ever. We have to get to The Machine as quickly as we can."

"What do you expect us to do?" Dave asked him. "Conjure up some sort of express train?"

"Yes, something like that."

"Maybe we ought to let nature take its course," Danny said. "You know, what will be, will be?"

"If we do nothing, that is what will be – nothing."

"What? We'll all disintegrate, and the world will end?" Ringo asked him, still sneering.

Seth nodded. "At times you can be very astute. It's a shame those times are so infrequent."

This was music to Danny's ears. 'Nothing' was exactly the black hole he yearned for. He didn't really understand what Seth expected from Dave and himself, but it seemed as if it would need their joint cooperation. Maybe the end was really nigh.

"What do you want us to do?" Dave asked.

"You may be tired of your own life, Danny," said Seth. "Your reticence, however, will damn the rest of your earth to your choice of fate. Is that what you want?"

Danny was still fighting his demons, that was clear and to be expected. The darkness Dave had seen in his mind didn't disappear within the blink of an eye. He could see the torment in his eyes. He took him to one side.

"I know this isn't easy for you, Danny. At this moment, you probably want to curl up into a ball and roll away. Don't forget I've seen inside your head."

His face was a mask, chiselled from despair, his eyes prisoners. Dave had never seen such utter desolation before.

"I needed time," Danny said.

Dave sighed. "I know, mate, but we don't seem to have much of that left, if the big man's right, and I don't see any reason to doubt him, do you?"

Danny shook his head. "I guess not."

Dave put his hands on Danny's shoulders. "Look Danny, you're a good man, better than all of us. This is no longer just about you. If we don't do this, we all go to hell in a handcart – everybody."

"I don't even know if I can."

Dave looked into his eyes. "You've got to try, mate. It seems we're out of options."

Danny took a deep breath and let it out slowly. He patted Dave on the back and turned to Seth. "What do you want us to do?"

"We need to move quickly," Seth said. "You two have to absorb as much old magic as you can. Then, you carry the rest of us to The Machine."

"I thought it would be something difficult," Danny said flatly. "How are we going to do that?"

Dave grabbed his arm. "Look what you did when you saved Blue and Charlie."

"Yeah, and sent the rest of us to fucking Siberia," said Ringo.

Dave shot him a glance. "That was accidental, and you know it."

Ringo shrugged. "Just saying, that's all."

"If you can't say anything helpful, best to keep it buttoned, man," Dave said. There were times when Ringo really irritated him. He turned back to Danny. "Come on, Danny, we've got to give this a shot, okay?"

Danny took more deep breaths and nodded. "Let's do it."

Normally that phrase is accompanied by a gut full of enthusiasm. It wasn't this time.

"Just feel it out to start with," Dave said.

He grabbed Danny's hand and closed his eyes. He could feel the power under their feet, like a rippling carpet. He opened up and let it flow. He could feel Danny doing the same. It was like filling a jug with water but, from the bottom not the top. He felt enormous, a giant. He probed Danny's mind and found a marked difference. The old magic was filling him and calming him, at the same time. It seemed as if it might be a panacea. Dave hoped so. As Danny's brain let go of the desperation that plagued it, the old magic swirled in, like oil in water. Slowly, he experienced a salving sensation as the force increased. He began to absorb as much as he could, its energy becoming *his* energy. He reached out to Dave and, mentally, they became one unit, a glowing ember turning to a burning flame, then a shimmering inferno of magic. He was having trouble holding it and he could tell Dave was too.

They were totally in sync, their minds linked. There was no longer any need for words.

Danny thought, 'throw it around the others.' They pushed out the magic until it enveloped the whole group. 'Now let it go.'

He vaguely remembered hearing Ringo shout, "Holy shit." They were travelling at speed towards the clamouring, the power increasing rather than being depleted. It seemed the nearer they came to The Machine the more the old magic helped them. He could feel Seth's jubilation and was glad to be helping achieve his purpose.

Dave's voice was in his mind. 'We're doing it, man. How are you doing?'

'I'm good, bordering on euphoric.'

'I know, it's incredible. It seems like my mind has separated from the rest of me, flying like a bastard, untouchable. It's insane,'

'Aladdin sane.' Danny laughed. It felt so good to laugh.

'Across the fucking universe. We are the men.' Dave laughed as well.

It seemed as if the misery was being shredded away. Strands were falling into the whistling wind. Death no longer seemed to be Danny's primary interest. He was helping his friends. He was helping humanity, although that term appeared to be incorrect, under present circumstances.

Fleetingly, he wondered what they actually were.

EIGHT

The barrarhawks were reaching true hawk stature, as they cut the gas. If this was The Machine, it was a crumbling, rocky edifice in the middle of nowhere.

"Is this it," Danny asked Seth.

"Appearances can be deceptive," Seth said, with a smile.

"We felt a shift in the old magic, is he here?"

Seth's smile turned to a frown. He nodded his head. "Oh yes, he's here somewhere, there is little doubt of that."

"Why doesn't the fucker show himself?" Ringo said, drawing his sword.

"Put it away mate," Dave said to him. "Don't forget, he could turn that into a molten, steel canapé and ram it down your throat. You'd better leave the bastard to Danny and me."

Ringo shook his head and grimaced. "I think that should be 'Danny and I'."

"Well, your thoughts would be wrong," said Seth. "Now – less of the talking, more of the looking."

Ringo glared at him, waited until he turned away and gave him the finger.

They reached the base of what looked like a small mountain viewed from a distance.

On closer inspection, the walls of the construction weren't crumbling at all, but shimmering. Danny reached out a hand. Seth grabbed his arm.

"Don't touch it – not yet."

They all stood there, and Danny couldn't help thinking this was the biggest anti-climax ever. Whatever he'd been expecting, it wasn't this.

"So, what are we supposed to do?"

Seth looked up and whistled. The hawks were circling, but one of them broke away from the rest and swooped down. Seth held out his arm and the bird flapped its wings to slow itself down and folded its claws over his wrist. Seth brought the bird's head to his face and whispered to it. The hawk let out a strange, keening sound, punctuated by sharp squawks.

"Is he talking to that...thing?" Pete asked Ringo. Ringo shrugged. "I pity it, if he is."

"He's already in there," Seth said. He kissed the barrarhawk's head and raised his arm, the bird taking flight and joining its brothers and sisters above The Machine.

"So, what's the plan?" Dave asked him.

"We go in and hope we're not too late." Seth's expression said it all.

"You think we will be, don't you?" Danny said. Seth let out a heavy sigh. "I hope not."

"Well, let's get on with it," Dave said. "How do we get in there?"

Danny suddenly thought of Gandalf, Bilbo Baggins and co. at the entrance to the Misty Mountains and almost laughed. Seth could be Gandalf, but, as for the rest of them – no chance.

"Have you got your staff?" He asked the big man.

"Is this thing supposed to have doors?" Dave asked.

"It would be rather stupid to leave The Machine open to every Tom, Dick and Harry, wouldn't it?" Seth said impatiently.

Harry looked hurt.

"So, is there some mumbo jumbo you've got to do to get in?"

"I have to find the entrance first – it changes every time." He looked at Danny. "That's why I asked you not to touch it. If you did, as you're not the appropriate guardian, The Machine would go into lockdown mode, making it almost impossible to enter."

"So, if that's the case, how did that other bastard get in?" Ringo asked the question that all of them wanted answering.

"He has been within The Grid since The Machine's conception. The fact that he has only just managed to reach it, is immaterial. He is considered by The Machine to be the last part of the maintenance team, along with the barrarhawks."

"But that's insane," Dave said.

"Don't forget – all of the exiles were supposed to be that – exiled. The Machine was never programmed to recognise them, as there didn't seem to be any point."

"So, due to a balls-up in the programming, he's in there doing what he wants?" Dave asked.

"There are a number of safeguards he has to find out how to disable first. He, obviously, hasn't managed to do that yet, otherwise we wouldn't be here."

"I don't understand," Danny said. "What does he get out of destroying The Machine. If everything and everyone is sucked into some black hole, surely he's finished as well."

"There is a pod," said Seth. "If he can get past all the protocol necessary to enable him to shut The Machine down, he will be able to avoid destruction by entering the pod and remaining there for three months. He will be the only man on this planet."

"Who would want that?" Dave asked.

"I think that is why he took Phil. He was after a mate."

"Well, he hasn't got her now. Why would he go ahead, knowing he's destined to wander a wasteland – for the rest of his life."

Seth sighed. "I think it's become more of a game to him. Whatever the outcome, he must win."

"That's ridiculous."

"Well, stop trapping on and find the bloody door," said Ringo. "This ain't going to get the donkey a new fucking hat."

Seth shook his head, sighed and lay both hands on the surface of the Machine, putting his ear to it as if he were trying to crack the code of a safe. He began to hum in a tuneless monotone. Danny could see Ringo struggling not to burst into uncontrollable laughter. He gave him a slight mental jab. Ringo winced and looked at Dave.

"What did you do that for?"

"Do what?"

"You don't even know you're doing it."

"Ringo – be quiet, it was me," Danny told him.
"Let Seth do his stuff without playing silly
beggars."

He was about to protest until Danny jabbed him
again, a little more forcefully.

"Okay, okay," he said.

Seth crept along the shimmering wall, eyes closed,
still humming. He was a strange sight, to say the
least, and Danny could see why Ringo found it
amusing. They waited patiently, the only sound –
Seth's monotonous hum. Danny was about to sit
on the ground when The Machine began to hum as
well. Seth kept moving, eyes still closed, but now,
there was a faint smile on his face. The humming
from the machine increased in volume until it was
drowning out Seth. The smile on his face widened
and he stopped, listening intently. He took another
short step, lifted his head away from the machine
and brought his hands together. The hum became
a drone and the barrarhawks swept down, flapping
their wings slowly to hover above him.

The wall beneath Seth's hands began to tremble,
causing a rippling effect. He stood back and
dropped his hands to his sides.

"The guardian requests access," he said softly. "I
am the next in line, the appropriate one. I
command The Machine to allow access for myself
and my fellow guardians and associates. Open your
wings and let me take my place within."

This time Ringo couldn't hold back, and he almost
choked on his giggles. Seth was in the zone and no

matter how much noise the Liverpudlian made, he waited for The Machine to do his bidding.

The drone suddenly ceased, and Seth raised his arms above his head. The wall before them seemed to dissolve before their eyes, replaced by a honeycomb structure, the apertures about two feet across. The hum was back, accompanied by a soft, green hue.

"We don't appear to be any further forward, do we?" Ringo asked the big man.

"On the contrary. I've told you before – appearances can be deceptive."

Seth stepped forward and melted into the honeycomb.

Dave looked at Danny and Danny looked at him. They both shrugged and followed Seth into The Machine.

"We don't have much time," said Seth, as Ringo, Pete and Harry joined them. "He's close to shutting everything down. Be careful and listen to me. The Machine is an extremely dangerous place if you don't abide by the rules."

There was another wall in front of them and it was swinging back and forth like a pendulum, revealing passageways, solid rock and gaping holes. There was no pattern.

"Is this a case of picking the moment and going for it?" Pete asked.

"It is knowing," said Seth. "This is not a game of chance."

"And you know?" Harry said.

"I will do, if you stop wittering in my ear," Seth said sharply.

Pete and Harry exchanged – is he up his own arse, or what – expressions.

"That thing seems to be swinging fairly swiftly," Danny said. "Will there be enough time for us all to get through?"

Seth let out an exasperated breath through gritted teeth. "I told you to listen to me. Is that so difficult?"

Ringo gave his back the finger again, Dave looked at Danny and held out a hand towards Seth. 'He's the man,' he said telepathically.

Once again, they were playing a waiting game. Danny sucked on the old magic, like a cocaine addict might snort a line. He was enjoying the euphoria it produced. The fact that he was using it like a drug didn't perturb him in the slightest. It was good to feel full of life, instead of being eager to end it. He hoped, that if Seth managed to get them to the exile in time to save The Machine and he fulfilled his destiny, it wouldn't all disappear. If time ran out, it wouldn't matter.

"Get ready," Seth said. "When I move, follow as quickly as you can. There will be a window of approximately ten seconds."

"How approximate is that?" Ringo asked.

"I'm assuming even you can count to ten."

"Please, man, stop being fucking awkward," Dave said. "You're starting to irritate everybody now."

Ringo shook his head. "You just can't see him for what he really is, can you? He's a fucking charlatan."

"Shut up, Ringo," Danny said, following it up with a mental jab. Ringo winced and gave him the evil eye.

"You're going to regret that, magic boy."

Danny glanced at him and looked away. His obnoxious attitude was becoming wearing, to put it mildly. His empty threats were – just that. He threw a – can't you do something about him? – to Dave.

'Leave him, he'll be alright.' he threw back.

They all focused on the pendulum-like wall, waiting for Seth to give the command.

The swinging wall showed no signs of slowing, never mind stopping. But, as Seth kept saying, appearances can be deceptive. Ringo was twitching at the side of Dave and starting to worry him.

"What's the matter with you now?" Dave asked him.

Ringo glanced at him and looked back to the wall. "You'll find out soon enough."

Dave was about to ask what he meant when he leapt forward, the wall nearly cutting off his foot as he just made it into the passageway.

He stood and looked back at us. "See you later losers." He pointed to Phil. "You'll be coming with us; you'll make a good brood bitch." He turned and ran.

"It can't be him," Danny said. He looked at Dave. "I thought it might be you."

Dave was confused, firstly by Ringo's sudden change of sides, secondly by Danny's apparent knowledge of a traitor.

"What do you mean?"

"Bobby told me that someone I thought was a friend wasn't, or words to that effect."

"Ringo was the man," said Harry. "Our own bolshy Beatle-head."

"This is insane," said Pete.

"Now," Seth shouted, leaping forward. The wall was still swinging or seemed to be. He sailed through. The rest of them made the leap of faith, before the ten seconds was up. Once in the passageway, Dave said to Seth, "Did you know anything about this?"

Seth shook his head. "That was as much of a surprise to me as it was to you. I just thought he was an irritating idiot, but a loyal one."

"Why would he change sides? It makes no sense."

"He's had nothing to do with the exile," Danny said.

Dave was devastated. Ringo was his friend; they'd been through so much together. He knew he had never hit it off with Seth, but that was just a clash of personalities. He was a good human being; this couldn't be happening.

"Could that bastard have brainwashed him somehow?" He asked Seth.

"I don't see how. You were the one fighting him. I don't recall any contact between the two of them. Maybe, he thinks we're going to lose, and he wants to be on the winning side."

"No, Ringo's not like that. He's a diamond."

NINE

With all the excitement and urgency, Danny had
forgotten about Blue and Charlie. They would still
be standing in front of the machine. He just hoped
that Blue would not try and follow them.

"We will come out of this, won't we?" He said to
Seth. "Only there's a dog and horse that sort of
rely on me."

"If we are in time to stop our enemies from
hurling us into oblivion, you will all leave The
Machine. As I've said before, Dave and the others
are an unknown quantity. As for your animal
friends, they will be there waiting."

"What if Blue tries to follow us? She could get cut
in half."

"Once we entered, the portal closed. She won't be
able to follow. So please Danny, try and forget
them and focus on the job in hand, your help is
imperative, especially now Dave's pal has decided
to throw in his lot with the exile."

"But Ringo can't access the old magic."

"Now we're in The Machine and he has changed
sides, there's no telling what can happen. The
nearer they get to the centre, the more power the
exile will command. This situation is unique. I have
no idea how it will play."

At least Danny's concern for Blue and Charlie had
been put to bed. "It can't be far now we're inside,
surely?"

"Hopefully not. It depends on his knowledge and ability."

"What do you mean?"

Seth sighed. "The closer he comes to destroying The Machine, the more he can manipulate it. He will be able to use it against us."

"But you're the appropriate guardian."

"I'm sorry Danny, I don't have all of the answers. This we, literally, must play by ear. We have to stop him or it's all over, and there's only one way to do that."

"Kill the son of a bitch."

"I couldn't have put it better myself."

Danny picked up the pace. For the first time in a while, he wanted to keep this heart of his beating and pumping his revitalised blood. He remembered Ringo's last words to Phil and hoped he could persuade the exile to hold fire until they had their brood bitch. The idea had, obviously, been in his head when he took her the first time, and, if he could, somehow, inject some old magic into his new recruit, he would be feeling more confident. On the other hand, he could reject Ringo totally, kill him and continue with his mad plan. He could think Ringo's sudden change of allegiance was a trick. It was pointless thinking about it, what would be, would be. They needed to find him before he could pull the pin. As Seth had said, play it by ear. He looked over to Dave and gave him a smile and a tentative thumbs up. Dave grinned back and trumped Danny's thumb with a thumb and forefinger circle. Once more, Danny was reminded of emojis. He sucked up more magic and almost sighed like a junkie after a fix.

Dave tried to put as much conviction as he could behind the smile, he gave Danny but really, he had a bad feeling about the whole deal. He was still smarting from Ringo's actions and still unable to accept it all. This was a bloke who was more like a brother than any brother he may have had, could have been. He had never experienced such a rapport with another human being. He felt like he knew him inside out and this was totally out of character. He picked up Danny's thoughts and latched onto the double bluff thing. As much as he wanted it to be true, he found it hard to believe. Ringo was a 'kick their asses' sort, not a tactician, it wasn't in his nature. He just wanted to see him again and ask him what he was playing at.

"I mean mate, what the fuck?" It was Harry.

"I still can't believe it," Dave said.

Pete twirled his finger by the side of his head. "Maybe he's gone.......you know?"

Dave shook his head. "Nah, he's stronger mentally than all of us."

"Well, it looks like he's sold us down the river," Harry said.

Dave wanted to stick up for Ringo but couldn't. "Like the big man says – appearances can be deceptive," he said weakly.

"He basically stuck two fingers up to us," said Pete. "I don't think there's anything deceptive about that, do you?"

Dave looked at him and shook his head again.

"No. I guess I just don't want to believe it."

"You can lead a horse to water, but you can't make it drink," said Harry with a shrug.

They both stared at him.

"What?"

"Oh, forget it," Dave said. There seemed little point in delving into Harry's weird mental meanderings. Dave was so involved in his own emotional tussle, he nearly ran into the back of Danny. He stopped just in time and looked over Danny's shoulder. Seth was stock still as a stream of shapes floated before his eyes. The path that they'd been following was now a massive crevasse, the other side a good ten metres away.

"What the......." Dave said, unable to think of any other utterance worthy of the situation.

"Quiet," Seth snapped.

They all watched as his head moved from left to right, as if he were watching a tennis match. He lifted his right hand, extended his index finger and flicked a triangle to the left. He followed it up with a circle, a rectangle and something that resembled a rhombus. The crevasse disappeared and the path returned, shaky at first but, soon solidifying. Before following the big man, Danny gave it a good stamping, just to make sure.

He walked gingerly across the newly reformed path, hoping there weren't pressure points that would cause a huge, stone ball to be hurled at them – a la Indiana Jones. Dave, Harry and Pete followed, and he could feel their trepidation.

"I'm not easily bored," said Harry, "but I am getting tired of all this now."

"I concur," Pete said.

"Ain't a cur, a dog?" Harry asked.

"Are you serious?" Pete said.

"You must think I'm stupid," said Harry with a grin.

"The thought had crossed my mind," muttered Pete.

"You what?"

"I said – I thought nothing of the kind," Pete said.

Danny smiled at the banter. If Ringo were here, he'd be leading the proceedings. No matter which way he looked at it, he just couldn't believe Ringo would suddenly change sides like that. He was a pain in the arse at times, but he was solid. If he'd had to choose the most loyal member of their merry band, he'd have struggled between him and Dave. He didn't know if Dave had picked up on his thoughts, he wasn't inside his head, but his friend caught him up.

"You okay mate?"

"Just thinking about Ringo."

"I know, that's what you call a real, fucking bummer. I'd sort of got it in my head that when this shit was all over, we'd hang out together, him and me, you know? I thought we were mates."

"No amount of regurgitating it is going to change the situation," said Seth. "It is what it is. Get used to it."

"Have a little compassion, Seth," Danny said. "Dave's just lost his best friend."

"Friends like that, you don't need."

'He's an understanding sort,' Dave said mentally. 'He just wants to get to The Machine before it's too late, everything else is secondary.'

"How much further?" Dave asked Seth.

"How many more times – I – don't – know."

"Alright, keep your wig on, I was only asking."

Danny tapped Dave on the shoulder and when he looked at him, he shook his head and made a 'keep it zipped' motion with his right hand.

'Miserable git,' Dave said in Danny's head.

Danny smiled and nodded. He was in a similar state of mind to Harry.

Considering they were supposed to be inside a machine, it bore little resemblance to anything mechanical or digital. They were in yet another passage that appeared to have been hewn from the uneven rock surrounding them. But as Seth kept reminding them – appearances etc.

Dave was totally pissed off with the situation. Before they reached The Machine, getting there seemed to be their goal, the end of this irritating quest. Now they were here, Seth still had no idea how much further they had to go. Dave thought – how big can a machine be? He wanted to ask Seth but knew the kind of response he'd get. If it supposedly kept the world, as they knew it, going through its daily motions, it couldn't be the size of a sub-station. Maybe it was the size of Texas – they could be here for the rest of their lives.

He started to think back to when the five of them had been thrown back in time. It had been kind of fun, even his own near beheading. They were a bunch of mates and it was them against the rest of the bastards. He'd liked the way that felt, knowing that they had each other's back. How the hell had they become embroiled in this maniacal mess? Life is full of decisions, he thought, it's just a shame you can't be shown the options before you make your choice. The strange thing was – if he could have turned back the clock, knowing everything he now knew, he would still answer that ad. He'd met some top blokes, seen a load of weird shit and been loaded up with magic. Compared to a life on the dole, living from day to day, eating cold baked beans from the can, when the power had been cut off, shivering under a summer quilt whilst arctic winds forced their way through the gaps between the walls and the warped window frames, it was a no brainer. Being trained to be a fighting machine, transported back to the twelfth century, before squeezing through some rift into 'The Grid' had to be preferable, surely?

Years ago, when he was about ten, he used to read Richmal Crompton's 'Just William' books, thinking how awesome it would be to write something like that, something other kids devoured. Maybe, after all this was over, he might attempt to put it all down on paper. It could make a fucking, great read.

"What are you doing?" Seth snapped as he bumped into him.

"Oh, sorry." He had been in a world of his own and not noticed him stopping in front of him.

"Penny for 'em?" Danny asked.

"Just reminiscing," Dave said.

"I keep forgetting how to do that," said Harry.

"Now I know you're taking the piss," Pete said.

"Yeah, but I had you going for a while there, didn't I?"

"Especially with the horse and the water, yeah."

"What do you mean, I meant that."

The four of them cracked up.

"Will you try and keep your wits about you?" Seth said through gritted teeth. "This is not a scouts' jamboree."

"Do you ever laugh?" Dave asked him.

"I wonder if you will, when your skin starts to melt, and your bones begin to crumble."

"You didn't say anything about that before," Harry said, his smile turning into a frown.

"I didn't think I had to. I was mistaken."

It was obvious the banter was starting to annoy Seth, not being one for frivolous humour himself. He didn't realise it was a type of coping mechanism employed by the less cerebral. Like Dave, Danny wondered what it would take to make him laugh, not just a chuckle but a real gut busting belly-laugh, or even, if he was capable of such. He imagined this wasn't the time to ask him and as they were on their way to his leaving them for greater things, so to speak, it was highly likely that that time would never arise.

"Who wants to play I spy?" Harry asked.

Despite Seth's words of warning and the look he shot Harry, the rest of them fell about. The sour faced old bugger didn't know what he was missing.

"It would appear that no amount of advice makes the slightest difference," Seth said. "From now on, you either take notice of what I say, or you don't – the choice is yours. I am here to try and save your world and I will do my utmost. Your assistance would be, possibly, helpful, or maybe a hindrance, I no longer know. All I do know is that if you persist in this puerile nonsense, the latter is more likely."

Harry looked genuinely deflated. "Look Seth, I'm sorry but, just because we laugh and joke, it doesn't mean we're not concentrating. It's just the way we are. We're all different man. You're a miser.......I mean, a profoundly serious man and we're.......not."

"This is a serious situation and, therefore requires total concentration. Whilst your brain is involved with silly, little games and ludicrous banter, that is not possible, believe me. Once this is over, providing we are successful, you can laugh and joke as much as you want. Luckily, I won't be there to hear it."

"The banter is over, Seth," Danny said. "Isn't it lads?"

"Absolutely," said Dave.

"Yeah, we'll try harder," said Pete.

Harry had a mischievous expression and Danny gave him a little jolt of the old magic before he could say anything else to upset their leader. Harry winced and looked from him to Dave. "I was only going to say 'yes'," he said, rubbing his temple.

"For the time being, a little peace and quiet wouldn't go amiss," said Seth.

They trudged on along a stone floored, stone walled, stone ceilinged passageway in total silence. Without a little badinage, it soon became tedious in the extreme. Danny was sure they were all eager for something to happen, even if it was life threatening. He sucked up a little more magic to alleviate the boredom and felt a difference in its feel.

"Will the old magic change, the closer we get to The Machine?" He asked Seth.

"It should become more concentrated. You'll need to take care managing it."

"I think I can feel it changing," said Dave.

Danny nodded. "Maybe there is finally light at the end of this tunnel."

"Only if we can stop our enemies," said Seth. "If not, none of us will see light ever again."

TEN

There was definitely a shift of some sort, probably like a mini power surge. Seth had made it quite clear that he'd said all he was prepared to on the subject. As they neared his purpose, he was becoming a man of fewer words. Dave wondered if he was nervous considering he was going to cease to exist as a being and become a part of something much bigger. How can anybody, guardian or mere pleb, get his or her head around that. He decided to leave it; he was in danger of getting deep again. He was about to send Danny a mental message when he heard a low growling sound.

"Ah," said Seth, a slight smile lifting one corner of his mouth.

"Ah?"

"You are about to meet the 'Vodra'"

"The whata?"

"You'll see."

Up ahead the passage curved to the left and as they neared the bend, the growling became louder. It sounded like a cross between a large dog and a lion or tiger. It was clear there was a group of 'Vodra', slight differences in tone and volume evident. Dave didn't know what he was expecting but it wasn't what came into view as they turned the corner. He automatically drew his sword, hearing Harry and Pete following suit.

"Put your weapons away," said Seth. "They will serve little purpose here."

"What – are – they?" Harry asked, his eyes nearly popping out of his head.

"I've told you, the Vodra."

There were nine of these creatures blocking their way completely. They looked like Great Danes with the heads of Velociraptors. Their heads moved back and forth, beady eyes fixed on their group. Dave had no idea how many razor-sharp teeth there were in each of those massive jaws and he didn't really want to find out. Ignoring Seth, he held his sword out before him.

"If you did manage to kill one, which is highly unlikely, three more would take its place. They are unbeatable." Seth still had this silly sort of grin across his mush and Dave wondered why.

"If they are unbeatable, why are you smiling?"

"I just have to find the leader."

"But they're all fucking identical."

"All identically vicious," Pete said.

"They look some mean sons of bitches," said Harry.

"What happens if you find the leader?" Danny asked.

"I will show him this." He pulled up his sleeve and showed them a tattoo on his forearm. It looked like a pentagram with snakes twisted around the sides.

"Mm, nice work," said Harry. "I always wanted a tattoo. My old man was dead against 'em though."

"What happens when you show it to him?" Dave asked. "Does he bite your bloody arm off?"

"Just give me a little time and try to have a bit more faith."

"How would that traitorous bastard have got past the big, fucking hole in the floor, never mind these........things?" Phil asked.

She'd been quiet ever since Ringo had taken his leap of faith, telling her that she would become a brood bitch, if the exile was successful. Dave felt like a bastard for ignoring her in favour of the banter and their increasingly ridiculous situation. Mind, it was unlike her to be silent for so long.

"They won't win, you know," he said to her.

"How do you know? You can't even answer my question."

"Either he has had the exile's help, or he is dead," Seth said flatly, still scrutinising the Vodra.

Phil looked at Dave, her eyes soft and earnest.

"Promise me one thing."

"Anything."

"If it looks like it's all going tits up and they're going to grab me, kill me first. Will you do that, Dave?"

"It won't come to that."

"But if it does."

"It won't."

"Promise me."

Dave looked into those brown eyes and he wanted to cry. How on earth could he promise to kill the girl he could be falling in love with. By the same token, he wouldn't let Ringo and his new best mate take her – that would be a fate worse than death.

He placed his hands on her shoulders. "You know I'd die for you, don't you?"

She grabbed his hands and pushed him back. "I don't want you breathing your last, fucking breath as you watch that filthy twat slobbering as he grabs my arse. Promise me you'll kill me before that happens."

He took a deep breath and let it out slowly. "I promise I won't let either of them take you, and, yes, if it comes down to a choice, I will kill you before I die myself. Is that good enough for you?"

She smiled a sad smile. "Your word will always be good enough for me." She turned her attention to Seth, as if that were one bit of business out of the way. "Now, will you stop pissing about and get us past these overgrown Labradors."

"I think that's the one," he said, pointing to the second from the left.

"You think," said Phil. "What happens if you're wrong?"

He shrugged. "It's an educated guess."

He stepped forward, making eye contact with the beast he'd singled out. They all crouched down, as if ready to pounce. Dave, Harry and Pete had their swords at the ready as they stepped behind Seth, pushing Danny and Phil behind them.

"I hope to fuck he's right," said Harry.

"I guess we'll soon find out," Dave said.

Danny hadn't thought about Ringo manoeuvring his way through The Machine's entry system until Phil mentioned it. He couldn't see the exile waiting around in case one of them decided to defect, that just didn't make sense. Seth seemed to think he had a good head start on them. That being the case, he could only surmise that the latter of the two options offered by the big man was the most likely. But then, Ringo wasn't stupid, wanting to throw himself into a pit or get eaten by prehistoric canines. He had left them defiantly, not a pitiful soul wanting his life to be over.

"The exile must have helped Ringo," he said as Seth chose his favourite Velocalabrador and Dave pushed Danny behind him.

"Please – not now, Danny. I need to concentrate," Seth said.

He took another step forward and the beast he had chosen bared its teeth and raised its head.

"For Christ's sake, Seth, are you quite sure you've got the right one," said Pete, lifting his blade a little higher.

With a flourish, Seth snapped his arm out in front of those horrific jaws, the tattoo centimetres from the most prolific set of vampiric teeth Danny had ever set eyes on. The creature opened its mouth and bracketed Seth's arm. Danny waited for closure, wincing, closing one eye. He said to Dave – 'Should we do something?'

He sent back a mental shake of the head – 'No – look!'

The jaws drew back and the dog-like thing sniffed Seth's arm. It shuddered and threw itself against the rest of the pack. The sound it made was like a thousand nails being scraped across a thousand blackboards and they all put their hands over their ears. The creatures seemed to blend into the walls of the passage, and it was as if they'd never existed.

"How sure were you of that?" Danny asked him.

"As sure as I could be."

"So, you could have been wrong?" Harry said.

"Nothing is ever certain; you should remember that. The best we can expect is a nine to one choice, and even that is our own interpretation. We all must take chances in our lives, otherwise there really is no point existing. In your world, you have people who sit in front of television, day and night, playing games where they risk a character's life, whilst they, themselves, grow more obese, less active, sinking into an early grave, their hearts giving up the tedious fight with cholesterol and blocked arteries. Which would you rather have?"

"I quite like computer games," said Harry.

"I rest my case," said Seth. "Now let's move it."

"Do you really think he's with the exile?" Dave asked Danny.

"He has to be. I'm sorry mate."

"No, I hope he is. Rather that, than, you know. I still can't believe he's gone to the dark side."

"Don't let that cloud your judgement when the time comes." Danny nodded to Phil. "Don't forget, you made a promise."

"You don't have to remind me."

The old magic was becoming stronger. Danny began to see the seams of stone and flint in the walls of the passage, the colours sharp, textures almost tangible.

'I've never taken LSD, but I bet it's just like this,' Dave said over their mental link, his wonder evident.

'I guess it *is* like a drug.'

Suddenly a face with black hair and beard emerged from the stone. It hovered before Danny's eyes, grinning, eyes dark and menacing, teeth whiter than snow.

'It's him,' Dave said. 'The exile.'

The grin widened and Danny's head almost exploded with pain. 'Shut it out,' he screamed to Dave, bringing up the walls. He lost contact with him as they both summoned their mental defences. The pain subsided and the face disappeared.

"Shit," said Dave, still wincing.

"What's wrong with you?" Pete asked.

"We've just had a meeting of minds," Danny answered for him. "And it was painful."

"Felt like my head was going to explode," said Dave.

"He's taunting you," Seth said. "Time is running out."

Danny couldn't get that face out of his mind, but thinking about it, raised a question.

"If he can do that – I mean, appear to the two of us like he did, surely we can do the same?"

Seth thought about it for a minute. "Theoretically, yes, but what you must understand is this – he has had a lot more time to learn how to control his power than you have. It would be similar to a novice going up against a grand master in a chess game."

"Correction," said Dave. "Two novices. Have you never heard of the old pincer movement? Plus, we're learning all the time, we're not complete greenhorns."

"Did you see Ringo?" Harry asked Dave.

"No mate, just that hairy faced bastard."

"We don't really have the time to wait whilst you try and..........project your minds. We need to move as quickly as we can," said Seth, although his tone lacked conviction.

"But, if we can see how near he is to The Machine, surely it's worth a try," Danny said. "If we find it difficult and time consuming, we call it a day and carry on as we are. I think we have more to gain than lose."

"Just give us five minutes," Dave said. "If we can't, what d'you call it – project our minds – it's back to the drawing board. Come on man, we're wasting time here."

"Okay, five minutes. If nothing happens in that amount of time, we move on. Agreed?"

Dave and Danny nodded. Harry looked at the three of them as if they were aliens.

"I don't have the slightest idea what you're talking about."

ELEVEN

"How do we do this?" Dave asked Danny.

"It'll be like meditating, I suppose," said Phil.

"And I suppose you know all about meditation," Danny said, a look of comical inquisitiveness gracing his features.

"I tried it once," Phil said defensively.

"Time's running out," said Seth.

"Okay," said Danny. "Sit down next to me and hold my hand."

Pete and Harry started to throw kisses at each other, and Dave gave them the finger before parking his arse next to Danny's. He grabbed his hand.

"Let's do this."

"Just let your mind drift up with mine. Think about Ringo, think about finding him. I'll think about our other friend. Use the old magic to push you along. Once we're free of our bodies, I think it'll be much easier. Now, close your eyes and concentrate. The rest of you – keep quiet please."

Dave closed his eyes and thought of his old mate. 'Where are you, man?' He thought, letting his body go limp. He could smell everybody's sweat, mixed with the mustiness of the passageway. The Beatles playing 'In My Life' entered his mind, carrying it along. He felt like a cloud on a magic carpet, floating above the group below. He could see through his cloud-eyes, his and Danny's bodies slumped against the wall, the other four watching them intently. A puff of air escaped Danny's lips, blossoming into his wispy brother. It floated up until it sat at Dave's side.

'You okay, mate?' Dave asked him.

'Put the pedal to the metal,' Danny replied.

Within seconds they were speeding along, drifting in and out of the walls. It seemed they were ghost-like.

'Think about Ringo,' Danny said.

The walls came and went, turning from stone to a strange malleable metal that appeared to breath.

'Look,'

Dave looked down and saw the exile and Ringo in cahoots, bent over a strange looking control panel. It seemed to be continually changing shape.

"We probably don't have a lot of time," Dave heard Ringo say, with far more reverence than he would have thought him capable of.

"We're nearly there," said the exile. "In any case, we can't leave without the bitch. We can only destroy the rest when we have her. Relax my friend and draw in the magic. The next time they see you, they'll see a Titan."

'I think we've seen enough,' said Danny.

The exile turned his head. "They're here," he said with a smile. "They've learnt how to eavesdrop.'

The pain began. 'Close it down and let's get back to the others,' Danny said before they threw up the walls.

Their minds raced back, screaming through rock, like a hot knife through butter.

When they reached their friends, they were still gazing at their inert bodies. They let their minds drop slowly back into place. Dave opened his eyes. "How long were we gone?"

"Only a couple of minutes," Seth said. "Did you see anything?"

"The exile and Ringo bent over some weird and wonderful control panel," Danny replied.

"So, he's alive," said Harry, unable to stifle a grin.

"Alive and in cahoots with that bastard," Dave said. "Maybe it would have been better if he had been dead."

"You can't mean that man," said Pete.

Dave looked him in the eye. "I believe I do, Pete. I hate to admit it, but he is now the enemy."

"Have you any idea how far away they are?" Seth asked.

Danny and Dave both shook their heads. "We sort of whizzed along, going through walls half the time, so it's impossible to say."

"Well, we'd better get going. They're at the final hurdle now. For him to unlock the final doors will not be an easy task, there will be a lot of trial and error involved. We just have to hope we can reach them before he manages it."

"I'm afraid the exile seems to have found a way for Ringo to absorb the old magic," Dave said. "He said he'll be like a 'Titan'."

"The exile is so close to The Machine, the power he is drawing will be immense. It will give him abilities otherwise denied. The upside is – the nearer you two get, the stronger you will become as well. I won't lie to you, it won't be a fair fight, they will have the advantage."

"There are six of us though" Phil said.

"Without the old magic, we can be no more than irritating or diversionary. We do not pose any threat whatsoever. We will be little more than wasps buzzing around their heads."

"In that case, I'll make sure I sting the fuckers as much as I can. And – Dave?"

Dave looked at her, knowing what she was going to say. "Don't worry, I won't forget," he said.

Seth was already on his way, striding out, his shoulders slumped. Dave wondered if he thought he was fighting a losing battle. If he and the others weren't going to be able to make any real difference, it would be down to himself and Danny. Before all of this, if he'd have had to put money on who would win if Ringo and he went head-to-head, his cash would have been on him. It would have been close, but Dave thought he'd have had the edge. When they finally did meet, if the exile didn't manage to blow them to fuck beforehand, they would have had control of massive amounts of power much longer than them. Up until now he had felt quite positive, now he wasn't so sure.

The power Danny was absorbing was intense and, after what Seth had said, it meant, surely, they weren't that far away. He looked at Dave, his sword hanging at his side and realised he was weapon-less. It hadn't really bothered him before.

These, however, were different times, and as Seth, Harry, Pete and Phil weren't going to be able to help much in the way of combat, it seemed logical that he should have something ready-made. Something he could transfer the magic into rather than having to manufacture his own at a time when time would be, no doubt, of the essence.

"Considering what Seth has just said," he said to Harry. "Do you think it might be an idea if I had your sword?"

Harry looked at him as if he'd just raped his Granny. "Erm, I don't know. Me and Gloria have been through a lot together and I still believe I can contribute." He jerked a thumb in Seth's direction. "He can't be right about everything."

"Gloria?" Pete asked mockingly. "You call your sword – Gloria?"

"After my favourite aunt, yeah. What's wrong with that?"

"You are sad, man. I mean – Gloria." He unbuckled his own sword. "There you go Danny, you can have Mabel. I mean, how can you call a fucking sword Gloria?"

"You're taking the piss now, aren't you?" said Harry uncertainly.

Pete shook his head. "I tell you what mate, you decide."

Danny took the sword off Pete, stuck it around his waist, adjusted the belt a notch and felt like a musketeer.

"Nice to meet you, Aramis," said Dave, reading his mind.

407

"Yeah, and you, Athos."

"Bugger that, I'm D'Artagnan, the good looking one."

"In your dreams," said Phil.

"Do you even know how to use it?" Harry asked Danny.

Danny shrugged. "I was trained to box by a master of the noble art. This will just become an extension of my fist. I will swing, jab and parry and, if I get the chance, chop that bastard's head off."

Suddenly, Dave was in his head. 'We've got to win this mate, I mean it. We cannot lose.'

'You won't have to keep your promise, we'll make sure of that,' Danny told him. The confidence he relayed settled Dave; he could tell. The doubt that was bubbling, he buried before Dave could pick up on it. He knew Seth was right, this wasn't going to be a fair fight. Still, aren't they the best?

He couldn't help thinking back to Lawrence Carter. It seemed that was when his life changed, and he stopped being a kid and had to grow a pair. The good times had been short lived. He was looking forward to the fight. He was sucking up that much of the old magic, he was on fire. He took Pete's sword in his hand, hefted it. It felt good. He felt good, better than he'd felt in a long time. The exile was just another bully who was about to be shown the error of his ways. He was under no illusion; he knew it wouldn't be as easy as Carter and his henchmen.

'Do you feel that?' Dave asked him over their link.

Danny felt it all right. The old magic was swirling like a twister. 'We need to be ready. I think they're coming to stop us getting any further.' Dave drew his sword and they moved forward to the head of the group.

"Are we close?" Seth asked.

"They're coming to stop us," Danny said. "Phil, stay at the back. The rest of you, don't try any heroics. This is down to Dave and me."

"Is there nothing we can do?" Harry asked.

"Just try and stay out of the way, mate," Dave said. "I know it's going to be hard, but this is a fight you have no chance of winning."

Harry's hand was on the hilt of his sword and the look in his eye was not one of submission. Danny put his hand on Harry's shoulder.

"Really Harry. Stay out of this."

The air seemed to grow heavy, and Danny's stomach churned, the power lurching within his body. It raced through his muscles, making them expand and contract. He felt like a marionette.

"What's the matter with you two?" Phil asked. "This is no time for pissing break dancing."

'Shit, Danny, we've got to get a hold of this, or we done for,' Dave said in his head.

'Don't fight it,' Danny told him. 'It's here to help us. The Machine's trying to feed us as much as it can.'

He looked back at Phil and smiled. "It's okay, we're being supercharged."

"You ain't kidding, yours eyes are like 100-watt bulbs, man."

'You okay Dave?'

'I feel like I could carry the world on my shoulders,' he said, his lips pulled back from his teeth in a mad grin.

The passage was lit up. The blades of their swords shimmered like mercury. The old magic felt as if it were queuing to enter his body and he didn't know how much more he could take. He knew the more he could absorb, the better their chances would be when the time came.

It began as a low growl, quickly growing in volume and pitch. It was inside their heads. Danny tried to shut it out by raising the walls, but the sound became a tumour pulsating and reaching around the edges of their barricades with cancerous tentacles.

He sucked up a huge wedge of magic and hurled it into his brain. The walls moved outward, trapping and cutting those fibrous fingers. The scream was no longer directed at them but because of them.

The sound was excruciating. It felt as if Dave's mind was splitting in two. He could feel Danny sucking up more power and he followed suit. They were becoming a unit. They both hurled great gouts of old magic at their attackers and erected the walls again. They were no longer novices, learning quickly, as they had to. Even with the walls in place, they managed to leave the mental link open and protected.

'That was supposed to disable us and get a quick kill,' Danny said.

'They obviously don't know who they're fucking with. Ringo should have known better.'

'I get the impression he's along for the ride. I wouldn't imagine his opinion is worth jack shit to the exile. He's probably just another trophy, like he plans Phil to be. If we don't win this, I think his life will be almost as miserable as hers.'

'Why can't he see that? I still can't believe he did what he did. That's just not Ringo.'

'I think this place has changed us all.'

'Yeah, but not to that extent.'

'I don't know what to say, Dave. It is what it is. Now, shut up and get ready. I have a feeling they'll push forward sooner rather than later.'

'It's gone sort of quiet.'

'Have you never heard of the calm before the storm?'

The heaviness retreated, leaving the air thin and fragile. Whilst it didn't affect Dave or himself, the other four began to wheeze and cough. He let out a bit of the magic and threw it around them like an oxygen chamber. He knew this was another ploy to distract them, but he couldn't see their friends gasping for breath.

"Come on you fucking cowards," Dave yelled.

As if in response a wind of some force blew their hair back from their heads, tugging at their clothes. The scream was back, but it was audible to all, filling the passage like a war cry.

"Time to put the game face on, my man," Dave said to Danny.

"Don't worry mate, it's been on for a time. You ready?"

"Damned right I am."

Danny grinned. "Well, in that case, let's hope this pair of clowns stop squealing like girls and show us what they're made of. Typical bullies, shit scared, when somebody stands up to them."

The scream morphed into a roar.

Dave laughed. "Does he really think his pathetic lion impression cuts any ice. The phrase – all mouth and trousers – comes to mind."

The roar filled the cavern. It seemed the exile was quite easy to wind up.

"What's that?" Phil asked shakily. "It looks like........oh shit the bed, the filthy bastards.

The floor of the passageway became a carpet of rats. Phil jumped onto Harry's back.

They swarmed around their feet, nipping at their ankles.

"I hate rats," Pete said shakily. "Shit, that fucking hurts. Can't you do something?" He was pleading.

"It's a diversionary tactic," said Seth through gritted teeth, kicking rats in the air.

"Deal with them," Danny said to Dave. "I'll stay focused. We can't be caught off guard."

Dave nodded. This had to be quick. He forced the power down and imagined the vermin bursting into flame. He closed his eyes and pushed.

"That'll teach you, you dirty little fuckers," Phil said gleefully.

Dave looked down and saw the rats melting into the stone floor. He was about to turn to Danny when he heard him yell.

"Come on then." His blade was above his head, incandescent.

In the passage just ahead of him stood the exile, his own axe before him. It appeared to be smoking, flickering red and black. By his side was Dave's old friend. Ringo's face had changed. The humour that always twinkled around the corner of his eyes was gone. The man who stood there now was harsh and hard faced. This was not the man he'd called his best friend. He thought that when they met again, Ringo would remember and come to his senses. Sadness welled inside when Dave realised that was not going to happen. Ringo grinned at him.

"What's the matter 'Pansy', you lost your bottle?"

"You don't want to do this mate, you really don't."

"Oooh, I'm scared," Ringo said mockingly.

'Attack is the best form of defence,' Danny sent across their private link. 'You have to stop thinking of him as your friend, he wants to kill you. It's you or him. Let's do this.'

Danny leapt forward to meet the exile. Dave was by his side, sword raised, dreading what he had to do. Ringo came at him, the grin widening as he swung his own blade. "You can always change sides, my man, join the winning side. This is your last chance."

Dave looked him in the eye. "Go to hell, you fucking traitorous bastard." He drew in all the old

413

magic he could, before their blades met. He was shocked at the power behind Ringo's thrust. He was almost knocked off his feet. Ringo laughed and shook his head.

"I expected more from you, Dave. Where's your fight, you spineless bastard?"

Dave pulled back, took a deep breath and attacked again. Ringo parried the blow easily. Dave sucked up more power and managed to drive him back an inch or so.

"Give it up, while you still have a chance," he said. Ringo laughed in his face.

"You're weak, Dave, you always have been. You've never really had that killer instinct, have you?"

Danny launched himself at the exile as Dave took on Ringo. This was now a fight between two even sides, and it would be a fight to the death. He drew in the power and channelled every ounce of advice Billy Arnold had given him. He feinted to the left, trying to wrong foot his opponent. It was as if the exile could read his mind, he stood firm and blocked the jab Danny sent up towards his throat. His face was a mask of malevolence. As he parried Danny's next swing, he looked at Phil and winked. Danny glanced over to Dave and saw him attempting to gain a firmer footing under the barrage of Ringo's sword. It was obvious, from the start, they were stronger than himself and Dave. Harry ignored everything they'd said and dashed forward, bringing his sword forward. The exile shot out his left foot and caught him in the chest, sending him sprawling, the blade skittering across the floor of the passage.

"Stay back, Harry," Danny managed to say as he avoided another effort at a beheading. The exile's blade nicked his ear, and he could feel the blood trickling down his neck. He lunged forward and was batted away like a fly.

'They're too strong,' He sent over to Dave. 'Any suggestions?'

All he sent back was, 'We can't lose.'

Danny summoned all his strength and sucked up as much old magic as he could. He leapt at the exile, going for a kill shot. The exile brought his sword around and it smashed into Danny's, splintering it. He was left with the hilt and a jagged piece of steel, the size of a small dagger. The exile kicked him, and he fell onto his back, holding his excuse for a weapon out in front of him.

"I think your days are numbered," the exile said, grinning. "Unless you have a rocket launcher in your pocket." His laughter filled the cavern. Danny just caught sight of Dave nicking Ringo's arm before his ex-friend pushed him to the floor. He could hear Phil screaming about his promise to her. He had never felt so helpless.

'You've got to keep your promise,' Danny said to Dave. 'It's over, we can't beat them.'

The exile lifted his blade and Danny waited for it to pierce his heart and release him from this life.

"Have that, you bearded fucker," He heard Ringo shout. The exile's head left his body in a bloody shower. His body swayed and slumped to the floor

415

by Danny's side, his arm across Danny's chest. He threw it off and leapt to his feet. Dave was sat on the floor staring up at Ringo, who was shaking his head.

"What the fuck was all that?" He asked.

Dave jumped up and threw his arms around the man. "I knew it, man, I knew it."

Ringo patted him on the back. "All right, mate, don't go overboard. Was that the bastard? The fucking exile?"

Phil rushed forward and hugged him as well.

"I'm getting to quite like this," he said, holding his hand an inch from Phil's left buttock.

"You might have just saved our lives," she said in his ear. "But if you squeeze my arse, I'll bite your fucking nose off."

TWELVE

"What happened mate?" Dave asked him.

Ringo shook his head. "I dunno, I was waiting with you lot watching that bloody wall swinging and then I was fighting with you. Why was I fighting my best mate?"

There were tears in his eyes. "I could have killed you man. What the fuck has happened to me?"

"I believe, because of your dislike for me and your apparent prowess, the exile thought you would be the best choice for an ally," said Seth.

"What?" Ringo looked confused. "I don't understand."

"He got into your head mate," Dave said. He hugged him again. "I knew you wouldn't turn on us intentionally."

"So, he......brainwashed me?"

Seth nodded. "Something like that. I believe when Dave caught you with his sword, it brought you back, woke you up, whatever you want to call it."

Ringo looked down at his arm, where the blood was already drying. "That's all it took?"

"Your power was incredible," said Dave. "No matter how much old magic I sucked up it didn't cut the mustard. You were just too strong."

"You mean, I had that magic shit?"

"You probably still have."

"I think, as it was the exile who bequeathed it to you, you might find it left when you beheaded him," said Seth.

417

"Do you feel any different?" Danny asked him.

He stood for a few seconds, staring into space.

"Apart from feeling a total bastard – no."

"We're just happy to have you back, you ugly fucker," said Harry, with a grin.

"And so say all of us," Pete added.

"Eh, come on, I might be a bastard, but ugly? You are joking, right?"

They all laughed, even Seth. The big man held out his hand. "Thanks for everything, Ringo, you saved humanity, and I mean that."

Ringo shook his hand, his face reddening.

"You're blushing like a little girl," said Phil, winking at him.

"I'm just a bit hot, that's all," Ringo said, grinning from ear to ear. "You know how it is when you've just saved humanity. Oh no, 'course you don't, do you?" He winked back.

At that moment, they all felt happy and relaxed. The threat to Seth's final journey had been eradicated, thanks to Ringo's awakening and all the urgency and stress had disappeared. They were close to their destination and it seemed their quest would soon be over. The only question now was what would happen after Seth joined his predecessors in the machine. Phil and Danny, even Blue, should return to their previous lives. Whether the rest would join them was still a mystery.

Dave couldn't take his eyes of Ringo. He'd only just accepted that he'd become the biggest shit head in the world, yet here he was – a hero.

"Will you stop staring at me, Dave, you're starting to give me a complex."

"Sorry mate, it's just so good to have you back. I thought I'd lost my best mate."

Ringo punched him in the shoulder. "You know I hate this sort of stuff." He looked at Seth. "Hadn't we better get this show back on the road, boss?"

Seth smiled. "I think we've got a few minutes to enjoy your triumph. I believe Mr. Lennon would have been proud of you."

At the mention of his hero, Ringo beamed. "I just did what any of you would have done under the circumstances."

"Oh, absolutely," said Pete, nodding.

"'Course we would," Harry said, swinging his sword with a flourish.

"I was about to grab Harry's sword, leap over Danny's head and do it myself," said Phil.

Ringo looked from one to the other. "Yeah, but......it was me that did the business, wasn't it?"

"For Christ's sake mate, they're winding you up," Dave said. "None of us had any chance. You were the only one with the power and the element of surprise."

"If you hadn't come to your senses, we were done for," said Danny. "We'd thrown everything we'd got at the pair of you and fallen way short."

Ringo soaked up the praise like a pro. Dave almost expected him to take a bow. Instead, he gave an embarrassed cough. "I really think we ought to be making a move."

Seth smiled. "He's probably right. It's time to renew The Machine."

"Then what happens?" Harry asked.

"Danny and Phil will be sent back and, in due course, will learn the identities of the next guardians. As for the rest of you, I can't say, I'm afraid. You're not from The Grid, so my best guess is that you will either go back with the guardians or return to the place you were prior to entering The Grid. I really don't know."

"So, we could end up back in the twelfth century," said Pete.

"You'll probably come back with us," Danny said.

"Yeah, I bet that's what'll happen, "Phil agreed.

Neither of them was convinced. How could they be?

"Well, I guess we'll soon find out," Dave said. "Lead on Seth."

He walked by Ringo's side. "You know, I don't really give a shit. Wherever we land up, we'll have a laugh."

Ringo put his arm around his shoulders. "Yeah, we will. It's just a fucking bummer Jack won't be with us."

Dave took out his sword, held it in the air. "To lost friends."

The other three took out their blades, Pete's a little shorter than the others, and chinked them like wine glasses.

"Lost friends."

Danny smiled. It was good to see Dave and his mates having a laugh again. It appeared that all their differences had faded to nothing. They were a gang once more. He envied them. Returning to his previous life with Phil didn't fill him with elation. As far as being furnished with details of the next two guardians was concerned, it seemed like a massive chore. He was about to suck up more of the old magic but decided against it. Soon, he would have to do without it and live in the real world. At least, if everything Seth had told them was true, Blue should be there by his side. He would miss Charlie; they had become a strange but wonderful trio. He wondered what would happen to him when Seth 'reset' The Machine and was about to ask. Instead, he let it go. He didn't really want to know. He wanted to remember him as he was the last time he saw him.

"Watch it, too much thinking can damage your health, Danny boy," said Phil, clapping him on the back. "Don't tell me, you're thinking about what happens when this shit is all over and 'his knibs' has taken his rightful place. Am I right?"

Danny nodded. "Yeah, something like that."

"Depressing, ain't it?"

He nodded again. "I mean, you look at Seth and he's all over it. Going into this bloody machine is all he can think about. I can't imagine myself ever feeling like that, can you/"

"Shit, no; and meeting the next guardians and baby-sitting the bastards." She let out a heavy sigh. "For fuck's sake, kill me now."

"Maybe we'll feel differently once he's gone in there," he said hopefully.

"Like Paul on the road to Damascus," said Harry. "Sorry, I wasn't ear wigging, I just couldn't help hearing you. We're not exactly in an area that provides any sort of privacy, know what I mean?"

"I didn't realise you were religious," Danny said to him.

He shook his head vigorously. "Oh no, I'm not. It's just something my old man used to say when someone had an unexpected change of view or something."

"I'm surprised you turned out so dumb, when your old feller was so knowledgeable," said Phil.

Harry looked hurt.

"She's joking mate," Danny said, glaring at her. She was about to pile on in but had a change of heart (another Damascus moment).

"Yeah, 'course I am, you muppet."

He looked at her. "You know something? You're not a very nice person. I don't see what Dave sees in you."

Phil's expression was one of utter shock. "I was trying to save your feelings there...."

"I'll leave you two to it," said Harry, turning away. Phil looked at Danny and held her hands up in a – what was all that about – gesture.

"I can't disagree with him," he said. "You really need to start thinking before you open your trap, unless you want to end up a lonely, old crone."

Dave, Ringo, Harry and Pete sheathed their swords and gave Jack a few minutes silence. The five of them had started this ridiculous journey as a unit, a gang of misfits but a gang, nevertheless. The situation with Ringo had taken all their attention, they feared they'd lost another of their group to the ravages of The Grid. To have him back had been overwhelming, to say the least. Dave felt guilty for forgetting about Jack, but he was gone, and nothing would bring him back. Life is for the living even if the dead are like shadows by our sides. He couldn't say he was in a better place because he hadn't a clue what was supposed to be what anymore. He'd never been the religious sort but, maybe, erred on the side that there may be a place where we went when this pile of shit did for us. He supposed, deep down, we all hope that once we expire in this world, we don't just end, that we have something resembling a soul and that it drifts off to a cloudy world where we meet up with our old friends and relatives.

"What happens when you go into The Machine?" He asked Seth.

"I revitalise it."

"Yeah, but what happens to you, you know, the thing that makes you who you are?"

He smiled. "You're talking about souls, aren't you?"

Dave shrugged. "I don't know. I've always thought there was something inside all of us that made us individual and, maybe left our bodies when we died. If I'm honest, I haven't really thought about it much before – before coming to this place and you telling us we're all kept alive by some machine."

"All I know is that if I don't join The Machine, we may as well have let the exile do his worst. It is a privilege to be a guardian and I'm eager to play my part."

"Aren't you scared?"

Seth looked into Dave's eyes and all he saw was serenity. "Why would I be scared? I'm about to achieve my destiny."

"Okay. I'm happy for you – I suppose."

Seth laughed. It had a good ring to it. "You don't sound too sure, Dave."

"That's because I'm not. If you hadn't noticed, I haven't been sure about anything for a long time."

"I just hope that you all end up in the same place when it's done."

"Ah, don't worry about us. We'll be all right, we've got each other."

"Are you telling me there is no-one you'll miss?" He nodded in Phil's direction.

Dave couldn't help it, he blushed. "I don't think the feeling is really mutual. Maybe it would be better if we were separated."

"I'm not an authority on affairs of the heart," Seth said, "but I'm quite sure that young lady is carrying a torch for you, young man."

Dave blushed a bit more. "As some woman sang – what will be, will be."

"I think it was Doris Day – Que Sera Sera."

"Yeah, that's her. I suppose we'll just have to wait and see. Thanks for the talk, I'd like to say it helped but, if I did, I'd be lying."

For the first time, Danny thought he'd got through that hard exterior to the person that lay beneath. "You know me, Danny, I'm a feisty cow, that's how I've managed to get through life. I didn't mean anything." She looked sorry.

He sighed. "That's not a problem mate, but hurting your friends is. They're not some loser who's trying to jump you. You even treat Dave like shit and he's really sweet on you."

She almost blushed. "I really like him as well." She looked him in the eye. "The trouble is, I've been like this for so long now, I don't know how to be anything else. It's who I am."

Danny held her gaze. "No, it's not who you are, it's who you want people to think you are, which is fine, if they are people who don't care about you. For the ones that do, you've got to let them in."

A tear clouded the corner of her eye. "I don't know if I can."

He patted her hand. "You can, trust me. Now, why don't you go and apologise to Harry properly, it might start the ball rolling." She nodded and he gave her a wink. "Go."

He watched her approach Harry and put her arm through his. He tried to pull away, but she held on. As she began to talk to him, his shoulders relaxed, and he nodded his head a couple of times. A few minutes later she pecked him on the cheek and came back to Danny's side.

"He's a nice bloke," she said.

"They're all nice blokes, if you let them be."

"I hope we don't get split up after Seth's done his party trick."

"Same here," he said. "I've never really had much in the way of mates before."

"Shit, we're a sad pair of bastards, ain't we?"

He laughed. "Yeah, I suppose we are – Bill and Phil no mates."

Dave joined them. "What's the joke?"

"Us, we're the joke, a couple of misfits who can't stop feeling sorry for ourselves."

"Mate – you're a diamond and you." He looked at Phil. "Well, you know what I think about you."

"Why do you like mc, Dave, I'm a bitch."

He shrugged. "Maybe I like bitches."

She punched him in the arm. "Wrong answer arsehole."

The three of them burst out laughing. This is more like it, Danny thought. He just hoped it continued after Seth's departure.

Suddenly the big man called back from up ahead. "We're here." The joy in his voice was apparent.

"The moment of truth," said Ringo, joining them.

"I'm sort of nervous," said Pete.

"Me too," said Phil, gazing at Dave.

Seth turned and put his hand on Dave's shoulder. "You're a good man, Dave." He looked at Ringo,

Pete and Harry. "You're all good men, even if I don't share your sense of humour."

"You just need more time, that's all," said Ringo, winking at him.

"I'm afraid we won't be able to test that theory," said Seth. "Unfortunately." He winked back.

Ringo held out his hand. "At least shake before you get a frontal robotomy."

Seth shook his hand and smiled. "Maybe, if we had time, I may be more receptive to your particular brand of humour. It's doubtful, but stranger things have happened."

For the first time, Dave was aware that their journey together was close to ending. Seth was about to press the reset button and, apart from Danny and Phil, the rest of them had no idea what that would mean.

"If we go back to where we were before we were slung into that time machine, will I keep the old magic?" He asked Seth.

"As far as I know, the old magic cannot leave The Grid, so I would have to say no." He shrugged. "I'm afraid I can't tell you anything for certain, Dave."

"I know – just ignore me. Come on, let's get to that bloody machine before it seizes up. I'm going to miss you man."

"Just keep your friend from doing anything stupid. He's a bit hot headed, you know."

"I'm standing just here," said Ringo grinning. "I'd rather be hot headed than a cold fish, any day."

They stood for a few minutes, none of them wanting to complete the final leg of their journey now that all obstacles had been removed. It was Danny who broke the silence.

"Do we need a group hug?"

"I think not," said Phil, eyeing Ringo and Harry and turning up her nose. Ringo blew her a kiss.

Normal service has been resumed, Dave thought.

"Time to go," said Seth with a mixture of eagerness and regret.

"Lead the way, big man," said Ringo. "I can't wait to see this 'Machine'.

"You've already seen it," Dave said.

"Yeah, but I wasn't compos mentis, was I?"

"Are you ever?" Pete asked.

Ringo punched him in the bicep. "Piss off Parsnip before I glaze you with honey and roast the bollocks off you."

"Promises, promises."

They all laughed. This was what it was all about, the camaraderie, the craic.

"I hate parsnips," said Harry. "They're the food of the devil." He shivered. "Dirty bastards."

This was it, the end of this particular journey. Dave was resigned to being sent back to the 12th century. If that turned out to be the case, they'd have no option but to carry on with the original plan of searching for Poulson in order to return to present day. Just as Phil was starting to show her softer side as well, a side, he wasn't sure she possessed. Ringo was back in the fold and getting on reasonably well with Seth, a fact that, in itself, was sad as the boss man's time with them was severely limited. He was really hyped about fulfilling his destiny and Dave, for one, felt happy for him. He couldn't understand how anyone could look forward to letting some machine suck the life out of them but hey, what did he know?

"Getting to medieval Scotland and finding that Poulson twat will be a cake-walk after all this shite," said Ringo.

"So, you think that's what's going to happen?"

"I've never been a betting man, but if I was, I'd put a sizeable amount on it, yeah."

Dave nodded and looked at Phil. Ringo followed his gaze.

"But who knows?" He said, "You know me – I'm so full of shit I could be a labourers' khazi after a bank holiday weekend."

"Well, I guess we'll soon find out," said Pete. They followed Seth around a bend in the tunnel and were in the cavern Danny and Dave had seen when they left their bodies and saw the exile and Ringo bent over the weird control panel. The big feller was already there, flicking images and numbers left and right on an invisible screen in front of him. They seemed to be a combination of equations and peculiar, animated shapes. Every so often a silver light flashed, and Seth let out a satisfied grunt. As far as Dave could make out, there was nothing else here. If he were supposed to enter a machine of some sort, he couldn't see it. Seth's fingers were like a blur as they moved the figures from one side to the other, flicking some upward and some down. Watching him was both mesmerising and relaxing at the same time.

"He's like a conductor," Ringo said softly.

Normally one of them would have mentioned the absence of a 'bus' but they were all so immersed in his calculations, the opportunity passed without the slightest murmur.

Dave was sure none of them knew the amount of time that had flown by before Seth let out a satisfied 'Aahh' and sat back. The cavern wall in front of them shimmered and dissolved, revealing The Machine. They let out a communal gasp. Dave didn't know what the others had been expecting but he doubted if it was anything like the vision before them.

"The Machine," said Seth proudly.

"That is incredible," said Ringo. "Abso-fucking-lutely incredible."

"That is huge," said Pete.

"I think the word is 'magnificent'," said Danny.

They stood in awe. The Machine towered above them, its colour changing every few seconds. It pulsed like a beating heart as flashes of what appeared to be lightning crackled from the moving portals.

"Is it alive?" Dave asked Seth. "It looks alive."

"Not in the way you mean, no, but it exists on more plains than we do. If I had to try and describe it, I would have to say it is like a million computers, all programmed for different applications, combined with brains from beings far superior to the likes of Einstein, Darwin, Da Vinci – even John Lennon." He winked at Ringo. He was like a different man.

"How do you get into it, man?" Ringo said. "I don't see anything that resembles a door. Wow, does it ever stop moving? It's like a cross between a massive chameleon and a rubber Empire State Building."

"When I touch it, it will recognise me as the appropriate guardian and welcome me," Seth said, beaming.

"I guess this is goodbye then," said Phil. She wiped a tear from her eye, disgusted with herself.

Seth nodded. "It is indeed, my dear" He held out his arms and Phil walked into them and hugged him.

"You've been like a father to me," she said. "I'm going to miss you telling me off."

"You'll be fine, you know you will."

"Well.........all the best," said Harry. "What else can I say?"

Seth laughed. "Nothing, that's as good as anything Harry." He looked around the group. "Look after each other. Who knows, maybe I'll see you on the other side."

"Is there another side then?" Pete asked.

Seth laughed again. "Probably not. Maybe best for me to take a leaf out of Harry's book. All the best to you all. Now, it's time for me to go."

He reached out towards The Machine and as his hand drew close, the pulsing increased, and the lightning streaked wildly. It was like a puppy welcoming its master back home. If it had a tail it would have wagged profusely. Dave held his breath as Seth's fingers caressed its surface. The Machine shuddered and a large maw opened, blood red inside. Seth turned his head and gave them a last wave.

"Goodbye my friends."

He walked inside, a happy man, finally at peace. The mouth closed over him and he was gone. Dave exhaled. They looked at each other, waiting to see what would happen next.

The ground began to tremble, The Machine began to fade into the rock, the lightning becoming fairy lights. They waited.

Danny could feel the old magic leaving him. He tried to hold onto it, but it was like sand slipping through his fingers. Their time in The Grid was coming to an abrupt end.

"I think we should hold hands," he said.

Ringo looked at him as if he'd just propositioned him. "You're a mate and all that but..."

Phil grabbed Danny's hand and his. "Do you want us to stay together, meathead?"

Dave grabbed Ringo's other hand.

"Come on you two, we don't have much time," he said to Pete and Harry.

As The Machine became a wall of rock and the trembling became a shaking, it was obvious that whatever was going to happen was going to occur imminently. Pete grasped Dave's hand, gripping Harry's with his other. Danny reached out to Harry and completed the circle. Whether this would do any good or not was anyone's guess, but it had to be worth a try. As everything around them started to break down and lose all definition, his vision started to blur, and he felt faint. Seconds later, it felt like he was spinning through air as thick as soup and all he could think of was keeping hold of Phil's and Harry's hands. A wild screech assaulted his eardrums, and he could feel consciousness going the same way as the old magic.

"Keep hold guys," he managed to say before he sank into a cotton wool world, grateful for the oblivion. Even his mind seemed to be shutting down and his last thought was - this is death. He welcomed it with open arms and sank into obscurity.

THIRTEEN

"Danny, Danny, come on man, wake up."
Danny opened his eyes, trying to focus, part of him wanting to sink back into nothingness.
He blinked a few times and focused on Dave's face hovering above him.
"Christ mate, we thought you were dead."
Danny sat up and looked around. They were all there. Something wet tickled his ear. He turned his head and let out a cry of joy. Blue was licking his face, her tail wagging twenty to the dozen.
"Oh girl, it's so good to see you again." He hugged her and then looked back at his friends. There seemed to be a stranger in their midst.
"Who's he?" He said pointing to the interloper.
Ringo had his arm around the man. He was about five eight, slim build, intelligent eyes above a pointed nose.
"This is the bloke we were sent to find," Ringo said, hugging the chap tighter. "This here is Martin Poulson, genius and thief."
"Is he the bloke who nipped off with an integral part to this time machine of yours?"
"The very same," said Dave. "It seems we came back at an extremely opportune moment. Apparently, his vacation in 12th century Scotland was terminated rather abruptly, and he was returned to England with a bump."
"So, we're all in the twelfth century?"

"Just briefly," said Ringo with a grin. "Now you're back with us, we can catch a ride back to the future."

Blue was crying as she jumped around him. No-one in his life – ever, had been that pleased to see him, and he doubted if he'd ever been as glad to see anyone else as he was to see her.

"Okay, calm down," he said, laughing. She wouldn't stop licking his face and he was having difficulty catching his breath. "You're smothering me, gorgeous girl."

"I think she might be happy to see you," said Dave.

Danny managed to calm her down eventually. "So, we're all in the twelfth century. So much for us returning to our old lives and Seth's uncertainty about your future." He waved his hand in Dave and Co.'s direction.

"Yeah, weird," said Harry.

"I can only assume," Dave said, "that because there are four of us and only two of you, and we were all holding onto each other that we sort of cancelled you out."

"Maybe that's why your man is here," Danny said gesturing towards Poulson. "To right the wrong."

"What, you mean, because we dragged you back here, The Machine has dragged him back here too, so you can get back to present day?" Ringo looked both perplexed and doubtful, a hard look to pull off. "Why not just take us all there in the first place. It would have been much easier."

435

"A good point, well made," Danny agreed. "I'm afraid I'm as much in the dark as you are. I've given up trying to understand. Let's face it – The Machine works in mysterious ways its wonders to perform."

"What's The Machine?" Poulsen asked.

They all looked at him and burst out laughing.

"You think you've had a weird time, my man," said Phil. "You don't know the fucking half of it."

Poulsen was visibly shocked by Phil's bad language.

"Don't worry, most geeks are prudes," said Pete.

"I ain't worried about this puny, little bastard," said Phil, making a fist in front of Poulsen's face. The poor man flinched.

"Leave him alone, Phil," said Dave. "He's going to have enough to contend with when we get back. He's definitely off Christian's Christmas card list, that's for sure."

"Where is this 'Tardis' then?" She asked.

"It's camouflaged," said Poulsen.

"How do we know where it is then?"

Poulsen smiled. "You don't, but I do."

"Well, are you going to share, little man?" She put her face inches from his.

"Best do as she says, mate," said Ringo. "None of us are going to protect you."

Poulsen reached inside his jerkin and pulled out a tiny piece of equipment.

"Is that it," Dave asked.

Poulsen nodded.

He held what looked like a Zippo cigarette lighter.

436

"That piece of the puzzle allows us to get back?" Dave said.

He nodded. "Yep."

"What is it?"

"A time and light converter. It responds to light, much the same way as a solar panel does. It has a memory, like a 'sat-nav' and therefore logs locations, those travelled from and those travelled to. Without this, this wonderful time machine is in neutral; it can neither go forward nor back, in fact it's useless."

"What I don't understand, China, is why you nicked it in the first place and why you decided to come back to the century that has as much appeal for life as the eighties had for music. Unless you're a dentist, of course – a good dentist could make a fortune here," Ringo said.

"I meant to go back nine months," he said with a shrug. "Unfortunately, I was disturbed whilst I was inputting the data and had to rush things a little. I still don't know how I managed to select the twelfth century. I guess I was distracted by the men with guns, wanting to kill me."

Dave stuck out his bottom lip. "I'm thinking that hasn't really changed, Martin, my old pal."

"They're not going to let you go either, you know," Poulson said. "You know too much, you're as dead as I am."

"So, what happened?" Phil asked him.

"I've no idea, one minute I was in Scotland, eating a tasteless, grisly stew, the next, I was here, surrounded by you lot."

That seemed to have proved the point. Danny and Phil (and Blue) had been yanked back in time and amends had to be made.

"So where does that leave us?" Ringo asked, looking at Dave.

"The way I see it is, we can't stay here, we have to go back."

"Christian said that if we brought him back, we'd be free to go," said Pete.

Poulsen shook his head. "You can't honestly believe that."

Dave knew Poulsen was right. When they hurtled back to present day, there would be a firing squad waiting for them.

"Can you do anything to give us an edge," he asked the scientist.

Poulson thought for a minute. "If I can make it so Christian expects us to arrive at – say ten past and we get in a couple of minutes early – would that help?"

"The element of fucking surprise is what it's all about," said Ringo. "If we can surprise the bastards, we can chop their bollocks off before they realise that eunuchism was ever an option."

"Nicely put," said Harry, an expression of admiration gracing the features of a nodding head. "If that is actually a word."

"He has a way with words," said Pete.

"If you can give us ten, or five even – two's a bit close for comfort."

Poulsen looked at Dave and he could almost see the cogs turning. "At a stretch I might be able to manage five, but no more."

"Do what you can, man, every second counts." Dave put his hand on the hilt of his sword and looked around their little band of misfits. Danny and Phil stood out, being the only ones dressed in modern day clobber but, also the only two without weapons.

"I wish we had more blades," he said.

Phil looked at him and winked. "Don't you worry about me, Davey boy, these are all I need." She held up her fists and kicked out her right foot, lifting it higher as she pivoted on her left.

"Same here Dave," said Danny. "I'd be useless with a sword, without the old magic – at least I've been trained to use these." He waved his hands in the air.

"Look mate, it is what it is," said Ringo. "We'll be outnumbered, they'll have guns. We've just got to hit the ground running, make the most of our advantage and go in hard. We snatch a couple of Uzis and we level the playing field a bit and, don't forget, they're just doing what they get paid for, we're fighting for our lives. Let's just go fuck the bastards up the arse."

"I told you he had a way with words," said Pete.

"How long will it take you to set it all up?" Dave asked Poulsen.

He shrugged. "About fifteen minutes. At least I'll be able to concentrate this time."

"Are you sure we can trust this weasel?" Phil said, looking at Poulsen as if he was something nasty, she'd stepped in.

"I don't think you have a lot of choice," said Poulsen. "Look, I'm kind of relying on you to help me stay alive. I can't fight, I'm a scientist. If you die, I die, and I'd rather not do that. I'm thirty-six years old and I quite fancy reaching retirement age, if that's possible. We're all in the same boat."

"Believe me, he can't have any agenda," Dave said to Phil. "We were sent here to bring him back. Once Christian gets that back." He pointed to the Zippo. "He's surplus to requirements and needs to be shown the error of his ways."

"And Christian is an evil bastard," said Harry.

"I wonder if poor old Jerome's still there or if Christian has disposed of him," said Pete.

"Now there is a gentleman," said Poulsen.

"Yeah, he was a decent sort," said Ringo.

"Let's hope he still is," Dave said. "Now, I think you need to get this show on the road."

"Yeah, show us the money," said Ringo.

Poulsen counted from the left of the copse they were in. When he reached seven, he stepped forward.

As he approached the tree, a thought occurred to Danny.

"If this time machine is useless without this bit of kit, how did they get here in the first place?"

Dave, Ringo, Harry and Pete did a bit of communal nodding, a fine thing to see when it's done well.

440

"That is a good question," said Ringo. "One that needs answering in the next five seconds." He took a step towards Poulsen, gripping the hilt of his sword. "If you're fucking with us...." He didn't need to say anymore.

Poulsen held his hands up. "Come on guys, this is getting a little tedious. I'm not your enemy."

"Answer the question," said Dave.

"Any time machine requires a time and light converter at both points – exit and entry. This is the one from the exit port which renders this side of the machine ineffectual. The entry port is still viable but can only transport its subjects to the last, selected destination, i.e., here."

"I guess that makes sense," Danny said.

Ringo relaxed the grip on his weapon and Dave did a bit of solo nodding.

"Yeah, I can see that," he said.

"I still don't trust him," said Phil. "He looks shifty."

Poulsen sighed. "I'm not going to apologise for my appearance. Either you want me to do this, or you don't. I can quite easily go back to sleeping on straw and eating scraps that taste like shit. At least I won't be looking down the barrel of a gun. The choice is yours."

Danny shrugged and looked at Dave. "I don't see that we have a choice unless you want to spend the rest of your days here. Personally, I would like to go back and take my chances."

"Me too," said Phil.

Dave looked at Ringo, Harry and Pete. A single, synchronised nod was all that was needed.

"Work your magic," he said to Poulsen. "Let's go home."

"Are you sure?"

"We're sure," Danny said.

Poulsen bent down, reached behind the tree and pulled out something covered with leaves and branches. He brushed them away, revealing a silver box about the size of a small suitcase.

"Is that it?" Harry asked.

"Don't be deceived by the size," said Poulsen, stroking the top of the box. "This unit can produce a considerable inverted force field. If you found the outward journey uncomfortable, the return will be – how shall we say – a little more turbulent."

Poulsen open the box and it immediately came to life. It began to make a whirring sound similar to a laptop and LED displays glowed brightly.

"So, what sort of place are we going back to?" Danny asked Dave.

"Yeah, I suppose I haven't given you the low down on our previous lodgings, have I? It's sort of like.... a training school, I suppose. Apart from proper school I haven't had any experience of those sort of places, if you know what I mean. When we arrived, there were loads of us. We were all sorted out into different groups and trained within an inch of our lives. Guess what – we were the team that put the rest to shame. Lucky us, eh?"

"So, what happened to the rest of them?"

Dave shrugged. "To be honest Danny, I have no idea, but I wouldn't be surprised if, after we were sent back here, they weren't lined up against a wall and..."

He made a reasonable impression of a firing squad with his hands.

"You've got to be joking."

"I wish I were. I wouldn't put anything past Christian and, like Poulsen says – we all know too much."

"But the others didn't know about the time machine, did they?"

"No, I suppose not. I don't know mate; he might have let them go with a decent payoff or not. I just know he's an evil bastard who takes pleasure in others' pain. He's twisted."

"What do you think our chances are – really?"

"If we can get the jump on them, grab a couple of Uzis, we could do 'em. If not, we're probably dead. Swords are no match for machine guns. We have to rely on Poulsen getting us that leg up. What else can I tell you?"

"Maybe The Machine will come into play, if two guardians' lives are at stake," Danny said. "It brought him back here." He jerked a thumb at Poulsen.

"Mate, after all we've been through, anything is possible. All I'd say though is this – don't rely on it. When we get there, fight for your life."

"I don't know if it's worth fighting for," Danny said, missing the lift the old magic had given him.

"Don't fucking start that shit again," Dave said through gritted teeth. "If you don't want to fight for yourself, fight for your friends. Remember, we're all in this together."

"Hey, I'm alright." Danny grinned. "If I'm clocking off, I'll kick some ass before I do. You know I wouldn't let any of you down. I just miss the old magic."

"Yeah well, it is what it is. As usual, it's us against the world."

Danny looked back at Poulsen as he pressed buttons and slid sliders (what else would you do with them?). After ten minutes or so the scientist said, "I think we're about ready to go."

Dave looked around the group. They all nodded. "Let's do this."

Poulsen pressed his finger to the centre of the box and a flap glided open.

He placed the convertor into the gap and closed the aperture. His finger hovered over a silver button.

"Once I press this, there's no going back," he said.

"That's good," said Ringo. "It's forwards we're after. Just press the fucker and let's have less of the pissing drama."

"Have you managed to programme in our little leeway?" Dave asked him.

"Yes, I believe I have."

"Believe?" Ringo looked at him with disdain. "Believe?"

"I've done all I can and if I was a betting man, which I'm not, I would say we have a ninety-nine per cent chance of entering the future at least four minutes before our arrival is heralded," said Poulsen. "Nothing in this world is ever one hundred per cent positive. Now, do I press the button?"

He turned away from Ringo and looked from Danny to Dave and back again. It was obvious he wasn't sure which one of them was the leader of the group. He wasn't the only one. Dave took the initiative.

"Take us back to the future 'Doc'."

Poulsen shook his head. "Very droll." He pushed the button.

The box became silent, and they all stared at it, imagining the worst. Dave was wondering where the components had been produced when the light was sucked from around them. He felt as if he'd been hit by punch-bag swung by the World's Strongest man. He fell forward putting out his hands to break his fall. He was spun onto his back and buffeted back and forth. A keen wind stuck his hair to his head and stretched the skin across his face. He tried to look for the others but couldn't even open his eyes. He stopped trying to fight the force and let it take him. He'd never been in the midst of a tornado, but he was sure it would be like this. He imagined the years falling away like pages torn from a diary.

Before they landed, a screech nearly burst his eardrums. He used the term 'land' because he didn't really know what the appropriate wordage was for reaching one's destination after travelling through time. He was sure in about twenty years when such a thing was commonplace; a hip expression would be devised. Plus, the journey would be less baggage class and more business. He hit the floor with a hefty bump, Ringo falling on top of him. They were all trying to scrabble away from each other. Dave's ears were blocked, and he had to work the lobes to get them to pop. "Fucking hell," said Phil, rubbing her hip. "Did you do that on purpose?" She glared at Poulsen. "I did say it would be a little turbulent."

Dave got to his feet and looked around. Sure enough, they were back in Christian's prison camp, and, at the moment, alone.

FOURTEEN

They faced the metal door that they had been pushed through prior to their outward journey. The lights flickered around them.

"We're in a metal, fucking box," said Phil. "No, correction – we're in a metal, fucking box with fairy lights."

"Well spotted," said Ringo, winking at her.

"The point is," Dave said, "we're in a metal box on our own at the moment. Had our friend here not managed to give us those extra minutes, we'd be in a metal box facing a firing squad."

"There's not much in the way of hiding places," said Danny, pulling a – sorry to mention it – sort of face.

It was true. The room was a box. From the time machine, the walls led, in parallel to the wall containing the metal door. There were about two metres of bare wall either side of the door.

"The door opens inwards," Dave said, "I suggest Ringo, Pete, Harry and myself line up on that wall. You, Danny and you, Phil put Poulsen behind you and hide behind the door when it opens. Christian isn't expecting us to have picked up a couple of hitchhikers, so he won't be looking for anyone else. As soon as they come in, we'll go in as hard as possible. You two take them from behind. Knock seven bells out of the bastards and, if you can grab a gun or two, all the better. I really think we can do this if we keep our heads. What do you say Danny?"

"I think it's a plan and I'm up for a scrap. What about you Phil?"

She planted her hands on her hips. "Bring it on."

Dave looked at Poulsen, who resembled a rabbit caught in a car's headlights.

"You just stay out of the way and if you get a sudden urge to try and help, curb it – understand?"

"I...er...don't think I'll be getting any sudden urges; you needn't worry about that."

Phil looked at him with disgust.

"Right, we've probably got less than a minute before they come to welcome us back, so I think we'd better take up our positions. Good luck everybody."

Danny and Phil got themselves behind the door, Phil pushing Poulsen, a little too forcefully, to the back. Blue took her place by Danny. The rest of them flattened themselves against the wall to the other side of the door. They all drew their blades in readiness.

"Whoever comes through that door first is going to end up a fucking kebab," said Ringo. "I just hope it's that arsehole, Christian."

"I wouldn't hold your breath, he's bound to send, at least, a couple of his goons first." Dave put his ear to the door. He could hear footsteps – a lot of them. "Quiet, they're coming."

They all held their breath and waited. There was a heavy clunk as the magnetic lock released and the bolts slid back.

The door began to swing inward. Danny put his fingers to his mouth to shush Blue. Her beautiful, brown eyes shone with understanding. She turned her attention to the open door. Two armed guards entered, their focus on the machine ahead. Ringo and Dave were on them immediately, forcing them back into the room and spinning them around. Danny heard a voice shout, "Get them, cut them down." He assumed it was the chap they called Christian. Two more goons entered, looking towards Harry and Pete, their weapons raised. Danny nodded to Phil and they leapt from their hiding place. Danny grabbed one of them round the neck, stuck his knee in his back and yanked with all his might. Blue nipped at his heels. The guard dropped his gun, trying to find some purchase. Phil slid her hand between the other's legs and grabbed his nether regions. He squealed like a banshee as she squeezed and yanked at the same time. Harry and Pete were there in a second, taking the two Uzis. Danny glanced over to Ringo and Dave. They stood, Uzis pointing to the door, the two guards dead at their feet. Danny threw the one he had by the throat into the corner. Because he didn't have the history that they had with these boys, just disarming them was good enough for him. Phil had turned her goon around and battered him, her knuckles bloody from the onslaught. She finished him off with a roundhouse to the throat. He fell in a heap, holding his throat, gasping for breath.

Dave, Ringo, Harry and Pete held their Uzis on the rest of the party. Danny came from behind the door to see some weaselly looking character standing there with his hands up, his expression a mixture of fear and annoyance. By his side, a round faced man was smiling. The other four guards had dropped their weapons and had their hands in the air as well.

"How the devil are you Christian, you ugly motherfucker?" Ringo asked their host.

"I suppose you think you're clever McGee," Christian said, licking his lips.

Ringo stepped forward and jabbed the barrel of his gun in his gut. "Put it this way, tosser, if this was a game of chess, this would be fucking checkmate." He lifted the gun and swiped him across the face with the butt. Christian fell to his knees, blood pouring from his nose.

"You lot," said Dave, gesturing to the other guards. "Get yourselves in here, against that wall. Harry, Pete, if they so much as scratch their arses, spread their brains across that nice, white wall. Who knows, we might even win the Turner prize." The goons did as they were told, fear in their eyes. They eyed their fallen comrades, not wishing to join them.

"How are you Jerome?" Dave asked the round-faced man.

"Much better now, Dave," he replied stepping away from Christian. "I thought you were all dead men."

Poulsen stepped out from behind Phil. Jerome stepped forward and hugged him.

"Oh Martin, I didn't think I'd ever see you again. What did we do?"

"We made a terrible misjudgement, Jerome, a terrible misjudgement."

Christian glared up at Ringo, wiping the blood from his nose with the back of his hand.

"What's the matter big man?" Dave asked him, not trying to hide the hatred in the grin he gave him. He stepped forward, raising his own gun above his head. Christian raised his hands and cowered back against the wall.

"Not such a big man now, are you?" Ringo said, jabbing him with the barrel of his Uzi. He looked over at the goons. "Ah, Carter, my old friend, so good to see you again. Last time we met, I believe you had the gun." Ringo handed his gun to Danny. "This time, let's make it a bit fairer, shall we. Come on hard case, get up." He unbuckled his sword belt and let it fall to the floor. Carter gazed up at him, swallowing hard. Ringo grabbed him by the front of his tunic and yanked him to his feet. "You can go first arsehole, but you'd better make it a good one."

"They'll all pile in," said Carter looking nervously round their group.

"This is between me and you, Carter – no-one else. You see I'm not a snivelling, little coward like you. Come on, give it your best shot. If you don't, I'll pick that sword up and separate your head from

451

your body. I'm not going to give you another chance."

Carter licked his lips, clenching and unclenching his fists. He glanced at the sword and made up his mind. He swung a looping right hook. Even Danny could see it coming. Ringo leaned back as Carter's fist whistled past his chin, a huge smile on his face.

"Now that wasn't very good Carter, was it?" He shot out a left jab, spreading Carter's nose across his face and sitting him on his arse. "Come on, you can do better than that, you're a fucking hard man."

Carter sat with his hand over his face, tears running down his face. "I...I'm sorry," he said almost sobbing. "He made us do it." He pointed toward Christian.

Danny walked over to Christian, grabbed him by the throat and smacked him across the face with the back of his hand. "I hate bullies," was all he said.

"What are you going to do with us?" Christian asked, unable to hide the fear anymore.

"I don't know. What would you do if the positions were reversed, I wonder?" Dave said.

Christian didn't seem to be enjoying the game anymore.

"It would be a shame to kill them all," said Ringo. "Where's the fun in that?"

"What do you think, Jerome?" Dave asked Christian's ex-partner.

Jerome looked at Christian with a mixture of hatred and pity. "I'm not normally a vengeful man and have never been vindictive but, in this case, I believe a quick death would be much too kind. I have never known so much evil in one man." He glanced across at Poulsen. "How about you Martin, any suggestions?"

"I think that the man who took over the running of our machine and had no qualms sending others into unknown danger with minimal chance of returning ought to put his money where his mouth is, so to speak," he said softly.

"Before we go any further, I'm intrigued," Dave said. "What were his plans for the machine?"

"To make as much money as he possibly could," Jerome replied.

"He wanted to send his men back to steal paintings, manuscripts, musical scores – anything he could sell for a fortune. Imagine how much an unknown Van Gogh would fetch or a lost Shakespeare play, an unheard concerto by Mozart. The possibilities were endless."

"Very clever," said Ringo.

"I got the impression from what you said earlier, the time machine was your baby," said Pete, looking from Jerome to Poulsen.

Jerome nodded. "It was Martin's creation; I merely financed the venture. Trouble is – the money ran out just as we were on the verge of a breakthrough."

"A friend of mine, who I had confided in, put forward Spalding's name and offered to introduce us. At least I thought he was a friend."

"At first, he was very charming," said Jerome. "Eager to help with the financial side but willing to leave the rest to Martin and myself. He even offered us the use of this facility. Before that we were working in a small factory unit in the middle of nowhere."

"If something seems too good to be true, it normally is," said Harry with a nod of his head, trying for maturity but only managing semi vacant.

"Indeed," said Jerome.

"And what about you two, what were your plans?"

"At first, it was just a question of whether it was possible," said Martin. "I believed I had managed to instigate an Einstein-Rosen bridge and with the correct magnetic field and energy conditions I was hopeful. The time and light convertors were the last piece of the puzzle. We tested it first by sending Jerome back from October to September."

"Once he'd seen it work," Jerome said, pointing to Christian. "He started to show his true colours. That's when the guards came in. Shortly after that you all applied to the advertisement he posted. The rest, as they say, is history."

"Where were you supposed to be going when you were forced back to the twelfth century? Dave asked Poulsen.

"The plan was to go back to the time before we allowed the evil bastard into our midst," he replied.

"It seemed the easiest way out of the whole predicament."

"But surely that would mean the machine wouldn't be finished," said Danny.

"That would seem logical," said Martin. "But the truth is this – once the time machine has been conceived and operated, it cannot cease to be. History can be changed but the machine itself can never be unmade."

Phil yawned. "I always hated Physics at school. Can we get back to sorting these shitheads out?"

"A spirited girl," said Jerome.

"Yeah, a lot more spirited than you, by all accounts," she said with disdain.

"Leave him be, Phil, he's one of the good guys," Dave said. "He was put in an impossible situation, that's all."

She looked Jerome up and down. "If you say so."

"Anyway, where did you pick up your travelling companions?" Jerome asked, changing the subject.

"Well, that – is an awfully long and complicated story. One we'll tell you when we've decided what to do with our friends here."

"If he loves this time machine so much, why don't we let him use it?" Harry asked.

"Yeah, I think a one-way ticket may be in order," said Pete.

Christian was looking from one to another, panic beginning to set it. "Look...er....I'm sure we can sort this out. I've got lots of money. You let me go and it's all yours. You can do what you like with these idiots." He waved a hand toward his guards.

"What do you think of that fellers?" Ringo asked, grinning. "I think that might be called leading from the rear."

Christian's guards looked at him with a mixture of pure hatred and psychosis. It was a pleasure to witness.

"I think I have the ideal destination," said Poulsen.

"Spill H.G.," said Ringo.

"London, July 1348."

"What's so special about that date?" Harry asked.

"The Great Plague," said Jerome.

"What – you mean the Black Death?" Dave said.

Poulsen and Jerome indulged in a bit of their own mutual nodding.

"I like it," said Ringo. "Who knows chaps, with all the antibiotics and shit you've taken over the years, you might find you're immune. It's sort of a fifty-fifty job. Let's face it, you ain't going to get better odds than that."

One of the guards made a run for it. Pete halted his progress with a bullet to the head.

"Better odds than that," Ringo said with a nod.

"The choice is yours chaps but make up your mind, I'm getting kind of hungry, know what I mean?"

"Can't we talk about this?" Christian pleaded, tears running down his face.

"We've heard as much of your voice as we can suffer," Dave said. "Martin, set the controls for the heart of the sun."

"Eh?" said Harry.

"Pink Floyd — sorry couldn't resist it. Anyone else want to opt for the quick release?"

Danny realised why Dave and the gang were acting the way they were. The bloke they called Christian, and his paid thugs had put them through hell, and they were after revenge. It was natural. If he'd been part of their journey, he'd probably have felt the same. As it was, all he saw were frightened, defenceless men faced with a fate that would probably be worse than a quick death.

"If we do this, doesn't it just make us like him?" He asked Dave.

Before he could answer, Ringo jumped in. "No disrespect, Danny, but you have no idea what this bastard and his shitehawks have put us through. Nothing is bad enough for them. Nothing."

Dave shrugged. "He's evil mate." He looked at the guards. "Okay, they were doing what he told them to do, because he was paying them well. Not once did a single one show any remorse for what they did to us — not once. All they thought about were their bank balances. I know this seems brutal and........abhorrent. That's because it is. But people like these can't be allowed to get away with treating human beings that way. Yes — it's payback, but it's also necessary. Either they die here and now, or they suffer the same fate we did."

"It's fair Danny," said Harry bluntly.

"They deserve everything they get," Pete added.

"You're obviously a good man," said Jerome. "But so are your friends here. They are also right – evil must be eradicated. Are you a religious person?"

Phil burst out laughing. "Fuck me man, this is turning into some sort of comedy show."

Jerome looked at her perplexed.

"Are you religious?" She asked him.

"No, I'm an atheist," he replied. "Why?"

"What about you Martin?" Danny asked him.

"I'm a scientist. A supreme being goes against all I know to be true. Why are we having this discussion now?"

Dave held up his hands. "There's plenty of time for this after we've dealt with our current business. As I said before – set the, I mean, get on with it Martin?"

"We're ready to go – or should I say – they're ready to go."

"If you've got any final requests, put them in an email when you reach your holiday destination," said Ringo. "And don't forget, you probably have more chance than the other, poor bastards had. Bon voyage."

"You're going to regret this," Christian said, trying for defiance but managing wretched.

"You mind how you go now," said Pete, waving.

"Yeah, and have a nice time," said Harry.

Danny wondered if this was an end to it all, and, if it was – what happened next. All he really knew was – he was tired. As Martin pressed the final button on his keypad and Christian and his men became distorted and opaque, he hugged Blue.

FIFTEEN

They gazed at the space where Christian and his guards had been a couple of seconds ago. Danny wondered if the fact that they'd lived in present day England and had had the benefit of the latest medication would make any difference when they pitched up in plague-ridden London. He, somehow, didn't think so.

"I know how you feel mate," said Dave. "They were just pathetic, defenceless sorts to you. We have no idea what they did to the other recruits, but you can guarantee it wouldn't have been nice. That man was as evil as Hitler – I mean, would you feel sorry if we'd just sent the Fuehrer back to the Black Death?"

"Shit, no – that would be too good for him."

"Now you're starting to see things our way. Who knows, they may survive. I fucking hope they don't, but I wouldn't put anything past that bastard. At least he won't be able to torment anyone else."

The reference to Adolph had put things a little more in perspective. If this bloke was as bad as that, and Danny had no reason to believe that Dave would lie to him, then good riddance.

"So, what now?" He asked no-one in particular.

"Why were you asking if we were religious?" Jerome asked.

Phil looked disappointed. "Shame you're not, I was looking forward to bursting your bubble."

"You have a nasty streak," Danny told her.

She grinned. "Yeah, I know."

"Well?" Jerome said.

"We haven't just been back to the twelfth century," Dave said. "We've been to The Machine."

Jerome continued to look puzzled. Martin pricked up his ears.

"The Machine?" He asked.

"Yeah, apparently it's what keeps this shithole they call the earth turning," said Ringo. "I tell you man, we've been through some weird shit, and I mean – weird."

Phil and Danny sat back while Dave, Ringo, Pete and Harry related the whole, extraordinary story. Blue was fast asleep on Danny's lap.

"Do you feel any different?" He asked her.

"No – you?"

He shook his head. "I thought once Seth had done his bit, we'd be hit by some strange, Machine related emotion. There are supposed to be two new guardians out there somewhere."

"To be honest, I couldn't give a toss. I'm in no hurry to revisit that place, I'm telling you."

Blue's back legs were twitching, and her muzzle kept drawing back from her teeth. Maybe she was dreaming about one of their little skirmishes. Danny stroked her belly wishing he could stay like that forever.

Jerome listened intently, a look of wonderment spread across his chops. Martin was more animated. He looked across to Danny and Phil.

"So, you're guardians of The Machine?"

"Apparently so," said Danny, stroking Blue. He didn't appear to be too interested in the conversation.

"And this 'Seth' just disappeared into it?"

"Yeah," said Ringo. "Penn and Teller couldn't have done it any better."

"So, this must have happened after the 'Big Bang'. There was life on other planets even then."

"Big Bang?" Harry said.

"The Big Bang Theory," said Martin impatiently.

"I love that programme."

"He's talking about a scientific view of how the universe began," said Ringo, shaking his head. "Not shit American comedy."

Harry looked hurt. "It isn't shit, it's funny."

"This is amazing," said Martin. He turned to Danny. "Can you go into 'The Grid' anytime you like? Could you take me?"

"Calm down professor," said Phil. "It ain't as easy as that."

"It will probably be years before we have to go back," said Danny. "Before that, the identities of the next two guardians have to be passed on to us. It's not like getting on the sixty-seven bus. We will only be able to enter The Grid when the time comes for one of us to do what Seth did."

"That's me," said Phil. "I'm next in line. I mean – what a bummer."

Martin gazed around the group, looking into their eyes. "No, I believe you're telling the truth, extraordinary as it is."

Dave had to admit, he was a bit pissed off. "What, did you think we made the whole thing up? Are you serious?"

"It seems so fantastic," Poulsen said apologetically.

"What – like a time machine?" Pete said.

"I suppose I'm used to that."

"If we found life on another planet now, would everyone who believes in God suddenly stop believing?" Danny asked.

"I wouldn't think so – no," said Jerome. "Why would they?"

"So, theoretically, God could still exist. He could have created the race that took over earth. The Machine may keep some sort of status quo here or it may be a ludicrous illusion."

"That's ridiculous," said Martin.

"Maybe we all believe what we want to believe."

"Not the scientific fraternity, " said Martin. "We require proof."

"But you have no proof that God doesn't exist," Dave said, getting on Danny's wavelength. "He just doesn't fit into your regimented, little ideas. I mean, the Bible might be the best lump of fiction ever written but it still doesn't mean there isn't a God. There is no proof either way."

"There is no scientific proof for a supreme being, none at all," Martin said, looking Dave in the eye. "It's all just an elaborate plan to make money from the gullible, those who require some sort of crutch to help them through the miseries of this life. Something to believe in. Heaven is peddled like a five-star hotel at the end of an arduous journey – and I mean peddled."

Dave shrugged. "Show me proof that God doesn't exist," he persisted.

"Show me proof he does."

Dave laughed. "I can't – the same way you can't prove he doesn't."

"All the information we have discounts any such theory."

"I think you're going round in circles," said Ringo. "What the fuck difference does it make anyway?"

"I suppose it'd be nice to know, one way or the other," said Harry.

"That's the point mate – there is no way of knowing," said Ringo, shaking his head.

"Maybe Seth knows," said Pete.

"Well, we can hardly ask him now, can we?" Dave was getting a little tired of the conversation. He'd only jumped on the bandwagon to wind Poulsen up.

"We'll just have to agree to disagree," Martin said.

Dave held his hands up. "Hold on, I didn't say I believed in God. I was merely pointing out that his existence could neither be proven nor disproven."

"Can't we just go and get something to eat, I'm fucking starving," said Phil, rubbing her stomach. "I've always hated intellectual debates, but I hate knob-heads attempting to sound intellectual more."

Dave smiled and looked at Jerome. "I take it he hasn't killed the chefs yet."

"No, but I think he put the fear of God into one or two – pardon the religious reference."

"By the way, what did happen to the other recruits?"

"I'm afraid they're still here."

"You're joking?"

"I wish I were. They have been kept as prisoners, basic rations, stuck in dormitories – six in rooms meant for three. I think they should be our priority, don't you?"

"Lead the way," said Ringo. "Let's go and release the poor buggers. Get onto the chefs, it's time for a party. I bet that ugly bastard has got some bottles of extremely expensive wine in his cellar."

"Indeed, he has," said Jerome smiling. "Some excellent malts and cognacs as well. In fact, there's enough alcohol in here to sink a ship."

"I think we could do with a shower and a change of clothes as well," Dave said. "We're used to smelling like polecats, but it would be nice feel human again."

"Yeah, then we can start on that ship," said Ringo.

Danny hadn't realised how hungry he was before Phil mentioned food. Then Dave talked about a shower and clean clothes. He nearly lifted his arm and sniffed his pit but there was no need. As Dave had said – they stank.

"I'll go to the office and take the automatic lock off all doors." said Jerome. "Your old clothes have been laundered and left in your old rooms," he said to Dave, Ringo, Pete and Harry. It was then that he realised they were one short. "What happened to Jack?"

"I'm afraid we lost him in The Grid," said Dave.

"What? Do you mean he's still in there?"

"No – when I say we lost him, I mean, he's dead."

"I'm so sorry," said Jerome. Dave could tell he was sincere.

There was an awkward silence until Ringo broke it.

"What about these two?" He said pointing at Danny and Phil. "Can you rustle up some rags for them?"

"I'm sure we can find something. The two rooms next to yours are reasonable," he said to Dave. "We'll have some clothes dropped off."

"Follow me," said Dave.

As they walked down the corridors Danny began to fantasize about standing under a jet of hot water. It seemed like years since he'd taken a shower.

"What do we do after this?" Phil asked him.

"I don't know – go back to our lives?"

"Well, I hope you don't take up from where you left off."

Danny laughed. "No, I've got a dependent now," he said, stroking Blue's head. "She'll keep me on the straight and narrow. What about you? Are you going with Dave?"

She shrugged. "I dunno. He ain't said anything and I don't know if he'd get on my tits. I like him and all that, but I've always been on my own, you know what I mean?"

Danny nodded. "Sure do. It's not all is cracked up to be."

"Yeah well, I never had parents like yours, or brothers or sisters. It's always been me against the fucking world. You and me – we're different."

Danny looked into her eyes. "We're not all that different. We're both fucked up."

She laughed. "You're not wrong there, Sherlock."

"Dave thinks the sun shines out of your backside."

"Maybe."

"For Christ's sake Phil, let your guard down a bit. Dave is a bloody good bloke and he'll look after you."

She snorted. "I can look after myself, always have."

"There's no hope for you."

She looked at him and smiled. It was a sad smile. "You only just realised that?"

Pete, Harry and Ringo slipped into their rooms. Dave stopped at the door to his.

"Home sweet home," he said. "The next two are yours. See you out here in an hour – yeah?"

Phil entered the room next to Dave's without looking at him. His expression said it all.

"I know she doesn't show it, but she really does like you mate," Danny said to him.

"I think she's got to start liking herself before she can show any affection for anyone else." His tone was flat and forlorn. Danny had never looked at it that way before but now he did, he realised Dave was right. Phil had lived for years being a hard ass, never letting anyone in. She had existed behind her own walls for so long she didn't know how to break them down.

"She's not your run of the mill girl, that's for sure." Dave gave a tired laugh. "That's why I think so much of her. She's not like any other girl I've ever met."

Danny slapped him on the back. "Don't give up, eh? If he exists, God loves a trier."

"Yeah, but there's only so much trying a bloke can do, you know what I mean?"

Danny nodded. "I've got faith in you. You can knock those walls of hers down."

"It'd be nice just to punch a small hole in one of 'em. Anyway, let's go and get cleaned up, she might like me more when I don't smell like a rancid vest." They went into their rooms, Blue following Danny. "You can shower after me," he told her. She wagged her tail and let out a single yap.

The room was on a par with a four-star hotel. He went straight to the en-suite and threw off his dirty clothes. He turned on the shower and stepped under the powerful jets. It was heaven. He washed his hair and soaped himself down, watching the filthy water run down the plughole. He stood there for a good ten minutes, enjoying the feeling of the hot water on his skin. He turned it off just as Blue began to bark. He grabbed the robe from the hook on the door and padded out to see what was bothering her. A thin, spotty youth stood by the door with an armful of clean clothes. Blue was barking at him, her teeth barred, hackles up.

"I.....I've brought clean clothes," he said not taking his eyes off Blue.

"It's okay Blue," Danny said to her. She let out a final bark and curled up at his feet.

"Sorry about that," he said to the spotty youth. "She's very protective, we've been through some tough times together."

The youth held out the clothes. Blue growled. Danny took them off him. "Thanks, I really appreciate it. She wouldn't have hurt you, unless you'd tried to hurt me of course, or, unless I told her to."

"Can I go now?"

"Sure, and thanks again for the clothes."

As he left Danny bent down and rubbed Blue's ears. "Good girl."

He led her into the en-suite and coaxed her into the shower. It turned out she liked water and they had a rare, old time washing her. When they were done, she stepped out and shook herself, water going everywhere. It was at that time he realised just how much he loved her. Just as she would die for him, he would do the same for her. They sat on the tiled floor while he rubbed her with one of the fluffiest towels he'd ever encountered. She nuzzled him and licked his face. The bloke who had been contemplating suicide before Seth and Phil had drugged him was gone. He was back in a relationship and he knew this one would last.

Dave entered the room he'd been assigned at the start of this ridiculous adventure. It was weird how dirty he felt. Until they'd found themselves back in the here and now, he'd known he needed a bath or shower but never actually felt disgustingly filthy. Now he did. He peeled off the twelfth century garb and hit the shower. After ten minutes in there, he filled a bath and had a good, old soak. He couldn't stop thinking about Phil, wondering if there was any real future for the pair of them. He was starting to nod off, feeling the most relaxed he'd felt in a long, long time when there was a knock at the door. He cursed, got out of the bath and pulled on a robe. When he opened the door, his jaw dropped in total, joyful surprise.

"Are you going to let me in then?" Phil asked impatiently. She was in a similar robe, her hair plastered to her head. She looked beautiful. He stood aside to let her in, staring like a village idiot. "What's the matter with you, the cat got your tongue?"

"Quite possibly."

"I don't need anybody to look after me. Are we clear?"

"I never said you did."

"If you try and play the butch, protective boyfriend, we're done, Understand?"

Dave nodded. "Is that what I am – your boyfriend?"

"I don't know. I guess we could try it – see how it works out. If you want?"

"That's all I've ever wanted. From the first time I saw you."

They stood facing each other, a wedge of awkwardness between them.

"Well, are you going to kiss me?"

He had only been alive for twenty-nine years, but he couldn't remember anyone saying anything more enticing and exciting before. He leant forward and their lips touched, gently at first. She pulled him closer, and the rest was a wonderful blur.

They managed to make it to the bedroom, their robes entwined on the floor. Their lovemaking was short but intense.

Afterwards, she lay with her head on his chest. He was the happiest man in the world. He kissed the top of her head.

"You're amazing, do you know that?"

She lifted he head. "Shut up and kiss me."

They lay like that until there was a sharp knock at the door, Ringo shouting, "Come on Dave, it's party time."

"Be with you in a minute mate," he called back. He kissed Phil again. "I guess we'd better go babe."

She sat bolt upright. "Don't ever call me that," she said with a snarl. "That's what he used to call me."

"I'm sorry, I didn't know. I'm so sorry." He thought he'd managed to blow it again. Instead, she said, "It's alright, you weren't to know." She looked him in the eyes. "Now you do, yeah?"

He hugged her. "I do, yeah."

Dave's clothes had been washed and ironed, as Jerome had indicated. A selection of skirts and dresses, tops and jeans had been left for Phil. He picked up a pretty, little, blue number.

"Don't even think about it," Phil said grinning. "What do you think that'd do to my street cred?"

"You'd look gorgeous in it," he said, meaning every word.

"Maybe I'll wear it for you later." She winked and started sorting through the underwear that had been supplied. "This is good stuff – expensive shit. All my size as well. How do they know?"

He shrugged. "I have no idea, and to be honest, I don't care. I'm the happiest man in the world."

She finished hooking up her bra and looked at him. "You'd better not fuck me about, Dave."

He put his hands on her shoulders and kissed her neck. "That is something I'd never do, I'm crazy about you. Haven't I made that clear?"

She put her hands over his. "Yeah well, you wouldn't be the first bloke to say that just to get into a girl's pants."

He put his forehead against hers. "Phil – I love you. I'd die for you; you must know that."

She kissed him on the lips. "You'd better mean that, I'm letting my guard down here. You hurt me and I'll kill you."

"I won't hurt you; I promise."

"Have you got a bird in there?" Ringo's dulcet tones cut the atmosphere like a chainsaw.

"Are you ready to go public?" He asked her.

She pulled on a burgundy sweater to compliment the beige jeans she had picked. "Let's do it handsome."

472

He opened the door. Ringo grinned like a loon. "About fucking time. I was beginning to wonder if you batted for the other side." He shook Dave's hand and gave Phil a gentlemanly hug, something he must have found difficult. "Now, come on, let's go and tie a fucker on, my throat's drier than a nun's twat – pardon my French."

"You're an uncouth bastard," Phil said, slapping him on the back.

"I know, I'm the same," he said, smiling. "I'm glad you two have got it together – really."

"Cheers mate, that means a lot. There were times I thought you fancied her."

"Oh, Christ on a tandem, I've always fancied her – who wouldn't? I guess us uncouth bastards are destined for higher things though, know what I mean?"

They linked arms, Phil in the middle, and made their way to the canteen, Ringo starting them off with 'All you need is love'.

SIXTEEN

The clothes that Blue's new friend had brought appeared to be pristine and excellent quality, definitely out of Danny's price range, under normal circumstances.

There were pants, socks, a pair of white Nike trainers and a pair of navy desert boots as well as a variety of shirts and jeans. Everything was his size. There was even a posh, leather collar for Blue. He picked it up, showed it to her and laughed.

Her expression was one of disgust.

"That's just what I thought, girl," he said. "You don't need one of those things." He threw it on the chair by the door. For himself, he chose a pair of black Levi's, a midnight blue satin shirt and the desert boots. He stood before the full-length mirror, brushed his hair back with his fingers and nodded – not bad. Positivity was finally chasing away the crap that had been cluttering up his mind. To be honest, he wanted to be out of this place and finding a place for the two of them. This was going to be a new start and he was excited about it. If any possible return to The Grid was years off, he wanted to enjoy as many of those as he could with his dog. He was already thinking of setting up his own boxing gym. Maybe a place with a small flat above. He still had nearly a quarter of a million quid in the bank from the sale of his family home. He couldn't remember the last time he'd felt so buoyant. Before that, however, they had a bit of a shindig to attend.

"Are you ready to party, girl?" He said to Blue. She stood, wagging her tail and barking at the door.

"I think that might be a yes."

They left their room and wandered along the corridor, not really knowing where they were going. Danny was hungry, that was for sure, but had already decided that no alcohol would be passing his lips. He was following his nose when Harry emerged from one of the other rooms.

"Hey Danny, do you know where you're going?"

"Not a clue mate."

"Best follow me then, Pete's gone on ahead, got a thing about vol-au-vents, wants to make sure he gets his fair share."

Danny smiled. "Oh...right."

"I know, mad ain't it. They've got enough bleeding vol-au-vents here to bury the Eiffel Tower. Should be a good do though. It'll just be nice to kick off and relax."

"I'll second that. Lead on, my friend."

The canteen was heaving with food and drink. Music played through a top end system and a large mirror-ball reflected subdued lighting. It reminded Dave of one of discos he used to go to in his early teens, apart from the masses of grub and bottles of booze, of course.

"The first thing I'm going to do when we get out of here is get myself outside a few pints of real ale," said Ringo, eyeing the bottles of Budweiser,

Becks, Desperado and Bulmer's with distaste. He picked up a bottle of Merlot and a glass, looked at them both, put the glass back on the table, picked up a tumbler and filled it to the brim. He took a slug. "A cheeky, little number," he said, grinning and belching at the same time.

"Who said blokes can't multi-task," Dave said, clapping him on the back.

'You Really Got Me' by The Kinks gave way to 'Please, Please Me' by The Beatles. Ringo started throwing a few shapes, making sure he didn't spill any wine.

"Wine?" Dave asked Phil.

"Nah, chuck us a Bud."

He cracked open a couple and they both started to do a bit of grazing. It was good stuff. Pete was ramming as many vol-au-vents into his mouth as possible. There were about thirty blokes in there, some of whom looked vaguely familiar. These were obviously the other candidates, the ones not chosen to be sent to a distant hell but to have to suffer a more domestic version. Dave didn't envy them. Deep down, he thanked Spalding for putting them all together and sending them back in time. He thanked whatever it was that had caused the rift and thrown them into The Grid. Without all of that he wouldn't have met Phil. He popped a sausage roll into his mouth and put his arm around her shoulders. She slipped her arm around his waist and he was on cloud nine.

The place was a maze of corridors but, after about five minutes, Danny and Harry could hear music and excited chatter. They rounded a corner and found themselves in the canteen. There were tables against the two side walls, all heaving with food and drink. A large mirror-ball hung from the ceiling deflecting and spreading squares of light across the room. The Beatles – who else – were singing 'Please, Please Me'. There were about thirty blokes in the room he'd never seen before. Ringo had an exceptionally large glass of red wine in his hand as he swayed and sang along to his heroes. Dave had his arm around Phil's shoulders and hers was around his waist. Thank God for that, he thought. Pete was, indeed, tucking into a large plateful of vol-au-vents.

Danny took a slice of roast beef and gave it to Blue. It was gone in a second.
"That didn't touch the sides girl."
He was about to give her another slice when Jerome walked up with two stainless steel dog bowls.
"Maybe she'll appreciate this a little more," he said, putting the bowls in front of her. One was piled high with raw steak, the other filled with clean water. Blue looked at Danny for permission. He nodded. "Go on girl but take it easy." She dived in, ignoring the 'take it easy' suggestion.
"Thank you, Jerome, you're very kind."

"It's the least I can do. Any friend of Dave's is a friend of mine." He held out his hand and Danny shook it.

"What happens next? Are you going public with Martin's invention?"

He shook his head. "I don't think the public are ready for such a revelation. Luckily, Spalding has left us well provided for research capital. I'm sure he would want us to put it to good use, don't you?"

"After our brief but informative meeting earlier, I think he would love you to," Danny said, with a grin.

"And what about you? I would love to hear all about your adventures in The Grid, especially with regard to this mysterious machine."

"I'll leave Dave and the gang to fill you in." He patted Blue as she took a drink to wash down her steak. "We're wanting to find some sort of normality. How far away from Warwick are we?"

"About a hundred miles. Enjoy tonight, sleep in a comfortable bed and tomorrow, we'll have someone drive you to wherever you want to go. How does that sound?"

"That sounds extremely generous, thank you."

"Don't mention it. Now go and enjoy yourselves." Jerome left them and went over to Dave and Phil. Danny picked up a paper plate and filled it with food, even managing to grab a couple of mushroom vol-au-vents before Pete could devour them. Pete looked at him accusingly and then laughed.

"I've eaten nineteen," he said, letting out a thunderous belch. "You've just done me a favour."
A waiter appeared from nowhere with another tray piled high with salmon and asparagus vol-au-vents. Pete groaned. "I love salmon and asparagus."
"Maybe better to take a rest, mate. I don't think there's going to a shortage of anything tonight. Pace yourself."
Danny stood munching on a chunk of quiche, looking around the room. Everyone was having a good time, everything prior to tonight forgotten. He felt happy for them but realised it wasn't for him. He'd give it another half hour or so and then go back to his room. The idea of sleeping in a real bed was enticing, to say the least.
"Tomorrow's a new day, girl," he said to Blue. "You ready for our new life?"
She yapped her agreement, yawned and lay on the floor and closed her eyes. Danny smiled.

Dave had never realised that happiness of this nature could exist. He couldn't stop smiling.
"Enjoying yourselves?" It was Jerome. Although Dave liked the bloke, he didn't appreciate him spoiling the moment. Nevertheless, he smiled at him.
"Yeah, it's great, Jerome – a marvellous spread." He suddenly felt like some old codger at a wake. "It's good to be back."
"You don't need me to tell you how good it is to have you back, all of you. I'm sorry about Jack."

"Thanks." Dave didn't really know what else to say.

"I'd be very interested to hear about your exploits."

"We just want to chill, you know. I'm sure Ringo will be glad to tell you all about it."

"I feel like a ball in a pinball machine," he said.

"Sorry?"

"Never mind, you deserve to take it easy after all you've been through. By the way, the fee you were originally promised will be doubled. Maybe a deposit on a house?" He winked at Dave, something Dave wouldn't have thought him capable of.

Dave put his hand on Jerome's shoulder, manoeuvring him away from Phil before she decided to take umbrage. "It's early days," he said quietly.

"Oh, understood," Jerome said, nodding. "I'll go and talk to Frank, shall I?"

"Good idea."

Danny watched Ringo throwing himself about the dance floor like a demented marionette. He was lapping up all the attention, even if it was mostly amazement at his ridiculous and out of time movements. He was amusing a lot of people. It was good to watch. Danny was going to miss his new friends, but he needed to get his head together and focus on himself and Blue. She was fast asleep at his feet and he didn't want to disturb her. He picked up a Coke from an ice bucket, opened it and took a swig, thinking about the crazy journey he'd been on – they'd all been on. It seemed a lifetime away since he was sat in the 'Red Lion' with a bottle of vodka, contemplating ending it all.

"Help me out mate." Pete's pleading voice cut through his reverie. He held a depleted plate of vol-au-vents in his hand. "I think I'm fucking addicted." He patted his belly. "I look like I'm pregnant." His stomach was bulging considerably.

"Just stop eating," Danny said, unable to see his problem.

"That's the problem – I can't."

Danny took the plate from him and put it behind him. "All gone," he said, as if talking to a child.

"They're not though, are they?"

"What are you going to do when you leave here?" He asked him, trying to change the subject.

"Me and Harry are going to start our own limo business. With what we get from Jerome, we'll be able to get a couple of nice motors. What about you?"

Danny told him about his intention of opening his own boxing gym and Pete nodded.

"Nice one." He was still trying to look behind him.

"Leave the bloody vol-au-vents alone," Danny said sharply. "You've had enough."

Pete looked shocked. "No need to be like that, I'm full anyway."

"Exactly. Now go and talk to Harry about your prospective business venture. Start making plans, you know, the type of cars you want to get, the name you're going to use."

"Oh, we've sorted that out already." He lifted his arms in the air as if he were holding a banner.

"H.P. Limos," he said with pride.

"Very catchy. Now go."

"What are you saying? You don't want to live with me, is that it?" Phil said to Dave, her face like thunder.

"Shit, no," Dave said. "I didn't want you to feel pressured or rushed. I was just...."

She laughed. "I'm winding you up, you muppet. I don't mind people thinking we're a couple. Do you?"

"'Course I don't, I love it."

"Good. Now, tell me how much money you're going to be getting."

"Fifty grand."

"Shit the bed, that's serious wedge."

"I know. We have earned it though. It's just a pity Jack's not here to collect his share."

"Yeah, that is a real bummer."

Phil gave it a minute before she asked, "So what are you going to do with it?"

"Maybe a deposit, like Jerome suggested. Then a job. What do you think?"

"Hey, it's your money, you do what you want."

"I meant, if I get a place – will you move in with me?"

She looked at him, sticking out her bottom lip. After a few seconds she said, "I suppose I haven't got anything better to do."

"Is that a 'yes' then?"

"Suppose so."

He threw his arms around her. "You'll never know how much that means to me."

"Of course, I do." She stood back, held out her arms. "Let's face it – who wouldn't want to live with this?"

"I would," said Ringo, sidling up beside Dave.

"You two shacking up together then?"

"I believe we are," Dave said with the widest grin any human could manage. "What about you mate?"

"Go back to the 'pool, get a guitar and get some gigs. Who knows, maybe even play The Cavern."

"Good on you, you've certainly got the voice for it."

"Yeah, the guitar playing might be a bit of a problem though. I can't play," he said with a wry smile.

"I'm sure a man of your talent will soon learn."

"Yeah, how hard can it be?"

'A Hard Day's Night, came on and Ringo was off again, resembling a cross between Liam Gallagher and Mick Jagger.

"I hope his guitar playing turns out to be better than his dancing," Dave said to Phil.

"It can't possibly be any worse," she said, putting her head to one side, a puzzled expression on her face, as she watched Ringo's cavorting.

He nodded. "You're right there, nothing can be worse than that."

It was nice to chill out and have a good feed and drink. After three 'Buds' Phil burped and giggled.

"I think I'm getting a little tipsy Mr. Potter."

Dave picked up his fourth. "I think I need to do a bit of catching up." He kissed her on the tip of her nose. "You're beautiful."

"Tell me something I don't know."

"Oh look, Danny's off. I think he's had enough."

"I don't think it's his scene," she said. "I think he's a bit of a loner really."

"I know he's had a bad time, what with his parents and his brother and sister. I can't imagine how you come through something like that."

Phil watched Blue follow him out of the canteen.

"He nearly didn't. If me and Seth hadn't found him when we did, who knows what would have happened. I think that dog has saved him. If anything happens to her...." She paused. "Well, I dread to think."

"I'm sweating like a pig." Ringo was back and he wasn't lying. His shirt was sticking to him and his face was red and extremely moist.

"Maybe you're getting too old for this lark, mate," Dave said, grinning.

Ringo grabbed a bottle of 'Bud' knocked the top off and downed half of it.

"I think I might take a breather. Where's old Danny gone?"

"I think he's called it a night."

"Call the fucker what you want, I don't know about you, but I've got room for another gallon or so."

Jerome saw his chance and came up to their little group. "Ah, Frank, I wondered if I might have a little chat with you?"

Ringo looked him up and down. "Go on then, my old mucker. Grab a bottle of the most expensive malt that shithead had in his cellar and we'll take the weight off and chew the fat." He put his hand on Jerome's shoulder. "But it's Ringo now, I've dispensed with Frank, alright?"

Jerome nodded, unable to hide his enthusiasm. "Ringo it is – I'll get that malt, don't go away."

"I'm rooted." Ringo shook his head. "He wants to hear all the shit, doesn't he," he said to Dave. "I bet you swerved him and told him to grab me, didn't you?"

Dave held up his hands. "In the words of George Washington or whoever, I cannot tell a lie."

"The night is still young, and that malt had better be ancient. Like I said, I could do with a breather."

Jerome came back, cleaning the dust of a bottle of amber liquid. "Douglas Laing's Xtra Old Particular," he said. "Probably set him back over a thousand pounds."

Ringo nodded. "How old?"

"About fifty years."

"I suppose that'll have to do. Lead on young man."

They partied on into the night, all of them getting drunker and drunker. It was good to let their hair down and not think about anyone but themselves. Ringo had given Jerome the low down on their exploits in The Grid and the older man had seemed both intrigued and flabbergasted. He had begun to start a debate with Ringo, but old 'Beatle-head' was having none of it.

"Look man, I've told you what happened, I don't understand it any more than you do. Now, I just want to get pissed. If you want to chew the fat with someone, go and find H.G. Wells. I'm sure he'd love to discuss the fact that this world of ours might have been created by an alien race. He doesn't believe in God, so it should be right up his street. Now, if you'll excuse me, old bean, I'll be off. You don't mind if I take this with me, do you?" He held up the bottle of expensive malt. Jerome waved him away, a look of disbelief combined with confusion, topped with fascination covering his mush. Ringo went over to Dave and Phil, swigging from the bottle.

"You really are a pig," Phil said to him.

"Don't start trying to sweet talk me now, darling – not now you've plighted your.........whatever it is you plight..........to Davey boy here." He started to gyrate, doing his perverted version of 'The Twist' and they all burst out laughing.

"I'm going to miss you man," Dave said to him.

"Hey, we're going to stay in touch mate. Who else are you going to ask to be the Godfather to your firstborn?"

He drifted away, slugging scotch and moving in a weird cross between a jog and a shuffle. It was a sight to see, but dancing, it was not.

Dave had moved on to red wine and picked up his glass of Merlot. Phil was on white, a crisp, fruity

Sauvignon Blanc – or so she told him. He yawned.

"I don't know about you, but I'm shattered."

"Yeah, I think I'll be out cold as soon as my head hits the pillow," Phil said.

"Oh," Dave said, unable to hide his disappointment.

"You are so transparent; do you know that?"

He smiled. "I just thought we might..........you know?"

"Oh, I know alright, you want to get your leg over."

"I'd rather call it making love," he said, meaning every word.

She put her arm around his waist and laid her head on his shoulder. "I'll get there, don't worry," she said. "It's just going to take a while to lower my guard completely, you know?"

"We've got all the time in the world."

"Fuck me, have you turned into Louis Armstrong now?" She laughed and then apologised again.

"Look, I love you the way you are."

"What – a bitch?" She was grinning and Dave loved that grin.

"You can be what you want to be, but don't ever try to be something you're not. Now give us a kiss."

She gave him a peck on the cheek. "That's a down payment. Now shift your arse."

SEVENTEEN

Danny awoke in the morning just before nine. Blue was already awake and staring at him, willing him to open his eyes.

"Morning girl, did you sleep as well as I did?"

She wagged her tail, happy that he was back in the land of the living. He couldn't remember the last time he'd slept like that. If he'd dreamt, he had no recollection of the content. He felt rested and replenished and was even more eager to get started on their new life.

"I'll just grab a quick shower, girl, and then we'll go and see if there's any breakfast going. How's that sound?"

Blue's tail wagged faster, and she licked his face, as if to say – get a bloody move on then. He was just beginning to see how a lot of humans humanise their pets and match the dog or cat's conversational skills to their own. Having said that, he was one hundred per cent certain that Blue understood everything he said to her. He guessed he wasn't the first pet owner to say that either.

He jumped in the shower and washed off the remnants of that wonderful slumber, feeling more positive about his life than he had since he'd first met Joey. He hoped this chapter was going to turn out a lot better than that one had. He towelled himself dry, dressed in the jeans he'd worn the night before and put on a clean t shirt.

"Ready?"

Blue barked three times, her tail going ninety to the dozen.

Danny opened the door, and they made the journey to the canteen again. It was transformed. Tables, seating from two to eight were placed around the room, all laid for breakfast. Half a dozen blokes were already there tucking into bowls of cereals. Danny nodded at them and was on his way to get himself some Corn Flakes and look for something for Blue when Jerome appeared from nowhere.

"I thought you might be an early bird," he said. "I think your friends might be a while yet – a little overindulgence, if you get my meaning."

Danny smiled. "I think I get the idea, Jerome. Do you have anything for Blue? I don't want to be a pain."

"Not at all, we have some chicken fillets that might be agreeable, and I'll bring her some fresh water. How does that sound?"

"That sounds marvellous, thank you so much."

"My pleasure." He rushed off and Danny tipped some cereal into a bowl and added milk. "Yours will be here shortly, girl."

He walked over to a table and sat down, Blue laying at his feet, whining. The other recruits looked over, whispering. He didn't know what they were saying, and he didn't care. He was halfway through his Corn Flakes when Jerome brought Blue's breakfast. He put it down and she looked at

Danny expectantly. "Go, girl," he said softly, and she dove in.

"Would you like a full English, Danny? Set you up for your journey back?"

"I would like that very much. Thank you, Jerome."

He left again and Danny sighed. He felt at peace. He'd eaten his bacon and eggs, toast and marmalade and was on his second cup of coffee before any of his friends made an appearance. Most of the other recruits, if not all, were already there. There was a feeling of expectancy.

The first to arrive were Dave and Phil and they were looking pleased with themselves. It was good to see a genuine smile on Phil's face, instead of a sneer or an aggressive grin.

"You two look happy,"

"That's because we are, Danny. Am I right?" Dave looked at Phil and she sighed.

"You don't have to keep looking for confirmation and approval," she said. "I'm not suddenly going to turn on you like a black widow spider, you know?"

"That is definitely good to know," Dave said grinning.

"Where are the others?" Danny asked.

"Ringo popped his head out as we were passing. He looks like shit. I'm sure they'll all be here soon."

On cue, Pete and Harry came in, Ringo trailing behind. He did, indeed, look like shit.

"You want a fry up mate," Dave asked the Liverpudlian.

"Ringo tried to glare at him through bloodshot eyes but winced instead. "How much did I fucking drink last night?"

"Apart from about a gallon of red wine, you downed almost a whole bottle of £1,000.00 malt."

"Never mix the grape with the grain," said Harry with a nod.

Ringo sat down and grabbed the jug of orange juice. He didn't bother with a glass. He downed half of it and let out a savage belch. "Shit, I nearly followed through there."

"You really are a heathen," said Phil.

"Since when did you become Princess, Fucking Leia?"

"Since you became Stig of the fucking dump," she replied, sticking out her tongue.

"Touché."

"Are we all here?" Danny turned around to see Jerome walking into the room. Mumbles rippled through the room.

"Well, I'm sure you're all eager to get back to your old lives, start new ones or just go on a spending spree. I have envelopes here for you all. Inside, each of you will find a considerable amount of money, more than you were originally promised. I must apologise for the treatment you've all had to suffer, especially those who were sent on the secret mission. That, by the way, must remain secret. Is that understood?" He looked at their little group. They all muttered their agreement, Ringo raising his hand in a thumbs up salute.

"If you can come up and receive your payment when I call your name. We have transport laid on to take you to your desired destinations. I apologise once again for Christian Spalding's behaviour. Please take comfort in the knowledge that he has been well and truly punished and none of you will ever set eyes on him again. Now, Ryan Ackles, please come forward."

All the other recruits were paid off and led off to their transport, all grinning. Dave didn't know how much Jerome had given them, but it was apparently enough to make them forget their unlawful imprisonment.

"So," he said. "This is it – a new beginning."

"I wish all of you, all the luck in the world," Jerome said, handing out their envelopes. "There are mobile phones in there as well. Each one is programmed with the others' numbers, plus mine. If any of you need anything and I can help, I will. I apologise again for that man's behaviour."

"Don't sweat it man," Ringo said. "You can't blame yourself for that arsehole's actions. You've done right by us."

"Yeah, you've been nothing but a gentleman, Jerome," Dave said. "I'm only glad the bastard won't get the chance to torment anyone else. Hopefully, by now, he's a puss ridden bag of rags."

"That's a really sweet picture, mate," said Ringo, nodding his head. "Really fucking sweet."

"We've got four cars ready to take you wherever you wish to go. I'm not normally presumptuous but I'm assuming that you – Dave and Phil will be travelling together, Harry and Pete, you'll be off to start your new business venture, Frank – I mean Ringo – you'll be going back to Liverpool and you, Danny will be taking Blue back to Warwickshire?" They stood there for a couple of minutes, none of them knowing what to say. When a group of people have been through what they had, it's not easy to just say goodbye and walk away. Eventually, Danny coughed and said, "I'll miss you lot, but now we're back in this section of existence, we have to behave accordingly and do what we have to do."

He held out his hand and they all shook it. Blue had her ears rubbed and her head stroked.

"I'll miss her more than you," said Phil with a wink. "Take care of yourself Danny." She looked at Jerome. "Does he get a phone?"

"Oh yes, of course." He reached into his pocket and took out a silver Samsung.

"Sorry Danny, I forgot. All the numbers are in there."

"You start thinking about doing anything stupid," Phil said to Danny. "You ring me, yeah? I'll be there before you can scratch your arse."

Danny stepped forward and hugged her. "Don't worry about us, we'll be fine. Let's all keep in touch, especially you, Ringo. I'll want to know when your first album's coming out."

Ringo grinned. "You'll be the first to know Danny boy. Now let's get this show on the fucking road, I've got a guitar to buy."

They said their goodbyes and settled themselves in their assigned Range Rovers. Dave was sad to see the others go but was excited about his new life with Phil. As the driver put the pedal to the metal, he wondered if he'd ever see any of them again.

EPILOGUE

It was dark and the stench was overpowering. Raw sewage flowed through the streets. Rats, not already destroyed by the plague, ran or ambled along in plain sight.

"Oh Christ, we're going to die a fucking horrible death," said one of Christian's former guards.

"We have to make sure we don't become contaminated," said Christian.

"And how do we do that. smartarse?" Another of the group of five asked.

"From what I remember, it was carried by the rats and the fleas that fed on them. We have to get away from the city, for a start."

A third member grabbed Splading by the arm. "D'you know about this shit?"

"As much as you would do, if you'd paid more attention at school," Christian said sharply. "We have to work together if we're going to survive this."

"Work together? You don't even know our names," said the one who'd called him a smartarse. Christian looked at him, narrowing his eyes.

"There are leaders and there are followers. I am a leader and I suggest you carry on being followers if you want to live. I'm quite happy to leave you here to suffer his fate." He pointed at a hunched figure on the other side of the street, puking blood, his neck black and swollen.

"Has he got it?"

"It was called 'The Black Death' because, after the initial symptoms, the lymph nodes became swollen and black. Death followed shortly after that. The disease can be transmitted by fleas, rats, or any bodily fluid from an infected person. We have to find somewhere to hide out until it passes."

"And how long will that be?"

"Maybe a couple of years, maybe less. I'm not a bloody historian. I'm trying to recall my history lessons at school."

The fourth guard spoke up for the first time. "If we're all in this together, we need to be able to communicate, and to do that we need to know each other's names. The four of us," he waved a hand around the four guards, "have worked together for a considerable time and so, there is no problem there. The four of us all know you, again – no problem. Unfortunately, the only one of us that you knew by name was the one that was killed before we were sent to this hellhole. You may have a greater I.Q. than the rest of us but, I believe, if we are to get through this, it will be as a group. If you want to exercise your leadership qualities and fuck off, please, be our guest. I'll give you a week, at most, before one of those poor bastards throws up over you. What do you say – boss?"

Christian smiled. "You will take Harvey's place. What is your name?"

The guard shook his head. "My name is Alan and, from now on, there will be no pecking order. We already know what to avoid in order to give us the best chance. The only question is – are you willing to stop being a megalomaniac – or not?"

Christian was not used to being spoken to like this, especially so eloquently, and he didn't want to be alone, no matter how much false bravado he managed to create.

"I am," he said. "I guess it's time for introductions."

Alan hated the man but thought his knowledge and devious mind might be of use down the line. He turned his attention back to the pitiful figure across the street, hoping that wouldn't be him soon. The man fell to his knees, retching. As Alan watched, the air shimmered, as in a heat haze, and the man disappeared. He rubbed his eyes, looked again and watched the man fall face down, his face in the stream of sewage. Alan shivered.

TO BE CONTINUED

Printed in Great Britain
by Amazon